Christmas at Lilac Cottage

HOLLY MARTIN

ZAFFRE

First published in eBook in 2015 by Bookouture

This paperback edition published in Great Britain in 2016 by
ZAFFRE
80–81 Wimpole St, London W1G 9RE

A CIP catalogue record for this book is
available from the British Library.

ISBN: 978–1–785–76270–3

5 7 9 10 8 6 4

Typeset by IDSUK (Data Connection) Ltd
Printed and bound by Clays Ltd, Elcograf S.p.A.

MIX
Paper from
responsible sources
FSC
www.fsc.org   FSC® C018072

Zaffre is an imprint of Bonnier Books UK
www.bonnierbooks.co.uk

Christmas at Lilac Cottage

*To the wonderful bloggers who constantly tweet,
retweet, blog, review, share, shout, gush and generally
get very overexcited for me. You guys are amazing
and I couldn't do it without you. I love you all.
I hope one day we can all meet in a room where there's
lots of cake and I can come round and hug you all
personally. Until that day, this book is for you.*

Chapter 1

The timer went off on the oven and Penny quickly dropped her sketch book and grabbed her oven gloves. Opening the oven door released a waft of gorgeous, rich fruity smells into the kitchen, making Penny smile with excitement. The mince pies looked golden, crisp and perfectly done. She quickly transferred them to a wire rack to cool and gave the warm mulled wine a quick stir as it simmered on the hob.

She looked around at the green-leafed garlands that covered the fireplace and the white fairy lights that twinkled from in between the leaves, the lights that lined the windows also lending a sparkling glow to the room in the dullness of the late winter afternoon. She knew that next door, in the annexe, looked equally inviting now that she had spent hours decorating it in suitable festive attire ready for the new arrivals.

Everything was perfect and Penny couldn't wait to meet them.

Henry and Daisy Travis had been referred to her by the agency in charge of finding tenants for her annexe. Although Penny would have preferred a single woman like her, the young couple came with great references and no children.

Not that she had an issue with children; she loved them. She had even thought at one point in her life that she might have some of her own but that had passed her by. She just wanted to make friends with people who were at the same point in their life as she was.

One by one all her friends had got married and had children, and each time a new child in the town was born it seemed to add weight to her solitary existence. Everyone had someone to love and look after. Penny had a fat, lazy dog called Bernard. The loneliness inside her had grown recently to an almost tangible thing. Whenever people asked if she ever felt isolated up on the hill on her own, she always batted it away with a cheery smile and talk of how she never had time to feel that way with her job. And while it was true that her job as the town's only ice carver did keep her very busy, she knew she took on a lot of work to try to distract herself from how utterly alone she really felt.

She had always lived in Lilac Cottage and she could never imagine living anywhere else. The view over the town of White Cliff Bay and the rugged white coastline that lent the town its name was stunning; she could look at it for hours and never grow tired of it. But the hustle and bustle of the town was a good ten minutes' drive from where she lived and, although she loved the remoteness of her home, she was starting to hate it too.

Renting the annexe out would be a good way to make some new friends and, even though they would still lead separate lives, Penny hoped they would be able to chat from time to time.

Penny checked her watch again, a nervous excitement pulsing through her. She had cooked lasagne for them and she hoped they could spend the night chatting over wine and a good meal and really get to know each other.

It was going to be perfect and she couldn't wait to start this next chapter of her life.

Henry slammed his hands on the steering wheel as another red light forced him to stop. In a town that was probably no more than a few miles long they seemed to have traffic lights on every corner and every single one of them had been red so far.

This had to be the worst moving day ever. The expression of you get what you pay for couldn't be more true today. As the annexe he was moving into was fully furnished, he only needed a small van to bring his other belongings. He'd stupidly hired the cheapest company to move his stuff and now the van was sitting in White Cliff Beach in the furthest reaches of Yorkshire instead of White Cliff Bay in rural Devon.

And what was with the people in the town? They asked so many questions. Stopping for petrol in the town's only petrol station, stopping at a supermarket, and then a café for lunch with Daisy, he had been accosted by about thirty different people who wanted his whole life story. Daisy was lovely and sweet and would chat to anyone and everyone, the complete opposite to him; he just wanted to tell everyone to sod off and leave them alone.

Daisy was staying with his sister tonight, which was a good job too as he was in a foul mood. All he wanted now was to get to this house, unpack the few things he had brought with him and fall asleep in front of the TV or over a good book.

He just hoped that Penny Meadows, his landlady, wasn't a talker. Living up on the hilltops all by herself and completely cut off from the town, he presumed she was some kind of hermit and liked to keep herself to herself. That suited him fine. He didn't want to make friends, he didn't want to chat to anyone. He just wanted to be left alone.

He turned onto the long driveway leading up to what he hoped was Lilac Cottage. He had got lost three times trying to find the blasted place and when he stopped to ask directions, people seemed to close ranks and send him the opposite way, as if they were trying to keep the place hidden. As he drove over the crest of the hill he saw it. The house was a pale purple colour. He had presumed the name Lilac Cottage would come from nearby lilac trees, not the actual colour of the house. It looked like somewhere Barbie might live. With the lights twinkling happily in a multitude of colours from every tree, bush and fence surrounding the home, it just added to the sickeningly cutesy feel. Daisy would love it. He glared at the lights as if they were causing him great offence. Bloody Christmas. Humbug.

A silver Range Rover pulled up on Penny's drive and she nearly cheered with excitement. She ran to the front door to greet her new tenants, but then held back for a few seconds. Yanking the door open before they'd even turned off the engine might seem a bit over-enthusiastic. She didn't want to come across as too keen. She counted to ten, quickly, then opened the door. The man standing on her doorstep with light snowflakes swirling around him was... beautiful. He was so tall she had to crane her neck to look him in the eyes, slate-grey angry eyes hidden underneath long, dark eyelashes. He was muscular too. He had dark, stubbly hair and a deep frown that was marring his otherwise gorgeous features.

'I'm Henry Travis.'

Penny supposed she should say something but annoyingly any coherent words seemed to elude her. His frown deepened some more at her inadequate silence and she finally found her voice.

'Penny Meadows, pleased to meet you. Come in, I'll show you your new home.'

She ushered him in but, as she looked out, Daisy was nowhere in sight. Maybe she was coming later. She closed the door and stepped back into her front room, which seemed so much smaller all of a sudden now Henry was filling it with his enormous size. She tried to get past him to lead him into the kitchen but he was too big to squeeze past. He stared down at her with confusion as she tried to slide through the tiny gap and then finally he stepped to one side.

She walked into the kitchen, feeling awkward and clumsy in his presence.

'This is the connecting door,' Penny said lamely, showing him the obviously connecting door. Next she'd be saying things like, 'This is the door handle and this is the sofa.'

'But we have our own separate front door, don't we?' Henry said.

'Of course, but this will always be open so feel free to pop in any time.'

Henry's scowl deepened so much she could barely see his eyes. He stepped through the door, banging his head on the low door frame. He swore softly as he rubbed it.

'Oh god, I'm so sorry. I didn't realise it was that low.'

He glared at her as he stepped into his lounge. 'Jeez, it's tiny.'

Penny had always thought it was cute and cosy, but with his massive build the place looked like a doll house.

'Erm. . . through there is your kitchen and your front door, which leads out onto the back garden. So I suppose technically it's your back door.' She giggled, nervously, mentally slapping her forehead with how stupid she sounded. 'Upstairs are the two bedrooms and the bathroom.' Penny winced at how small the bathroom was going to be for Henry. He'd have to bend almost double to fit his head under the sloped roof of the shower.

He took two giant steps and ducked into the kitchen, shaking his head incredulously, probably at the size of it.

He looked back at Penny and must have seen the desperate hope in her eyes as his features softened slightly. 'It's lovely, and it's only for a few months so I'm sure I can remember to duck when I walk between the rooms until we find somewhere bet. . . bigger.'

Penny's face fell. 'You're not staying?'

Henry shook his head. 'We have our name down for a house in the town. Rob at the agency said he thinks he will have somewhere by March or April at the latest. Did he not tell you this was short term?'

Penny swallowed down the disappointment and shook her head. She had been trying for months to rent out the annexe without any success and in the end left it in the hands of the agency, and even they had struggled to fill it. Now it seemed that, in a few months, Henry and Daisy would be gone, leaving Penny all alone again.

She forced a smile on her face, determined to make those months count. 'So I've put a bed in the second bedroom but if you wish to use it as a study or something else, then I can easily remove it.'

Henry looked at her as if she was stupid. 'No, we'll obviously be needing the second bed.'

Penny blinked. Maybe they had separate bedrooms. She knew lots of couples who slept apart for one reason or another.

She could never imagine sleeping apart from her husband, but then she didn't have one of those, so who was she to judge?

'That's fine. I, erm. . . made some mince pies and some mulled wine if you wanted to have something to eat before you unpack.'

'No, I'd rather just get everything in before it gets dark. Most of my stuff won't arrive until tomorrow – the bloody removal people got lost and ended up in a different part of the country.'

'Oh, how frustrating for you,' Penny said. Maybe that explained the almost permanent frown. 'Well, I can help you bring things in from the car and I've made a lasagne for later, so if you didn't fancy cooking, you and Daisy are more than welcome to come round later to share it with me.'

'Daisy is staying with my sister tonight.'

'Well, you can still come over. . .' Penny trailed off. Was it inappropriate to share dinner with another woman's husband? It was just dinner but the cosy night in with her new neighbours was suddenly turning into something a bit more intimate now it was just the two of them. Henry obviously thought so too as his eyebrows had shot up at her suggestion. 'Or I can plate some up and bring it here for you to have on your own.' There was something even sadder about that, both of them sitting in their separate kitchens eating by themselves.

'I need to get unpacked tonight. Get it all out the way before all Daisy's rubbish gets here. She could fill this whole annexe with all her junk so I better get my stuff put away first. I'll probably just get a pizza and eat it whilst I work.'

Penny felt her shoulders slump in defeat, though she kept the bright smile plastered on her face. 'Well, let me help you with all your boxes.'

'I'd really rather. . .'

7

'It won't take too long with the two of us at it and as it's starting to snow now, maybe the quicker we get it in the better.'

Henry reluctantly nodded. She followed him out to the car and couldn't help her eyes wandering down to his bum before she tore them away. What was wrong with her? He was married.

She was disappointed that he hadn't even glanced at the incredible view yet, the sun covering the waves with garlands of scarlet and gold. He opened the boot and grabbed a box, passing it to her. With the easy way he handled the box, she wasn't expecting it to be so heavy, but the weight snatched the box out of her fingers and it tumbled to the floor, sending a pile of books over the gravel driveway.

'Oh god, I'm so sorry. I didn't realise it was so heavy.'

He stared at her incredulously. Penny sank to the floor and started scooping the books back up into the box, noticing wonderful delights from Ernest Hemingway, John Steinbeck, James Lee Burke, classics from Dickens and Thomas Hardy intermingled with Tolkien, Dan Brown and Iain Banks. She loved a man who liked to read.

Henry sighed, softly. 'Here, I'll get these, you take this. It's pillows so it should be a bit lighter for you.'

Penny took the box, unable to miss the sarcasm in Henry's words. This wasn't going well at all. She walked back into her house and into his lounge. She wondered where would be best to put the box that would be out of his way, but everywhere was going to be in his way – he filled the whole room. As it was pillows, she thought she could just put them upstairs for him. She turned and walked straight into him as he ducked into the room. She bounced off him, hit a plant on the shelf behind her and watched in horror as it fell to the floor, sending dirt cascading all over the cream carpet.

He rolled his eyes and sighed, heavily.

'Oh crap, I'll get my hoover, I'll clean it up.'

'Please don't take this the wrong way, but I think it's best if I just unpack myself. This place is small enough without the two of us banging into each other.'

'Of course, sorry, I'm not really helping, am I? Let me just clean this up for you and—'

'Just leave it.' Henry was clearly trying to stay calm when he was well and truly pissed off.

Penny nodded, stepping back out into her own kitchen. 'Well, feel free to cut through my house, it will probably be quicker—'

'I think I'll just use my own front door, start as we mean to go on.'

Disappointment slammed into her at that obvious statement of segregation.

'Shall I run through a few things with you, how the oven works and—'

'I'm sure I can work it out and I know where to find you if I get stuck.' He forced a smile onto his face. 'Thanks for your help, I'll see you around some time.'

He closed the door between them and Penny stood staring at his shadow in the frosted glass.

She rolled his words around her head. 'I'll see you around *some time.*'

She swallowed, sadly. Of course it was stupid of her to expect they might use the connecting door as their front door, that they would let themselves in through her kitchen and they'd chat over a cup of tea or dinner on a daily basis. They would have their own lives to lead. They had rented a property and that was it. Making friends with her was clearly not on the top of their to-do list, especially as they were planning on moving out soon.

She watched Henry look around the room and then he moved away. She heard the sound of furniture being dragged across the floor. The huge shadow of the bookcase was pulled in front of the door, blocking out all the light from the window, and then it stopped, resting against the door. He clearly had no intention of ever using the connecting door, now or in the future. He had made a blockade to keep her out permanently. Penny felt the tears that sprang to her eyes at this gesture and she dashed them away angrily. She had been rejected.

Chapter 2

Penny zipped up her jacket and walked into the cool room that was attached to the kitchen. The heating was on very low in here and she felt the cold envelop her straight away, but in her warm clothes she didn't feel it too much on her body. It was only her face and hands that felt it.

She looked around her newly converted room; it was so much nicer and roomier to work in here than it was before. The room was large, with the ice-block-making machines up one end that made the metre-long blocks of ice, and there was a large space in the middle for her to work. The floor and walls were tiled to maintain the coolness of the room and for easy cleaning.

She opened up one of the block machines: the water was oscillating slowly inside to keep the ice pure and clear. The water was partly frozen at the bottom, the perfect time to add some of the decorations her clients had asked for. This particular one wanted fairy lights, interwoven with snowflakes. She placed the glittery snowflakes in a rough pattern in the middle of the block and weaved the fairy lights in between them, weighing them down so they didn't float to the top of the water and taping the cable for the lights to the side. It looked magical and she knew it would look even more so once the piece was finished.

The walk-in freezer was up the other end and she opened the door. Several blocks stood along the back wall, waiting patiently to be turned from large ice cubes into masterpieces. Along the side were about ten sculptures that were finished and ready to go out.

She had been carving ice for about ten years and she never tired of seeing the finished pieces, never failed to feel proud of turning a block of ice into something beautiful. She even enjoyed creating her most commonly requested piece, the swan, which almost every wedding party asked for.

She grabbed one of the ice blocks, which was resting on a wheeled platform, and pulled it out into the cool room, closing the freezer door behind her. She snapped the brakes on the wheels and looked at her blank canvas.

This one was going to be a Christmas tree. She had already stuck the template on a few hours before, now she was going to carve it. She pulled on her gloves, slid her safety goggles over her eyes and picked up the die grinder to trace the outlines of the template. The thin drill bit on the end was the perfect tool to sketch out the design. She pressed very lightly because the main detail would come later.

She could lose herself for hours in here, spending time perfecting each curve, swirl, feather or leaf. When she was in here, the only thing that filled her mind was carving, chiselling, scraping, sawing and creating something intricate and beautiful. That was why she loved it so much, because there was no time to think about how the whole town of White Cliff Bay seemed to be moving forwards with their lives while Penny's life had stagnated, frozen in time. There was no time to focus on her loneliness, or the heartbreaking feeling that her loneliness was probably going to last a lifetime. She could get lost in a sculpture for hours and never have to think about these things. It was only when she stepped out of the cocoon of her cool room to warm up that the real world invaded her thoughts.

Having finished marking out the lines of the template, she picked up the chainsaw and started lopping off the big pieces she wouldn't need. She wouldn't think about Henry and his slate-grey eyes and she wouldn't think about how her loneliness had seemed to have inexplicably doubled since he had pushed the bookcase in front of the connecting door.

Henry hovered at Penny's back door, unsure whether to knock or not. As he raised his hand to tap on the door, Penny stepped out from some room off the kitchen. She was wearing black waterproof trousers and a black jacket, which clung to all her wonderful curves, making her look sexy as hell. She looked like she was about to get on a motorbike and drive off into the sunset. She pulled off a pair of workman's boots and unzipped the jacket. He quickly looked away in case she was naked underneath. After a few seconds he chanced a very brief look back and was relieved to see she was wearing a tiny vest and, as the waterproof bottoms came off, he could see she was wearing black leggings underneath too. She hung the clothes up in a closet and pulled on a huge, oversized hoodie, obscuring that sexy body from view. Her conker brown hair that had cascaded in curls down her back earlier was pulled up in a messy ponytail. She looked dishevelled and messy and utterly adorable. Her green eyes looked sad and he wondered whether he'd put that look there or whether she always carried it with her.

He looked down at the white roses he was carrying and wondered whether it was too much. He didn't want her to attach any romantic motives to the gesture.

Penny suddenly spotted him and he waved. She didn't wave back; the cheery persona she had presented earlier had vanished, the sparkle in her green eyes had gone out. She visibly sighed and then came to open the door

Tiny flakes of snow swirled around them, settling on her eyelashes and in her hair. There was something about her that he felt drawn to. She was beautiful, there was no denying that, but there was much more to it than that.

Henry held out the roses. 'I wanted to apologise for my behaviour earlier. As moving days go, this had to be the worst. Even before I got here, everything that could go wrong did go wrong. I was grumpy and tired and I'm sorry. I was wondering whether that offer of lasagne and mince pies was still open.'

Penny stared at him in confusion. 'I, erm. . .' She looked around as if an excuse would suddenly present itself. She didn't want him there and he felt like an utter arse. He had a lot of making up to do. As she clearly couldn't think of somewhere important that she had to be, she nodded reluctantly and stepped back to let him in.

He handed her the roses and she took them.

'I see you moved the bookshelf,' Penny said, trying and failing to keep her voice casual as if she didn't care. He had hurt her with that too.

'I can move it back, I just. . . I'll move it back.'

'No, it's fine, it's your home, do what you want.' She shrugged.

He hadn't even thought what Penny would think about him blocking the door – of course she would be upset by that.

'Listen, the last place we lived, we not only locked all the doors and windows at night, but we locked the bedroom doors too and I slept with a baseball bat under my bed. We moved here because it's a better area, it's better for Daisy. It's just going to take a bit of getting used to that everyone is so friendly and helpful. I'm sorry if I upset you. I'll move it back tonight.'

Penny stared down at the flowers and softened. 'I'll put these in some water and make us some dinner.'

Henry breathed a sigh of relief.

'Would you like a glass of mulled wine while you wait?' She filled a vase with water and plonked the roses in some haphazard arrangement.

'Yes please, it smells wonderful,' Henry said, sitting down at the large dining table. He watched her as she moved around the kitchen. There was something so captivating about her, he couldn't take his eyes off her.

'It's my own recipe, I just sort of threw some ingredients together.' Penny lit the hob under the saucepan and gave it a stir. 'It's sort of a Sangria and mulled wine mix. Red wine, rum, brandy, fruit juice, fruit, some spices.'

'Sounds very potent.'

Penny laughed and he liked that he could see the warmth and spark back in her eyes.

'Yeah, it might be. I haven't tried it. At least neither of us are driving.'

A giant, deep red, shaggy beast ambled into the kitchen, sniffing at the lasagne that was warming in the oven. Henry laughed; he had never seen anything so ridiculous-looking in his entire life.

'Wow, what breed is he?'

Penny laughed. 'I don't think even he knows. Half red setter, half English sheepdog, half Newfoundland maybe.'

'That's a lot of halves.'

'I know. He thinks he's a tiny lap-sized dog too, always climbs on my lap for a cuddle and then squashes me to death. He must weigh seven stone. Seriously, he could give pony rides to small children.'

'He looks like a Muppet.'

'Don't say that, you'll upset him, but yes, I know. The vet says he has never seen any dog so red before and with his shaggy fur he does look as if he's just walked off *Sesame Street*. Henry, meet Bernard. Bernard, this is Henry, our new neighbour.'

Bernard came and sniffed him with a vague interest. Clearly Henry met with Bernard's approval as he sat on Henry's feet, demanding to be stroked. Henry stroked his head and rubbed his chest. He looked up to see Penny smiling at him and then she quickly looked away.

He watched as she poured two large glasses of the mulled wine concoction and brought them to the table. She passed Henry his glass.

'Should we make a toast?' she asked.

'How about. . . to new beginnings.'

She stared at him and then smiled, chinking her glass against his.

His grey eyes were so intense, like he was studying her, searching for answers to some unanswered question. He took a sip without taking his eyes off hers and she noticed straight away that he didn't have a wedding ring.

'Thank you for decorating next door for Christmas, by the way. Daisy will love it.'

'My pleasure. I didn't get you a tree. I guessed that you and Daisy would want to get one together.'

'She'd like that, thank you.' Henry smiled and Penny felt her heart leap. She had never been the sort of girl to fall in love with a smile before, but there was something about his smile that filled his whole face. He was married, she had to remember that.

She focussed her attention on Bernard for a moment so she wouldn't have to look at the smile.

'So what brings you to White Cliff Bay?' Penny asked, taking a sip of the wine.

'Work mainly. I have a job at the White Cliff Bay Furniture Company, starting after Christmas.'

Her eyes widened. 'As a carpenter?'

He nodded. That at least explained the lack of a wedding ring; he worked with tools like she did, and wearing jewellery could cause injury.

'Wow, they are so selective about who they take on,' Penny said. 'I hear they have something like five hundred applicants every time they advertise. Isn't there some crazy interview process?'

'Yes, it kind of felt like *The Generation Game* with all these tasks that we had to do. We were shown once how to do a process and then had to replicate it within a certain time with the utmost quality and care. It was a whole day thing with the woodwork skills demonstration in the morning and a panel of seven interviewers grilling me for over two hours in the afternoon. I came out feeling like I had run a marathon.'

'They only take on the very best so you clearly did something to impress them. It will be a huge feather in your cap if you ever decide to move on. Everyone knows how prestigious the company is.'

Henry took a big swig of the wine. 'We don't intend to move on. I hope to stay in White Cliff Bay for some time.'

The way he said that, staring right at her, sent shivers down her spine. Was he flirting with her? She shook that silly thought out of her head, taking a big gulp of the wine. It was spicy and fruity and, as Henry said, very potent.

She tried to tear her eyes away from Henry's gaze but struggled to do so. She quickly turned away from the table to dish up the lasagne.

'Have you always been a carpenter?'

'Yes, I love it. There is something wonderful about creating something beautiful with your own hands. I've made and sold my own furniture but I've also made wooden jewellery and statues too. That's more of a hobby, though, but it's something I like to do in my spare time. I know I asked the agency about this, but they said you would be happy for me to use the shed as a sort of workshop?'

Penny nodded. 'Yes, it's huge and I only really use a small part of it. Feel free. I would love to see some of your jewellery and statues. My job is quite similar.'

'What is it you do, Penny?'

'I'm an ice carver.'

'Oh, that's cool. And do you get enough work in that line of business?'

She placed the plate of lasagne down in front of him and sat down to eat hers. 'Do I get enough to pay for this place, you mean?'

Henry's eyes widened slightly. 'Sorry, that came across as very nosy, didn't it? Ignore me. I hate it when people ask me about my work and my money. It's absolutely none of my business.'

'The house belonged to my parents, I grew up here, but they emigrated to Italy several years ago and left the house to me and my brother. He lives in the next town and I bought him out of his half of the house. I'm the only ice carver for miles and there are weddings every weekend, business functions, parties. I have to turn down many jobs because I just don't have enough time to do them. It pays very well.'

Henry looked surprised but she'd got used to those comments by now; no one took her job very seriously and certainly didn't believe that she could support herself on it.

'And, erm. . . is there a Mr Meadows?'

Penny stabbed a piece of pasta with her fork. Why did people assume that she needed a man to keep her happy? She was perfectly fine on her own.

'I'm presuming by the way you are murdering that piece of lasagne that I've stepped on a sore nerve there. My apologies.'

Penny smiled as she looked at the massacred piece of lasagne.

'I only asked because that hoodie looks way too big to belong to you,' Henry said.

'I just like big jumpers or hoodies. They're comfortable. There isn't a Mr Meadows, there never has been. Everyone in the town says I should be married with babies by now so it gets a bit wearing. I. . . I've had my heart broken in the past and I guess I'm wary of falling in love again.'

She stared at her dinner in horror. Why did she feel the need to divulge that to him? She barely knew the man. How much wine had she drunk to loosen her tongue that much? It wasn't even true. She wasn't not with someone because she was scared of falling in love again, she was just happier on her own. It was easier this way. She took the last sip of wine in her glass and went to the stove to pour herself some more.

'So you'll have to go to the Christmas Eve ball now you're a resident of White Cliff Bay,' Penny said, desperately trying to change the subject. 'Daisy will love it, there's music and fine food and dancing, and there's also a big ice carving competition there this year.'

'I'm not sure a ball is really my sort of thing. I'm too big to dance gracefully.'

'Everyone goes, you have to go. It'll be a great way for you to meet people and I'm sure Daisy will be upset if you don't take her.'

Henry still seemed undecided.

'It's for charity, you sort of have to go.'

He smiled at her again and she cursed herself for reacting like a silly schoolgirl with a crush.

'Well, if it's for charity then I can't say no, can I?'

Penny grinned and shook her head. Noticing he had finished his lasagne, she stood up and took his plate to the sink. 'Shall we go into the front room? It's a bit cosier.'

What was she doing? She didn't need to get cosier with this beautiful man, with this beautiful *married* man. But Henry was already standing up and moving in there, taking his new best friend Bernard with him.

She watched him go. She could do this, be in the same room with a man she was insanely attracted to without launching herself at him. A giggle burst from her throat at this thought. She had never launched herself at anyone in her entire life; it was unlikely she was going to start now. She was rubbish when it came to approaching men or even talking to them. Henry was easy to talk to. Although she was attracted to him, being married meant he was safe and she had spoken more to him tonight than she had to almost any man recently. She would just enjoy his company tonight and hopefully tomorrow she could pick up in the same place with his wife too.

She plated up two mince pies and followed him. She stopped when she saw him on all fours in front of the fireplace trying to light the fire. Good lord, his arse was a sight to behold. She couldn't help but stare at it as he wiggled it around setting twigs and papers in between the bigger logs.

Bernard seemed transfixed by his arse too and she quickly grabbed his collar before he decided that humping Henry was a good idea. She had almost forgotten that Bernard liked to hump most of the guests who came to the house. She didn't get too many visitors up here, but poor Jill, her cleaning lady, had been humped several times over the years, especially when she got on all fours to dust or clean. Bernard thought the whole thing was clearly a game and the more his victims tried to wiggle or escape, the more Bernard clung on for dear life, like he was riding a bucking bronco.

'Bed!' Penny said, pointing to Bernard's basket. Bernard seemed to sigh theatrically at having his fun thwarted. 'Bed, now.' Bernard slunk off with disappointment and climbed into his basket.

'Erm, that's a very nice offer, but we've only just met,' Henry said and then laughed as he watched her flush.

She sat down on the sofa and to her surprise he sat down next to her. There were three other chairs that he could have sat in but he chose to sit next to her. She wanted to get up and move away from him but that would appear rude. His smell was intoxicating, sweet but spicy, like cinnamon, zest and cloves. He smelt of Christmas, of the pomanders she used to make with her parents when she was younger and hang over the fire. She wanted to press her nose to his neck and breathe him in.

He didn't say anything, he just stared at her like a starved man would stare at steak.

He suddenly leant forwards and brushed his finger across her cheek. Electricity sparked through her at the softest of touches and she leapt back away from him.

Henry's eyes widened in horror. 'I'm so sorry, I'm not normally this creepy, I promise. I don't normally go round touching strange women. You had sauce on your cheek, I was just wiping it off. With hindsight I probably should have just told you.' He stared down at his wine. 'What did you put in this thing? It's gone straight to my head.'

Penny tried to find her voice, to try to say something to put him at ease, but she could still feel his touch on her cheek. Had it really been that long since she was touched by a man that her body reacted this insanely over a simple graze of her cheek?

She cleared her throat. 'I didn't think it was creepy.'

'You didn't?'

'A bit inappropriate, maybe, but not creepy.'

'Very inappropriate, I'm sorry.'

Silence descended and sparks seemed to crackle between them like the flames in the fireplace.

Penny passed him a mince pie, suddenly feeling nervous around him for the first time that night. He took it and bit into it, obviously still embarrassed by his overly tactile moment earlier.

'Mmm, this is delicious. I'm so rubbish at making mince pies, I just can't seem to get them right.' He took another bite and moaned softly with pleasure. 'So tell me more about this ball – will I have to wear a suit?'

She was relieved to move the topic back onto safer ground, although the sudden vision of Henry in a suit was doing nothing to stop these inappropriate thoughts from swirling around her head.

'Erm, yes, everyone gets dressed up in their best clothes.'

Henry pulled a face.

'I'm sure you'll look very sexy in a suit.' Good lord, what *had* she put in the mulled wine, some kind of truth serum? His eyebrows shot up, the mince pie frozen halfway to his mouth. 'I'm sorry, I'm rubbish around men, I really am. I'm trying to say things to you that I'd say to my girlfriends: "Oh, you'd look beautiful in that dress, those shoes look so good on you." Please don't take it the wrong way, I'm not chatting you up.'

He resumed eating his pie and Penny was surprised to see what looked like a brief flash of disappointment cross his face, but then it was gone.

She took a sip of the wine.

'What charity is it for?'

'It changes every year. This year we're raising money for research into miscarriages, stillbirths and premature babies.'

'That sounds like a very worthy cause. My sister, Anna, miscarried. I know how utterly heartbreaking it can be. She just had her second child, but I don't think the pain of it ever really goes away.'

She stared at him, a huge lump forming in her throat. He understood. He stared right back, narrowing his eyes slightly. When he spoke his voice was soft. 'I'm guessing you've lost a baby too.'

She swallowed. 'You're very astute. It was a long time ago, eight years, in fact. I was only twenty-one.' It had been a long time since she had spoken about it too but he seemed to command so much honesty from her. 'You're very easy to talk to. I never talk about this with anyone. Chris and I had only been going out for three or four months but I just knew that he was my happy-ever-after, that we were going to be together forever. Then I fell pregnant. He didn't want to keep it, he wanted to travel the world, not be tied down by a baby. But there was no way I could get rid of it; from the moment that I found out, I loved that baby with everything I had. I was nearly four months when I lost it. Chris was so relieved, he practically cheered when I told him. I couldn't stop crying, for the baby, for his reaction to it. He left me a few days later. I was heartbroken.'

'I'm so sorry.'

'It's fine. Well, it's not, but it was a very long time ago. And looking back now, I'm so glad we never stayed together. He was wrong for me in every way. I cannot even begin to imagine raising a child with him. He was an arse. So maybe in some horrible way it was for the best.'

'I went through a similar thing myself when I was sixteen, got my girlfriend pregnant. She was horrified, kept saying that she wanted an abortion, that the baby would ruin her life. I couldn't bear the thought of that – this was my child and I couldn't believe that she hated this baby so much when it hadn't even been born. Thankfully her parents were Catholic and wouldn't let her have an abortion but they blamed me entirely and I wasn't allowed anywhere near her. They moved away and said the baby was going to be put up for adoption. I was absolutely gutted. I suppose I should have been relieved, a drunken fumble that turned into a pregnancy. I was sixteen years old with my whole life in front of me and her parents were giving me a way out, but I never saw it like that. I never saw my girlfriend again. Last I heard she ran away to Australia not long after the baby was born.'

Penny stared at him in horror. Was it worse that Penny had lost her baby or that Henry had a baby somewhere that he wasn't allowed to see? 'What happened to your baby?'

Just then Bernard leapt up from his position at the window and started barking furiously at something unseen outside.

Henry quickly moved to the front door as if he was ready to take on the world. She giggled at his over-protectiveness as he flung the door open and Bernard ran out into the night.

'It's just rabbits, Bernard hates them.'

She followed Henry to the door as he stood on the doorstep with his fists clenched, scanning the darkness for any threat. Bernard was sniffing around the rabbit holes, clawing at the grass with his big paws, with the obvious hope that one day one of the rabbits would run straight out the hole and into his mouth.

Seeing that there was no one waiting outside ready to kill them, Henry turned back and banged into her, nearly sending her flying. His hands shot out and grabbed her arms. She looked up at him, silhouetted against the night sky, tiny flakes of snow fluttering around him like icing sugar, his sweet, spicy scent washing over her as he was standing so close. She had bared her soul to this man tonight and, for the first time in a very long time, she wanted nothing more than to reach up and kiss him. Weirdly enough he looked like he wanted the same thing, as his eyes darkened with desire and then scanned down to her lips. What the hell? He was married. It was bad enough that she was having inappropriate thoughts about a married man; it was absolutely not OK for him to be having those same thoughts about her.

She took a definite step back. 'Well, it's getting late and I have to be up early tomorrow so maybe you should go.'

He stared down at her with confusion and she knew she had been sending some very mixed messages that night.

'Yes, of course. I'll let you get to bed,' he said, softly.

'And I look forward to meeting Daisy tomorrow,' Penny said, waiting for the guilt to cross his face at the mention of his wife. But there was no remorse there at all. He just nodded, walked through her kitchen and out the back door, not giving her a single backward glance.

She breathed in the cool night air, determined to clear her mind, then called Bernard in. He ran in, shook wet snowflakes all over her and then launched himself at the sofa where they had been sitting just moments before. She sighed and went into the kitchen.

How unfair was it that the first man in years that she'd had any kind of feelings for was beautiful, intriguing, intelligent, worked with his hands, kind and. . . married?

She was better off alone – that had been her mantra for the last eight years and she was sticking to it.

She jolted at a sudden noise from next door and she watched as the bookshelf was pushed away from the connecting door. He'd done that for her and she wanted to hug him and shake him in equal measure. He was married and it seemed he needed reminding of that even more than she did.

Daisy would be back tomorrow; hopefully that would stop any of that chemistry that was sparking between them.

Henry turned the downstairs light off and wandered upstairs to bed. There was something so attractive about Penny. Even wearing that oversized hoodie over black leggings and her hair pulled up in a messy ponytail, she looked adorable. She was fascinating too; he could have chatted to her all night. But she didn't seem to know what she wanted. Flirting with him one moment and completely back-pedalling the next. He didn't need another complicated woman in his life; Daisy was his entire world. But as he lay down in bed, it was Penny's smile and those intense green-gold eyes that he thought of before he drifted off to sleep.

Chapter 3

Henry strode along the steep, narrow, winding lanes with his niece Bea on his hip. She was too little to keep up with his long-legged stride so it was easier to carry her. She didn't seem to mind.

He passed cute little cottages that were jutting out onto the cobbled streets, their front doors opening right out onto the road. The homes were a higgledy-piggledy mess – there was no order, they just seemed to have one house piled almost on top of the next one. They were all brightly coloured, but none were the same style as the previous one he had passed; some were tiny bungalows whereas some were large three-storey houses. But it just sort of worked.

He stepped into a coffee shop and looked up at the board to see what was on offer. He had to smile when the limited choices ran to cappuccino, espresso and a few herbal teas. This was definitely not Starbucks.

'Jesus, who is that fine piece of arse?' said a voice behind him in a stage whisper.

'Jade, keep your voice down. I'm sure he can hear you.'

'But look at him, we never get men like that in White Cliff Bay.'

'That's Henry Travis, Anna Kent's brother, and that's his niece. He's moved into Penny's annexe.'

Henry winced that they were talking about him so openly, like he was a piece of meat.

There was a loud bark of a laugh from a third woman. 'I bet Penny thinks all her Christmases have come at once.'

'He's not going to go out with Penny,' Jade said. 'A man like that only goes out with beautiful women. Besides, she wouldn't have the first clue what to do with him. She wouldn't know how to please him.'

'And you would?'

'Oh yes. I could make him cry with joy.'

'You're so full of yourself.'

'Shut up, Beth, do you want to have a go?'

'I could do better than you.'

'Want to have a bet? A hundred pounds to whoever can get him into bed first.'

Henry stared at the counter incredulously as he waited for his turn in the queue. How old were these girls – twelve? He glanced briefly in their direction: three bleached blondes with long manicured nails and completely overdressed for a coffee shop on a Saturday morning. Their type did nothing for him.

'Deal,' said one, holding out her hand for the other to shake.

'Well, as I saw him first, I get the first go,' Jade said, standing up. Henry quickly looked away.

He heard the click-clack of heels over the tiled floor as she came towards him.

'Excuse me, you must be Henry Travis. I'm Jade Ambleside.' She held out a manicured hand for him to shake, which he ignored.

'Sorry, I've sort of got my hands full.' He gestured with his head towards Bea.

'Well, aren't you the cutest thing ever?' Jade said in a sing-song voice. 'What's your name?'

Bea stared at her with unblinking eyes. She wouldn't speak to Jade. She didn't speak to anyone outside her home. It was a worry for Anna that Bea would chat non-stop inside the house to her family but as soon as she left the home she wouldn't say a word.

'Her name's Bea, she's very shy.'

'Oh, you don't have to be shy with me, sweetheart,' Jade sang, trying to pull a cutesy face. Bea just stared at her as if she was stupid. 'I love children so much, I love playing with them and talking to them. Kids love me.'

Henry doubted that statement to be true. He looked to the front of the queue where the same person who had been at the front when he came in was still happily chatting to the owner of the coffee shop.

'Henry, I think we should get together some time, for a date?' Jade said, thrusting her chest towards him.

'Like a play date? Do you have children too?' Henry said, deliberately misunderstanding her. 'Anna would love to take Bea to a play date with you. There's a kids' indoor play area on the far side of town – it's very noisy, very sweaty, but the kids love it. I'll tell Anna you'd be interested in going. Well, I must go, I'm in a bit of a rush. I'll get Anna to give you a call.'

He turned and walked out the shop. Maybe he should start wearing a wedding ring so people would know he was not in the market for a relationship. Though knowing women like Jade, that wouldn't stop her.

Penny sat in the bakery window, eating a freshly baked chocolate croissant. It was Saturday and the kids from the local school were chasing each other around the giant Christmas tree in the town square, throwing lumps of slush at each other and squealing with delight as the ice made contact with their skin. It hadn't properly snowed. It never did in White Cliff Bay. They'd had tiny flurries of snow over the last few days, which had gathered at the roadsides and frozen overnight, but any beautiful picturesque snow-topped village scenes were very far away.

The multi-coloured lights from the tree danced and flickered in the dull morning light, casting puddles of blues, greens, purples and reds across the wet cobbles. Every shop window twinkled with festive lights, candy canes, Santas, reindeer and the odd baby Jesus. Some were beautifully decorated, with every star, twinkle or speck of glitter strategically placed; some were a hodgepodge of fun and character.

Being in the town amongst all the hustle and bustle always cheered her up. People were so friendly and chatty. A walk of a hundred yards would sometimes take over half an hour or more because people wanted to stop and chat, even if they had only seen her the day before.

The door to the bakery burst open and the warmth and delicious cake smells were interrupted briefly with a blast of cold air.

Penny smiled at her friend Maggie as she waddled through the door. She was huge, and getting bigger by the minute. She'd never dream of saying that to Maggie's face though, as everyone else in the town thought they should.

Maggie flopped down in the brown leather armchair opposite Penny and took a large bite of the croissant Penny had bought for her.

'Where are your little angels today?' Penny asked, looking around for Maggie's sons, conspicuous by their absence.

'Daniel has taken them to watch football, so I get some peace for a few hours, but I actually miss them when they're not with me, it's way too quiet.'

'You'll have another little one to add to the menagerie soon. How is my godson today?' Penny asked.

Maggie rubbed her oversized belly affectionately. 'He's fast asleep now, but he never stays still at night, feels like he's doing the samba in there.'

'He's eager to come out.'

'Well, he needs to keep that eagerness to himself for another six weeks. January thirteenth and not a moment before. I'm too busy for him to come now.'

'How are the preparations for the Christmas Eve ball going?' With only ten days until the ball, Penny was sure that Maggie had everything organised with military precision.

'Good, I think. The marquee is being delivered a few days before. Food is sorted, tables, chairs and heaters will be delivered on the day, and I have a crew of people who will set everything up. You know what I'm like, these were all organised months ago. But I'm still getting twenty emails a day with queries or changes or demands. The band want their own dressing room, which is a headache, but it's the bloody ice carvers who are causing me the most stress.'

Penny smiled. The competitors were an odd bunch. There was probably going to be ten of them, including her, exhibiting their entries at the ball, with one smaller competition in the lead up to the ball. In the next few days some of the best ice carvers in Europe would descend on White Cliff Bay. It thrilled Penny to be rubbing shoulders with the elite but she had met a few of them before and knew that they were highly competitive and some were very bitchy.

'How are your new neighbours?' Maggie said, through a mouthful of croissant.

'I've only met Henry.'

Maggie took a big sip of tea, eyeing her suspiciously. 'What's with the look, Penny Meadows?'

'There was no look.'

'There was definitely a look.'

'He. . .' Penny rubbed her eyes, hating that Maggie knew her so well. 'He's the most beautiful man I've ever seen.'

Maggie clapped her hands and squealed with excitement.

'Mags, he's married.'

Maggie frowned. 'I know his sister, Anna – she was telling me how much she was looking forward to having him here at last. She never mentioned a wife.'

'Daisy,' Penny prompted.

'Oh yes, I do remember Anna saying something about her now; my brain is rubbish lately, I can't remember anything.'

'Anyway, the weird thing is. . . I think he sort of flirted with me.'

'Why is that weird? You're funny, sweet, beautiful, hugely talented.'

'Because he's married.'

'Oh yes. Urgh, what a creep, all men are the same. No loyalty.'

'You say that when you're married to one of the most devoted men I know.'

Maggie's face split into a huge grin. 'Daniel is pretty amazing, isn't he? He carried me home the other day because I was tired and couldn't face the one-minute walk up the hill. I haven't cooked a single meal since I became pregnant. I do love him.'

'He's so excited about becoming a dad again. I saw him the other day, it was all he could talk about.'

The door opened, sending a blast of cold air over them again. Penny looked up straight into the soft grey eyes of Henry. He was with a small girl, her tiny hand clutched in his. Penny recognised the little girl from around the town and guessed she must be his niece. He gave Penny a small wave before moving to the counter. She couldn't take her eyes off him and it seemed he was having trouble looking away from her too. Something had passed between them the night before and they both knew it.

Maggie hissed to gain Penny's attention and she tore her eyes away from her giant sexy neighbour.

'Is that him?' Maggie whispered, thankfully quietly enough that no one would hear her.

Penny nodded, subtly.

'He's hot.'

'Maggie!'

'What? Everyone is thinking it.' Maggie cast Henry an appreciative look. Sure enough, every woman in the shop – the old, the young, the happily married – was staring at him in complete adoration.

'Is that his niece?' Penny whispered, trying to change the subject slightly.

Maggie nodded. 'Bea. I think she's just started school.'

Penny sighed, forcing her attention out of the window and away from Henry. 'Mags, I think I need to start dating again. It's been too long.'

'I'm not surprised you've come to that decision after that gorgeous specimen moved in next door.'

'He's married,' Penny laughed with exasperation.

'Yes, yes, of course. Well, there are plenty of other single men in the town.' She looked out the window as if one might just happen to be walking past. 'What about George?' Maggie gestured to the curly-haired guy on the opposite side of the street. They had gone to school with George and, although she hadn't hung around with him, she knew he was lovely. 'He's sweet, nice-looking, very funny, divorced.'

Penny watched Libby come out of the shop opposite with two cream-topped hot chocolates. She passed one to George and he wiped the cream affectionately from her nose, then handed her what looked like a bag of sweets. Libby was obviously very excited about the contents and she kissed him on the cheek to say thank you. Penny smiled at the look he gave her.

'And he's completely in love with his best friend. I don't think I stand a chance.'

'Really?' Maggie peered across the road at the two of them. 'I thought he was in love with Polly.' Maggie gestured to the cute freckly red-head at the back of the shop, who worked there with her mum Linda.

Penny looked at Polly, who was busily chatting to Matt from the jewellery shop. 'No, but Matt is, and I'm pretty sure the feeling is mutual.'

Everyone had someone. She had always vowed that she didn't need anyone to make her happy, but in reality being alone was no fun.

Just then Linda Forbes, the owner of the bakery, came over with her little six-year-old granddaughter, Tilly, who had the biggest, toothiest grin and a mop of messy ginger curls. Penny was glad of the distraction, though she could still see Henry passing her little glances over Linda's shoulder.

'Tilly wants to know if you'd like to try our newest recipe – these are marshmallow snowmen biscuits.'

'Thank you,' Maggie signed with her hands at Tilly, before taking one and devouring it in seconds.

Penny smiled at Tilly and carefully signed. 'Did you make these?'

Tilly's face lit up and her hands flew into action as she signed her reply. Penny had to concentrate really hard to see what she was saying. 'I helped with putting the marshmallows on the icing and Nanny put the eyes and nose and mouth on. I decorated some myself but Nanny said that we could eat those rather than putting them in the shop for people to buy.'

Penny signed back. 'I want to see the ones that you made. I bet they're beautiful.'

Tilly grinned and turned and ran into the back of the shop, no doubt to retrieve her artfully made biscuits.

Linda smiled warmly at Penny. 'You're so good with her. When are you going to have children of your own? You would make such a wonderful mum.'

Penny felt the familiar pain in her chest at the thought of having her own family and even Maggie gave her a sympathetic smile as she wolfed down the last of her biscuit.

'All the girls in your year at school have kids now,' Linda said. 'In fact, you're the only one over the age of twenty-five not to have any children—'

'That's not true,' Maggie interrupted. 'Jade was in our class, she doesn't have any children, neither do Beth or Chelsea or any of the Blonde Bimbo Brigade.'

'And we all give thanks for that. What kind of mums would they make, going out and getting drunk and ending up in a different man's bed every night? But Penny here would make a fantastic mum.' Linda turned her attention back on Penny. 'How old are you now, twenty-nine, thirty? You don't want to leave it too late. Your biological clock is ticking. You don't even need a man these days, you can be artificially inseminated. You surely don't want to be alone for the rest of your life?'

Penny stared at her in horror. This wasn't the first time the people in the town had thought it was their business to talk about Penny's lack of children but it was the first time it had been put so bluntly. To her embarrassment, she knew Henry was listening to every word too.

'I don't really want children,' Penny said, quietly, even though it was a lie.

Linda stared at her as if she was some kind of monster. 'Why wouldn't you want children?'

'Excuse me.' Henry suddenly loomed over them all. 'Can I buy some cakes? I'm in a bit of a rush so. . .'

'Of course, sorry to keep you waiting.' Linda quickly moved back behind the counter and Henry flashed Penny a look of concern before he turned away.

He had stepped in to save her.

Tilly came running over to Penny carrying a plate of misshapen biscuits. Tilly's snowmen either looked drunk or as if they were based on Picasso paintings, with wonky eyes and manic grins.

'They're beautiful, I love them,' Penny signed and Tilly grinned, handing her one to eat. 'Oh no, I couldn't, these are yours.'

But Tilly insisted and Penny took a big bite. 'Delicious.'

Tilly skipped off behind the counter again, taking her creations with her.

Maggie leant over the table. 'Ignore the nosy old bat. Having children is no fun, they poo and cry all the time, you never get any sleep, you spend your whole life driving them around as they have far more of a social life than you, every penny you earn gets spent on them. You really are better off without them.'

'And this is your third child?' Penny laughed.

Maggie's face lit up as she smiled adoringly at her belly. 'I know, I never seem to learn my lesson.'

Penny stood up. 'I better go, I have a carving to finish before tonight.' She placed a kiss on Maggie's cheek. 'I'll see you later.'

Maggie waved at her as she was eyeing some of the other cakes that were on sale behind the glass counter.

Penny reached the door the same time as Henry did, and he opened it for her and let her go out ahead of him, hoisting Bea up onto his hip as he followed her out.

He walked up the street with her, but he didn't say anything.

'Thanks for, erm. . .' Penny gestured vaguely back towards the bakery.

'No problem. Is everyone in the town as rude as that?'

'She wasn't being rude, it's just people don't really mind their own business around here.'

'I don't like the sound of that. Where I come from, no one pokes their nose into what anyone else does with their life.'

'People care, they look out for each other. It might come across as nosy but it comes from people genuinely wanting the best for everyone. I like to pretend that I don't want my own children or family but in reality I do and the people of the town know that.'

Henry stared at her and she winced.

'I hate that I'm so brutally honest with you. There's something about you that brings all my secrets to the fore. I wish I could blame the mulled wine, but I can't even do that today.'

'What were you doing with your hands in there?' blurted out Bea from the safety of Henry's arms. Henry stared at Bea in confusion.

'The little girl in the bakery, Tilly, she's hearing impaired, which means she can't hear anything. . .'

'She can't hear anything?' Bea's eyes were wide with surprise.

'No, so when people talk to her she can't hear what they say. So she communicates with her hands. It's called sign language and she makes different movements with her hands to say different words.'

Bea nodded solemnly, with all the seriousness of a four-year-old taking the weight of the world on her tiny shoulders.

'Shall I teach you how to sign your name and the next time you see Tilly you could introduce yourself?'

Bea nodded keenly and Penny showed her the three simple gestures for the letters B, E and A, acutely aware that Henry was staring at her the whole time. What was it about this man? He wasn't watching her hands and what she was doing, he was just staring at her. She glanced up briefly from Bea into his eyes and was thrown by the sheer hunger there. He looked away first, clearly embarrassed by being caught staring.

He cleared his throat. 'So you learned sign language so you can communicate with Tilly?'

Penny smiled. 'The whole town did. When Tilly's mum, Polly, found out she was hearing impaired, she came to the town meeting and said she was going to arrange sign language lessons at her house and asked if anyone wanted to attend so they could communicate with her daughter when she was older. Almost everybody in the town turned up. They had to move the lessons from her house to the town hall to accommodate everybody. Some only learned the basics, but most people can converse quite fluently now. Tilly is such a confident little girl because of it, she can talk to anyone in the town now and not feel excluded. People care here, and I know they don't always go about it in the right way – and they gossip and stick their noses in where they're not wanted – but they genuinely do care.'

Henry nodded, thoughtfully. 'I can see that it has—'

Just then Beth, second in command of the Blonde Bimbo Brigade, came striding over. She sidestepped Penny and managed to slide in between her and Henry with the practised art of someone who had done it a thousand times before. Beth was beautiful and had a much softer way about her than her friend, Jade; most men were putty in her hands.

'Henry, I'm Beth. . .'

Henry stopped dead in the street. Penny wasn't surprised – Beth seemed to have that effect on all men.

Penny paused awkwardly for a moment, before realising that her and Henry's conversation was now over – he only had eyes for Beth.

She had turned away, when she heard Henry speak.

'Do you have any idea how rude it is to come over and interrupt me when I'm talking to someone?'

Penny turned back in shock.

Beth looked around and saw Penny, as if for the first time, and giggled. 'Oh, it's only Penny. You don't mind, do you, Penny?'

Penny shook her head; there was no point in kicking up a fuss over it.

'Well, I do,' Henry said, storming past Beth so he was at Penny's side again. He put his hand on the small of her back, encouraging her up the hill. 'I'm sorry, was she a friend of yours?'

'No, she was in my class at school but we're definitely not friends.'

'I can't abide rude people. Look, I better go, I have to pick Daisy up.'

'I love Daisy,' Bea said, cuddling into Henry's chest. 'Do you love Daisy, Uncle Henry?'

'Very much.'

'And do you love me?'

'Of course.'

Bea seemed satisfied by this answer. He had a lovely way with his niece. He would have made a great dad to his child and it broke Penny's heart that he had never been given that chance. But at the age of sixteen, when he was still a child himself, he probably would have struggled. There weren't many children who had the maturity to raise a child at that age, so maybe his kid being put up for adoption had been for the best.

'We'll pop by later so you can meet Daisy, if that's OK. She's dying to see you.'

Penny nodded and Henry rushed off up the hill, with Bea waving madly over his shoulder.

Penny watched him go, sparks zinging through her body. Even without any sign language, the signals that he was giving off were those of somebody who was physically attracted to her. No one ever looked at her like that. She was damaged goods to most of the men in the town. Chris had seen to that, telling all his friends how messed up she was after the miscarriage, how she'd sit and cry for hours on end. A lot of the men her age had been too scared to go anywhere near her after that. Even after all this time, there was a wariness from the men in the town, as if she might burst into tears at any moment. Henry was different, like he just saw her and none of the other baggage mattered. It infuriated her that she liked him so much, that he had kept her awake all night, her thoughts filled with him. He was married, he loved Daisy. There was no way this could end happily for her.

Penny pulled up behind Henry's car a while later and could see him standing on the edge of the hill with his arm wrapped around a woman with bright blonde hair. They were looking out on the view and the woman was pointing out certain things down in the town. She was tiny, maybe a bit smaller than Penny, and stick-thin; even her arms and legs were tiny like a child's. She was wearing flowery jeans and a black t-shirt, and was clinging on to Henry like she adored him.

Penny got out of her car and Henry looked over his shoulder at her. He must have said something to his wife because the blonde suddenly turned around, a huge grin splitting her face as she looked at Penny. Penny approached, unable to take her eyes off Henry's wife. She couldn't be any older than eighteen. She had large blue eyes and rosy cheeks and was undeniably beautiful, but she looked like she was fresh out of college. Penny noticed that the t-shirt she was wearing had a kitten on it. She was a child, and Henry suddenly sank down quite considerably in her estimation.

'Daisy, this is our landlady, Penny; Penny, this is Daisy.'

'Hi,' Penny said, quietly, suddenly feeling old and haggard in the face of his young, beautiful wife.

'Hi, I'm so pleased to meet you, I saw Bernard through your window, can I meet him, Bernard is the coolest name for a dog ever,' Daisy chattered with the over-exuberance of a puppy.

'Sure,' Penny said, gesturing for Daisy to follow her in. Daisy looked up at Henry with complete adoration as if asking his permission, which he actually gave with a nod of his head.

'I'm just going to check on lunch, you girls go ahead,' Henry said, disappearing through his own front door.

Daisy followed her in and Bernard fell off the sofa and ambled over to greet the new visitor, wagging his tail and sending the magazines and newspapers on the coffee table flying.

Daisy immediately sank to her knees to stroke him. 'Aren't you the cutest thing ever?' Bernard rolled over onto his back so Daisy could stroke his belly and Daisy giggled. 'I love dogs, but my dad would never let me get one.'

Penny watched her getting over-excited about Bernard. Not only was she physically like a child but she had the maturity of one too. She was very sweet and endearing but she wasn't at all what she'd imagined when she thought of Henry's wife.

'So, Daisy, are you at university or. . .' She trailed off before she said college; she didn't want to offend her. Maybe she just looked a lot younger than she was.

Daisy giggled again. 'Everyone always thinks I'm a lot older than I am. I'm sixteen, just. It was my birthday last week. I'm at school, taking my GCSEs this year, but I'll be going to college in September.'

Penny's gut twisted with a sick rage. She was barely sixteen, Henry had taken her away from her family and shacked up in some sick lovers' nest in her home. There was no way she was going to condone that.

'Would you mind staying here with Bernard for a moment? I just need a quick word with Henry.'

'Sure.' Daisy barely looked up as she stroked Bernard all over.

Penny let herself in through the connecting door, not even caring that she was entering his home without his permission. Henry poked his head through the kitchen door and was surprised to see her and not Daisy.

His eyebrows furrowed with concern at her face as he walked into the lounge. 'You OK?'

Penny closed the door behind her. 'She's a child,' she spat.

'Very astute.'

'And you're married to her. How is that even legal? Surely someone has to be eighteen to get married. Look at the size of her and look at the size of you. You make me sick.' She slammed her finger into his hard chest.

Henry couldn't have looked more shocked if she'd come into his house stark naked dancing the conga. 'Wait, wait a minute. I'm not married to her.'

'That doesn't make it any better.' Penny realised she was shouting. 'I thought you were a decent, kind man and now I find you're nothing more than a disgusting pervert.'

His eyebrows shot up and then immediately slashed down in a furious scowl. 'Firstly, just because you are my landlady doesn't mean you have the right to walk into my home any time you feel like it.' Henry opened the door behind her. 'Secondly, Daisy isn't my wife, or my girlfriend, she's my daughter. Now get out of my house before you see me get really mad.'

Chapter 4

Penny drove up through the steep, winding lanes as the houses got scarcer on the way up towards her home.

How had she been so stupid? Why hadn't she asked for more information on the people that were moving into her home? Had she been so desperate for some company that she would have accepted anyone? The agency had never said that it was a father and daughter, they'd just said Henry and Daisy Travis and she had wrongly assumed they were a couple. Maybe they deliberately hadn't told her because she might have had reservations about a teenager moving in next door, or maybe they just hadn't thought to pass that kind of information on.

She hadn't seen Henry all afternoon as she finished her ice carving and not even later when her assistant Josh had come round to help her load it into the van. Daisy had gone out earlier to explore the town, but although Henry had been in, there had been no sound at all from next door, the silence somehow foreboding.

She had to make it up to him.

It was just starting to get dark, the twilight sky filled with clouds of blueberry and plum.

As she bumped up the tiny dirt track that traversed across the hills towards her home, she saw Daisy walking back towards the house. She stopped and buzzed down the van window.

'It's not far, but do you want a lift?' Penny asked and Daisy climbed in keenly.

'That hill is steep, eh. I'm sure going to get fit climbing up and down that all day,' Daisy said, shutting the door behind her.

'You'll get used to it.'

'Dad's really mad at you, and he very rarely gets angry. I mean, he can be grumpy sometimes, but never angry.'

'I called him a pervert, which would upset the calmest of souls.'

Daisy giggled. 'I can't believe you thought we were together. I mean, he's so old.'

Penny smiled at her. 'I'm glad you found it funny; I wish Henry could see the funny side.'

'He will. Come for dinner tonight, he won't be angry with you when I'm there. I won't let him.'

'I really don't think he wants to see me right now, let alone eat with me.'

'Come on, what's the worst that can happen? He can't possibly be angrier than he is now.'

Penny conceded this as she pulled up next to Henry's Range Rover.

'I bought him some flowers,' she said lamely, as she got out the van, holding the bunch of bright orange and purple blooms aloft.

Daisy laughed. 'You bought him flowers, that's hilarious.'

Penny cringed inside – it was a terrible idea, but as he had bought her flowers to apologise the night before she thought he might get a laugh out of her doing the same for him.

Daisy encouraged Penny to follow her to the door and then told her to hold back a second. This was ridiculous, he was going to take one look at her and slam the door in her face.

'Hi Daddy,' Daisy sang.

'I was just about to come looking for you. I said to get home before it's dark.'

Although Henry was keeping it light, Penny noticed the protectiveness to his voice.

'That hill took a lot longer to walk up than I thought. Besides, it's not dark, it's twilight, dusk at best. I've brought a friend with me – can she stay for dinner?'

'You've made a friend already? Of course she can stay for dinner. Where is she?'

'She's outside, she's a bit scared of you,' Daisy giggled.

'That's ridiculous, I don't bite.'

Penny saw the huge shadow of Henry looming towards the door, then he poked his head out. His face fell when he saw Penny.

'She's my friend, and you said she could come for dinner, so you have to let her in,' Daisy laughed with the confidence of someone who knew she had her dad wrapped around her little finger.

Henry sighed heavily and stepped back to let her in.

'I, erm, bought you some flowers to apologise.' Penny proffered the small bouquet.

Henry stared at them in confusion. 'No one has ever bought me flowers before. That's normally a woman thing.'

'Why should it be, though, Dad? They don't come with labels saying for women only,' Daisy protested. 'I think it's a fantastic idea.'

Penny stepped into the warmth of the kitchen, eyeing Daisy, who obviously thought the whole thing was hilarious.

Henry took the flowers, holding them like they were an unexploded bomb. He found a pint glass, filled it with water and shoved the stems into the glass, the flowers still wrapped in their plastic.

He turned back to face her, folding his arms across his chest, his eyebrows slashing down across his eyes.

'I really am very sorry.'

'You said that.'

Wow, he really wasn't going to make this easy on her.

'I'm just going to send an email,' Daisy said. 'How long until dinner?'

'About five minutes,' Henry said, not taking his eyes off Penny.

Daisy turned from the room and Penny heard her race upstairs.

He stared at her for a moment, the awkward tension hanging over them like a black cloud.

'It's OK, I don't have to stay for dinner. I just wanted to apologise and I've done that. I certainly don't want to make you uncomfortable in your own home. Tell Daisy I'm really sorry I couldn't stay, but something came up.'

She moved to the door and he didn't even try to stop her.

She stepped outside, let herself into her own kitchen and switched on all the lights. Bernard popped his head over the arm of the sofa, but seeing it was her and not a burglar he went back to sleep again. Even if she had been a burglar she was pretty sure she'd get the same reaction from him.

She sat down at the kitchen table with her head in her hands. Life was going to be pretty unbearable between them. If there had been a fledgling friendship developing between her and Henry, it was well and truly gone now.

The connecting door suddenly opened and when she looked up, Henry was leaning on the door frame.

'Are you coming for dinner or what?'

Penny stared at him. She knew the tension would be excruciating and she didn't think she could face it. 'No, I'm fine, I'm just going to get a sandwich.'

'Putting up with my grumpy face has surely got to be better than sitting in here on your own. Daisy will talk to you even if I don't.'

It was hardly the best offer she'd ever had but it didn't seem there was any room for arguments as he disappeared back into his own home again.

She stood up and followed him in. He was already dishing up three plates of a cheesy tomato pasta bake.

'Daisy, get your arse down here,' Henry called, but it was said in good humour and she heard Daisy laughing from upstairs.

Henry put the plate down on the table in front of Penny. 'Help yourself to salad and garlic bread,' he said, gruffly. He sat down opposite her and turned his attention to his own dinner, not looking up again. Penny sat at the table and tried to force some pasta down. Really, eating a sandwich on her own was going to be better than this.

Daisy came running into the kitchen and sat between them. She tucked into her pasta, grabbed three slices of garlic bread and was halfway through the first slice when she realised that the atmosphere hanging between Penny and Henry was intense and unbearably awkward.

'Dad, don't be an arse,' Daisy said.

Henry sighed and put down his knife and fork. Penny focussed on her food; there was no way she was going to apologise again.

Suddenly a piece of pasta splatted against the side of Penny's face, sliding down her chin and landing with a plop against her shirt.

Penny looked up in shock and Daisy burst out laughing. She was surprised to see Henry fighting a smirk.

'Don't ever call me a pervert again.'

'Did you just throw your pasta at me?' Penny said, still unable to believe that the evening had taken this bizarre turn.

'He and his sister do it all the time, you'd wouldn't believe they were grown adults,' Daisy said.

Henry shrugged. 'I think we're even.'

Penny scooped up a piece of pasta and weighed it in her hand, taunting him.

'No, don't you dare,' Henry laughed.

Penny launched it across the table and it hit Henry in the middle of his forehead. A laugh erupted from Penny's throat, a huge, genuine laugh that she hadn't heard from herself for a very long time. Another one joined it, followed by a snort.

Henry's face lit up at hearing it. 'Did you just snort?'

Penny shook her head, unable to stop laughing, and just to call her a liar another snort escaped.

Henry's big booming laugh filled the kitchen and he picked up his knife and fork and carried on eating. The atmosphere between them had vanished.

Henry watched Penny across the table, tucking into her food with much more enthusiasm than she had been a few minutes before. He was an arse and he shouldn't have overreacted about her comments that afternoon. It was a perfectly reasonable mis-understanding and he should have just laughed it off.

He really liked having her here. He and Daisy so rarely had company; any women that he dated he normally did so away from his home, wanting to keep that part of his social life separate from his daughter. But this little family dinner with the three of them seemed so right. Penny fitted in with them perfectly. There was something about her that he found he was attracted to that went way beyond her looks. She was fascinating and he could have watched her all night and never got tired of it.

'So Daisy, you'll be going to White Cliff Senior School?' Penny asked.

'After Christmas,' Daisy said, over a mouthful of garlic bread.

'Don't talk with your mouth full,' Henry said.

Daisy swallowed. 'I'm going in for a day to meet people and some of the teachers but I won't start properly till after Christmas because they won't have the room for me. One of the kids is leaving so it works out well for me, otherwise I'd have to go to the school in the next town and the bus ride is over an hour. And the art teacher here is fantastic, he's had work in galleries in London.'

'Mr Cartwright?'

Daisy's face lit up. 'Yes, you know him?'

'He used to be my teacher too. So you like art?'

'I love it. Just to be able to watch something brought to life with your hands is wonderful.'

Henry smiled as he watched his daughter come alive as she talked about her passion.

'Dad said you were an ice carver?'

'I am.'

Daisy started bombarding Penny with a hundred questions about the process and Henry watched as Penny explained in detail about how she did it. It was clearly a great passion for Penny too. He liked that Penny was talking to Daisy like she was an adult, she wasn't dumbing down any of the explanations. Most of the women he had been with still spoke to Daisy like a child and she hated that. Lots of people didn't know how to behave around a teenager, but for Penny it was the most natural thing in the world. She had behaved the same with Bea in town; there was no singsong voice or cutesy face like Jade.

He finished his dinner and was standing up to take his plate to the sink when there was a knock at the door. He looked up to see Jade outside. He sighed – speak of the devil. She clearly hadn't gotten the message earlier in the café. She looked like she was about to go on a glamour shoot dressed in a red clingy dress and high heels.

He opened the door and Jade immediately leant into him, engulfing him in a sickly cloud of perfume. He took a step back and she pouted slightly.

'Henry, I brought you some dinner. I figured you'd be tired from all the unpacking and I went to The Olive Branch and got you some Italian. I figured we could share it together.'

'That's very thoughtful of you, thank you, but I've just eaten, though me and Daisy can reheat it tomorrow. We still have a ton of unpacking to do so this will be a huge help.'

He heard Daisy snigger at his polite rebuttal and he tried to suppress a smile.

'Daisy?' Jade asked in confusion.

'My daughter.' He gestured to the dining table. Jade hadn't even registered there was anyone else in the room with them. He didn't know whether to be flattered by that or annoyed that she hadn't even acknowledged Penny and Daisy.

Jade looked over and Daisy smiled, with pasta hanging out of her mouth. Henry scowled at Daisy's rudeness but had to keep the laughter that bubbled in his throat under control.

'Oh, she's so cute.'

She still hadn't acknowledged Penny, which annoyed him and he didn't know why.

'Penny, do you like Italian?' Henry called over to her. 'Looks like Jade has brought a ton of food here, so you can come and share it with me and Daisy tomorrow.'

Penny nodded in confusion. She'd gone very quiet again, scuttling back inside her shell just as she was starting to come out of it.

Jade laughed nervously at the new cosy arrangement that Henry had created with Penny.

'I hope you are settling in OK? Is there anything I can do to help?' Jade said, curling her hair around her finger, leaving him with no doubt as to how Jade would like to help him settle in.

'Well, actually there is. Me and Penny are going out on a date on Tuesday – would you be able to babysit Daisy for me?'

Daisy choked on her pasta. It had been a long time since he'd needed a babysitter for her. He glanced over at Penny, who was looking like a rabbit in the headlights.

'I'd normally ask my sister but she's busy with the new baby, so could you do it, Jade? I know how much you love children.'

Jade's sultry smile slipped from her face. 'You're going out with Penny?'

She said it with such disgust that he felt anger slam through him at her reaction. He bit back the retort he wanted to make. It had been kind of Jade to bring him dinner, even if she had an ulterior motive.

'Yes, we just hit it off the moment we met. It would be so kind if you could babysit?'

'I, erm. . . I'm busy that day.'

'Ah, that's too bad, I'm sure we can find someone. Thanks for this. Did you want to come in and share dessert with us all? We have Funny Feet ice lollies or I think we might have a Magnum or two at the bottom of the freezer.' Henry moved to the fridge, knowing Jade would be the last person in the world to sit down at the table with Daisy and Penny and suck on a Magnum.

Jade shook her head, still clearly in shock over the Penny revelation. 'No, I better go, I, erm. . . have somewhere I need to be.'

'Oh, that's a shame. Thanks for popping by though.'

Jade stumbled out and disappeared around the back of the house. Henry closed the door softly after her.

He went and sat down at the table again.

'Dad, you're so rude,' Daisy giggled.

'She's rude. I don't like her much.' He turned to Penny. 'Another classmate of yours?'

Penny nodded.

'How many times has she been up here over the years?'

'Tonight was the first. I'm surprised she even knew the way. She, erm. . .' she looked at Daisy as she tried to find the right words '. . .went out with Chris for a while.'

'Who's Chris?' Daisy asked.

'My ex.'

'Let me guess, she *went out* with him whilst he was seeing you,' Henry said.

Penny nodded.

Bitch.

He took a sip of water and stared at Penny across the table. Jade's attitude to Penny disgusted him. And Beth's too. He had a sudden desire to stick two fingers up at all the arseholes in the town who didn't think Penny was worthy of paying attention to.

'You know what this means? You and I have a date on Tuesday.'

Penny's eyebrows shot up and Daisy grinned at him.

Chapter 5

Penny woke in the night to mumbles and cries of panic coming from the lounge. She quickly got up and ran downstairs.

She was surprised to see Daisy lying on her sofa with Bernard by her side. She was clearly having a nightmare. She didn't know whether to wake her or not and she certainly didn't want to scare her by doing so. She didn't know why Daisy was in her lounge either.

'Daisy,' she said softly, but there was no response. What should she do? What kind of mum would she have made when she didn't even know how to deal with a child who was having a nightmare? Her first reaction was to stroke Daisy's head and hug her, but Daisy wasn't her daughter, she couldn't do that.

Leaving her lying on the sofa with Bernard staying guard, she went through the open connecting door and crept upstairs.

Henry's door was ajar and she stole a brief moment to admire him sleeping, the blankets bunched around his waist, his bare muscular chest gleaming in the moonlight that spilt through the open curtains.

She reached forwards and touched his arm, the feel of his smooth velvety skin making her stomach clench with a need she hadn't felt for years.

He didn't stir, so she shook him gently.

He opened his eyes blearily and suddenly smiled, running his hand up her arm.

She was here, in his bedroom. He hadn't been able to stop think-ing about her as he fell asleep earlier and now she was here. He was dreaming but she sure felt real, her skin was so soft. She wasn't dressed in the sexy lingerie the women of his dreams were normally wearing, but she still looked heavenly dressed in cute snowflake pyjama bottoms and an oversized t-shirt. He wanted to pull her into bed with him and see the gorgeous body she hid underneath these big clothes.

He slid his hand down to her fingers and entwined them with his own. He shifted back into the bed a bit and pulled her gently towards him. For one wonderful moment, she came willingly, before she stopped and pulled her hand from his.

'Henry, it's me, it's Penny.'

He was well aware who she was. Although as he became more awake it was very obvious she hadn't pitched up in his bedroom for a night of hot sex.

He cleared his throat and rubbed his face to try to dispel the images that were playing through his mind.

'Are you OK?' he said as he sat up and looked at her.

'Daisy's having a nightmare.'

He shot out of bed, all thoughts of passionate sex vanishing. 'Where is she?'

'In my front room. I didn't want to wake her in case I scared her.'

He raced downstairs. Why was Daisy in Penny's front room? He knew she hadn't been able to sleep earlier and he'd heard her go downstairs, presumably to watch TV or read. Quite why she had gone next door he didn't know.

Penny followed him down the stairs and back into her front room. She watched him carefully scoop Daisy up into his arms and place a tender kiss on her head, before he carried her back into the safety of his home.

She wondered briefly if she should follow him but Henry knew how to deal with it; she would only be in his way.

Sleep was a long way off now, especially after what had passed between them in the bedroom.

He had tried to pull her into bed with him and for a moment, maybe a few seconds, she had nearly done just that. What would he have done when he woke properly to find her in bed with him and not some gorgeous model that he had been imagining?

She was pouring some milk in a saucepan to make a hot chocolate, when suddenly there was a noise behind her. She turned to see Henry standing in her kitchen, looking incredible still only dressed in a pair of tight boxer briefs. He had his robe in his hand but he hadn't bothered to put it on. She quickly looked away.

'Is she OK?'

'Yes, she's fast asleep, and the nightmare seems to have passed.' He sighed heavily and Penny's heart ached for him.

'Does it happen a lot?'

'More often than I would like, but a lot less now she's older than when she was a child.'

Penny turned around to look at him, hearing the angst in his voice. He clocked the look of sympathy and smiled sadly.

'Mainly they revolve around her being abandoned or rejected, despite me doing everything in my power to reassure her that I would never leave her. She had attachment issues for the first ten years of her life; I couldn't leave her with anyone but my parents or Anna, and even that was a struggle. She was two months old when her mum walked out and, although Daisy has no memory of her, as a baby it was clearly hard for her to understand why her mum was no longer there. She was three months old when her maternal grandparents left her with me for a weekend and never came back to collect her, just as she was getting used to them raising her instead. She was so clingy for the first few years, and understandably so – even putting her down and staying in the same room as her would cause her to cry buckets. I'm sure subconsciously she was waiting for me to abandon her too. For the first six months she lived with me she would only sleep in my bed, with me lying next to her. I couldn't even leave her once she was asleep as she would be completely inconsolable if she woke and I wasn't there. It took a long time for her to realise that I was in it for the long haul but obviously she still doesn't totally trust me now if she is still having nightmares.' He rubbed his face to clear it of sleep and then suddenly looked horrified as he realised he had said too much. 'Sorry, I shouldn't have talked about that with you.'

'It's OK, I won't say anything, to her or to anyone else. But her nightmares don't reflect badly on you.'

'Of course they do. She has nightmares because she thinks I'm going to leave her.'

'You stood by her when no one else did. You raised her when you were no more than a child yourself and you should be incredibly proud of that and of the wonderful girl she is because of you. You put her first above everything else. Don't ever doubt your parenting skills – you gave her love and she can't ask for anything more than that.'

He smiled at her. 'Thank you.'

She watched him, unable to take her eyes off him, and he stared right back, the tension fizzing between them like lightning about to strike. She looked away, focussing on the task of making the hot chocolate.

'I'm sorry she was in your house. I have no idea what she was doing here. I'll speak to her tomorrow.'

She felt him move behind her, her body embarrassingly erupting in goosebumps at his proximity. Why was she so attracted to this man? Sure, he was good-looking, any idiot could see that, but there were lots of good-looking men in the town and she'd never reacted like this around them before. Was it the way he stared at her, as if he saw deep inside her? Was it having him in her home, the one place she always felt safe, and she just felt nervous about him being in her space? He wouldn't hurt her, she knew that, well, not physically, but he was exactly the sort of man who would ruin her. She feared for that.

'You're cold. Here, put this on,' Henry said, draping his soft towelling robe around her shoulders. The scent of him washed over her, sweet, intoxicatingly spicy. She pushed her arms through the sleeves. The warmth of the robe did nothing to dispel the goosebumps.

'I'm sorry she woke you.'

She turned around to face him, determinedly looking at his eyes and not at those abs that she just wanted to reach out and touch.

'It's no problem at all.'

He stared at her. What was with all the staring, that solid, unblinking, grey gaze? It made her want to run away and hide from it.

'I'm sorry about. . .' He gestured vaguely to upstairs and his bedroom. 'I'd just woken up and thought I was dreaming.'

She smiled, wanting to tease him to break the tension between them. 'I gathered you were dreaming when you tried to pull me into bed with you. Who did you think I was, Angelina Jolie or

Keira Knightley? I had a dream once that I was in bed with Brad Pitt and when I woke up I was cuddled up to poor Bernard.'

He frowned. 'I was dreaming about you and then I woke up and you were there.'

There were no words in Penny's head, nothing at all.

Henry stepped a bit closer and pulled the robe tighter around her, fastening it with the belt. 'Best dream I've ever had.'

Part of her felt euphoric at the attention he was giving her but part of her was annoyed. He wasn't really interested in her – flirting for him was like breathing. Henry could have any woman he wanted; he certainly wasn't going to choose someone like her.

He moved in, he was so close she could feel his warmth, feel his breath on her face, but he didn't touch her, just leant around her to pick the saucepan off the stove.

'Your milk is boiling over.' He poured the milk into the mug filled with the drinking chocolate and gave it a good stir, then pushed the mug into her hands. 'Now drink this and get back to bed.'

He flashed her a devastating smile and walked out without a look back.

Penny woke to the smell of bacon cooking the next morning and she smiled. Bright winter sunshine was already filtering through the crack in the curtains, indicating that it was a lot later in the day than she would have liked. She had barely slept at all after Henry had left, as she tried to work out whether the looks, comments, little touches amounted to anything or nothing. She had finally fallen asleep at six in the morning when the darkness of her room had turned to a muted grey.

She climbed out of bed, her hand hovering over Henry's robe for a moment before she decided against wearing it for a whole host of reasons and settled on her own robe.

She padded downstairs and smiled at her friend Jill standing in the kitchen frying bacon.

Penny walked up behind her and wrapped her arms around Jill's waist, leaning her head on her back. Jill jolted with shock for a second, before squeezing Penny's hand and then resuming her cooking.

'That's a lovely greeting for this time in the morning,' Jill said.

'It's lovely to be woken with the smell of bacon, but you know you don't have to cook for me any more.'

'And you know I like to. Tea is in the pot. You can pour me a mug too.'

Penny smiled with love for her. She had known Jill Stratton her whole life as she had been the housekeeper, cook and unofficial nanny to her and her brother growing up. She wasn't sure why Jill still came round once or twice a week to clean for her when Jill blatantly didn't need the money and Penny didn't need the help, but it was an arrangement that just seemed to have stuck over the years. Penny was beyond grateful for the company and the unwavering friendship, so she wasn't going to stop her coming any time soon.

Penny poured out two mugs of tea and sat down to watch Jill finish off the bacon. She was one of the most glamorous people that Penny knew. Even today, faced with a load of dusting and vacuuming, Jill was dressed in a pale blue trouser suit that would be more suitable for a high society wedding than a spot of cleaning. She had a deep blue satin scarf tied around her neck and a pair of diamond and sapphire earrings that Penny knew to be real. She was wearing an apron over her clothes but this did nothing to detract from her effortless grace and beauty. With her brown hair cut into a sleek bob, she hadn't aged a single day in all the time Penny had known her.

Jill placed a bacon sandwich in front of Penny and sat down opposite her to eat her own.

'How are the new neighbours? Henry and Daisy, was it?'

'Fine, they seem nice, but Daisy is Henry's daughter *not* his wife. . .'

'Oh.' Jill took a bite of her sandwich and chewed it thoughtfully, staring at Penny the whole time. She swallowed. 'And what is Henry like?'

Penny blushed. 'He's. . . very big and, erm. . .' Hot as hell, grumpy but kind and very, very flirty. She couldn't say any of those things but it didn't seem she needed to as Jill was smiling into her mug of tea. 'Daisy is very sweet, I really like her.'

There was a knock at the connecting door behind Penny and she heard it open. Jill's eyes lit up, indicating that it was most likely Henry standing there and not Daisy.

Penny turned around and eyed Henry standing in the doorway. He'd at least had the decency to put on a t-shirt since the night before, which covered his tight boxer shorts, but he hadn't put on any jeans to cover up his fabulous muscular thighs.

'Hi, sorry to bother you ladies. Penny, I was wondering if I could have my robe back?'

'Yes, of course, it's in my room, I'll just get it.'

She ignored the look of surprise from Jill that Henry's robe was in her bedroom as she stood up and quickly ran upstairs. When she returned a moment later, Henry was sitting down at the table talking to Jill as if he had known her for years. Jill had even made him a mug of tea.

Penny held out Henry's robe and he took it but didn't get up. He was sitting right next to where Penny had been sitting moments

63

before so when she sat down to resume eating, her thigh brushed against his momentarily. His touch zapped through her before she shuffled a few inches away.

'I see you two have met,' Penny said, half frowning at the new cosy family breakfast and half loving it too.

'Yes, Jill was just asking me if I was single.' Henry smirked and then, in a theatrical whisper, 'I think she fancies me.'

Jill laughed. 'Maybe if I was twenty years younger, but I have been very happily married to my Thomas for nearly twenty-five years now, so I don't think I'll be running off to have an illicit affair any time soon, despite how gorgeous you are.'

Henry smiled at Jill then transferred his smile to Penny. 'Besides, I don't think we can see each other anyway, Jill. I've got a date with Penny on Tuesday.'

Penny glanced over at Jill to see her smile widen into a full-blown grin.

'It's not a proper date,' Penny explained.

'Isn't it?' Henry asked, his eyes alight with amusement.

'No, you're just doing it to piss Jade off.'

'That's one of the reasons but it's not the only reason.'

She stared at him, his eyes not wavering from her face.

There was a movement behind them and, as they both turned around to see Daisy, Henry purposefully moved away from Penny.

'Can I smell bacon?' Daisy said, hopefully.

'Here, I'll make you a sandwich,' Jill said, standing up.

Henry frowned. 'No, Jill, it's OK. We have bacon next door. The lazy little tyke can make some for herself.'

'Or, if you were any kind of dad, you could make it for me rather than leaving me to starve.' Daisy grinned sweetly at her dad and Henry smirked again.

Jill was already at the oven. 'It's no bother. Henry, would you like some too?'

'Well, if you're making some for lazy bum here, then sure.'

Penny patted the bench next to her and Daisy dropped onto it in between her and Henry. Henry nudged her playfully and she nudged him right back. They had such a lovely way between them. Penny wondered whether Henry would bring up the subject of Daisy sleeping in Penny's lounge the night before but he didn't, so she decided not to mention it either.

'Daisy, this is my lovely friend Jill,' Penny said.

'I love your name,' Jill said, laying bacon in the pan. 'It's very pretty.'

'I hate it. I think Daisy is a cute name for little girls but I don't think people will take me seriously as an adult.'

'Daisy's a lovely name,' Penny said. 'I could think of much worse names. I saw an article on weird baby names the other day: there was a Frodo, Bilbo, Hashtag and Goldilocks.'

Daisy laughed. 'No one would call their kid Goldilocks.'

'I wish I was lying but I'm not. And do you want to know what Penny is short for?'

'I'm guessing Penelope.'

Penny shook her head. 'Tuppence.'

Daisy's eyes lit up and Henry gave a loud bark of a laugh.

'You're called Tuppence. That's your real name?' Daisy was clearly delighted by this turn of events.

'Yes. My brother got the worst deal though. His name is Rainbow Sky.'

'Seriously?' Daisy giggled.

'What can I say, our parents were hippies. Everyone just calls him Sky now. I think he had it officially changed by deed poll a few years ago. Although if you ever meet him don't tell him you know. He never tells anyone his real name.'

Daisy laughed. 'Thank god you didn't call me Rainbow or Moonshine.'

'You see, Daisy is actually quite a normal name,' Henry said.

Daisy nodded. Her phone beeped in her pocket and she pulled it out. 'Oh sorry, the battery is dying, I'll just turn it off.' She pressed a few buttons and slipped it back into her pocket. 'That's what I wanted to ask: the phone reception isn't great here – are there any places that get better reception?'

'Yeah, it's a bit rubbish. The shed is a good place or about twenty metres down the drive. I get very sporadic access in the kitchen. Weirdly I get excellent reception in the freezer.'

'So if I want to make a call to my friends, I need to freeze my arse. . . bum off to do it.' Daisy laughed, ignoring the pointed look from Henry over her use of the word 'arse'.

'The shed is actually quite warm, so feel free to use that whenever you want – there's a heater in there too. You might get some reception from the very back of Henry's bedroom. Wi-Fi is good though, so you can always Skype or WhatsApp your friends instead.'

'Oh, that's a good idea. WhatsApp is pretty much the only social media thing I'm allowed on; Dad doesn't like the prospect of me talking to strangers on Twitter or Facebook.' Daisy glanced at him and then whispered to Penny loud enough for Henry to hear, 'He's a bit over-protective.'

'I am not, I just don't like the idea of you chatting to bloody perverts, that's all.'

Penny could see this was a bone of contention between the two of them so decided to change the subject.

'What are you up to today?' Penny asked Daisy.

'Not a lot, probably just play some video games or read.' Daisy shrugged.

'Or unpack all your junk,' Henry said.

'Well, if you want to, maybe after you've unpacked a few boxes you can come and watch me carve. I can show you how it's done. I have two to do today. December is such a busy month.'

'I'd love that. Is that OK, Dad?'

'You unpack that big box at the top of the stairs, then yes.'

Daisy frowned.

'Well, I'll be at it most of the day so pop by any time. I'll be in my cool room, so just come on in.' Penny indicated the room off the kitchen.

'Is it like a freezer?'

'No, it's just cooler than the house because the heating is either on low in there or not on at all. The doors to the walk-in freezer are in there too. You should dress quite warmly, but nothing too cumbersome.'

'Here you go,' Jill said, handing out two more plates of bacon sandwiches.

'Thank you, this looks delicious. Dad normally burns the bacon so I end up doing it for us,' Daisy said, nudging Henry playfully in the ribs.

Henry smiled. 'Thanks Jill, this is very kind.'

Penny watched them both smother their sandwiches in a thick layer of ketchup and smiled.

'There's an open-air ice skating rink in town. Can we go?' Daisy asked, before wolfing down almost half her sandwich in one big bite.

'Sure, we can go tonight,' Henry said, mirroring her actions with his own sandwich.

Penny focussed on the crumbs on her plate, arranging them into some kind of pattern. They were so close, so familiar with each other, she could never be a part of that. They had sixteen years of history together. Henry might flirt with her and they might share the odd dinner or breakfast, but she would never be part of their world, not really.

'Well, I've got a box to unpack. I'll see you later, Penny. Thanks for the sandwich,' Daisy said, waving at Jill, and she disappeared with a thunder of feet going upstairs in the annexe a moment later.

Penny could see Henry staring at her out the corner of her eye, but he didn't say anything, so she didn't either.

Eventually he stood up and wrapped the robe around himself, tying it at his waist just as he'd done to her the night before. He moved around the table towards Jill, who was deliberately reading the paper and trying to pretend she wasn't there.

'Jill, it was a pleasure meeting you and thank you so much for breakfast,' Henry said, placing a kiss on her cheek. 'I'll see you guys later, I'm sure.'

He walked back around the table towards Penny and she wondered for one brief, brilliant moment whether she would get a kiss too, but she didn't. He gave her a small smile and then disappeared back into his home, closing the door softly behind him.

Jill surveyed Penny over her mug of tea with a smile. 'Well, he's easy on the eye, isn't he?'

Penny couldn't even deny it.

'And he's keen on you.'

Penny shook her head. 'No, I really just think he's like that with everyone. He was flirting with you. I think it's the way he is.'

'There was a huge difference between how he treated me and how he treated you. The sexual tension between you two is blazing hot.'

Penny didn't have anything she could say to that. She had noticed it too but she didn't think it was anything Henry was going to act on any time soon.

'What are you afraid of?'

'Having my heart broken again.'

Jill's face softened and she moved around the table, enveloping Penny in a big hug. 'Honey, you deserve to be happy and loved, but you're never ever going to have that unless you take a risk. Henry seems like a good man – take a chance with him and just see what happens.'

Penny nodded. For the first time in over eight years she was attracted to someone and in ways she had never felt before. She would be a fool to throw that away before even giving it a go. She just had to hope that Henry was willing to give her a chance too.

Henry leant against the bedroom door, watching Daisy move around the room, putting glittery picture frames of her friends on shelves, soft toys on her bed, and rearranging her CDs. There just wasn't enough room for all her stuff in here; there wouldn't be enough room for all her stuff in the whole annexe, let alone in the tiny bedroom. Most of it was going to have to stay in boxes in the shed that Penny said they could use until they moved out.

Daisy caught him watching and smiled up at him.

'Are you OK about moving here? I know you'll miss your friends but. . .'

'It's fine. I will miss them, of course I will, but I've always wanted to live near the sea and this place is beautiful. Besides, this is a fantastic opportunity for you to work for a company like White Cliff Bay Furniture Company. It means more money, regular hours. Plus we can be here to help Anna with the baby when she needs it too. I really think we did the right thing in coming here.'

Henry smiled. Through her endless, almost innocent, enthusiasm for everything, especially Christmas, there was a very wise young lady underneath her childlike exterior.

'I really like it here in Lilac Cottage. Can we stay? I know you wanted to move into the town and you wanted somewhere a bit bigger for us but. . . this feels like home. I know that's a weird thing to say after being here for such a short time but we've moved around so much over the last few years and this is the first place that I've really wanted to stay. I don't know if it's that incredible view from my bedroom window or having Penny and Bernard next door, but it feels good here.'

'I like it here too.'

'Penny is good company, I like her. She might be the only friend I make down here so. . .' She trailed off, awkwardly.

Henry felt a kick to the stomach, hating that Daisy felt that way. 'You're going to make a ton of friends. You're bright, funny, sweet, kind. What's not to like?'

Daisy shrugged and looked away, and Henry wondered if the fear of making friends and settling in was at the root of the nightmare.

'What were you doing in Penny's house last night? She came to get me because you were having a nightmare on her sofa.'

Although it was inappropriate for Daisy to go in Penny's house, it was the nightmare that troubled him more than anything. Daisy only normally had nightmares when something was bothering her.

'Oh god, I'm sorry. I was in our lounge and the door was open and I thought I'd just go and see Bernard for a while. I must have fallen asleep.'

'And the nightmare?'

Daisy shrugged. 'No idea.'

'I was concerned something might be worrying you. Is it starting at a new school or. . . about Penny?'

She looked confused. 'Why would I be worried about Penny? She's absolutely lovely.'

'That I'm sort of going on a date with her on Tuesday. It's not a proper date, I can cancel if you want.'

'Dad, I want you to go out on dates. It's high time you got yourself a nice woman to look after you. I'm certainly tired of doing it.' She grinned mischievously. 'Just pick someone lovely, not anyone like that bitch Emily.'

'Watch your language.'

'It's true though, she was.'

'I know she was, but I still don't want you to use words like that.'

'Give me one word to describe your ex-girlfriend that isn't a swear word.'

Henry couldn't. 'OK, no one like Emily, I promise.'

'But I don't think you should go out with Penny either, not properly,' Daisy said, and Henry couldn't help the huge wave of disappointment that crashed through him at those words.

'Why not?'

'She's. . . vulnerable. She's like those puppies you see in the advert for the dogs' homes, those ones that have been beaten or neglected.'

Jeez, the kid was astute.

'I know there have been other women beyond the ones that you have dated seriously, the ones that never get brought back to the house, that you meet up with occasionally and. . .' Daisy waved her hand vaguely. Henry blushed. Shit, he thought he had been discreet. 'Penny is an all-or-nothing kind of girl. Don't use her and then cast her aside for the next. Either give her everything or don't go out with her at all.'

'Wise words for someone so young.'

Daisy smiled and carried on with her unpacking.

Could he give Penny everything? She was wonderful and warm and funny and sexy as hell, but despite Daisy's magnanimous attitude towards him dating, it wouldn't be that easy to change their cosy two to a three. Everything was great with Daisy now and he didn't want to do anything to upset their happy little equilibrium again. Penny couldn't be a casual thing either, he knew that, he wouldn't hurt her like that. So it looked like she was out of bounds.

Chapter 6

Penny was busy carving a giant angel for the forthcoming competition the next night, which had been taking a back seat for all the Christmas orders. This one was quite tricky with all the folds in the angel's dress, the long flowing hair, and the feathers on the wings, but she loved the challenge. She was listening to her beloved Westlife album, singing – or probably wailing – as she chipped away the detail on the angel's face. A movement caught her eye and she whirled around to see Henry and Daisy watching her from the doorway.

She quickly pulled out her headphones. 'How long have you two being standing there?'

'Long enough to hear your beautiful voice.' Henry smiled.

'And long enough to see your wonderful dancing,' Daisy said, trying to hold back a giggle.

Penny blushed, knowing her dancing had consisted of a lot of bum wiggling.

'I'm just checking it's OK for Daisy to hang out with you for a few hours?' Henry said, wrapping an affectionate arm around his daughter.

'Of course you can.' Penny smiled at Daisy.

'Just tell her to clear out if she starts to annoy you, she won't be offended.'

Daisy laughed.

'There's an old jacket of mine next door in the cloakroom. It's thin and lightweight but will keep you warm. There's also an old pair of steel-toecapped boots and some gloves – go and put them on and then I'll show you a few things.'

Daisy disappeared into the cloakroom, leaving Henry standing there staring at her.

After a long while he finally spoke. 'Thank you for doing this, you're very kind. She has a huge passion for art, especially sculpture. She took a wood carving course over the summer so she loves stuff like this. But, seriously, if she gets in your way just tell her to get out.'

'She won't be in my way.'

Henry continued to stare at her. He ran his hand over the stubble on his face awkwardly. 'Listen, about our date on Tuesday. . .'

'I'm ready,' Daisy announced, coming to stand in the freezer with her hands on her hips, looking like some kind of superhero.

Penny laughed. 'Well, come in then.'

Daisy walked in and looked at the sculpture in awe and Penny wondered what it looked like through her eyes.

'Can I touch it?'

'Yes, of course,' Penny said at the same time as Henry said, 'No.'

'It's fine, you can't harm it. It's perfectly dry too. It hasn't been out of the freezer long enough for it to start to melt yet.'

Daisy tentatively reached out to touch it. Penny looked over towards Henry, wondering what he had been going to say before Daisy came in.

'I'll leave you ladies to it.' Henry smiled at her sadly and then left, closing the door behind him, leaving Penny guessing that he had wanted to cancel their date. She tried to ignore the disappointment that twisted in her gut before turning back to Daisy.

'So I thought you might want to have a go yourself, if I show you the basic skills.'

Daisy turned to her with wonder and excitement in her eyes. 'Really?'

'Yes, it's quite easy to learn the basics and your dad says that you've already learned some wood carving, so the skills are completely transferable. I've cut up a block into two smaller blocks for you to have a play with, create whatever you want. Now normally I put a template on the side of the ice and go over the lines lightly with this chisel, but you can just draw your own design with it.' Penny hammered the chisel into a large block of ice that stood on the table. She quickly marked out a basic star outline. 'Once you've done that you can go over the lines with a die grinder, which makes the outline a bit deeper, like this.' She fired up the die grinder and very carefully used the short drill bit to go over one of the lines. She saw Daisy watching her intently the whole time, watching the angle at which she held the power tool, how much pressure was used, taking it all in. 'I can then use the chainsaw to cut out the bits you don't want.'

'Can I use the chainsaw?' Daisy said, keenly.

Penny smiled at her enthusiasm. 'Not today. It's very powerful and one slip and your whole hand would come off. I don't think your dad will thank me for that. But I will show you how to use the other tools, safely. Once I've used the chainsaw, you can use this v-shaped chisel to scrape away the bits you don't want. Once you've done that, I can show you which tools to use depending on what effect you want or what design you are making. There's different techniques to create feathers or clothes or fur, so I can show you those, depending on what you're making. I'd go for something simple first like a bell or a Christmas tree or. . .'

'An angel,' Daisy said, staring at Penny's piece in awe.

'Yes, if you want to, but that's quite a tricky piece to do, especially on a small scale. But go for it, if that's what you want.' Penny handed her a pair of goggles.

Daisy picked up the chisel and held it in her hand and then started chipping away, very carefully, onto the flat face of one of the smaller ice blocks Penny had laid out for her. Penny watched her for a moment, so she could improve her technique if she needed to, but Daisy was an absolute natural. She was taking her time, each mark she made considered and thoughtful, not going too deep. Penny smiled as what appeared to be an intricate snowflake started to appear. The girl had high hopes, but she liked that about her; Daisy obviously liked a challenge too.

'Give me a shout when you want to use the die grinder and I'll start you off,' Penny said, moving back to her angel.

Daisy chipped away silently for a few minutes. It was nice for Penny to have someone to work alongside for a change. Even though they weren't talking, it was still good to have the company.

'So do you like my dad?' Daisy said, without taking her eyes off the block of ice.

That wasn't really a conversation Penny was willing to have with anyone, least of all Henry's daughter.

'All the women like him,' Daisy went on. 'I can't see the attraction myself.'

'Well, you're not supposed to.'

'Ha. No, I suppose not. But women fall over themselves to be with him. I guess he must be nice to look at.'

'So he has a lot of girlfriends?' Penny asked, still trying to avoid saying whether she found him attractive.

'Yes. I mean, not girlfriends, just women that he sort of sees on a casual basis, the ones I'm not supposed to know about.

They never last long though, a few dates here or there before he moves on to the next. I don't think he has any interest in anything serious. There've only been two semi-serious girlfriends over the years. Rosie was lovely, but the other one was awful. He generally tries to avoid relationships because of me, which I feel really bad about. He thinks he can't do both – be a dad *and* a boyfriend – but he can. He'd make someone a wonderful husband one day and I'm sure he'd like more kids, he's so good with Bea and Oliver.' Daisy continued to work on her block, making gentle taps here and there.

Penny bent down to smooth off some of the scratch marks from the angel's dress. 'How would you feel if he got married, had another baby?'

'Honestly, I'd love it. He's been stuck with me ever since he was sixteen; he deserves to be happy.'

'Your dad adores you. I don't think he would consider raising you as being stuck with you.'

'Oh, I know he loves me, I see that every day, but I've obviously put a dent in the life he would have led. I want him to find someone he loves, who loves him. I always try to be understanding about him dating women as he should have a life outside of being a dad, but the last one was a complete bitch. Don't tell him I said that, he hates hearing me swear. So I want him to choose someone lovely, though I totally get that who I would choose for him and who he would choose for himself would probably be two different people. Although I think he likes you, which is a first for us both to like the same woman.'

Penny felt a tightening in her throat and she tried to clear it before she spoke. 'Really?'

Daisy nodded. 'But he went through a bad break-up with his last girlfriend and it got all messy because of me so he's not looking for anything serious at the moment. I told him not to mess around with you unless he thinks he can cope with something serious and he really doesn't do serious.'

Penny stared at her angel without even seeing it. So that was why he had tried to cancel their date earlier – because Henry didn't want anything serious with her. Well, if he was only interested in a quick fling, then it was a good job it had stopped before it had started.

'I didn't say the wrong thing, did I? I just didn't want to see you getting hurt,' Daisy said, obviously noticing Penny's disappointment with this new turn of events.

Was she that needy and pathetic that even a sixteen-year-old girl had noticed it?

'No, it's totally fine. I'm happy on my own. I like Henry, but I don't *like* him.'

'Well, that's cool then, you two can be friends. He needs friends in White Cliff Bay and I expect it gets lonely for you up here sometimes. You'll be good for each other.'

And that was true. She hadn't rented out the annexe with the hope of finding a man, she'd done it with the hope of finding a friend, and it seemed that she had done that with Henry and even with Daisy. She would be grateful for that.

'You should come ice skating with us tonight.'

Penny couldn't think of anything worse than being the pity date, even if the alternative was a night in watching old reruns of *Quantum Leap* with a tub of Ben & Jerry's. 'I can't really skate.'

'My dad will help you, he's really good, he used to have lessons when he was younger. That's how he and my mum met, apparently, at the ice rink. She was so impressed with his skills that. . . well, nine months later I arrived.'

Penny blinked, surprised at her candour. 'Do you ever see your mum?'

'No. Thank god. Apparently she's heavily involved in drink and drugs. Lucky escape for me.' She gave the ice a hard whack.

'Henry told you that?'

'No, my aunt Caitlyn did, my mum's sister. I still see her and my grandparents from time to time, though they never see my mum at all. Whenever they come round they always pick holes in the way that my dad raises me, but at least he stuck by me, didn't run off to Australia as soon as I was born.'

There was bitterness there and Penny just wanted to hug Daisy but she didn't know her well enough to be able to do that.

Daisy stepped back to inspect her work. 'I think I'm ready to use the die grinder now.'

Penny picked up the power tool and moved to have a look at what Daisy had created. The sketch of the snowflake was beautiful and very intricate. It would be unlikely that Daisy would be able to carve it successfully but it would be a great design for practising several different skills on. She powered up the die grinder and went over one of the lines that Daisy had made with the chisel.

'Don't push too hard, just let the grinder do the work for you,' Penny explained before carefully passing the tool to Daisy's greedy hands. She watched Daisy push the drill bit carefully into the ice. 'That's it, just go really slow and then you shouldn't stray from the lines.'

'What if I make a mistake?'

Penny shrugged. 'Most mistakes can be incorporated into the design. Besides, it's your first time, you're going to make mistakes. Just don't panic if you do.'

She stepped back to watch Daisy move the die grinder with all the concentration of a Grand Master at a chess match.

Satisfied that she was doing it safely she moved back to the angel on the pretence of doing her own work, though surreptitiously keeping an eye on Daisy at the same time, but Daisy's focus didn't waver once.

She watched her work and felt her heart twinge. Daisy's mum had missed out on this beautiful child growing up into a wonderful, talented, smart young lady. How could she have turned her back on that? Henry had done an incredible job on his own and Daisy was someone he could be very proud of. But it was clear why he didn't want a serious relationship. He didn't want anyone to hurt Daisy like her mum had.

As disappointing as it was, Penny would accept the friendship and not hope for any more. She ignored the ache in her heart that told her that would be easier said than done.

Henry popped his head around the connecting door later to see if Daisy had emerged from the cool room. He knew Daisy was very easy to get along with but he didn't want her outstaying her welcome. Jill was cutting into a huge loaf of bread and looked up and smiled when she saw him.

'Hello there,' she said, resuming her carving. 'Can I make you some lunch?'

'Oh no. I'm fine. I was just making sure Daisy wasn't getting on Penny's nerves.'

Jill gestured for him to sit down at the table and, recognising that she wasn't the sort of person that you ever argued with, he did as he was told.

'Penny hasn't got a bad bone in her body; I think she is physically incapable of thinking bad of someone. Daisy could pitch up in her house every day and I don't think Penny would ever get annoyed with her – she just hasn't got it in her.'

'Yes, she's very sweet.'

'You like her.'

It wasn't a question and Jill seemed to command honesty. 'Yes.'

'She's not someone you can have a fling with. She is fragile and I never want to see her get hurt again.'

'She told me briefly about Chris and the baby. I bet she was devastated.'

'She was, but Chris was an arsehole. You'll never hear me swear but there is no other word that I can use to describe him. Well, there are plenty of worse words. I think she would have been fine had he stayed with her just for a month or two after the miscarriage. She would have been upset for the baby, of course, but for him to leave her just two days after the miscarriage was the worst thing he could have ever done. She found out later there had been someone else too, which was a double betrayal. But the worst part of it was how he acted afterwards. The people of the town realised what he had done and so many of them were angry with him, and to save face he bad-mouthed her to anyone and everyone who would listen, told everyone she was deranged and crazy, said some really horrible things about her. Although most people didn't believe it and he ended up just making it worse for himself, there were some that did, especially his friends. Her parents protected her from most of it but it was still a tough blow for her when she was dealing with everything else. There has been no one for her since and I know it's because she doesn't want to get hurt like that again.'

'I'm not going to hurt her. I'm not sure what will happen between us. I'd like to be her friend more than anything. Maybe in time that friendship will turn into something more, and maybe not, but I have no intention of ever hurting her.'

Jill nodded seriously and then blushed. 'My apologies, it was wrong of me to talk to you about her like this. I'm sure she won't thank me for it. But if you spend any length of time in her company you will see what a truly wonderful person she is. I love her like she was my own daughter and I only want the best for her.'

'I want that too.'

'Oh, let's change the subject, she'll kill me if she knows I've said all this. Do you want tomatoes in your sandwich?'

Henry nodded and watched as Jill busied herself with making the food. The truth was he had already seen what kind of person Penny was and he was having a hard time coming up with reasons why he should stay away. Something serious was not good for Daisy, not so soon after the disaster with Emily, but any kind of relationship with Penny was only ever going to be that.

'Come on.' Penny ignored the pout from Daisy, after telling her that they had to stop. 'We'll have some lunch and then we can go back to it later this afternoon. It's important to take breaks when working at low temperatures and it's not exactly warm in here. I normally give myself a maximum of two hours of carving before taking a long break. Your snowflake will still be here later.'

Penny moved to admire Daisy's work. 'This is really good. If you ever wanted a job, I'd be happy to employ you. I turn down so many jobs because I just don't have the time to do them.'

'I would love that!' Daisy almost shouted and Penny regretted saying something before checking with Henry first. It was an offhand comment, but Daisy clearly did have the talent for it and Penny could easily teach her the skills she didn't know; she was obviously a fast learner.

'Well, we'll chat to your dad; if he's OK with it then you could help out at weekends, providing it didn't interfere with any homework. I can help you with any tricky bits and I'd pay you, of course.'

Daisy had the biggest grin on her face as Penny pushed both sculptures back into the freezer and then walked out into the kitchen.

Penny looked pleased when she saw two plates of sandwiches waiting for her and Daisy. Jill had obviously made lunch for them. But her smile grew even more when she saw Henry sitting at the table, drinking a mug of tea. She quickly tried to wipe the expression away and the feeling him being there gave her.

Henry looked up and flashed her a huge smile, and she hated that something as simple as that warmed her from the inside.

'Jill made us all lunch. She just left and she didn't want to disturb you by saying goodbye. She's a gem, that one, isn't she? Where did you find her?'

'She was our live-in housekeeper, cook and nanny growing up. She's never stopped coming round, even though it's only me here now. I feel bad, especially when I'm more than capable of cleaning myself, but when I once tried to stop her she laid the biggest guilt trip on me about everything that she'd done for us and then didn't speak to me for over two weeks, despite all my apologies. Then one day she turned back up here cleaning again as if the whole argument had never happened. We've never spoken about it since nor would I ever suggest that she didn't clean again. I love her, she's literally like a second mum to me.'

'Maybe she needs the money.'

'Her husband is probably one of the richest people in the area, so I doubt that. He owns the White Cliff Bay Furniture Company.'

Henry paled significantly, backtracking over every comment he had made to Jill to make sure he hadn't said anything untoward.

'Oh, don't worry, he has nothing to do with the company any more. He took early retirement from being CEO many years ago. He still has shares in the company and he's on the board of directors but he leaves all the management side of things to his son and daughter.'

Penny watched Daisy grab her sandwich and take a massive bite before even sitting down, but at a glare from Henry she quickly sat at the table. Penny washed her hands and then joined her.

'I got the impression that Jill didn't have any children?'

'She doesn't; Clara and Edward are her step-children, from Thomas's previous marriage. She was housekeeper for them too, which is how she and Thomas met. When his wife died she was there for him a lot. A year later he married her and they've been happily married ever since.'

'I think I met Edward at the interview,' Henry said, thoughtfully.

'I'm sure you did, he is very hands-on. He knows everyone's name at the factory and oversees everything that happens. He seems a lovely man.'

'Don't think I met Clara, though.'

'You probably didn't. I don't think she gets involved in that side of the business at all. She's joint CEO but I think her role is more design or publicity or something like that. Well, her team is in charge of that. I've never met her but by all accounts she isn't a nice person.'

Penny looked at Henry's empty plate in front of him. 'Did Jill make you lunch too?'

He nodded. 'I popped by to see if Daisy had finished about half an hour ago and she insisted I stayed for lunch. Sorry, we'll be eating you out of house and home at this rate. But you can come for dinner tonight before we go ice skating. We have that Italian that Jade kindly brought round.'

Penny bit into her sandwich, her stomach twisting with a sudden unease. What had he and Jill been talking about for half an hour? Jill was a wonderful friend and she'd never say anything bad about her, but she did wonder how far Jill's over-protective streak for her might stretch in her conversation with Henry.

'We had a lovely chat about the cruise she and Thomas went on this year,' Henry said, as if reading her mind.

She tried to relax a little bit, but the way that he was staring at her left her in no doubt that she probably came up in conversation at some point.

'I've invited Penny to come ice skating with us tonight,' Daisy said before she stuffed the last piece of sandwich in her mouth.

Henry hesitated before speaking, just long enough for Penny to think he didn't really want her to come.

'Of course you should come with us.'

'Oh no, it's fine. I have work to do here and there's a movie I really wanted to see on TV...' It sounded lame and pathetic even to her ears.

'Come on, it'll be fun. It's Christmas, you have to enjoy the festivities,' Daisy insisted.

'No, I don't want to intrude. I think it's lovely that you two are going together. But I'm very happy staying here.'

'But—' Daisy started.

'Daisy, if she doesn't want to come then we're not going to force her,' Henry said.

Penny frowned as she sipped her tea. Although she couldn't think of anything worse than going with Henry because his daughter had forced Penny on him, she was a bit sad how quickly Henry had closed down the topic of her going. He was clearly relieved that Penny had said she wouldn't come.

'But she's only saying no because she can't skate. Of course she doesn't want to be sitting up here on her own, while the rest of the town is enjoying the festivities.'

'Is that true, you can't skate?' Henry asked, his soft grey eyes watching her intensely.

'I know, it's kind of ironic, isn't it, being an ice carver and all, but no, I can't.'

'Well, I can teach you, if that's the reason.'

'No, really, I don't want to be in the way.'

Henry leant across the table towards her, his eyes focussed only on her. When he spoke his voice was low. 'If you want to come then come, if you don't then don't, but don't not come because of any other weird reason floating around in your head about me not wanting you there, because I do.'

Daisy stared between them as if she was watching a tennis match.

'OK,' Penny said, quietly. She wasn't entirely sure what the right answer was. She did want to go but she didn't want Henry to be forced into taking her.

'OK, you'll come?'

Penny nodded, feeling suddenly very silly for making such a fuss.

'Good,' Henry said. Putting his mug down, he got up and walked out.

'I'm sorry about him, he has no patience at all. But if he didn't want you to come, he would say so. Look how he was with Jade the other night,' Daisy said.

'Daisy, get your arse in here and let Penny have some peace for a few hours,' Henry called through the open door, and Daisy smiled with love for her dad.

'I'll see you later,' she said and ran quickly after him. After a few moments Henry appeared in the doorway, flashing Penny a brief tiny smile before closing the door.

Penny sat staring at the door in confusion. What the hell had just happened?

Chapter 7

Penny could see Henry in the shed, moving around and looking completely at ease as he worked.

Feeling the need to repair their tentative friendship, though she wasn't sure why, she cut a big slice of Christmas cake, made a mug of tea and carried it out to the shed.

He didn't notice her at first. A foot-long piece of wood was clamped to the table and he was chipping into it with a small chisel. It looked like the beginnings of a reindeer.

She watched him run his hands lovingly over the wood, brushing away the sawdust. His hands were big and strong and very capable. He had a huge smile on his face as he worked, evidently loving the creativity of what he was doing. He was obviously very talented and if he could create something this detailed and small by hand, it was little wonder White Cliff Bay Furniture Company had hired him. He paused for a moment and she stepped forwards.

Either sensing or hearing her move, he turned around and his face lit up into a grin when he saw her, which warmed her from the inside. That feeling faded very quickly as she suddenly felt very foolish for coming to apologise to him when clearly he hadn't been bothered at all by what had passed between them a few hours before. Now, standing there with a slice of cake and a redundant apology drying on her lips, the offer of a cake looked flirtier than she had wanted. It reminded her of Jade arriving with an Italian the night before.

She really didn't want to be lumped in with the women of the town throwing themselves at him. She groaned inwardly. Why was he making her second-guess everything? She felt so raw around him, as if a plaster covering an eight-year-old wound had been ripped off and he was poking at it without even realising it.

'Hi,' he said, the grin not disappearing from his face.

'I thought you might be hungry,' Penny said, cringing at how awkward this was, though he hadn't seemed to notice.

'Thank you.' In two large strides he was in front of her. He took the cake gratefully, taking a huge bite. His eyes locked on hers.

She forced her gaze away from him and focussed on the reindeer. Now he had stepped away from it, she could see it in all its glory and it was stunning.

She stepped away from him and his intense proximity to look more closely at it. 'This is beautiful.' She ran her fingers over the tiny intricate antlers. 'Do you make them to sell?'

He shook his head as he swallowed down the cake. 'No, just for fun. I always make a new tree decoration every year for Daisy, it's kind of a tradition, that and making terrible mince pies on Christmas Day. Daisy has started making her own wooden tree decorations too and we exchange them on Christmas morning.'

'I love that idea.'

He stepped closer. 'You do? Maybe I'll make one for you this year too.'

She looked up at him and then back at the reindeer. His flirting was making her uncomfortable. He would hurt her. If she let herself be swept away by the comments and looks of affection, she had no doubt that he would break her heart after a few weeks. He didn't want anything serious.

'You're very talented,' Penny said, annoyed at the crack in her voice. She didn't want him to know how much he affected her. She blushed as she realised that what she had just said was very flirty too. She really had no idea how to act around men. She had never properly dated. Chris had been her only real boyfriend and he had instigated their relationship. She had never tried to impress him or say the right things because in the first month or so he had been completely smitten with her. Though her shine had clearly rubbed off very quickly.

'Making furniture is what I'm most comfortable with. This is just a bit of fun for me, it's nothing like the kind of sculptures you produce,' Henry said, leaning around her to brush away some more sawdust. 'I bet you could do something like this very easily. Have you ever carved with wood before?'

Penny swallowed as his sweet, spicy, Christmassy scent enveloped her. She shook her head.

'Have a go.' He picked up a tiny chisel and offered it to her.

'Oh, I couldn't, I don't want to ruin it.'

He leant around her, bracketing her with his arms as he took her hands and placed them on the chisel. Goosebumps exploded on her body at his touch. She moved the chisel to the thick fur around the reindeer's neck. Henry's hands stayed over hers, even though they both knew it wasn't necessary. As Penny had told Daisy this morning, the skills were completely transferable. She obligingly chipped a few small chunks of wood away, making the fur collar more defined. It was fun to work on a different canvas. This one was a lot more permanent than the carvings she created.

A cough came from behind them and Henry immediately stepped back, away from Penny.

Daisy was standing in the doorway, with a slight scowl on her face. She turned her attention away from her dad and looked at Penny. 'There's a man here to see you. Josh?'

Penny nodded. 'Can you tell him I won't be a second?'

Daisy hesitated for a moment then left.

Penny let out a breath she hadn't realised she had been holding and brushed the hair off her face in frustration.

'I'm not sure what is going on here, whether all this – the flirting, looks, touches and comments – is just some kind of game for you, or you are just incapable of not flirting with a woman, but nothing is going to happen between us, so you can stop it now.'

Henry looked stunned. 'You're flirting with me.'

'I am not.'

'You brought me cake,' Henry said, with exasperation.

'I'm sorry, I didn't realise cake was the international sign language for I want to get you into bed. If that's the case I must have been flirting with my friend Maggie every Saturday for the last five or six years.'

'I'm rubbish at reading women, but I thought you made it pretty bloody obvious you were attracted to me.'

Penny felt her mouth fall open. What had she done to give him that impression?

He stepped closer. 'Your breathing accelerates when I come near you, your pupils dilate, I can see your pulse hammering against your throat, your body goes into goosebump overdrive whenever I touch you,' he said, softly laying his finger on her arm as her body betrayed her by proving his point.

'Fine. I am attracted to you.'

'I'm very attracted to you, so what's the problem?'

'You.' She gestured frantically at him and all his spectacular gorgeousness. She suddenly stopped her protests for a second to appreciate his wonderful words. He was attracted to her. The endless flirting hadn't just been a bit of silly fun for him; he actually was attracted to her. *Very* was the word he used.

'What's the problem with me?' Henry asked.

She stared at him, realising he wasn't the problem, she was.

'I can't do a relationship. I go into them with everything I have. I'm sure that's not the kind of thing you're looking for.'

He didn't argue against it but finally he spoke. 'You're right, I'm not looking for anything serious right now.'

'And I'm not looking for anything casual. I haven't been in a relationship since the last one ended in the most heartbreaking way possible. If I go into a relationship again, it has to be with someone I can trust not to hurt me. You seem lovely and kind and Daisy adores you, but you also seem the sort that can get any woman he wants and I certainly don't think you want to put up with all my insecurities and baggage and crap. So can we please put a stop to all of this flirting, because it's killing me.'

Penny was suddenly aware of Daisy standing in the door again. She quickly turned to face her.

'Sorry, Penny, Josh says he's in a bit of a rush.'

Penny nodded and, with one more glance at Henry's dumbfounded face, she hurried out. Well, if she wanted to put Henry off her for good, she'd certainly done that with all her crazy. The men of the town really were right. She was damaged goods.

92

Henry watched her go, confused by how quickly and disastrously that conversation had gone. He didn't know why he was so drawn to Penny; only a few hours before he had sworn to himself that he wouldn't pursue things with her, but he couldn't seem to stay away from her. He looked back at Daisy, who fixed him with a glare as she folded her arms across her chest.

'What?'

'You said you weren't going to get involved with her.'

'I didn't say that.'

'We agreed that she was an all-or-nothing kind of girl. You're not capable of anything serious. You're going to hurt her and I really like her. She's said she's happy to teach me about carving and that I can work with her part-time around school and she will pay me to carve. You have no idea how much I want to work with her. My first proper job doing something I absolutely love and you're going to screw it all up for me.'

'I won't screw it up. I have no intention of hurting her, that's the last thing I want.'

'But you will. Look at Rosie. You broke her heart.'

'Rosie was never anything serious.'

'It was for her.'

He knew he had hurt Rosie when he broke up with her and he felt bad for that, but the worst thing was how upset Daisy had been by the break-up too. He shook his head. Why was he trying to justify his relationships to his sixteen-year-old daughter? Surely it should be the other way around.

'She was never going to be a good fit for us.'

'She doesn't need to be a fit for us, she needs to be a fit for you. You finished it with her because she was getting too close.'

It was true that he found it hard to imagine ever trusting or loving someone enough to have them in his and Daisy's life permanently. He always kept women at a distance. But Daisy had lectured him about his commitment issues after he had split with Rosie and he had tried to prove he didn't have these issues by bringing Emily into their life, which had resulted in the very thing he had tried for years to protect Daisy from. Daisy feared rejection, he knew that; she was scared that one day he would leave her just as her mum had. But what Henry feared was any woman he was with rejecting Daisy, making her feel for one second unloved and unwanted, and Emily had done just that. It would be a long time before he could trust someone enough to let them into his life again.

'Look, I like Penny and the ice carving is important to me. If you break her heart she is hardly likely to want me around any more. Be nice to her, be friends with her, but please don't sleep with her,' Daisy said.

'Hang on, you don't get to dictate who I do or don't go out with. I would never presume to tell you who you can or can't date.'

'Oh, if that's the case, you'll be OK with me dating the huge tattooed guy who was just flirting with me in the kitchen.'

Henry let out an involuntary growl. 'That's different and you know it.'

'I have never asked you not to date anyone before, not even bitches like Emily.'

'Watch your language.'

'The point being I hope you can see how important this job is to me. I like living here. I know it's small but the views are incredible and I really like living next door to Penny and Bernard. I think she's lovely.'

'I do too.'

'So do you really want to ruin what could be a fantastic friendship for you two and ruin my first job just for a few weeks of fun?'

Henry couldn't help feeling like the naughty child called in front of the headmaster.

Daisy walked back towards the house and Henry rubbed his head with the sudden complications. But if it really was that important to Daisy, he would have to forget about being with Penny once and for all.

Daisy was right, he didn't want anything serious and Penny didn't want to get hurt. It was better all round if he stayed away from her.

Henry knocked softly on the connecting door later that night as Daisy tucked into the Italian with great relish. The girl was like a gannet, eating everything and anything in sight, and she still stayed stick-thin.

'Save some for the rest of us, greedy guts.'

Daisy grinned up at him with her winning smile and carried on eating at full speed.

There was no answer from Penny so Henry tentatively let himself in.

He didn't want to call out if she was working in the cool room; if he scared her while she was working with some of those tools she could end up cutting off one of her fingers. He opened the cool room door but the room was empty. He closed it and that was when he saw her lying on the sofa in the darkness of the front room.

He moved closer and noticed she had fallen asleep reading some romance book. He carefully took the book out of her hands, marked the place with a piece of paper and put it on the coffee table. She was sleeping peacefully, her mouth parted slightly, her long eyelashes dusting her cheeks. He sat down on the coffee table, feeling mildly creepy watching her sleep, but finding her peaceful slumber incredibly alluring too.

He ran his hand up her arm, giving her a gentle shake, and her eyes fluttered open.

'Hey,' he said softly. 'Dinner is ready and if we don't get in there soon, the hungry caterpillar in there will eat it all.'

She looked around in confusion. 'Did I fall asleep?'

'Evidently.'

She sat up and swung her legs off the sofa, but he put a hand on her shoulder to stop her getting up. 'Give yourself a moment to wake up.'

'I never fall asleep during the day.' She rubbed her face and looked up at him. Her hair was sticking out at all angles and there was something just so achingly endearing about her.

She stood up and shivered. He grabbed the blanket from the back of the sofa and wrapped it around her and, with his hand on her back, he guided her towards the connecting door.

As they walked into the kitchen, Daisy looked up at them in horror at Penny's appearance. With the bright red blanket, pale face and hair everywhere she did look like she'd just been rescued from a hurricane or plane crash. Henry made frantic gestures behind Penny's back so Daisy wouldn't say anything to make Penny feel self-conscious. Thankfully, after sixteen years of living together, she knew him well enough to understand him.

'Here, sit down,' Daisy said gently, as if Penny had just received some bad news and needed tender loving care.

Daisy patted the seat next to her and Penny sat down, obviously still waking up.

Penny started helping herself to some of the food and Daisy mouthed over her head, asking if she was OK. Henry nodded and mimed that she had been sleeping. Daisy sighed with relief.

Daisy liked Penny and it was easy to see why. He really liked her too. But it was almost unheard of for Daisy to like the same women he did. She had never really liked any of his girlfriends apart from Rosie and, although he hadn't the best track record for choosing wisely, he did wonder whether some of it was to do with not wanting to share him after she'd had him to herself for the last sixteen years. He didn't want to upset Daisy and he worried over how much his daughter would still like Penny if he ever got involved with her, or if she would find fault in her just like all the others. Daisy had practically made him promise not to pursue things with Penny and he had to remember that.

They ate and chatted about the upcoming ball for a while and then Daisy got up and started clearing away the plates.

'We better get going,' Henry said, glancing at his watch.

Penny nodded. 'I'll just grab my shoes and coat, I won't be a second.'

Sure enough, she was back in the kitchen a few seconds later, with her shoes on, fastening her coat, her hair still a wild, tangled bush.

Henry bit his lip. As much as it didn't bother him in the slightest going out with her looking like this, he knew it would bother her.

'Erm. . . maybe you should, er, brush your hair first,' Henry said.

Penny looked at him in shock. 'Why, what's the matter with it?' She glanced at herself in the reflection of the window and her eyes widened. 'Oh my god, why didn't you tell me I looked such a state?'

'Because we're friends, and if you came to dinner in your tattiest stained pyjamas, I wouldn't give a shit.'

Penny turned to look at him, a huge, genuine smile forming on her face. 'We're friends?'

'Yes, of course.' He wasn't sure what had caused her to smile so much but he liked it a lot. Penny didn't say anything else, she just walked out, presumably to do something about her wayward hair, but she had the biggest grin on her face.

He looked at Daisy in confusion and she came and hugged him. 'You know, for all your grumpiness you can be very sweet sometimes.'

'What did I do?'

Daisy let him go. 'I'm just going to grab my hat.'

She ran upstairs and he stared after her. Women, he'd never understand them.

Penny came back in with her hair suitably brushed and swept up in a loose ponytail. He caught her arm as she moved towards the door.

'Look, I'm sorry about –' he gestured towards the shed – 'the flirting and everything. I don't want to do anything that makes you feel uncomfortable and I certainly don't want to do anything to hurt you, but I would like to be friends. I promise no more flirting from now on.'

She eyed him speculatively for a moment and then smiled. 'I'd really like to be friends too.'

She stuck out her hand for him to shake and he smiled as he took it. The feel of her skin against his was like a jolt to the stomach. Her eyes were alight with happiness, trusting him so easily, when he barely trusted himself. Being friends was for the best.

Penny's heart sank a little as they walked down towards the seafront and she realised that the ice rink was directly outside The Pilchard, Chris's parents' pub, a place she had tried to avoid for the last eight years. His parents had been lovely while they were dating and had been very excited about the arrival of their first grandchild, even if her pregnancy had come very early in their relationship. But after the miscarriage, and shortly after the break-up, Chris had tried to tell anyone who looked badly on him for leaving her mere days after she had lost their child that she was unhinged, deranged and completely psychotic. Thankfully, most people hadn't believed it. She wasn't sure what his parents believed, but the fact they had never been to see her in the months after their grandchild had died probably meant they had believed everything their son had fed them. She'd seen them around town occasionally but they always scurried off in the opposite direction whenever they saw her, making an already awkward situation worse. Thankfully Chris didn't live in White Cliff Bay any more, but he did pop back now and then to see his parents and the thought of running into him when she still felt so much anger towards him was not one she relished.

She looked at the ice skating rink, determined she was going to enjoy her night out and not let any of her feelings ruin it for Henry and Daisy.

Standing just in front of the rink was a fire breather, mesmerising the crowds with his fiery talent, and the golden glow of the flames stood dramatically against the icy backdrop of the ice rink.

The ice rink looked magical and enticing as they approached. Fairy lights were strewn across the top of the rink in a criss-cross star pattern and they sent orbs of lights over the black waves immediately behind the rink. With only nine days until the Christmas Eve ball, it seemed that the Christmas festivities were well underway.

Penny smiled as couples old and young clung to each other as they slid gracefully past, families with small children linked between them creating small chains of people as they skated around the rink.

They paid and got changed into their skates. Penny stood up, wobbling on the blades. How was anyone supposed to walk in these things, let alone move with any kind of skill or grace? Her feet really hurt inside them, but she guessed that was to do with the muscles she was using to stay upright. She hobbled towards the entrance, knowing that if she had been trying to impress Henry, she was a million miles away from looking sexy right now. Daisy got on the ice first, skating off and zooming around with all the ease of someone who had been doing it for years. Henry got on and patiently waited for her, both hands out towards her for her to hold.

She grabbed them and stepped onto the ice. Immediately her legs were like Bambi's underneath her, sliding in opposite directions to each other, and she tried to run on the spot to stop herself from falling. She squealed, drawing a lot of unnecessary attention on herself. Henry immediately hauled her up against him, holding her steady, with his arms around her back and her face squashed against his chest.

Oh god, it felt too good in his arms. He was warm and strong and so solid. She tentatively rested her hands on his hips, trying to steady herself, but the rush of emotions that stormed through her at being held did nothing to quell her nerves.

'Don't panic, I've got you, I'm not going to let you fall, trust me,' Henry said softly, with all the patience and tenderness of addressing a frightened child.

Holding on to her forearms firmly, he pulled back slightly, holding her up.

'OK, relax, bend your legs a little and lean forwards slightly. I'm going to pull you round. Look at me, not your feet.'

She stared up at him and unbelievably he started skating backwards, taking her with him. He cast an odd glance over his shoulder now and again, but other than that his eyes stayed on hers the whole time.

'You're doing great, don't look down.'

She cast a look around and was surprised to see almost everyone on the rink and the spectators were watching her and Henry. Was she doing that badly that she was keeping everyone entertained with her wobbly gait? She flushed with embarrassment.

'What's wrong?'

'People are staring.'

'They're not, don't be so self-conscious.'

She glanced around again. 'No, they're definitely staring.'

Henry looked around as well, and she saw him frown as he saw all the eyes that were watching them.

'They're probably looking at me, you know, the new guy in town. People are curious,' he said, trying to placate her.

She looked at some of the townsfolk. Some were smiling at her encouragingly, and Suzanna, one elderly lady she knew quite well, gave her a big thumbs up and a toothy wink as they passed. Suddenly Penny realised why they were getting all the attention: they thought she and Henry were a couple and they were all smiling because it was the first time that Penny had been with a man in over eight years. It was embarrassing because it wasn't true.

'They think we're together,' Penny said, quietly. 'Sorry, these guys don't get out too much and me holding hands with a man is big news.'

Henry smiled. 'I'm not remotely bothered by it, so you shouldn't be either. If they want to think I'm going out with a beautiful woman, then I'm totally fine with that.'

Penny flushed again at the compliment.

'Right, start picking your feet up a little like this, so you can practise distributing your weight onto different feet.' He demonstrated lifting each of his feet off the ice ever so slightly and repeating it several times.

Penny blocked out the stares, studied his feet and attempted to do the same. It was surprisingly easy.

He gave her a few more pointers about pushing her legs back so that soon she was propelling herself across the ice. Even though he was still holding her hands, she felt like she was doing most of the work. He was a great teacher, so patient and demonstrative.

He stopped her and moved to her side, still holding one of her hands. 'Let's try it like this for a while. I won't let you fall.'

She knew he wouldn't. She tentatively pushed off and was pleased that she seemed to have the hang of it, though her legs felt like they were shaking under the strain. Her feet were still hurting and there were muscles screaming in her legs that she never knew she had. She caught sight of Daisy staring at them. The last thing she wanted was for Daisy to feel left out so she pulled to a stop, clinging on to the side.

'I'm just going to have a rest for a little while. Why don't you skate with Daisy for a bit and I'll get back on in a few minutes?'

Henry nodded and escorted her safely off the ice, before tearing after Daisy and chasing her around the rink.

Penny sat down on a bench, took her skates off and leant back against the sea wall. The waves were crashing onto the rocks about twenty metres below and she looked out at the little red and white striped lighthouse warning ships of the rocky islets that surrounded the bay.

Over the sound of the waves, she heard a shout of laughter come from the other side of the sea wall.

Penny knelt up and peered over the wall. The slipway behind her, used for the launch of boats, looked empty, but suddenly movement at the very bottom of the slip where it joined the water caught her eye.

She squinted against the bright lights of the ice rink to see two boys, Sam and Alex, playing just a few feet from the water's edge. The waves were crashing theatrically against the sea wall, mere inches from where they were standing, and the boys didn't seem fazed at all.

Where were Mike and Pippa, the kids' parents?

Loads of kids played on the slip during the day, but normally only when the tide was out. Three big shipwrecks had happened in the cove over the years and wonderful treasures – like cups, plates, coins, jewellery and various sailing paraphernalia – washed up on the slip on an almost weekly basis. Most of it was completely worthless, but for the children of the town it was like a little trove down there. She watched Sam and Alex now, filling their buckets up with bits of sea glass and other wondrous delights.

She looked around for Mike and Pippa. Surely they hadn't let them go and play down there when the tide was in?

Suddenly a huge wave crashed against the slip, covering the boys completely, and to Penny's horror, when the water receded, there was only one boy left on the slipway.

Chapter 8

She was on her feet before she even knew what she was doing, leaping over the small barrier separating the ice rink from the public and running to the top of the slipway.

She spotted Daniel, Maggie's husband, with his two small boys in tow, and he looked at her in horror as she ran past.

'Get help, call the lifeboat,' she yelled at him as she ran down the slip, yanking her coat off.

Alex, the oldest of the boys, was standing on the edge of the slip, trying to reach Sam, who was struggling in the water, too far out for either of them to reach.

Penny grabbed Alex's arm and pulled him away from the edge. 'Get help now.'

'But. . .' Alex was sobbing.

'Go!'

Alex ran up the slope and Penny turned and dived straight into the water, the icy waves closing over her head, the weight of her clothes dragging her down. She swam as far as she could underwater towards where she had last seen Sam. It was easier under the surface without the waves surging around her. Eventually she surfaced, just as a wave crashed over her head. The cold penetrated every inch of her body and she blinked blearily to try to see Sam. A flash of blond hair appeared momentarily over the waves and disappeared behind another surge a second later. She swam towards him, pushing with everything she had against the impending waves. She saw him again mere feet from her but when she tried to grab him the waves pulled him from her reach. She swam and pushed and grabbed and finally made contact with the back of his hood, pulling him towards her, hauling his tiny body against her own and determinedly trying to keep his head above the water, when another wave crashed over them. She couldn't see, couldn't breathe but she held Sam's struggling body against her with every last ounce of strength. They broke through the surface again and she briefly saw a crowd of people lining the slip, before another wave crashed over them. She pushed towards the slip but the waves surged around them, forcing them further and further away. She kicked frantically with her legs but it was hopeless.

Suddenly everyone on the slip started waving and pointing frantically at her and Sam, some people even cheering.

She turned around in the water and saw the bright orange RIB from the lifeboat station ploughing through the water towards her. The lifeboat crew were looking in the water for them but couldn't see them. She didn't dare wave in case she lost her grip on Sam.

Waves crashed over her and she just hoped they would see them soon.

A shout rang out from the boat and the next thing Dave, a local farmer, a rope with a small float on the end threw towards her. Holding Sam tight, she grabbed hold of it and Dave dragged her towards the side of the boat.

She held Sam up out of the water for them to take, but that forced her under the water. A hand came down and grabbed her, yanking her back to the surface as Dave took the boy from her.

She looked up blearily into the eyes of her friend George, who was holding onto her with grim determination. Another hand grabbed her other arm and between George and another man she was hauled aboard.

George knelt down in front of her, pulling a lifejacket over her head. 'Are you OK?'

She nodded, not able to talk as the cold night air sliced into her skin.

George quickly stood up and manoeuvred the boat back to the side of the slip. Penny glanced over at Sam huddled in Dave's arms. He was shivering but clearly alive and seemingly uninjured.

The boat slammed against the side of the slip. Dave quickly stood up and leant over the side to hand Sam back to his dad.

George helped her to her feet and Dave held out a hand for her to guide her ashore. Suddenly Henry was in front of her and he quickly lifted her to safety. He pulled the lifejacket off her and wrapped his coat around her tightly, though it did very little to dull the effects of the cold. Henry stared down at her. He looked furious.

'Take her to The Pilchard,' someone said. 'They've got a fire in there.'

Oh god, please no.

Henry turned and marched through the crowd, dragging her with him.

'Where's the pub?' Henry asked someone from the crowd, and they must have told him because he started to head that way, not relinquishing his hold on her.

The crowd surged around her, helping to push her up the ramp as her legs seemed unwilling to walk on their own, but every movement from her and every touch from someone else caused her wet clothes to touch her skin, making her even colder.

She was vaguely aware that Henry was only in his socks too, having clearly ditched his skates at some point.

The Pilchard loomed over them and she tried to pull back but Henry and the rest of the crowd were having none of it. The warmth of the pub swallowed them and Penny just hoped with everything she had that Chris was not going to be amongst the regulars tonight. People jostled around her and there was lots of shouts of confusion and calls for everyone to get out the way as Henry dragged her towards the fire.

Where was Sam, surely they would have brought him in here too? Penny looked around as she was shoved into a seat right in front of the flames and locked eyes with Chris's mum, Kathleen, as she pushed her way through the crowd to see what the fuss was about.

To her credit Kathleen only hesitated for half a second when she saw who it was that was causing all the attention before she moved into action.

'Come on, Penny, let's get you into some dry clothes.' Kathleen grabbed her hand and pulled her through the door that led to their living quarters.

Through the cold and exhaustion, Penny noticed that nothing had changed since she had frequented these corridors and rooms almost every day when she had been going out with Chris. The dark wood panelling, the tiled floor, the photos on the walls, everything was exactly as it was.

Even Kathleen hadn't changed; maybe she had a few more lines around the eyes and a few more flecks of grey in her hair, but she had remained relatively the same. She was even wearing one of her favourite shirts that Penny had seen her wearing many times when she had been dating Chris.

The scents of various cleaning solutions and the ever-present odour of alcohol was as prevalent as it always had been, mixed with the smells of food from the kitchens.

She didn't need these memories; she had spent eight years carefully keeping them locked up. She had been here the night she had miscarried and everything about that night came flooding back to her now. Panic, fear and the devastating loss slammed through her, coupled with the memories of how badly Chris had treated her afterwards.

Kathleen pulled her upstairs towards the bedrooms and she must have felt how awkward this reunion was too.

'Would you like a shower or a bath to warm yourself up?'

Penny shook her head, wanting to be out of there as quickly as possible, and Kathleen nodded with understanding.

Kathleen laid out some clean clothes and a towel on her bed and then hovered awkwardly for a moment.

'Thank you for this,' Penny muttered.

Kathleen smiled weakly before leaving her alone in the room.

With fumbling cold fingers she managed to get out of her wet clothes, dried herself off and dressed in the warm, dry clothes of her ex-boyfriend's mum in record time. She needed to get out of here, her chest was tight, her throat was raw with suppressed emotion.

She looked around for a plastic bag to put her wet clothes in and saw one propped up against a chest of drawers. She picked it up and carefully removed the contents and laid them on the bed, but her heart missed a beat when she saw the abundance of tiny baby clothes and a bear that had the word 'Grandson' emblazoned across its chest. As Chris was an only child it was obvious this was for him, or rather, his son. She ran her fingers across the softness of the bear, feeling numb, and it wasn't anything to do with the cold any more. She had heard, through the grapevine, that Chris had got married but she'd had no idea that he'd had a son; the grapevine had spared her that. She closed her eyes and prayed that the little boy who received this bear would be loved and adored by his dad and not hated as her child would have been years before. She hoped with everything she had that Chris had turned into someone wonderful like Henry, who loved Daisy so much there was no room for anyone else in his heart.

She dumped her wet clothes in the bag and walked out. She walked down the stairs into the warmth of the pub again and a loud cheer went up when her 'fan club' saw her. They all surged around her, patting her on the back and trying to thrust drinks in her hand.

She was finding it difficult to breathe, the tightness in her chest becoming unbearable. Henry was suddenly in front of her, his eyes blazing with a myriad of emotions.

'I need to go home, I can't stay here.'

He grabbed her hand and forced their way out of the pub, despite all the moans of protest behind them. They obviously wanted to celebrate her heroism until the early hours of the morning, but she got the feeling they probably would even without her there.

It was freezing outside and Penny knew it felt worse than it was because she still hadn't thawed out yet. Her whole body was aching, her muscles screaming at her.

'You guys stay and enjoy the ice skating, I'll get a taxi,' Penny said quietly, as Henry pulled her a little way along the street.

'Daisy has gone to collect our shoes. The car is here, I brought it as close as I could.' He bundled her into the passenger seat, but before he could climb into the driver's seat, Daisy was already clambering into the back.

'I'm sorry I ruined your night.'

Henry stared at her incredulously. 'By saving a child's life, yes, how incredibly selfish of you. I saw you dive into the sea. I honestly don't know whether to applaud your bravery or berate your stupidity – you could have been killed.'

'Let's go with applauding her bravery then, eh, Dad?' Daisy said from the back seat as she squeezed Penny's shoulder. 'You're a hero.'

Penny didn't feel very heroic; in fact, she felt pretty devoid of all emotion at the moment.

Henry seemed to guess that she didn't want to talk and they drove back up the winding lanes in silence. The further away they got from The Pilchard the more the pressure on her chest lessened slightly. She tried to order her emotions; she had done all her grieving for the baby she had lost eight years before, it didn't make sense to be upset again now, but walking back into The Pilchard had brought back so many memories of that horrible night. She had been dealt one bad blow after another by Chris in the immediate aftermath of the baby's death, and for some reason she associated the pub with all of that. Not only had he left her two days after the miscarriage, but he had also spread cruel lies around town about her. Then to find he had been sleeping with Jade behind her back the entire time she had been pregnant had been the ultimate betrayal.

To find out that Chris was now a parent again was a shock, especially after he had been so against her keeping their child. He had been young, they both were. But somehow, knowing he

111

had grown up and moved on, that hopefully he was in a better place now, a much better person, made so much of that bitterness and hate she felt for him fade away. Maybe losing his baby all those years before would make him treat his little boy like a king and truly appreciate how precious he was. She would hope for that.

They pulled up outside their house and she said her goodbyes to Henry and Daisy and let herself into her house. She ran upstairs and quickly changed out of the clothes that, although clean, still smelt of the pub.

When she came back downstairs in her pyjamas, Henry was waiting for her. He'd lit a fire and the golden glow infused the room with warmth and light.

'Are you OK?'

She stepped closer to him, hesitant because she wanted nothing more than to step into his arms and have him hold her tight, but she didn't know how to ask for that. Yet somehow, instinctively, he knew what she wanted and gave her just that. In one large stride he was in front of her, enveloping her in his arms. She wrapped her arms around his waist and leant her head on his chest, hugging him back.

He felt so good, so warm and solid and dependable. She had known him such a short amount of time yet she inexplicably trusted him. Everything melted out of her: the adrenaline and fear from rescuing Sam from the sea, the memories the pub evoked, her anger towards Chris, her inability and fear of moving on from her past. In his arms, in that moment, for the first time in a long time she was looking to the future. And maybe her future wasn't with this man, but she sure as hell wasn't going to hide away any more.

She clung on to him for what felt like an eternity, until eventually she pulled away slightly.

She looked up at him. 'Thank you, you have no idea how much I needed that.'

He cupped her face in his large, rough hands and kissed her forehead. Need for him erupted through her so fast it was almost painful. He moved back a little to look at her and his eyes scanned down to her lips, and in the light of the fire she watched them darken. She didn't hesitate this time; she reached up and kissed him.

Chapter 9

His response was instant, his hands holding her face gently, his lips touching hers with the softest of kisses, his mouth lingering slowly. His tongue licked her bottom lip, ever so slightly, and she opened to him. As his tongue touched hers, the taste of him exploded through her and she flushed with embarrassment at the moan that escaped her throat. The sweet, spicy smell of him invaded her senses, his touch on her face, the feel of him against her mouth, it was too much all at once. She wanted to separate each sensation, each feeling, each moment and appreciate it all slowly, but there was no time for any of that.

Eventually he pulled back slightly to look at her. He smiled. 'I've been wanting to do that since you opened the door to me on that first night.'

She smiled. 'Me too.'

He moved to the sofa, taking her with him. He sat down in the corner of the sofa and pulled her onto his chest, wrapping his arm around her shoulders.

'Do you want to talk about what went on tonight?' he asked softly.

She nodded, telling him all about Chris and his parents and the new baby, and he listened without interrupting, without taking his eyes off hers. It was a cathartic release to talk about it with someone after so long keeping it locked up inside. While she talked he wrapped a blanket around her, warming her from the outside and from the inside with his kind gesture.

When she had finished she rested her head on his chest and closed her eyes, suddenly feeling like she had run a marathon. She wasn't sure what the future held for her and Henry, but it didn't seem to matter right then, lying in his arms.

He shifted slightly beneath her and she found her hand instinctively gripping his shirt, before she quickly released him. She opened her eyes to look at him and he smiled at her.

'Don't worry, I'm not going anywhere.'

She smiled and let herself drift off to sleep.

Henry woke the next morning to find he was stretched out on the sofa, Penny lying completely on top of him, her face buried in his neck. Her soft breath on his skin was one of the most wonderful feelings he'd ever had.

He couldn't stop thinking about that kiss, how it felt, how she tasted. He wanted so much more.

Guilt suddenly slammed into him. For the first time in his life, Daisy hadn't been at the forefront of his mind. She had specifically asked him not to do anything with Penny and, although he hadn't promised anything, he had decided to respect her wishes and not take things any further. But that hadn't even entered his head the night before when Penny had kissed him and he had most certainly kissed her back. Crap. The one thing Daisy had asked him not to do and he'd gone ahead and done it anyway. He really didn't want to do anything that might upset or hurt Daisy.

But he was already in way over his head here. He really liked Penny. Maybe he'd just see how things went over the next few days; maybe nothing would happen between them at all and there would be no point bringing it up with Daisy. Maybe the kiss would be the last of it. But he had only known Penny for a few days and he'd already kissed her and spent the night with her, albeit in a far more gentlemanly fashion than any other woman he'd spent the night with. Things were not looking good for something casual.

He eyed the clock above the fire and knew he had to get up, even though he would have quite liked to have stayed there all day. He was supposed to go to work for a few hours today so they could show him a few things and he could get used to some of the tools and equipment, meet his line manager and some of the people on his team.

He shifted, trying to get up without waking her, but her eyes shot open.

'Hi,' he said, resisting the urge to smooth her hair from her face.

'Hi.'

'I need to go. I have to pop to work today and I don't want Daisy to wake up and find I'm not there.'

'Of course you don't.' She sat up and shifted off him and he stood up, leaving her sitting on the sofa, looking sleepy and adorable.

'She'll probably try to hang around with you, but just tell her to sod off if she gets on your nerves.'

'I'm happy to have her around, she's lovely.'

He nodded, not really sure how to say goodbye.

'Thank you for being there last night and staying with me and for. . .' She trailed off, touching her lips. She was remembering the kiss and wonderful memories slammed into his mind too.

He smiled and gave her a little wave before walking out. God, that kiss had been sublime, he wanted nothing more than to go back and do it again. He made it halfway across the kitchen before his control snapped. He turned and strode back towards her, immediately taking her face in his hands and kissing her hard.

She started a little before her hands slid around his neck, running her fingers over the fine hairs at the back of his head and kissing him back. She smiled against his lips before she spoke.

'You need to go.'

He nodded, kissing her briefly. 'I'll see you tonight.'

He walked out, suddenly feeling a hell of a lot better about his day. He let himself through the connecting door and came face to face with Daisy as she came down the stairs. Guilt burned through his gut. Why had he not thought about Daisy when he had cuddled up on the sofa and decided to spend the night with his wonderful neighbour?

Her eyes widened as she took in the same clothes he was wearing the night before.

'Did you spend the night with her?'

He closed the door behind him. 'Yes, but not like that; she was upset, I was just comforting her. I fell asleep on her sofa, but I promise, no clothes were removed, I just stayed with her, that's all.'

That and two incredible kisses, but he didn't want to tell Daisy about that yet. He had to figure out how he felt about Penny before he told his daughter. She wouldn't be happy, he knew that.

'I need a shower and then I'm going to work for a few hours. Will you be OK around here for a bit?'

Daisy nodded. 'I'll see if Penny will mind me watching her ice carving again. Or maybe I can walk Bernard with her.'

'Well, don't harass her, I'm sure she's very busy with all the carving jobs she needs to do and I think she has a competition tonight.'

'I won't be in the way.'

He smiled. 'I'm sure you won't.'

He ran up the stairs. He never wanted her to feel in the way again.

Penny stared at the flowers. There were bouquets of every colour, flower, size and arrangement covering her table. She sipped her tea and wondered if it would be safe to go into town later or whether she would be lifted on people's shoulders and paraded through the streets. Maybe it would be easier to stay up here out the way.

She heard the connecting door open and peered through the blooms to see a pair of pink-socked feet, which she guessed belonged to Daisy.

'Wow, did someone die?' Daisy asked.

'These are from Sam and Alex's parents, grandparents, aunts, uncles, neighbours and anyone else in the town that heard about last night's little adventure. It doesn't help that Pippa, the boys' mum, is the Mayor of White Cliff Bay. There's a certain amount of glory that comes from saving the Mayor's kids.'

'In that case, surely you should get the Victoria Cross or some other kind of medal.'

Penny laughed. 'I have better than that: there's five cakes in the fridge and four bottles of wine. Would you like a slice of cake?'

'Oh yes, if there's some going spare.' Daisy sat down opposite Penny and cleared a small space so she could see her through the flowers. Penny stood up to get some cake. 'Did they come round then, Sam and Alex's parents?'

'Yeah, I'd just got back from walking Bernard and they were here waiting for me. There's been a steady stream of deliveries ever since.'

'What did they say? We saw who I presume was the boys' dad running out of a café when it all kicked off. What kind of parents would leave their kids to play outside on the street while they go and have a cup of tea in the café? Alex couldn't have been older than eight or nine and Sam looked about five. It's neglectful.'

Penny put the chocolate cake on a plate and cut two slices. 'Pippa is pregnant and she nearly passed out while they were watching the fire breather. Mike rushed her into the café and told the boys to stay where they were for a second. He was only gone for two minutes.'

'They shouldn't have been left at all.'

Penny smiled at the outrage of someone who had never had the responsibility of looking after a child twenty-four hours a day.

'You can't watch them every second of the day, and even when you do watch them, accidents still happen. Mike apparently asked Jade to watch them for a few minutes while he took care of Pippa.'

'What? That's even worse than leaving them on their own.'

'Well, yes, she was just the nearest person there at the time.'

'So did Jade just wander off and leave them?'

'Mike doesn't know, there was no sign of her at all when he came back out. They were both very apologetic and thankful. I don't think we should judge them too harshly.'

Penny passed Daisy her cake and sat down to eat her own. Daisy took a big bite and moaned with pleasure. 'Well, if they bring cakes like this round, I guess not. Dad loves chocolate cake, so if you want to find a way to his heart, definitely ply him with lots of this.'

Penny scooped a bit of chocolate icing up from the plate, deliberately not looking at Daisy. She got the sense that Daisy didn't want her to date Henry, though she wasn't sure why.

'I know he stayed the night last night.'

'Nothing happened,' Penny said, awkwardly. Apart from the best kiss she'd ever had. 'I was just a little upset.'

'What about?'

Penny smiled at her brazen confidence. 'The pub is owned by my ex-boyfriend's parents; it just brought back some memories. Do you want to carry on with your snowflake?'

Daisy didn't notice the subject change, and her eyes lit up at the prospect of carving again.

'I have a competition tonight, you're welcome to come with me if you want to. You can meet some of the other carvers too. I'd like to say they are a friendly bunch but some of them are a little weird, but it should be fun. Some of them have very different techniques to me and I can talk you through some of them when we see them.'

'I'd love that. I'm sure Dad won't mind.'

'Brilliant. Oh, and Josh will be there too.'

Daisy's face split into a grin. 'He's lovely. We chatted a little bit while we were waiting for you yesterday. Does he work for you?'

'He's my assistant and mainly my muscles. The ice sculptures are very heavy and you need two people to lift them and move them. He comes up here two or three times a week to help to take the ice blocks out of the machines and helps me transport all my sculptures to events. I put an advert in the local paper for a big, strong man and he applied. I got the piss taken out of me for months afterwards. He's very quiet, very sweet. He's only seventeen. I'm sure you'll get on with him.'

'It would certainly be nice to make some friends round here,' Daisy said, a mischievous glint in her eyes that Penny didn't like.

'Well, let's get changed and then we can carve for a bit before tonight's competition.'

Henry was definitely not going to thank her for setting his daughter up with a tattooed, muscular seventeen-year-old. Nothing was ever simple.

Henry stood on the warehouse floor of the White Cliff Bay Furniture Company. He looked around at the other workers and at the natural light flooding through the windows that sent ribbons of gold over the dark wood. He was going to enjoy working here. He was going to get to work with his hands every day, nurturing and perfecting beautiful pieces of handmade furniture. He was going to learn new processes and skills too, and that was always something he was keen to do. White Cliff Bay Furniture Company was one of the biggest names in the world for handmade pieces and he was going to be a part of that.

He had met several members of the team he would be working with after Christmas when he started properly. They all seemed happy, cheerful people, singing and chatting and laughing while they worked. He knew he was going to love working with them.

He was waiting for Daniel, his line manager, to come back with some paperwork for him to sign when he heard the click-clack of heels across the hard floor. As all the women who worked on the factory floor wore steel-toecapped boots, he turned to look at the foreign sound.

It was the fiery red hair he saw first, cascading in long curls down one side of her face. In a black trouser suit and sky-high red heels, she looked like a force to be reckoned with. She was beautiful, there was no denying that, but there was a cold arrogance that marred her features. She didn't look at anyone as she passed, almost as if they weren't good enough to be looked at.

She was walking straight towards him.

'Clara Stratton, CEO.' She offered out a hand, clearly hoping he would be impressed with that title. He wasn't. He'd already met who he considered to be the real CEO, Edward, who had stopped to talk to almost every person on the factory floor earlier. He shook her hand anyway, noting her eyes were as cold as ice, a direct contrast to her fiery hair.

'Henry Travis, I'm starting work here after Christmas.'

This news clearly surprised her; she obviously had no idea about new staff, whereas Edward had recognised him from the interviews and made a point of coming and chatting with him for a good half hour when he saw him earlier.

'Oh, that's a pleasant bit of good news. It's nice to have a bit of eye candy to look at every day at work.'

Henry refrained from letting his jaw drop. Surely if it had been Edward chatting to a new female employee like that, she could have slapped a sexual harassment suit on him faster than he could blink. But Henry would be nice to her; he had to. He couldn't do anything to risk his job here before he had even started. He forced a smile onto his face.

'I think you'll be very happy here. I can help you settle in if you like. We should go out for dinner one night and we can talk about the White Cliff Bay Furniture Company, the expectations we have for you.'

'Well, I think Edward and Daniel, my line manager, have explained that very clearly. I know how important the reputation of this company is and I'm delighted to be offered a place here based on my skills and experience.'

He hoped that would be the end of it.

'We're a family business here. I do like to know the people who work for our family. Dinner would let us get to know each other better.'

'Well, I was just about to join Daniel for lunch in the staff canteen – you're welcome to join us. I hear the cheese and pickle sandwiches are to die for.'

She narrowed her eyes at his deliberate obtuseness. Just then Daniel came back. He looked at Clara in confusion – obviously it wasn't the norm for her to be seen talking to the carpenters.

'Oh, hello, Ms Stratton,' Daniel said. 'Are you lost?'

Henry clenched his lips together to stop the laugh from bursting from his mouth.

Clara forced her eyes from Henry to look at Daniel.

'What do you mean, lost?'

'We don't normally see you down here; I thought you might have taken a wrong turn,' Daniel said, innocently. 'Henry, here are your papers, are you coming to lunch?'

'Yes, of course. Clara, are you joining us?'

Daniel gave a blatant laugh, which he turned into a coughing fit.

She glared at Daniel before returning her attention back to Henry. 'Perhaps another time.'

She turned and strode away, back the way she had come, her bum swaying frantically at the speed she was departing.

'Bloody hell, Henry, the last person you want to get involved with is Clara Stratton,' Daniel said, when she had gone. 'I'd try to stay out of her way from now on if I was you.'

Henry sighed. The perfect job was coming with a red-headed downside.

Penny stepped back to look at her finished sleigh. She had to drop it off at a party tonight before she went on to the competition. She loved the bulging sack with a tumble of presents coming out the back. The intricate bows and shapes of the presents had taken quite a long time to get right, but she was proud of the finished result.

She glanced over at Daisy, who had been working silently and diligently for the last hour, taking her time with her piece. Penny had showed her a few skills to work on that were particularly useful for this sculpture and, as she had picked it all up very quickly, Penny had pretty much left her to it.

She moved around to look at the snowflake now that it was largely finished and felt her mouth drop in awe. Daisy had already asked Penny to cut the block vertically in half so the snowflake was a lot thinner, even though Penny had warned Daisy that this could make carving a lot harder because the thin bits could be broken off. But Daisy had done a wonderful job. All the tiny delicate fingers of the snowflake had been carved to perfection, each branch rounded so the snowflake looked like it was made from thin tubes.

'Daisy, this is incredible.'

Daisy looked at her in shock. 'Really?'

'Yes, you have a real talent for this stuff. I can't believe this is your first time.'

'I did do that wood carving course in the summer, so that taught me a lot of things.'

'Yes, but even so you're an absolute natural at this stuff. The thing with carving and sculpture is you either have the eye or you don't, it's not something that can really be taught. You've definitely have the skills to actually do this professionally.'

'Nah, I mean it's OK, but it's not like yours.'

'It's better than mine, and I've been doing it for ten years. Why don't you enter it into the competition tonight?'

'Oh god, I couldn't. All those professionals and my crappy snowflake.'

'What have you got to lose?'

'My dignity, when I come last.'

'I never enter to win, I enter just to be a part of the experience. Come on. I promise you it's good enough to be entered.'

Daisy stared at the snowflake and then back at Penny, a grin slowly forming on her face.

'OK.'

'Brilliant. Come on, let's get warmed up and changed. Josh will be here soon and I need to wrap up the sculptures ready for moving them.'

Daisy helped Penny put the carvings back in the freezer and walked out the cool room, bumping straight into Henry as he came through her back door.

'Oh hey, Dad, you looking for me?' Daisy asked.

Henry flashed Penny a quick glance that told her he'd actually been looking for her. 'Yes, I wondered if you were in here.'

Daisy wrapped an arm around his waist and he planted a kiss on her forehead. Penny loved how tactile they were with each other.

'How was work?' Daisy asked.

'Interesting,' Henry said, giving Penny another glance. 'The people are great, I think I'm going to enjoy working there. And I love the furniture they make, it's so stylish, I can't wait to be a part of that. I met Clara too.'

Penny tried to keep her expression neutral. She'd seen Clara around town a few times and she knew how beautiful she was. She wondered what Henry's impression was of her.

'The boss lady?' Daisy asked.

'Yes, she came downstairs to talk to me specifically.'

'Oh, that's nice, maybe I was wrong about her,' Penny said, turning away. She wasn't wrong, Clara had come downstairs to speak to Henry because he was hot and that was the only reason.

'She asked me out for dinner.'

Penny opened up a can of beans and poured the contents into a saucepan, throwing the empty can into the bin a bit harder than was necessary.

What must it be like for Henry to have all these smart, beautiful, rich, successful women throwing themselves at him? He could have any woman he wanted, yet he had kissed her. Had he kissed her simply because she had been upset and he felt sorry for her? That would be an awful reason to kiss her. Now his boss was asking him out. Surely it would be professional suicide to turn her down. And as she was so beautiful it wasn't exactly a hardship.

'Eww, Dad, don't go out with your boss, that's such a cliché.'

'I have no intention of going out with her. It would be beyond awkward if things turned sour. Besides, she isn't my type.'

Penny glanced over at him, and although he was talking to Daisy she felt like he was saying all this for her benefit.

'You mean she didn't have sleek blonde hair, big tits and a tiny waist,' Daisy laughed. She grabbed an apple from the fruit bowl and went to take a bite out of it before Henry snatched it from her and put it back in the bowl again. Daisy pouted.

Penny looked down at her tiny breasts and definitely not tiny waist. This conversation was getting better and better.

'I don't just go for blondes. I don't have a type. I'm attracted to personalities, not looks,' Henry said.

'Yeah right. That's why all your girlfriends have been verging on the supermodel end of the spectrum.'

'You're not painting me in a good light here,' Henry growled at Daisy and she laughed, completely unperturbed with the idle threat in his voice.

'You create your own reputation, that's nothing to do with me.'

'Come on, trouble, we'll leave Penny to some peace and quiet.'

'She asked me to come with her to a competition tonight; it'll be great experience for me to see the other carvers and their work. Can I go?'

Penny waited for Daisy to tell Henry that she was submitting her own piece to the competition but she didn't.

Henry looked over at Penny. 'Is that OK?'

'Yes, of course.'

Henry shrugged. 'All right then. Well, let's go and have dinner and Penny can knock for you when she's ready to go.'

He ushered her out through the connecting door and gave Penny a little smile as he closed the door behind them.

If that conversation about Clara had been designed to make her feel better it'd had the complete opposite effect.

Chapter 10

Henry finished washing up the dinner things when a movement caught his eye outside the window. There was a huge man outside and, as Henry watched, he let himself into Penny's house through the back door.

Henry quickly rushed to the connecting door and opened it a crack. The man was big and muscular but quite young too, maybe early twenties. He was wearing a t-shirt and both arms were covered in tattoos. The man looked around the kitchen, spotted Penny's rucksack and loaded it with her purse and her mobile phone. He spotted a camera and threw that into the bag too. Then he opened the fridge and helped himself to a handful of chocolate bars, which joined the other stuff in the bag. He zipped up the bag and moved back towards the door.

Henry slammed the connecting door open, making the man jump out of his skin.

'Going somewhere with all that stuff?' Henry asked.

The man stared at him with wide, terrified eyes. He pointed vaguely to the open door, made some kind of squeak of pure fear and then bolted out the door, taking the bag with him.

Henry was hot on his heels. The guy was fast, but Henry was faster and, as the man sprinted around the corner of the house, Henry threw himself at his legs, bringing him face down onto the gravel driveway. The man let out a wail of pain as Henry used all his weight to keep him pinned to the floor.

'Henry, what the hell are you doing?' Penny said, running towards them from the front of the house.

'I caught this thieving little shit stealing your purse, phone and camera. Call the police.'

'Henry, this is Josh, a friend of mine. He helps me to take my carvings to events. I told him to grab my bag. And you just threw him down on the floor.'

'He's a friend of yours?'

'Yes. He works for me.'

Henry processed this and quickly scrabbled off Josh, and then pulled him to his feet, brushing the dirt and stones off him.

'Sorry about that, mate, I just saw you come into Penny's house and take her stuff, and I thought. . . Sorry, you're not hurt, I hope? Why on earth did you run? You could have just told me you were a friend of Penny's.'

Josh still looked absolutely terrified of him, obviously wondering if he was going to get a pummelling at any second.

'Because you probably scared him. Have you seen the size of yourself? You scare me too.'

Henry blinked at this new revelation. 'You're scared of me?'

'Oh, there's a million things that scare me about you. Josh, get in the van, we need to go.'

Penny handed her bag back to Josh and walked back around the side of the house towards her kitchen. Josh didn't move for a moment but Henry ran around the house after Penny, catching her arm just as she was about to open his back door.

'Why are you scared of me? I would never do anything to hurt you.'

Her face softened slightly and she ran her hand over his stubble. Her touch was like fire on his skin and he instinctively moved his hands to her waist.

'I'm not scared of you physically hurting me, though I suspect the end result will be the same.'

'What does that mean?'

'Why did you kiss me last night?'

'You know why.'

'But you told me you're not looking for anything serious, and I get that, I totally do. Daisy is your number one priority and I never want to get in the way of that, but we agreed we would just stay as friends. I know I kissed you, I know it's my fault. I really like you and I suspect that the discrepancies in what we want will be the thing that hurts the most.' She sighed. 'I have to go.'

She opened his back door and stuck her head inside. 'Daisy, we need to leave now, are you ready?'

He heard the thunder of feet as his daughter came down the stairs and he quickly dropped his hands from Penny's waist.

Penny looked at him pointedly as she stepped away.

Daisy ran outside, stepping between them as she shoved her feet into her Converse and dragged a coat on. He was surprised to see she had done her hair in curls and even put some make-up on.

'I'd like her back by ten,' Henry said, trying to distract himself from what Penny had just said.

'Dad!'

'Half ten then.'

Penny nodded. 'We shouldn't be too late.'

He watched Daisy link arms with Penny and they disappeared around the side of the house.

He went back inside, a little bit annoyed that his daughter was allowed to go out with Penny but he wasn't.

After setting up Penny's competition piece on the stand, Josh went back for Daisy's piece while Penny went to pay and register for her and Daisy. She hadn't even looked at the other competitors' pieces yet as they were so late getting there.

She moved back into the village hall and found Daisy pressed against the back wall, seemingly too nervous to mingle or look around. The room was dark, lit up only by the spotlights arranged underneath the sculptures, making them look ethereal and magical in silvery puddles of light. Penny watched Josh carry the small snowflake across the room as if he was carrying a newborn baby and unwrap it with the same care.

'Everyone will laugh at my snowflake when they see it. I shouldn't have entered.'

'Of course you should. You have a real talent. In all honesty I don't think either of us will win tonight. I've just seen the list of competitors and there're at least three other entrants who always enter something that is truly magnificent. Fabio is from Italy and apparently he has won some big international championship in America this year, so I don't think we can compete with that, but it's fantastic to see other people's work and skills.'

'I just don't want to come last, that would be so embarrassing.'

'There's nothing wrong with coming last. But as it happens these competitions choose first, second and third place, so there is no last. If you don't come in the top three you can say you came joint fourth.'

Daisy grinned up at her.

'I've come joint fourth on many occasions.'

'Have you ever won?'

'Once, last year, which is why the big competition is being hosted in White Cliff Bay this year, at the ball – the winner's

132

town hosts it. I've come second once and third a few times, but, as I said, some of these guys pull out all the stops. One year Octavia had a tiny village with moving people, cars and lights that went on and off, all made from ice, with some kind of radio-controlled pieces inside. The Ice Carving Federation had to create a ruling that only ice was allowed in competitions from now on because people were going crazy with flashing lights and other things they had frozen inside the ice. Those sorts of things are great at a party or a wedding but when you do a carving competition they take away from the focus of the carving skills, which is the thing that is supposed to be judged.'

Penny watched Josh walk over to them. Normally Josh would help her set up at the competition and then leave, he very rarely stayed. But he and Daisy had chatted quite a bit on the journey, first to the party to drop off the sleigh and then on the way here. He very rarely spoke at all so it was quite a revelation to hear him so vocal. He rubbed his wrist again and Penny wondered if he had hurt himself when Henry threw him to the ground.

'Shall we have a look around at the other sculptures? Watch out for the other carvers, they're a slightly weird bunch. Just stay out of their way and it's probably best to not talk to any of them unless I say it's OK. It gets highly competitive.'

'Is that why the police are here?' Daisy joked.

Penny winced. 'Yeah, last time there was a punch-up between Geoffrey and Fabio, and that wasn't the first time something happened between the two of them. One year Geoffrey got drunk and pissed all over Fabio's sculpture, which caused it to melt.'

'Ewww, that's disgusting.'

'I know, he's probably the weirdest of them all. He was banned for two years after that. But he came back last year and before the competition had even started there was a punch-up between them.'

They moved off to look at the first sculpture, a wonderful mermaid that was bursting from the waves. It was very well done, though some of the un-textured surfaces were not as smooth as they could be, suggesting that the carver was new to the craft. It was beautiful though. Penny looked at the name of the competitor to see it was created by a girl called Melody. It wasn't a name she recognised from previous competitions and she smiled that someone new had joined their crazy little group. Penny looked around for her but there was no one standing nearby. She made a note to come and say hello to her later.

They moved on to the next sculpture, a stunning dragon that looked ferocious and ready to attack. Its minute scales must have taken hours of painstaking work. Penny looked at the name of the competitor and noticed it was Geoffrey, the insane, hugely talented carver from the furthest shores of Scotland and possibly one of the rudest men she had ever met. Daisy reached out to touch the sculpture but Penny snatched her hand away, knowing if Geoffrey saw her touch his precious carving he would go ballistic. But it was already too late. He suddenly loomed from the shadows at the very edges of the room.

'Don't you dare touch my dragon,' Geoffrey spat and Daisy shrunk back in shock. 'Thirty-seven hours this took me to carve; thirty-seven hours where my hands were bleeding and raw from working with the ice. Do you have any idea what level of commitment and dedication it takes to achieve this level of talent?'

'She didn't touch it, she. . .' Penny said but trailed off as Josh suddenly stepped forwards like a silent bodyguard. With one hand on Geoffrey's chest he pushed him firmly away from Daisy.

Geoffrey turned to release his wrath on Josh but, seeing the sheer size of him, he thought better of it. With another glare at Daisy and Penny, Geoffrey shrank back into the shadows like a monster disappearing back inside his cave.

'Don't pay any attention to these carvers, some of them are the weirdest people I've ever met,' Penny muttered in Daisy's ear, taking her arm in the vain hope that she could protect her from the weirdness.

'Penny!' A loud, deep voice rang out and Penny winced as Fabio strode across the room. At some point Fabio had obviously looked up what a stereotypical Italian stallion looked like and dressed accordingly. He was the epitome of some eighties porn star, with waist-long, sleek black hair, which he swished over his shoulder as he walked, wearing black leather trousers and a shiny black shirt. His appearance was so dated, it was impossible to take him seriously. She found it hard to believe anyone would willingly dress like this unless it was for some fancy dress party. His face was strikingly handsome and he was toned in all the right places but he was a complete creep. But it seemed she was the only one who thought like this. He made all the women in the room swoon.

'*Bella donna*,' Fabio said, kissing Penny on both cheeks in some exuberant European gesture. 'Sooo pretty, ze stars they are nothing compared to you.'

Daisy stifled a giggle next to her. Penny had always thought that Fabio wasn't a real Italian, his accent sounded terrible and he was a walking stereotype, but she hadn't dared call him out on it. It certainly didn't do him any harm with the ladies.

'How are you, Fabio?'

'I am alls the better for zeeing you. When will you agree to marry me and make beautiful babies?'

When hell freezes over. Probably not even then. Fabio had been begging her to marry him for years, ever since she started doing these competitions. She had never taken it seriously because at the end of the night he always left on the arm of a different woman.

'Ah, I'm always so busy with work, I have no time for making babies.' Penny shrugged.

'When I win tonight, will you marry me then? These sculptures are nothing in comparison to mine.' He swept his hands out in a theatrical gesture and for a split second it seemed that tiny crystals flew from his hands, covering Geoffrey's dragon in a sprinkle of sparkling magic before they vanished from sight. Penny blinked. Had she imagined it? Dust was easier to spot under the translucent lights and the shafts of lights around the room showed hundreds of particles swirling in the air, so maybe it had just been dust from his clothes.

'You must come and zee, you will love it.'

Fabio took Penny's arm and guided her across the room. The crowd parted and Penny stared at it in confusion for a few seconds before she gasped in horror. Captured in ice was a life-size sculpture of her, naked and in a passionate embrace with Fabio. It was intricately carved with wonderful craftsmanship and was quite possibly the creepiest thing she had ever seen.

Daisy burst out laughing next to her and Josh quickly averted his gaze but Penny couldn't take her eyes off it.

'Do you like it, *bella donna*? It is you, *sì*?'

'I. . . Why?'

'Because I am in love with you and I want to marry you.' He got down on one knee in a theatrical gesture and the spectators around them gasped and then cheered. Penny glanced over at Daisy, who was filming the whole thing on her phone.

Just then there was a shout and a cry of pain from across the room. All eyes swivelled from the bizarre marriage proposal to Geoffrey, who was also on his knees in front of his dragon. Though Geoffrey's cry seemed to be made out of despair as his sculpture melted and bubbled like a fountain. Within seconds the six-foot dragon was reduced to nothing more than a small lump of ice and a big pool of water.

Penny had never seen anything like it. As much as she disliked Geoffrey for his rudeness, no one really deserved to have their hours of hard work dissolve in front of their eyes. Who would do that?

Although she knew one person who would be quite happy to destroy the other competitors' work. She looked down at Fabio, who was still kneeling at her feet. He gave her a wink and she snatched her hand from his, not wanting any part of his pettiness.

'YOU! You did this,' Geoffrey roared, a livid rage boiling behind his eyes as he charged across the room towards Fabio.

Josh was quick to move Daisy out the way and Penny stepped to one side as Fabio leapt up and Geoffrey bulldozed into him. They both crashed into Fabio's pornographic ice sculpture, which tottered on the table. Fabio punched Geoffrey in the stomach and Geoffrey pulled Fabio's hair, pushing him back against the table again. This time the sculpture wobbled and fell in slow motion onto the floor, smashing into a thousand pieces.

This was at least enough to stop the fight as Fabio wailed in horror.

The police finally made a move, obviously finding the whole spectacle far too entertaining to actually want to stop it. As Fabio launched himself at Geoffrey again, they pulled the two of them apart and dragged them both out the building.

'Get off me!' Fabio yelled in a perfect Essex accent as he struggled for his freedom.

The door closed behind them and the room fell into silence. Suddenly people started clapping and cheering, obviously thinking it was all part of the competition. Either that or it was the most excitement the people of White Cliff Bay had seen in a long time.

Penny turned around to make sure Daisy was OK, but she was laughing and clapping too.

Penny approached and Josh lessened his protective stance in front of Daisy slightly.

'I'm so sorry. I shouldn't have brought you. I never expected it to be like this.'

Daisy wiped away tears of laughter. 'Best thing I've seen for a long time. You have to bring me to all competitions from now on, even if I'm not competing.'

With the drama over, people went back to perusing the remaining sculptures. There were only four others now apart from Penny's and Daisy's.

'Gives us more of a chance now they are out of the competition,' Daisy said. 'Though that Hogwarts Castle over there is getting a lot of interest.'

Penny peered through the crowds at the castle with each tiny brick carved into the sides, the pointy turrets and even a dragon resting on the roof. It was stunning. 'That has to be Octavia's, she is ridiculously talented. She's bound to win.'

Suddenly there was a flurry of excitement as the judges arrived. Pippa, the Mayor of White Cliff Bay, came in first, her huge pregnant belly parting the crowds, overshadowing the gold chain of office that hung around her neck. Pippa waved at Penny as she walked in and a feeling of unease settled in

Penny's stomach, remembering how grateful Pippa had been towards Penny that morning over her saving Sam. Surely she wouldn't be so grateful as to award her first place over the magnificent Hogwarts Castle? Thankfully there was one other judge with her, Mr Cartwright, her art teacher from school. He would make the right decision.

Daisy made a squeak next to her. 'That's Jackson Cartwright. He's going to be my art teacher at White Cliff Bay Secondary School.'

'He was my art teacher when I was there.'

'How cool is that. He must have been very young when he was teaching you.'

'He was, all the girls fancied him. He rode a motorbike and wore a leather jacket and he smoked, so obviously that made him a hundred times cooler than all the other stuffy teachers.'

'He has all these cool sculptures in galleries in London. I'm such a fan of his work.'

'Would you like me to introduce you?'

Daisy nodded. 'No.'

Penny laughed at the mixed signals. 'Well, maybe I can chat to him and you can be standing next to me.'

'Yes, that sounds good.'

'Competitors, please take your places by your sculptures to meet the judges,' a loud voice boomed across the hall.

Penny noted the young red-head standing next to Melody's mermaid sculpture and gave her a friendly smile. She saw Octavia by the Hogwarts Castle as she suspected and Ignatius, a man with a long flowing white beard and long hair to match, standing by a splendid-looking lighthouse. On the other side of him was Frank, dressed in a dusty pink trouser suit and standing next to an intricately carved vase of flowers.

The Hogwarts Castle was obviously going to win, but Penny couldn't call second and third place at all. Even Daisy's snowflake, though simple in its design, showed a real talent.

The judges moved around the room, admiring the sculptures and chatting to the competitors.

Finally they came to Daisy. Penny watched them as they studied her piece and noticed how Daisy was standing almost in shock at being so close to her idol. She willed Jackson to say something nice about it; if he did that would make Daisy's entire night, even if she didn't make the top three.

'This is an incredible piece,' Jackson said. 'These branches are so thin and perfectly round. I'm very impressed with the detail that you've put into this.'

Penny's heart soared with happiness for Daisy. She could see she was already beaming from ear to ear.

He looked at the card with her name and then looked back at Daisy. 'How old are you?'

'Sixteen.'

His eyes widened in surprise. 'You're the new girl. You're going to be in my form after Christmas and I'll be teaching you for art too.'

'You're my form teacher?'

Jackson nodded. Now he'd made her entire year.

'I'm so impressed that you have this skill at such a young age. Have you had much training?'

'I did a wood carving course in the summer and Penny has been showing me lots of things.'

Jackson turned his eyes on Penny and smiled. 'Tuppence Meadows, how lovely to see you here, and inspiring a younger generation, I see. You'll be putting me out of a job.'

'Your job is quite safe,' Penny said. 'Working with Daisy has been a delight but I don't think I'd want to work with thirty teenagers.'

He laughed. 'Yes, they can be a handful at times.' He turned back to Daisy. 'Will you be popping in this week before the school closes for Christmas? It'd be nice for you to meet the rest of your form at least.'

'Yes, I think I'm coming in Thursday or Friday this week.'

'Well, I look forward to seeing you then.'

He moved on to Penny while Pippa chatted to Daisy.

'This angel is stunning, Tuppence.'

'Penny.'

Jackson smiled. 'Penny, my apologies. The detail of the hair is quite beautiful. I'm very impressed, but I had no doubt that you would go on to do fantastic things with your art. I've seen a lot of your sculptures around town over the years. It makes me very proud. If you ever did want to come to school and do an ice carving workshop with the kids, it would be very inspiring and I'd be there the whole time so they wouldn't give you any grief.'

Penny smiled at the idea. She had thought about teaching some kind of carving course at the local college; she loved being able to pass on her skills and inspire other people to carve too. She had done hen and stag ice carving parties before and a few corporate team building days, which were always a lot of fun, and she had loved working with Daisy over the last few days. Maybe working at the school for a few days would be an excellent way to dip her toe into that side of things.

'I'll give it some thought,' Penny said and Jackson smiled.

Pippa joined them.

'I love your angel, Penny, I think it's magnificent.'

'Thank you.'

Pippa and Jackson wandered off to the middle of the room to discuss the results. There was lots of gesturing around the room, especially towards Octavia's castle. The organiser of the event joined them and he nodded as they told him the result. Jackson didn't look too happy though.

'We have our winners here,' the organiser boomed in his deep voice. 'And I must say the level of quality we have seen has even got our judges arguing over the winner, but our lovely Mayor does have the final say. So, in third place, the judges have chosen. . .' He paused dramatically. 'Daisy Travis with her snowflake.'

There was a big round of applause from the crowd and Penny cheered the loudest. As she moved to hug her she realised Daisy was shaking.

'Well done, I'm so pleased for you, you totally deserve it,' Penny said.

'In second place is. . . Octavia Greene.'

There was a huge collective gasp from the crowd that Octavia hadn't come first. Every single person in this room knew that Octavia's sculpture should have won, including, it seemed, Octavia. Her mouth dropped open, not from pleasant surprise, but in pure outrage. Penny winced, knowing where this was going next. For Octavia to be awarded second place that meant that Penny had been awarded first as Pippa's attempt to say thank you for saving her son's life the day before.

'And first place goes to. . .'

Penny prayed that Frank's flowers or Ignatius's lighthouse had caught the judges' eye.

'Penny Meadows.'

There was a polite round of applause and lots of murmuring and shaking heads as people obviously disagreed with the final verdict.

Penny wanted the ground to swallow her up. She didn't want to win like this. She was proud of her angel – it was good – but Octavia's castle was incredible.

Daisy threw herself at Penny, squealing loudly, clearly not having any idea why Penny had won.

The judges came over to shake Penny's hand and award her a rosette. She could barely muster a smile of thanks. A few other people came to shake her hand and pat her on the back and then the competition was over and people started to leave.

Octavia stomped over to her and Penny knew it wasn't to congratulate her. 'You and I both know why you won tonight and it has nothing to do with your ice sculpture.'

She stormed out and Daisy looked at Penny in confusion. 'Talk about losing graciously.'

'Come on, let's go home,' Penny said, feeling thoroughly deflated despite the ribbon that was shimmering on her chest.

Josh and Daisy followed her out.

Daisy chatted to Josh all the way back to his house but Penny was annoyed. The whole evening had been a farce. She wanted to inspire Daisy to continue with her carving, show her that with hard work and commitment she could create beautiful sculptures that people would admire. Instead she had exposed her to the crazy world of fierce competition and showed her that, no matter how hard you worked, it came down to who you knew and whose back you had scratched. Was there any point entering the big competition at the ball in a week's time if the winning vote had already been cast?

Penny dropped Josh off and she smiled when she saw him give Daisy a quick peck on the cheek to say congratulations. Daisy sat in silence with a huge smile on her face the rest of the way home.

They pulled up outside their house and Daisy practically bounced to the door, overflowing with excitement. Penny let them in through her front door and after Daisy had greeted Bernard with enough affection to last him a lifetime, she burst through the connecting door into her lounge.

'I have had the best night ever,' Daisy announced to her dad as Penny moved to the doorway to watch her. Henry was sitting on the sofa, reading a book, which he immediately put down to give his undivided attention to Daisy. He was wearing glasses and his feet were bare and there was something that made her stomach leap with affection for him at these small little attributes.

'Dad, I came third. Admittedly it was only out of eight people, well six, but still I came third and Jackson Cartwright was a judge and he said he was so impressed by my sculpture and—'

'Wait, you entered into the competition? I didn't know you had been creating your own sculpture. Why didn't you tell me? I would have come.'

'I didn't think it was any good, it was my first attempt and. . . I don't know, I didn't want you to see me fail.'

'I've told you before, you can only fail if you don't have a go. I'm so proud of you for entering. I wish you would have told me.'

'Sometimes you get a bit funny about my art.'

Henry looked shocked. 'I've always supported your art. I've paid for courses, I've taken you to exhibitions, I've bought you art gear. . .'

'But whenever I tell you I want to be an artist when I'm older, you always tell me not to neglect my other subjects.'

'That has nothing to do with me not supporting your art and everything to do with you being a lazy sod when it comes to your homework.' He put on a high-pitched girly voice. 'Dad, I don't need to do my maths homework because I'm going to be an artist when I'm older. Dad, I don't need to do this history essay because I'm going to be an artist.'

Daisy giggled at the terrible impression.

'You're a clever girl, Daisy. You could be anything you want to be when you're older: a doctor, scientist, astronaut. If you want to be an artist then I'll be behind you one hundred percent, but that does not mean you get to take it easy in all your other subjects. In a few years' time you might decide that you don't want to be an artist any more, you might want to be a vet or a translator or prime minister. You can't do those things without your GCSEs. You have six months until you finish school and you can study whatever course you want at college but you're damned well going to work your arse off between now and then.'

Daisy smiled. 'OK.'

'And next time, tell me when you enter a competition and then I can cheer the loudest when you win, or boo really loudly at the winner if you lose.'

'Penny won,' Daisy said and Henry looked over at her.

'You did? That's fab. I wouldn't have booed at you if I'd been there,' Henry said and then to Daisy he whispered, loudly, 'Well, maybe I'd boo quietly.' Daisy and Penny laughed. 'I don't suppose there's photos of these wonderful sculptures.'

'I have photos on my phone,' Daisy said, grabbing her phone and, pressing a few buttons, she passed it to Henry. 'That's mine.'

'Wow, this is really great, and you did all this on your own?'

'Penny did the chainsaw bit, she wouldn't let me use that.'

'Good job too, some of those tools look lethal.' He flashed Penny a look of concern.

'She's very sensible when she uses the tools, and I've showed her the correct way to use them,' Penny said.

Henry still didn't look happy about this but he clearly decided to let it go. 'It's very good, you really do have a skill for this.'

'This is Penny's.'

Henry gave a low whistle. 'That's seriously good. Wait, what's this?'

Daisy leant over to look and laughed. 'That's Fabio's sculpture before it got broken.'

Penny flushed as Henry stared at it. 'This Fabio seems to be very familiar with his subject.'

'Hardly, he missed out all my wobbly bits.'

Henry's eyes cast over her. 'He seems to have done a good enough job. So you and he. . .?'

'No, definitely not, not ever,' Penny said.

'Not from lack of trying though,' Daisy giggled as she pressed a button on her phone and played the video of Fabio's bizarre proposal.

Henry burst out laughing.

'Oh, well, on that rather embarrassing note, I'll leave you all to it. Daisy, I'm really glad you came tonight. I hope the crazies didn't put you off.'

Daisy shook her head. 'I loved it, thank you.'

Penny smiled briefly at them and shut the door between them. She walked into the front room where Bernard was on the sofa, upside down, tongue sticking out of his mouth, snoring loudly.

She fiddled around with her iPod, choosing a random play-list and something soft, sweet and slow drifted out of the speakers. She lit a fire and a few candles that smelt of spiced apples and mulled wine. A perfect romantic night for one. She sighed. She didn't fancy reading or watching telly. She wasn't sure what to do with herself. Next door she could still hear the soft sounds of Henry and Daisy talking and laughing.

It had been an odd twenty-four hours, with the sea rescue, seeing Kathleen, the farce of the ice carving competition and that incredible kiss that seemed to have almost been forgotten by the man who had done it. She closed her eyes and touched her lips, remembering what it felt like to have his lips there. Her memories replayed the event perfectly: his softness, the way he had held her, the taste of him, his sweet, spicy smell. She could smell him now, the warmth of his scent wrapping around her.

Suddenly her eyes snapped open, realising that his warmth and scent was a real thing. She span around and he was standing right there in her body space.

'Sorry, I didn't want to scare you, you seemed miles away.'

She flushed. Did he know she had been thinking of him?

'I just wanted to say thank you for tonight. I haven't seen Daisy smile as much for a long time.'

Penny swallowed down the emotion of having him so close. 'No problem.'

He still didn't move as he stared down at her. She looked away briefly, to see the connecting door was closed. He hadn't just come to say that.

He reached out to touch her hair, running one finger down its length and rubbing the end over his thumb. She couldn't move away from him. He was going to ruin her and there was nothing she could do to stop it. He ran a finger down her cheek and everything in her melted, so she was surprised she was still standing. How could something so simple have such an effect on her?

He sighed heavily and stepped back slightly, breaking the spell between them.

'Daisy has always hated my girlfriends. Even when she was little if I went on a date with a woman she would cry and scream. There was never that many, anyway. Raising a child on your own, there isn't much time for anything. But I had invited one or two women back when she was six or seven and it always ended with her crying hysterically. I stopped bringing women to the house after that and dated women in secret for years. I vowed that I would never bring anyone home unless it was a serious relationship. Since she's got older, she's met quite a few of my girlfriends and never liked any of them either. I think Rosie was the only one she liked. They'd go out together, go shopping. When we broke up I think Daisy was more upset by it than Rosie was.'

He moved his hand to link his fingers with hers. 'Even though she has hated almost every single one of the girlfriends she has met, she has never asked me not to date anyone before. Until you.'

Penny took a step back, wounded. 'I'm not good enough for you.'

Henry shook his head. 'No, that's not it at all. *I'm* not good enough for *you*. She really likes you and she's scared I'll hurt you. I am rubbish at relationships, I generally pick people that I think I can have a good time with and don't think beyond that. I always end things before they get too close, mainly because of Daisy. It's hard to think about turning our team of two into a three on a permanent basis. It would have to be someone who Daisy gets on with and until Rosie there hadn't been anyone and I never saw Rosie as someone I wanted to spend the rest of my life with. I have never imagined waking up every day lying next to the same woman for the rest of my life, or sitting down to breakfast and dinner with the same woman every day. There has been no one that I wanted to do that with until now.' He let out another sigh. 'I'm really painting myself in a bad light here, aren't I, and I don't blame you at all if you just want to be friends but. . .'

'Until now?' Penny managed to croak out. Her throat was completely dry.

Henry stopped talking for a second as he realised what he had just said.

'I care about you. A lot. And that's new for me. I love spending time with you, listening to you talk, watching you work. We've had more meals together, the three of us, in the last few days than I've ever had with previous girlfriends, and I really like that too. I like making you laugh and that kiss last night. . . There was something there that I've never felt before. I know this sounds naff. Something pulls me to you, an attraction that's so deep that. . .' He looked around, trying to find the words.

'That it hurts,' Penny said, quietly.

He stared at her. 'Yes. It hurts, it aches in my chest when I think of you, like a physical yearning for you. Do you feel that too?'

She nodded. 'And it's silly. I don't even know you.'

'Exactly. I don't know what that means, whether it's lust and desire or something more, but I know I want to find out. But is it wrong of me to just want to keep it between us for now? To wait to see if it turns into something special and wonderful, as I hope it will, or just peters out in the next week or so. This is all so new to us both. Neither of us know whether this is going to turn into something or not. In a few days you could decide that you find me incredibly boring and that we are better off as friends. Or we could have one great night of hot, passionate sex and this intense spark between us could die out the very next day and we decide never to do it again, or we could fall head over heels in love with each other, get married, have lots of babies and grow old and grey together. We can't see what's round the next bend. There's no point in upsetting Daisy if you decide that you don't want to pursue this in a few weeks' time. We've had a tough year and. . .'

He trailed off, looking thoroughly miserable about the prospect of upsetting his daughter.

'You want to keep us secret?' Penny was still trying to process that he actually wanted there to be an 'us'.

'Yes, just for a little while. I think part of her asking me not to date you is wrapped up in her uncertainty and nervousness of moving to White Cliff Bay. She's just moved to a new town and I know she's still feeling worried about starting school and making friends. I don't want her to feel in the way or awkward at home too. She likes it here at Lilac Cottage, she's settled in here really quickly because of you and the ice carving and her new job and. . .' Bernard gave a loud snore on the sofa. 'And him. She thinks if I start dating you and it all goes wrong then we won't be able to live here any more. I was happy to move out as soon as the agency could find us our own place but if she wants to stay here, I'd take smacking my head on that tiny shower every day just to keep her happy. Can we just get Christmas out the way, let her get a bit more settled and if it's still going strong between us then, then I promise we'll tell her and deal with the fall-out then. If we're not. . . then there would have been no point upsetting her over nothing.'

'I don't want to lie to her.'

'I don't either, that's the last thing I want. But can we just see if we have anything worth fighting for first? I'm not the easiest man to get along with, I'm grumpy, lack any kind of patience

150

and you will probably run a mile from me in a few days. Most women do. If we get past that and you still want me around, I promise we'll tell her then.'

Penny nodded. 'OK. So we're. . . dating?'

'Yes, if that's what you want?' He looked concerned.

She couldn't help the grin that spread across her face as she nodded.

'Daisy wants me to take you out, she thinks you need some company and friendship, so we can still do all the normal dating stuff but maybe keep all the snogging and passionate sex behind closed doors.'

She laughed. 'Damn, and I thought we'd strip naked and do it in the middle of the town square.'

His eyes flashed with warmth and mischief. 'Maybe one day. It's Tuesday tomorrow so we have our first proper date night anyway. We can celebrate our secret partnership then.'

'OK.'

She wasn't exactly being coherent and sparkling company at the moment. Her heart was pounding, she was shaking, all thoughts seemed to have gone out of her head completely.

He smiled at her stunned appearance. He ran his hand up her arm and cupped the back of her head. Moving in slowly, he kissed her again, with the same consideration and tenderness as he had the night before, as if she was someone to be cherished and adored. She ran her hands into the stubble at the back of his neck as he moved his hands down to cup her waist, pulling her against him. God, the feel of him was too much, the emotions for him slamming through her hard and fast.

He pulled back slightly, breathing heavily. 'OK?'

She nodded and he pulled away.

'I'll see you tomorrow.'

She smiled as he walked away, glancing over his shoulder at her as he closed the door. She was going on a date and she knew that tonight, for the first time in a very long time, she would be going to sleep with a smile on her face.

Chapter 11

Penny was shaken gently awake the next morning and opened her eyes to see Henry standing by the side of the bed.

Oh god, she knew her hair was everywhere, she probably had pillow face and she most certainly had morning breath. And he was offering a mug of tea with a big smile on his face, looking at her as if she was the most beautiful woman in the world. He was dressed in his robe and didn't seem to be wearing a lot underneath.

'I, erm. . .' Great, the ability to make sparkling conversation was back.

'I thought you might want a cup of tea and I made you breakfast in bed.' He indicated the bowl of cereal on the small chest of drawers next to her and she laughed.

'Wow, a lot of time and effort went into that breakfast, didn't it?'

'I'll have you know those cereal boxes are quite heavy.' He put the mug down next to the cereal.

'What's the weather doing out there?' Penny asked and he turned away to look out the window for a moment, giving her the perfect chance to grab some mints from her handbag and run her fingers through her hair.

'It snowed again last night. Not heavily, but Daisy is hopeful we might get a white Christmas.'

'This is very sweet, thank you, but you didn't have to do this.'

He turned and moved back to the bed. 'I'm trying to score all the good boyfriend points now because I'm sure I'll be losing them soon enough.'

'Why do you say that?'

'Because I'm rubbish with women, despite having spent the last sixteen years raising one. I don't know the first thing about romance. You may have to point me in the right direction now and again. Budge over.'

He must have caught the look of horror on her face and he laughed. 'I promise not to jump on you. But we can have a cuddle, can't we?'

She hesitated and then shuffled over.

He slid into bed next to her and pulled her onto his chest, wrapping his arms around her. It was such a comfortable gesture, as if they had known each other for years as opposed to just a few days. She couldn't help smiling.

'What?' he said, smiling too.

'This. It's nice. You're doing a good job so far at the romance stuff.'

He kissed her sweetly on the forehead; his tenderness was so endearing.

'Well, Daisy has gone to the big mall in the next town with Anna for some last-minute Christmas shopping, so we could stay here all day if you want.'

'That sounds lovely, but I'm meeting Maggie for lunch.'

'Damn it. Well, Daisy's staying over at Anna's tonight, so. . . if you want you could. . . stay over with me.'

A million excuses and reasons ran through her mind. She wasn't ready, she wouldn't be very good, she'd disappoint him, her bikini line was probably a bit of a state.

He must have seen all of that running across her face. 'I promise, we don't have to do anything, we can just do this. I like this. I like the idea of falling asleep with you in my arms again. I get the impression there hasn't been anyone for you since Chris?'

154

She flushed with embarrassment. 'No, for one reason or another, there hasn't been anyone for eight years. He was my first boyfriend too.'

She thought he might laugh at this. She was nearly thirty and had only ever been with one man, whereas Henry had probably been with lots of women, whether they were serious or not. But he didn't laugh at all.

'So we're going to take this really slow, we won't do anything until you're ready. We can date and get to know each other and I promise I won't try to take it any further. Doesn't mean I'm not going to want lots of kisses though.'

She smiled with love for him. This wasn't real, men weren't patient when it came to sex – well, Chris never had been. Someone like Henry could have any woman he wanted, if the reactions of Jade, Beth and Clara had been anything to go by. So why would he waste his time waiting for her when he could have a quick shag with any single woman in the town, especially as when he arrived in White Cliff Bay he wasn't even looking for a serious relationship?

'I want this to work,' he said softly, obviously having a knack for reading her mind.

She reached up and kissed him softly, hoping the mint had done a good enough job. He pulled her tighter against him, deepening the kiss.

He pulled back slightly, his eyes alight with mischief. 'Or you know, if you didn't want to wait, we could get down to the hot, passionate sex now.'

He quickly rolled on top of her, pinning her with his weight and tickled her.

'NO!' she squealed, trying to escape from his merciless hands.

'Come on, give me all the sex.'

She laughed. 'No, you're not having it, never.'

She wriggled from his grasp, quickly climbed out of bed and ran laughing from the room, but he was hot on her heels. He caught her by the waist and pinned her up against the wall, kissing her again as he tried to suppress his laughter. As he kissed her, his tongue sliding slowly into her mouth, his hands skimming her sides, her body humming at his touch, she wondered why she was holding back. Would it be so wrong to go back to bed with him now and discover how deep this spark between them actually ran? She barely knew him, but everything about this man, his kiss, his touch, just screamed that he was perfect for her in every single way. She was falling for him, she knew that. She just had to hope he felt the same.

He frowned. 'What time are you meeting Maggie?'

'Maggie?'

He smiled. 'Your friend?'

'Oh, erm, twelve.'

'Pity, it's half eleven now.'

Her eyes widened as the fog cleared. 'What? How is it so late?'

'Well, if you were anything like me, I spent most of the night lying awake thinking about our date.'

She smiled. 'I did too.'

He pulled away, reluctantly. 'Go and get ready and I'll see you tonight. You'll stay with me, right?'

She nodded and he walked down the stairs, leaving her alone. Her face was aching from smiling so much. Renting out the annexe was the best decision she had ever made.

Penny burst into the bakery and looked around. She was ten minutes late but it seemed she had still managed to beat Maggie. She walked up to the counter and joined the short queue. It seemed busier than usual for a Tuesday and Linda seemed a bit stressed out by the additional customers.

Tilly suddenly came running up to Penny, chocolate around her face, coupled with a huge grin.

Penny crouched down and carefully signed. 'Hello, what are you doing here, has your school closed for the holidays already?'

Tilly nodded excitedly and then signed back. 'The heating has broken so the school is closed. It probably won't be fixed before Friday.'

Well, that explained the extra customers and probably why Maggie was late if she was looking after her two boys.

'How cool, you get an extra long break. Are you helping your mummy and nanny today?'

'I've been making mince pies. Do you want one?'

'That would be lovely.'

Tilly ran off and Penny stepped forwards to place her order of a cheese sandwich for her and a bacon sandwich for Maggie. She was surprised when Linda handed her over two doughnuts as well as the sandwiches.

'You need to keep your energy up.' Linda winked and her daughter Polly, standing next to her, giggled.

Confused slightly, she found a table just as a young couple were leaving, and a moment later Maggie burst into the bakery.

'I'm so sorry.' Maggie took an appreciative bite out of her bacon sandwich, moaning with pleasure. 'The kids are off from school and I've been trying to keep them entertained all morning as I finish off the preparations for the ball. Seven days and

I'm starting to panic that I've forgotten something big. The pregnancy is playing havoc with my brain.'

'I'm sure you have everything planned to the finest detail. Is there anything I can help you with?'

'No, I think we're nearly there. The marquee arrives tomorrow, which is being used for the gingerbread house competition on Saturday and your workshop on Sunday, then everything else is arriving on Tuesday, the day of the ball,' Maggie rattled off her mental list of preparations from her head. 'Anyway, my mum has the boys for an hour, I told her I had an emergency lunch meeting with you.'

Penny blinked. 'What's the emergency?'

'Your big date tonight.'

She felt her eyes widen. 'How do you know about that?'

'Well, Jade was quite vocal about it in the pub on Saturday night after she had been spectacularly rejected by Henry, although she obviously didn't put it like that, and it's been quite the talk of the town ever since.'

'The talk of the town?' Penny suddenly felt cold at the thought of everyone talking about her. She knew that the town thrived on gossip and poking their nose into other people's business, but she had never been the subject of it before; her life was way too dull for that. She thought back to the time of her miscarriage and how everyone must have talked about her then, but she had been too far removed from it, closeted in her home up on the hill.

'Everyone is happy for you, they're all very excited,' Maggie soothed, though Penny could find nothing in these words to calm her down. How embarrassing. She and Henry were still trying to get to know each other; they didn't need the whole of White Cliff Bay digging their noses in before their relationship had even got off the ground. Plus the fact that Daisy wasn't supposed to know.

'We've had a meeting and—'

'A meeting? Who's "we"?' Penny squeaked, wanting suddenly to run back to her house and hide.

'The book club,' Maggie said, talking of the little group of mothers who would escape their families once a week to go round each other's houses, get drunk and let their hair down. No actual reading or discussions of books ever went on in their club meetings if the drunken photos on Facebook were anything to go by.

'I was the subject of a book club meeting.'

'Yes, now, the girls have all agreed to help. Natalie is going to do your hair and then Christine has you booked in for an all-over wax. Monica wants you to come to Silk & Lace afterwards and she's going to help you pick out some sexy underwear – I know you don't possess such things and all your bras and knickers are grey with holes in, which is not the look we need tonight and—'

'Wait, I'm not sleeping with him,' Penny shrieked and the bakery went quiet, all eyes swivelling in their direction.

'Sshhh, you don't want the whole town to know,' Maggie said as people resumed their conversations.

'I think the whole town does know. Did a message get put out on the town's emergency text system?'

'Look, everyone cares, this is the first date that you've had in eight years, we all want it to go well.'

'Can I not just screw it up on my own? Whether it does or doesn't go well is not going to depend on my hair or whether I have smooth legs or sexy underwear.'

'But those things will certainly help.'

'Maggie, I love you, but butt out.'

'Nonsense. If you loved me, you'd let me help you. Now eat up, your hair appointment is in fifteen minutes.'

'I'm not having my hair done.'

Why was Penny arguing against having her hair done? She'd been meaning to have it cut for ages.

'Come on, just a little trim. A cut and blow-dry. It's free,' Maggie wheedled.

'Fine, but I'm not having a wax or buying sexy underwear.'

'Well, see how you feel after your hair appointment.'

Penny sighed as she finished off her sandwich and then Maggie bustled her out the door, almost frogmarching her along the high street.

'I need to stop at the chemist first, I need a new toothbrush. I won't be a minute,' Penny said, abandoning Maggie outside.

'Don't think you can escape out the back door, Penny Meadows,' Maggie called after her as she sat down on the bench. 'I have spies everywhere.'

Penny didn't doubt it. She hurried along the aisles until she found the toothbrushes and was just trying to decide which one to buy when a lady came running up and perused the shelves next to her.

'It's so hard to know what to get, isn't it?' the lady said.

'I know.' Penny smiled politely. A firm toothbrush seemed a bit scary but soft probably wouldn't do the job properly.

'I like the ribbed ones though.' The lady winked at her and grabbed a box off the nearby shelf and ran off towards the tills.

Penny glanced at the shelf next to the toothbrushes in confusion and realised she was staring at a huge range of condoms. Words like Excite, Tickle, Pleasure, Extra Safe, Mutual Pleasure,

Ultra Thin, Latex Free, Extra Large and Intimate Feel leapt out at her from the shelves in an array of multi-coloured boxes. There were also different lubricants that were flavoured, warming or tingling, and one that promised to be orgasm-enhancing. Sex had moved on a long way since the quick shags she'd had with Chris. He always handled the contraception side of things, until that one drunken night when he obviously hadn't.

Suzanna, the old lady who ran the pharmacy, came bustling over and Penny quickly tried to look away from the condoms before Suzanna saw her, but she was too late.

'It's tricky, isn't it, dear, but if I were you I'd get the extra-large; that Henry looks like he's hung like a horse.'

Penny felt her cheeks flush blood red. 'I was looking at toothbrushes.'

'Of course you were, dear.' Suzanna picked a big box of extra-large condoms off the shelf and pressed them into Penny's hands, then escorted her to the tills. 'I have a load of free condoms from the family planning clinic we're supposed to give to the teenagers if they come asking for advice or any of that sort of thing. Why don't I give you a few of those too?'

Suzanna opened a drawer near the till and grabbed a huge handful of different condoms, shoving them into a paper bag. 'There's the extra safe ones in there and some of the thinner ones, plus some flavoured ones too. The strawberry isn't very nice but the chocolate is lovely, tastes almost like the real thing. These are all in date, dear, so you don't need to worry about that.'

She grabbed another huge handful and that went into the bag too.

Penny looked around at the other shoppers, who were watching the exchange in interest. She couldn't find any words at all to get out of this situation or laugh it away.

'Here, you put those extra-large ones in here, they're on the house,' Suzanna said, taking the box off her and putting it into the now bulging paper bag.

'I. . . It's only our first date, I wasn't planning on. . .'

'Of course not, dear, but you know, maybe the second date or the third. Don't keep him waiting too long though, dear; poor love will have testicles the size of watermelons otherwise.'

Penny grabbed her bag and ran out. Maggie hauled herself off the bench and waddled over.

'Took you long enough. What did you get?' Maggie eyed the bulging bag.

'Suzanna made me get some condoms and if you say one word about that I swear I'll pin you down and shave your eyebrows, pregnant or not, Maggie Stone.'

Maggie made a zipping her lips shut gesture, but Penny could see she was trying really hard not to laugh.

'Come on, Natalie will be waiting,' Maggie said, nobly.

Still dying with embarrassment, Penny thought it couldn't possibly get worse than that.

Chapter 12

Henry strode around the back of the house, whistling to himself. He had never looked forward to a date before as much as he was looking forward to his night with Penny. And it came with an almost guarantee of no sex, unlike his other dates, which were almost always guaranteed to end there. Bizarrely, he didn't care. He wanted to make love to Penny, he couldn't deny that, but it wasn't the end goal as it had been with other women. With Penny he wanted to get to know her more than anything, he wanted to spend time with her and make her laugh like she'd laughed that morning. He wanted to share himself with her, the good stuff and the bad, the small and the big. He'd bumped into an old man in town and had an interesting chat with him and Henry wanted to tell her about that too.

He peered through her back door to see if she was in and was surprised to see her pacing nervously around the kitchen. Maybe she was just nervous about the date. She had really big hair too, as if she had been in a wind tunnel, but on closer inspection it appeared it had been specifically styled that way.

He opened the door and let himself in. She looked at him with a terrified expression on her face. Was she having second thoughts about their date? He decided to ignore the big hair, as he certainly didn't want her to feel self-conscious about it, and just start a casual conversation with her to try to distract her from her nerves.

'I had an interesting conversation with someone in town. . .'

Penny groaned. 'I'm so so sorry. I don't know how it all started. It just snowballed out of control. They all know, everyone does. Apparently it's the most exciting thing that's happened in White Cliff Bay for years. I was the subject of a book club meeting, for Christ's sake. There was a plan hatched. I had no idea. And then I went to buy a toothbrush and they just happened to be next to the condom section. And I did look at them, but not for us, just because I was intrigued to see there were so many different types. The next thing Suzanna comes over and she starts talking to me about them and said that you needed extra-large and that it was best to have a range for our first time. I was mortified, but she wouldn't let me leave without taking some. Then Maggie took me to have my hair done and look at it, I look like an eighties porn star, it's huge and all I wanted was a trim. Before I could escape, Christine from the beauty place turns up and escorted me back to the salon. I told her that I didn't want anything but she wouldn't listen to my rebuttals and quite frankly she scares me. The next thing she is ripping hair from almost every single part of my body: my eyebrows, my legs, my bikini line. Honestly, I'm as bald as a coot down there now and it's chilly, believe me. And as I left, Monica from Silk & Lace was already waiting for me and whisked me off to her shop and persuaded me to buy some sexy lingerie. I've never bought sexy lingerie in my life and I now have two pairs of lacy pants with matching bras and tiny little rosebuds on them and a pair of black satin shorts that barely cover my bum embroidered with silver snowflakes and some kind of matching camisole top. Look.'

She pulled the short and top combo out of a paper bag and put it on the table.

'It's the tiniest, flimsiest piece of underwear I've ever seen, and I'd be way too embarrassed to ever wear anything like this.

But it didn't stop there: I was forced to buy a dress with a slit right up the side, ridiculous high-heel shoes, and a perfume that's supposed to bring men to their knees. I didn't want any of that stuff, I swear. I went into town for lunch and a new toothbrush, that's all. And now the whole town thinks we're going to have this night of passion and we've only kissed a few times and Daisy will probably find out and I'm so sorry if they've all been teasing you about it today,' she said, clearly out of breath from her sudden outburst.

Henry stared at her shock. He wanted to laugh, get angry and hug her all at the same time. He didn't know if he would ever get used to this level of nosiness but Penny had lived here her entire life and she was still clearly upset by it. His eyes cast down to the flimsy underwear on the table and he picked the top up, fingering the material. God, to see her in this would be a dream come true. Even if he had promised her that he wouldn't take it any further than a kiss, he would quite gladly cancel their date and spend the whole night holding her and kissing her in this underwear.

He looked up. She was waiting for him to freak out too, thinking he had been subjected to all of this when in fact no one had said a word to him. Although, come to think of it, he had noticed a few looks, smiles and winks but he'd just put it down to the oddness of the town. He had to reassure her that he hadn't been harassed like she was, but that wasn't going to make her feel better about her near-hysterical outburst.

Finally he cleared his throat. 'I was going to say that I spoke to someone in town today who had bought some of my handmade furniture years ago and he says it's still his favourite piece in his house.'

Penny paled.

'You didn't know I bought condoms or sexy lingerie?'

Henry shook his head.

Penny flushed, her pale cheeks going bright red. 'Oh god.'

She sank to the bench and put her head in her hands, clearly not wanting to look at him.

He smiled. The easiest thing for her would be to laugh it off.

'Where are the condoms?'

She pointed to a bag.

'I better take care of those; wouldn't want Daisy to see them.' She peered through her fingers at him as he looked in the bag. 'Wow, you bought a lot.'

'I didn't, the pharmacist just gave them all to me for free; she just filled the whole bag up, she was so excited that I was going to have sex after all this time and I didn't have the heart to say we wouldn't be.'

He nodded, trying to suppress a smile, but then he saw the twitches of a smile on her face too and he let out a loud laugh, which had her smile turning into a grin.

'I better go and get ready for our big date then. I'll pick you up at seven.' He moved to walk towards the door. 'Oh honey, wear the sexy snowflake set tonight for me. It'll make it much more fun when we're in bed later.'

'Ha, you wish. I'm going to wear my oldest, most grey, holey pair – that'll teach you for teasing me.'

He shrugged. 'That works too.'

She smiled and he closed the door between them. Tonight was going to be fun, regardless how it ended.

Penny nervously waited in the kitchen for Henry to come and collect her. She had managed to calm her hair down and pulled it into a loose side plait. She had worn the thigh-splitting dress, but only because the only other items of clothes in her wardrobe were jeans and hoodies or a smart trouser suit, which looked like she was ready for an interview. Part of her wanted to cancel the date because she didn't want to be subject to her whole dinner being under the watchful eye of the entire town. But if they were going to do this on a regular basis then they had to get the first time out the way and hopefully everyone would treat them normally after that.

It was still fifteen minutes till seven o'clock and she was trying to read a book, but the words weren't going in. Suddenly there was a soft knock on the connecting door and Henry walked in.

'Sorry, I couldn't wait to see you.'

Her stomach lurched at the sight of him. Dressed in a silvery grey suit and a white shirt that was open at the neck, he was a magnificent sight.

'If you're ready to go, we can leave now,' Henry said, when she had no words to fill the silence.

She quickly lurched to her feet, unsteady on her ridiculously high heels, and the dress that was split to the thigh fell open. She was completely overdressed and she suddenly wanted to sprint upstairs and change back into her favourite jeans again. She quickly pulled the dress straight, cursing that she hadn't gone for the trouser suit instead; the last thing she wanted was for people to be staring at her legs all night. But when she looked up at Henry, her fussing hands stilled. There was a complete and utter hunger in his eyes. Chris had never looked at her like that – at best he'd looked at her with a fondness, someone he quite liked spending time with. She'd had never been looked at as if she was about to be eaten. Her confidence soared, her doubts lay forgotten.

167

Henry moved towards her and grabbed her coat off the back of the chair, wrapping it around her shoulders and helping her to put it on.

He moved around the front and sweetly did the buttons up for her.

'I am quite capable of putting my own coat on,' she laughed.

'In all honesty, I had to cover you up or I really don't think we'd be leaving the house this evening.'

She smiled and leant up to kiss him, pulling on the lapels of his jacket. His arms wrapped around her in the biggest of hugs until she was so close to him there was no gap at all. God, she wanted more than this kiss, she wanted everything, to feel his skin next to hers, to taste every inch of his flesh. She had never had desires like this before, never wanted anyone with such a primal need before.

He pulled back. 'That's not helping us leave either. Come on, we can continue this when we get back. Maybe we skip the starters and the dessert, grab a quick McDonald's and come straight back here.'

'That sounds good.'

He escorted her out, opening his car door for her like the perfect gentleman.

'I need to ask a favour, actually,' Penny said.

'Of course, anything.'

'Well, it's your fault so you can't really say no. I had a phone call from Josh earlier – it seems he broke his wrist when you threw him to the floor.'

Henry paled. 'Oh god, no. Now I feel awful. I need to go over and apologise properly.'

'Well, you shouldn't feel too bad, you did do it with the best intentions, but going over there is not a good move. His mum is the most terrifying woman I have ever met. Josh told her he slipped on some ice and I really think she doesn't need to know the truth. She's a lawyer and I wouldn't be surprised if she managed to slap some criminal charges or lawsuit on you for abusing her son. If you feel really guilty buy him a new computer game for his Xbox and I'm sure he will love you forever. But he will be out of action for several weeks and that leaves me with a bit of a problem. I pay him to come and help me lift and move the ice blocks and carvings, and I can't do that alone. Looks like you might have a new job for the next few weeks.'

'You want to use me for my body?'

'Something like that.'

'And pay me for it? I feel so dirty and cheap.'

'You won't be paid for it; I'm still paying Josh whilst he's off sick and I'm not paying you too. You can do it out of guilt or the goodness of your heart, but I will cook you and Daisy dinner occasionally, so be grateful for that.'

'I don't mind helping you, but I do feel really bad about Josh.'

'He's fine. His mum is spoiling him rotten and he's enjoying the attention. He'll be completely fine in a few weeks.'

Henry drove down the bumpy drive but, instead of turning left to go towards the town, he turned right to take them away from White Cliff Bay. He caught her questioning gaze.

'I thought our first date should be just the two of us, not half of White Cliff Bay watching us like animals in the zoo.'

'Oh thank god, it would have been unbearable if we had gone into town but, you know, everyone will be very disappointed that we are a no-show.'

'They'll probably just think that we've decided to stay in and have hot, passionate sex instead.'

Penny laughed. 'What are we going to do if Daisy hears all these rumours?'

'I don't know, laugh it off, deny all knowledge. She knows we are going out tonight so we can just tell her the town have jumped to the wrong conclusion. As much as the town like to poke their noses in, I can't see anyone going up to a sixteen-year-old girl and saying, "Hey, did your dad get laid last night? Did you hear the bed squeaking? Do you know if he used the extra-large condoms or not?" I'd hope they'd have a bit more discretion than that.'

'I hope so too. I don't want to do anything to upset her. I really like her and she adores you.'

'Ha, she tolerates me.'

'You're her entire world.'

'I'm insanely over-protective and it drives her mad. Of course, I let her go out on her own, but it doesn't stop me worrying until she gets back home.'

'That's understandable. I don't suppose that feeling will ever go away. So you had her from when she was three months old? I know you said that her mum's parents wanted to put her up for adoption.'

'They did, but I begged them not to. They didn't really know what to do with her when she was born – they didn't want to raise her themselves and I think they hoped that Tina would fall in love with her and raise her properly, but she couldn't have cared less. I think they felt guilty about putting her up for adoption and my parents fought against it too. They brought her to stay with me quite frequently and one weekend they conveniently forgot to pick her back up again. I fell in love with her so quickly, so hard, that there was never a question of sending her somewhere else. My parents helped a lot and so did Anna – she absolutely adored Daisy too, we all did – but the night feeds, the dirty nappies, that was all down to me.'

'I admire you so much for that. So many sixteen-year-old boys would never have made that choice.'

'It was hard work, of course it was, but there was never a choice – she was my daughter.'

Penny watched him negotiate the roads and felt her heart fill with love for him.

'It must have affected your life though, the things that you wanted to do – travel, go to university – they would have been unattainable.'

'I had no idea what I wanted to do with my life at the age of sixteen; there were no plans that she got in the way of. I just wanted to provide for her and give her the best life possible. I lived with my parents until I was twenty-four, which gave me a tiny bit of freedom. I was always good with my hands, always enjoyed making things, so I would have probably got a job doing that anyway. I don't regret having her, not for one second. She's the best thing that ever happened to me.'

'So you've always been a carpenter?'

'Yes, making furniture, chairs, tables, chests. I worked in a small furniture shop for a while. I love the process, something that starts out as a little sketch on a piece of paper and with care and hard work it turns into a beautiful chest or a chair. How you finish the piece is crucial as well, whether the piece looks like faded driftwood or polished oak, the handles and hinges, the curves of the furniture. I loved it so much I started making my own stuff. I had a website and sold it online. I did well out of it. The White Cliff Bay Furniture Company approached me.'

'Wow, they must have been very impressed with what they saw.'

Henry nodded. 'Edward has one of my chests in his office. I saw it there the other day and I wonder if that was the thing that flagged me up to them. I'm going to keep making some of my own furniture as a little side line. If the job falls flat, I'll still have my own stuff to fall back on. The thing that worries me working at White Cliff Bay is not having the freedom to be able to design the pieces I want. But maybe I'll have to forgo that for financial job security.'

Henry turned down a little side road that led to a tiny cove. Penny frowned in confusion. There was nothing down here apart from the cove; there were no shops, toilets and especially not anywhere to eat.

'I think you might have taken a wrong turn,' Penny said.

'What's this, the outsider knows something the local doesn't?' Henry said.

He parked the car along the road near the path that led down to the beach. Surprisingly there were lots of other cars there too.

He got out and took her hand, leading her to the steps that curled down to the sand. It was well lit, with little lanterns sending puddles of light down the stairs and across a small wooden path that led across the beach towards the caves. She carefully picked her way down the stairs in her stupid high heels and onto the wooden path. The tide was in but it didn't reach all the way to the back of the beach, leaving a good twenty metres of sand untouched.

'I used to play here when I was a child, in the caves, but I haven't been down here for years,' Penny said, still wondering where they were going.

Henry helped her up a few stone steps into the cave and she followed him down a well-lit tunnel, but as she rounded the corner into what had been a large cavern, she stopped in shock.

There was a tiny lake in the middle of the cavern and dotted around the edges were about twenty tables lit up by lanterns and candles, the lights sparkling off the water like fireflies.

'Henry, it's beautiful. How long has this been here?'

'About two weeks, according to Anna. She and Steve came here last week.'

One of the waiters came over and Henry gave them his name and they ushered him to a table.

Penny looked around. In the darkness of the cave, the lights looked like orbs of gold, shimmering over the water. There were tall plants dotted between the tables along with outdoor heaters, lending a certain amount of privacy to the diners and giving it a slight Mediterranean feel, too.

'The menu is limited, a lot of it is barbequed or they have a large pizza oven, but apparently the food is amazing.'

Penny reached across the table and took his hand. 'Thank you for bringing me here, it's just wonderful.'

'I wanted something special for our first date and then I remembered Anna talking about this place.'

Penny smiled at the trouble he had taken to do something nice for her. 'It feels so secret, like no one knows it's here.'

'Secret place, secret meetings; I bet everyone here is having an affair.'

She laughed and looked around. At the next table was a young man in a very expensive suit sitting opposite a blonde with a very short skirt.

'I think he is a CEO of a big corporate company and that's his assistant that he is shagging behind his wife's back,' Penny said.

Henry glanced over and nodded. 'And look at that couple, she's old enough to be his mum. I bet she's sleeping with her daughter's husband.'

Penny looked over and laughed. 'That's Mary Buttercoombe and her son, Simon. So probably not sleeping together. White Cliff Bay may seem like an odd little town but I don't think incest is on our list of hobbies.'

'Ah, OK, what about those two?'

Penny glanced over at a slightly round man, dressed in leather with a long ginger beard and a bald head, sitting opposite a woman in a sweet flowery dress. 'They met online and this is their first date.'

The waitress came over to them. She was impossibly tall with a long curtain of blonde hair that was flicked over one shoulder. She had inexplicably large breasts. Henry glanced up at her, suppressed a smile and returned to looking at his menu.

They gave their drinks order and she left.

'What's made you laugh?'

'I was just thinking, if we are creating life stories for all the people in here, I think she is a secret porn star.'

Penny laughed. 'I must admit you're not anything like what I first thought when I met you.'

'What did you think of me when we first met?'

'That you were grumpy, moody, inappropriate because you were flirting with me when I thought you were married, and sexy as hell.'

He laughed so loudly it echoed around the cavern.

'And you don't think I'm sexy as hell now?'

'Ah, you're not bad to look at, I suppose.'

He laughed again and Penny loved the sight of him smiling so much.

'I am grumpy, thankfully not all the time, but when I get in a bad mood, everyone knows about it. I have a hell of a temper, which has only reared its ugly head a few times in my life but it isn't pretty when it does appear. And I am inappropriate because the thoughts that are currently running through my head about you are completely not acceptable for a first date where I promised to keep everything slow.'

'Oh.' Penny couldn't help but blush.

'You see, I am inappropriate. I shouldn't have said anything. I didn't mean to make you feel uncomfortable.'

'No, it's fine.' She ran her thumb over the back of his hand. 'I'm just not used to it, that's all. Chris never said things like that to me.'

'He never said how beautiful you were, how much you turned him on?'

'No. We just didn't have that kind of relationship. He... wasn't particularly tactile or loving. It's fine, different people work in different ways.'

'You deserve so much better than him. Let me tell you now, you look incredible tonight.'

Penny looked down at her menu.

'You don't like compliments,' Henry said. 'You're going to have to get used to them when you're with me.'

'I'll try.'

He smiled at her. 'You're also going to have to get used to standing up for yourself. I'm not going to allow people like Jade and Beth to think you are worthless. No one has the right to treat you badly and you need to tell them that. You deserve the best.'

She smiled, not quite sure what to make of this protective streak towards her.

'Do you want to share a starter?' he asked.

Penny nodded.

There was a lot she was going to have to get used to around Henry.

Henry pulled up outside their house and turned off the engine. They sat in silence for a moment. It had been a wonderful night. He was so easy to talk to and he made her laugh a lot. But now it suddenly felt like the evening was about to change. Even though Henry had promised to keep everything really slow and not to push her for anything more, she was still nervous about what the night would hold. She hadn't laid in bed with a man for over eight years. Part of her wanted to take that next step with Henry, she trusted him completely, and even though she had only known him a few days, she couldn't help the feelings that he caused in her.

He got out and came around to open the car door for her, taking her hand and pulling her out.

She looped her arms around his neck. 'Are you always such a gentleman?'

He smiled sheepishly, wrapping his arms around her tightly. 'Well, I was raised to have good manners with women, but I don't think any of my dates have suggested I'm a gentleman before. When I go out on dates there's pretty much only one thing on my mind.'

'Do all your first dates end in sex?'

'Most of them do.'

She sighed softly. Regardless of what he'd said that morning, he must be disappointed it wasn't going to end that way.

'It's different with you,' he said. 'I don't want that with you.'

'You don't want to make love to me?'

'Oh god, of course I do, but it's about more than that with us. I want it to be special and I've never wanted that before.

Normally I go back to the girl's place, we have a quick shag and then the women hate me because as soon as it's over I get up and come home to my daughter.'

'Do you ever bring them back to your house?'

'No, never, that's not the kind of thing that I want Daisy to see, hear or even know that that's what I'm doing. Even with the women that things got semi-serious with, I never had them stay over. I'd have them over for dinner so they could spend time with Daisy but then I'd take them back home again. Any sex always took place at the woman's house. Everything is different with you. It feels right. When you are ready, I want to make love to you in my bed.'

She stared at him, feeling her heart swell with love for him.

'Hey, look, a shooting star, make a wish,' Henry said, pointing out over the sea.

Penny watched as a slash of gold ripped open the inky blue night sky. She closed her eyes and wished, really hard.

'What did you wish for?'

'I can't tell you that, it won't come true.'

Henry took her hand and led her around the back of the house. He let them into his kitchen and undid her coat, not taking his eyes off hers for a second.

He stared down at her, as if he was trying to work her out. Whatever he saw made him smile. He kissed her, softly, sweetly, but, as with every time he had kissed her before, desire ripped through her at the slightest of touches.

'I want to spend the rest of the night kissing you in my bed,' he mumbled against her lips. 'Come on, let's go to bed.'

Henry started pulling her up the stairs.

'Wait,' Penny laughed at his urgency. 'I haven't got any pyjamas.'

'You can sleep in one of my t-shirts.'

He led her into his bedroom and she watched as he started undressing. She slipped off her shoes, and undid the plait, combing through her hair with her fingers as she watched his shirt and then his trousers come off so he was left only in his tight black boxers. He was watching her too and she felt suddenly shy about undressing in front of him.

He grabbed a t-shirt and put it on the bed in front of her.

'Why don't I leave you to get changed?' Henry said, softly.

'Wait, can you unzip my dress at the back?'

Henry moved behind her and the touch of his hands was like fire at the top of her neck. He unzipped the dress slowly, his hand caressing her back with the softest of touches.

'Oh,' Henry said, his hands parting the dress at the back. 'You wore the snowflake lingerie.'

'Well, yes, you seemed to like it so. . .' She trailed off as he moved his hands back to her shoulders and slid the straps down her arms. The dress slithered off her body into a puddle on the floor. At least the black satin camisole top and tiny shorts seemed to cover her body more than the skimpy bra and thong sets she had been forced to buy earlier.

He cupped her waist and pressed his mouth to her neck, sending desire and need hurtling through her as his hands wandered around to stroke across her satin-clad stomach.

'Do me a favour.' His voice was coarse. 'Just wear this tonight, forget the t-shirt.'

She tossed the t-shirt over the chair and climbed into bed. He was quick to follow, immediately pulling her to him and kissing her.

Where before the kisses had been slow and tender, now they were laced with an urgency and hunger. He moved slowly on top of her, pinning her with his weight as the kiss continued.

She could feel how turned on he was getting.

'Sorry, just ignore it,' he mumbled against her mouth and she giggled.

Knowing how his body had reacted to her just from a kiss made her heart soar and all thoughts of being slow and cautious went straight out the window.

'I don't want to ignore it,' she whispered.

He carried on kissing her for a few moments before he stopped. 'What?'

Flushing, Penny stroked his face. 'I want you to make love to me.'

He stared at her, not blinking. 'Now?'

She nodded.

'Are you sure?'

'Do I need to beg?'

'No, Christ no.' He immediately pulled her top off, and trailed reverential kisses across her shoulder down to her breast. His hands caressed her skin, moving slowly down to her hips and sliding her shorts down her legs. She ran her hands down his back, feeling the warm, soft velvet over a wall of muscle as he peppered kisses over every inch of her body, taking his time to touch, stroke, caress and adore her until her whole body was thrumming with need, responding to the slightest of touches.

Finally he knelt up and grabbed a condom from the nearby bulging bag. She laughed as he tried to find one he liked but he quickly did, and a few frustrating moments later he settled himself between her legs, carefully lowering his weight onto her. He kissed her deeply as he slid slowly inside her, capturing her moans with his mouth, letting out a deep guttural moan too.

He pulled back slightly to look at her as she ran her hands around the back of his neck and she was thrown by the look of pure love and adoration in his eyes. She was falling for this man and there was no way back now. Any hope of trying to protect her heart from the devastating pain she had felt eight years before was gone. It didn't make sense to fall this hard, this fast, and as he frowned slightly, she could see he was thinking it too.

'Do you know what I wished for?'

She shook her head.

'I wished that I can make all your wishes come true.'

He started moving, slowly, tenderly, without taking his eyes off hers, but with every breath, every movement, she knew she was falling deeper in love and deeper in trouble.

Chapter 13

Henry woke the next day to the winter sun pouring through the open curtains and a stark naked Penny lying asleep on his chest, wrapped tightly in his arms. He pulled the duvet over her shoulders and resumed his hold on her.

So much for taking things slow. He'd hoped to get to know her properly, date her, spend time with her, start a real relationship and not one that was based on sex. Two minutes kissing her in that unbelievably sexy underwear and he'd forgotten all his best intentions. He wanted this to work with Penny. She felt like the start of a wonderful new chapter in his life, one that he wanted to last a lifetime. He didn't know how Penny felt about them, whether for her this was a long-term thing or nothing more than a fling to get back in the saddle after all this time. But one thing was for sure, he wasn't letting her go without a fight.

She stirred and looked up at him, her conker brown hair sticking out everywhere and a huge grin spreading on her face as she remembered the events of the night before.

He brushed her hair from her face. 'Hi.'

'Hi.'

'I know last night didn't go according to plan but—'

'Last night was—'

A door slammed downstairs. 'Dad?' Daisy shouted. 'Get up, you lazy sod.'

Penny's eyes widened with fear.

181

'Crap. I didn't expect her back so soon,' Henry whispered.

'Dad!'

'Yeah, hang on, love, I'm just getting dressed, I'll be down in a second.'

Shit, he was going into full-blown panic mode here. He didn't want Daisy to know about him and Penny, not yet, and he absolutely did not want her to know that he'd slept with his neighbour just five days after meeting her. What kind of example was that to set for his daughter?

Henry scrabbled up and started throwing on his clothes. 'Get dressed.'

Penny quickly climbed out of bed too, her gorgeous, naked body disappearing into her underwear and dress. Jesus, there was no way to explain what she was doing upstairs in his room, clearly dressed in the clothes she had worn the night before. There was only one conclusion that Daisy could come to and that would be the right one.

'What do we do?' Penny said.

'I'll take her out somewhere and then you can escape.'

A thunder of feet came racing up the stairs and Henry thanked god that the door was closed and Daisy would never just walk in out of fear of seeing her dad naked.

'Dad, is the laptop in there? I want to Skype Melissa.'

Henry looked around and saw the laptop on top of the drawers. 'Yes, hang on, I'll bring it down to you.'

'It's OK, I was going to Skype her from my room. Come on.' She rattled the doorknob impatiently.

'In the wardrobe, quick,' Henry whispered, and he felt a stab of guilt and pain at the look of hurt that flashed across Penny's face as she stepped into the wardrobe and closed the door.

He grabbed the bag of condoms and hid it in the drawers, quickly straightened the duvet and pillows, kicked Penny's shoes under the bed, gave the room a quick cursory glance to make sure there was no other evidence, and then opened the door.

'Took you long enough.' Daisy grinned up at him.

'I'd just got out the shower when you came in; I didn't know I'd have to get dressed in record time.'

Daisy walked in and grabbed the laptop, sitting on the edge of the bed and firing it up.

'How was your date with Penny?'

'It was. . .' Brilliant, wonderful, fun and ended in the best sex he'd ever had. 'Fine.'

'Fine? That doesn't sound good. Was she boring or a terrible kisser or something?'

Could the morning after the most wonderful night end more badly than this?

'It wasn't a proper date, you know that, so there was no kissing and no, she wasn't boring, she was great fun.'

'But?'

'There's no but.'

'There was definitely a but.'

'There isn't. We went for a meal, we chatted, we had a lovely time and we came back here and went to bed.'

'Together?' Daisy's eyes lit up, mischievously.

'No, of course not.'

'Did she come on to you? Did she try to kiss you or something, because you're acting all weird?'

'No.'

'Did you kiss her and she rejected you?'

'No, what's with all the questions?'

'Because you never take a woman out on a date as friends, never, not once.'

'This was your idea.'

'I know, but I didn't think you'd actually go through with it. Do you like her?'

'No.' Horribly aware that Penny was listening to every single word that was being said and he had lied to his daughter about ten times in one conversation, he needed to say something that would rescue this situation. 'Yes, as friends.'

'Nothing more?'

'No. Maybe the friendship could turn into something more, but not yet. I need to get to know her a bit more first.'

'So more dates?'

Daisy looked down at the computer as she logged in, but not before he caught the flash of worry in her eyes.

'Yes, as friends.'

She nodded. 'I'm going to Skype Melissa.'

'OK, don't be long. I thought we could go out, catch a film, have some lunch.'

'Cool.' She got up and walked to the door. 'We can ask Penny too, if you want.'

'I think she's out.'

'Her car is here.'

'She could have gone for a walk.'

'Bernard is here.'

'Maybe she went out without him, I don't know, but there hasn't been a peep from her side of the house all morning. Come on, phone Melissa and we'll go out in ten minutes.'

'Make it fifteen.' Daisy grinned and walked off into her bedroom.

Henry waited a moment and then closed the door and rushed back to the wardrobe. He opened the door and saw Penny was sitting on the floor looking angry. Shit, it wasn't possible for it to get any worse.

He crouched down to her height. 'I'm so sorry, about all of this. I didn't mean. . .'

'I don't want to talk about this now, not here when I'm stuffed in the wardrobe like a terrible mistake that you're ashamed of. We can talk about this later.'

'I'm sorry, I—'

'Dad, Melissa isn't answering, we can go out now if you want,' Daisy called from her room and Henry quickly closed the wardrobe door again. He knew he was handling this terribly but he had no idea how to handle it in any other way.

'OK, I'll just grab my shoes and coat, give me a minute,' he called. He turned back to the wardrobe and whispered through the door, not wanting to see the hurt and anger in Penny's eyes again. 'Give us five minutes and then you can escape.'

There was no answer from inside. As he grabbed his coat and left the room, he knew he would have a lot of making up to do.

Penny was beating the eggs so furiously in the bowl that splashes were hitting the worktops. Feeling somehow dirty after it had all ended that morning, she'd had a shower, walked Bernard and tried doing some sketches for future ice sculptures, but had failed spectacularly to do even the simplest of drawings. She couldn't do any carving either because she was too angry for that. Cake-making seemed to be her best bet, she couldn't go too far wrong with that and couldn't really injure herself too much like she could if she was carving.

She heard a car pull up outside, doors closing and the sounds of Henry and Daisy chatting as they walked around the side of the house.

She saw them walk past her back door and then Daisy scooted back and let herself in.

'Hey, there you are, we didn't see you this morning. We were going to ask you to come to the cinema with us. Where were you?'

'Out.'

Daisy hovered awkwardly, clearly sensing how angry she was and not knowing why. Penny took a deep breath. She refused to be angry at Daisy; none of this was her fault.

She looked up at her and saw Henry waiting outside.

'Sorry, just had a bad morning. Did you enjoy the film?'

'Yeah, some Christmas fiasco, families warring thing – it was very funny. Can we do some more carving later?'

'Not today, honey, I'm going to be really busy. We can do some tomorrow though. I promise.'

Daisy seemed satisfied with this. 'Dad said you had a wonderful date last night.'

'It wasn't a date,' Penny said, adding the eggs to the cake mixture.

'But. . .'

'Daisy, come on, leave her alone,' Henry said. 'She just said she was really busy.'

'OK. Are you coming for dinner tonight?'

'No, sorry, love, I can't.'

'Tomorrow then?'

'Maybe.'

Daisy left, obviously knowing something was wrong, and she and Henry went back next door.

She added a splash of milk and gave it a good stir as the gentle murmur of voices continued next door. She heard the thunder of feet as Daisy went upstairs and a few moments later the connecting door opened.

She glanced up at Henry as he closed the door behind him.

'I'm really sorry about the stuff I said, about shoving you in a cupboard. I handled it terribly and I'm really sorry.'

She slammed the spoon down. 'And how should you have handled it?'

He had nothing to say. Eventually he spoke. 'We agreed that we wouldn't tell her.'

'We agreed that we wouldn't tell her unless it got serious between us. Last night it got pretty fucking serious. It was one of the best nights of my life and this morning you bundled me into a wardrobe like I was a shag that you regretted.'

'What did you want me to do? Bring you downstairs dressed only in my t-shirt? That was not the way for her to find out.'

He was angry now and she didn't think he had any right to be.

'No, but you could have had a sensible conversation with her.'

'How? She was standing outside my bedroom door and you were standing there in last night's clothes and just-fucked hair. What could I have said? "Hey, Daisy, I know me and Penny have only just met but last night we slept together and it was the best sex I've ever had in my life?"'

Penny stared at him in shock and he moved around the table towards her. When he spoke his voice was softer. 'Should I have told her that when I made love to you I could honestly see myself doing that every night for the rest of my life?'

She was horribly aware that she looked like a fish as her mouth moved but no words came out.

'Come in the lounge and let's talk.'

He waited for her and she led the way, sitting down on the sofa. He sat down next to her.

'She's happy here. She hasn't been really happy for a long time. We've moved around a bit in recent years because of work and one reason or another. She was bullied at the last two schools. I'm not sure whether it was because she was the new girl or because sometimes she's a bit shy. Teenagers are cruel and they just have to get a whiff of vulnerability and they attack like a pack of wolves. Having a mum who abandoned her a few weeks after her birth, well, that kind of stuff is like gold dust to a bully. Lots of kids come from single parent families but somehow it's different that she was raised by her dad and not her mum. Your mum is supposed to be the one person that sticks by you through thick and thin. There were comments about her being an ugly baby and how no one wants her, even comments that she wasn't mine because she's so blonde and I'm so dark.'

Penny gasped. 'Is that true, she might not be yours?'

Henry shrugged. 'I don't know and I don't care. It didn't occur to me at the time when she came to live with me, it was only later when she started school that a few of the other parents made snide comments about our differences. Her mum has dark hair too. But I've raised her ever since she was three months old; she's mine even if she isn't biologically.'

Penny stared at him, feeling her heart fit to burst with love for him.

'It hurts her though, when the other children pick on that. Another layer of doubt to add to her abandonment worries. If I'm not her dad then why would I stay? It breaks my heart. I think the only saving grace through all the bullying was her relationship with Rosie, my ex. I think Daisy saw her as her only friend at the time and it really upset Daisy when I broke up with her. I tried to make it up to her by bringing Emily into our life. She was all sweetness and light to Daisy in front of me but behind my back she brought her down, stomped on her confidence, said some absolutely horrible things. She told her things I'd supposedly said about how Daisy had ruined my life and I regretted having her and that I wished Tina had had an abortion and that I didn't think she was mine.'

'No!' Penny felt tears spring to her eyes. 'How could anyone say that to a child?'

'I don't know. I would never even think those things, let alone say them. Jesus, every insecurity Daisy has ever had, Emily played up to every single one of them. I'm not sure if Daisy believed her at the time or whether she didn't want to tell me because I was happy with Emily. I had no idea what was going on but Daisy ran away from home. She went off to school one day and never got there. She made her way down here instead, caught the train some of the way, walked a lot of it. Took her three days; she slept rough for two nights. It absolutely broke my heart. The police were out looking for her, it was horrible, the worst days of my life. I'm scared of it happening all over again. She got so lucky last time, no one found her or hurt her. She might not be so lucky if she runs away again. I promised her no one would ever come between us again. It's harder because this is her home, and you're part of it, and I never want her to feel in the way in her own home.'

'I understand.'

'No, you don't. Last night it did get serious between us – it wasn't just sex, you know that. There was a connection there that I've never felt before. But this is all happening way faster than any of us could have imagined. She specifically asked me not to date you and I went ahead and did it anyway, and I really don't want to upset her when she's smiling again for the first time this year. I just need to give her some time to get used to the idea. If you come round for dinner most nights, come out with us, she will get used to having you as part of our life, she will see how good we are together and trust that I'm not going to hurt you, and then I can introduce the idea of us seeing each other. After last time with Emily and Rosie, I just want to tread carefully with Daisy this time.'

Penny took his hand and he sighed with relief. 'I understand not wanting to tell her, but if she finds out we've been sneaking around behind her back and lying to her she is going to be even more hurt.'

'I know. I would just like to get to Christmas without upsetting her. I like seeing a smile back on her face again.'

'OK.'

'And we'll just be really careful for the next few days.'

She nodded.

'Now let's have a quick shag, whilst she's on the phone to her friend.' Henry reached for her, and she laughed, batting away his advances.

Henry chuckled. 'Come for dinner tonight. I'll cook you something special.'

Penny nodded. 'I'll bring some cake.'

'Well, if making cakes is your response to getting annoyed with me, I'm going to be as big as a house.'

'Then don't annoy me.'

Henry smiled, peered over her shoulder at the still closed connecting door and reached forwards to give her a brief, soft kiss, before walking out the door.

Chapter 14

Henry pulled his car into the furniture factory car park and got out. The car park was nearly deserted.

He had been surprised to get a phone call from Audrey, Clara's assistant, half an hour before, asking him to come in and discuss his designs with Clara and Edward. It was one of the things Henry had brought up in his interview, that he would love the opportunity to design his own furniture. Edward had seemed really interested but hadn't been sure whether at that stage they would be looking to design anything new when their current lines were selling so well, but he had promised to talk to the design team. Henry hadn't expected to hear any more about it and certainly hadn't expected to get a phone call from Clara so late on a Wednesday night just a week before Christmas, especially because, according to Daniel, although Clara headed up the design team, she basically did a big fat lot of nothing. But it wasn't an opportunity he was going to miss: designing and creating ideas from scratch was something he was passionate about. He loved building a piece that was individual and not like anything that could be bought in shops.

He grabbed his portfolio from the car and walked into the factory just as Daniel was walking out.

'Oh hey, mate, what are you doing here so late?' Daniel asked, shrugging on his coat and pulling his hat on over his messy hair.

'I've been asked to come in and talk to Edward and Clara about my designs for some new furniture.'

'Oh, that's cool. I hope they like your designs. Oh, before I forget, Maggie wants me to invite you round for dinner tomorrow. You can bring Daisy too, if you want.'

'Thank you, I'd love to. I'll ask Daisy, though I doubt she will come. What time?'

'About seven thirty is good. I'll see you then.'

Daniel left and Henry looked at his watch. The nice dinner and evening he had planned with Penny was quickly disappearing. She had been out walking Bernard when he left so he had asked Daisy to start dinner and to pass on a message that he had been called in to work but he would be back soon. He only hoped that this meeting didn't take too long.

He raced up the stairs and walked into Audrey's office, which led through to Clara's office. Audrey was just getting on her coat and scarf to leave too.

She looked at him apologetically. 'I'm sorry to call you in so late, but she insisted,' Audrey whispered as she walked past him and out the door, leaving him alone.

He approached the door to Clara's office. Clara was sitting behind her desk, a huge thing that took up almost the entire room. The whole room was covered in dark wood that matched the desk and modern art pictures that were slashes of brown and beige. There wasn't a single slash of colour in the room, in stark contrast to Edward's office, which was pale wood, lots of colourful photos of sunsets and beaches, and even a little Christmas tree in the corner. There was nothing that indicated that it was Christmas in here.

Clara's desk lacked any kind of work paraphernalia at all. It was devoid of all the papers that had littered Edward's desk. It was hard to see what she did with her time all day. Maybe she spent a lot of it on the phone, but he would still expect to see some kind of notes from her telephone conversations. The computer was switched on and she was working on it but there didn't look like there was anything work-related on there; in fact, the screen was filled with lots of photos of expensive-looking dresses.

He knocked softly on the door and she looked up and flashed him a huge smile when she saw him.

'Henry, do come in, shut the door behind you.'

He did as he was asked but, looking around, he could see they were alone, whereas Audrey had made it sound like there would be members of the design team there too. He took his coat off and left it over the sofa that was in the corner of the room, though he instantly regretted it when he turned to see her appreciative gaze raking over his body.

'Are Edward or the designers joining us?' Henry said, hesitantly.

'Edward has already left for the evening,' Clara said, coming around the desk towards him. 'He asked me to arrange a meeting with you and one of the designers but, as the managing director in charge of the design team, I wanted to look through your designs first. We are very hands-on at the White Cliff Bay Furniture Company. Something I'm sure you will appreciate about working here.'

Henry cleared his throat, not at all comfortable with the way she was staring at him like she wanted to eat him.

'Let's see what you've got,' Clara said, without taking her eyes off him.

He opened up his portfolio and pulled a few sheets from the folder, spreading them out on her desk as she stood just behind him.

'I know you've just started doing a range in chairs but I thought about maybe expanding it. The chairs we sell are very functional and nice but I think we could make them into something more.'

She moved in next to him, her body pressed close to his, though her eyes were still on him and not the designs. He subtly moved away a few inches.

'I've designed a chaise longue, which is classic but with traces of more contemporary styles at the same time. The chaise longue is a most sought-after piece with many women, it's romantic and will make a great addition to any lounge furniture or even the bedroom.'

'What would you do with it in the bedroom?' Clara said, raking her fingers seductively over the curves of the chair, her eyes returning to him almost immediately.

'Well, you would sit on it and read or. . .' He trailed off as her fingers skated over his knuckles as he leant over the desk. He removed his hand from under hers. 'I thought we could make it from white, black or beige leather, as that will fit in with most colour schemes, and we can add silver or gold to the legs to make it more—'

'Will it be big enough for two?' She stared up at him through long lashes as she ran her fingernails up his arm.

Henry glanced over to the closed door, a sick feeling of panic rushing through him. This was not good. She hadn't brought him here for the designs. There was only one portfolio she was interested in and it wasn't the one in his black folder but the one that was mere centimetres from her ever encroaching hand.

In a last-ditch attempt to change the subject and put the conversation back on track, he rifled in his folder for another drawing to show her, moving subtly away from her gold-painted talons.

'I have some other designs too.' He grabbed the first design that came to hand and laid it on the desk. His heart sank as soon as he saw which design it was. The two chairs facing in opposite directions, joined together by the S-shaped curves of the backrest and arms, was a very popular style in the late Victorian period and Henry's design was a modern twist on that but the name was vastly inappropriate for what Clara had planned for this meeting.

She glanced at it briefly. 'A love seat?'

'Yes. Also known as a tête-à-tête.'

'Face-to-face,' Clara whispered, and Henry cringed because the literal translation was not helpful either.

'They are making a comeback in garden furniture and I think we can—'

'I wouldn't have a love seat in the garden. Besides, these armrests between the couple are not exactly conducive to a romantic setting. I prefer a lover's chair with no boundaries,' Clara said, leaning up and pressing her lips to his throat.

He immediately took a step back. 'Clara, I'm flattered but I have a girlfriend.'

A girlfriend who was sitting at home waiting for him, someone he should have been having dinner with at this very moment. This whole meeting was a huge waste of his time.

'Yet you're here with me and not at home with her.' Clara cocked her head to one side, in what she clearly thought was a flirtatious move, running her tongue across her teeth as she surveyed her prey.

He took a step to grab his designs but she moved in between him and the desk.

'I came for purely professional reasons. Working in design is important to me.'

She stepped forwards, placing a hand on his chest. 'How important?'

He wanted to push her away, her perfume settling around him making it hard to breathe. He wouldn't touch her. Just the two of them in a closed room, she could claim anything had happened and it would be his word against hers. He took a step back, but her fingers had already closed over one of the buttons on his shirt and as he moved he heard the small tear of material as the button came off in her hand.

He stared at her in shock before he turned and grabbed his coat. 'If Edward is serious about looking at my designs then I'll make an appointment to see him.'

He opened the door and stormed out. He should have seen through the façade from the second he realised it was just going to be the two of them. He should have told her where to stick her inappropriate advances and most importantly he should have stayed at home with his lovely girlfriend.

He got in the car and drove quickly back towards Lilac Cottage. Rain lashed down on the windscreen and storm clouds rolled across the sky, lighting up the heavy clouds with periodic flashes of lightning, reflecting his mood perfectly. As he approached a little hut used for birdwatching, he nearly ran over a hooded figure who was cycling quickly away from it, dressed all in black, silhouetted against the rainy night sky; the boy was almost impossible to see. Henry cursed as he mounted the grass to avoid him and then turned down the driveway to his home, wanting nothing more now than to wrap his arms around Penny and know that there were still good people in this world.

He pulled up outside the house and strode straight into Penny's kitchen. She looked up from a book she was reading and gave him a half smile. He had let her down by not being there for dinner as promised.

'I made you and Daisy spaghetti bolognese, but it's probably all dried out now,' Penny said, moving towards the oven.

'I was going to cook for you, I'm sorry, something came up,' Henry said, catching her arm. She didn't shrug his hand off her but she distinctly moved out of his reach. Her stomach suddenly gurgled hungrily and he felt another wave of guilt. 'Have you not eaten?'

'No, pathetically, I thought I'd wait for you.'

'Where's Daisy?'

'She went out, about two minutes after you left.'

'What?' Henry looked outside into the inky black night, rain coming down in curtains as it ripped across the cliffs. 'And you let her go out in this?'

Penny stared at him incredulously. 'I was out walking Bernard when I saw you both leave. And I certainly don't have any authority over her.'

Suddenly the kitchen door banged open and Daisy came in with a huge grin on her face. She was soaking wet, and little stalks of grass were stuck to the legs of her jeans. Her trainers were covered in mud.

'Hey Daddio,' she sang, sitting down at Penny's table as if it was the most natural thing in the world.

'Where have you been?' Henry tried and failed to keep the angry, concerned tone from his voice.

'Nowhere. I was in the shed chatting to Melissa.'

'You got that wet running from the shed to the house?'

'I slipped over on the grass.'

She was lying and he didn't know why.

'Penny said she saw you go out.'

Daisy stared at Penny for a moment. 'I was. . . trying to get a signal down the drive but then it started to rain hard and I remembered that Penny said I could get a good signal in her shed so I came back a few minutes later. Penny must not have seen me. Is dinner ready?'

'The dinner I asked you to start for me,' Henry said.

Daisy shrugged, still unable to wipe the huge grin from her face. 'The phone call took a bit longer than I thought.'

'It's fine, I made dinner,' Penny said, deliberately stepping between them with a huge dish of bolognese.

He sat down and watched as she dished it up onto three plates and then sat down at the opposite end of the table to him. This was not how he had planned his evening at all. Outside the storm raged on, thunder rolling across the night sky, lit up periodically with spectacular forks of lightning. But inside the tension between the three of them was almost as tangible as the storm outside.

Henry sat staring at his spaghetti bolognese with as much concentration as he could muster for a plate full of meat and pasta. He glanced over to Penny, who was focussing on the art of wrapping a string of spaghetti around her fork as if it was the hardest job in the world.

Daisy looked between the two of them in confusion. She knew something was going on even if she had no idea what that something was.

'Did you guys have a row or something?' Daisy said.

'No, sorry, honey, it's just been a weird day,' Penny said.

Henry cast around for a suitable topic of conversation. It was ridiculous to sit in silence when conversation had flowed so easily whenever they'd been together before.

'Hey Dad, did you tell Penny about the huge penis we saw in town?'

Penny choked on her drink

That certainly wasn't a suitable topic of conversation, especially after what had gone on between them the night before. But Daisy wasn't to be deterred.

'It was hilarious, some woman dressed in this huge seven-foot costume chasing men down the streets and hugging them. White Cliff Bay is a little weird, eh? I bet it's a right little den of sin, people sleeping with their neighbours or having orgies.'

'Hey,' Henry reprimanded.

Daisy laughed. 'Orgy isn't a swear word.'

'It's not exactly an appropriate subject for the dinner table though, is it?'

Penny stifled a giggle and he sensed the mood between them was on the verge of passing. 'I've seen people do stuff like that before. I think it's to raise awareness or money for cancer. So don't judge our little town too harshly just yet.'

Henry needed to change the subject away from people having sex with their neighbours. He latched on to something Edward had said to him on Monday.

'Oh, that's what I wanted to talk to you about. Edward said there was some gingerbread house competition on Saturday. He asked if I wanted to come with my family and form a team. I don't really know what it's about, but it's for charity. Daisy, do you want to do it?'

'We make a gingerbread house? Do we get to eat it afterwards?'

Penny laughed. 'It's the annual Giant Gingerbread House Race. The White Cliff Bay Furniture Company holds it every year.

Everybody in the town goes to watch. But it's not real gingerbread, they use plastic walls and foam and plastic sweets and decorations. The gingerbread walls are six-foot panels and I'm pretty sure the icing they use isn't edible. There's normally around eight teams and you have about an hour to build your house into something wonderful. It's great fun.'

'So you can be in our team too,' Henry said, decisively.

'I can't, it's families of employees only.'

'You can be part of our family,' Daisy said simply and Henry smiled that his daughter had just given her seal of approval so readily and unknowingly.

'Edward isn't going to care too much about who is on my team; he won't exactly be demanding to see a marriage certificate before he lets us in,' Henry said.

'I'll do it if you do it, Penny,' Daisy said. 'And it is for charity so you can't really say no.'

Henry laughed at the exact same persuasion technique that Penny had pulled on him to get him to agree to the ball a few days before.

'I'm rubbish at building things. You really won't want me on your team. I'd be more of a hindrance than a help. When I built the barbeque in the summer, I ended up with pieces upside down and several pieces left over.'

'We need you on our team, you have the inside edge, you've seen what other people have done before to win and we don't have that. As newbies we need a fighting chance. And Daisy and I can't do it alone; other teams will have five or six people in them. You can't let us down, Penny. Will you be part of our family?'

He fixed her with his best puppy dog eyes and she laughed.

'OK, but don't say I didn't warn you.'

'Now you're part of our family, I think you should come for dinner every night,' Daisy said. 'It gets pretty boring looking at his ugly mug every night.'

'Hey!' Henry said.

'Well, that sounds lovely, it does get a bit dull talking to Bernard every night, especially as he doesn't talk back, but understand I'm only doing it for you, Daisy, to save you the tedium of talking to your dad.'

'Hey, I am sitting here, you know,' Henry protested and Daisy laughed.

'Except I can't come tomorrow night, I have plans.'

'Ooooh, do you have a hot date?' Daisy said, getting excited about the prospect of some gossip. Henry rolled his eyes; she was going to thrive in this town.

'No. I—'

'I saw Fabio come round earlier. Do you have plans with him?'

Henry was surprised by this. 'Fabio was here?'

'He was next door for over half an hour and when he left he was looking pretty pleased with himself,' Daisy said. 'I saw it all from my bedroom window.'

Henry stared at his daughter incredulously. 'I've raised a spy.'

'Well, as we've already established, living with you can be really boring so I have to provide myself with some entertainment.'

'What did Fabio want?'

'Nothing much, just to apologise for his behaviour the other night and to ask me out on a date.'

He cleared his throat. 'And you're going?'

'Dad, it'll be nice for Penny to go on a date. Let's face it, her dates with you aren't going to set her world on fire.'

'I don't think I did too badly last night.'

202

'It was OK.' Penny shrugged, fighting with a smirk. He couldn't help the smile from spreading across his face as she blushed bright red and focussed her attention on her spaghetti again.

'So you're going out with him?' Daisy asked.

'Sure, why not? I love a guy in leather trousers.'

'Hear that, Dad? If you really want to impress the ladies you need to wear leather trousers and maybe get a medallion too. It seems the old clichés never die.'

'I'll be sure to remember that, especially as my dazzling conversation skills clearly need a lot of work. I have plans too tomorrow night. I'm going for dinner with a guy from work. You can come if you want, Daisy?'

'Nah, I'm fine here. Shame though, there's a mince-pie-making class at Linda's bakery tomorrow night. I was going to suggest you go as your mince-pie-making skills are absolutely dire.'

'Hey, I'm not that bad,' Henry said, indignantly. 'Why don't I take you out for ice cream before I go out for dinner tomorrow night? I'm at work tomorrow too, someone has called in sick and there are a few jobs that need to be finished before the factory closes for the holidays, so you won't see me all day.'

'I'll cope.' Daisy flashed him a cheeky smile. 'But yes to ice cream. Can we do some more carving tomorrow, Penny?'

'We can, actually. I have a snowman carving that needs to be finished for a corporate party so you could help me do that if you wanted, or just have fun creating your own pieces.'

'You'd let me help with one of your professional pieces?'

'Yes, of course. You're an ice-carving champion now; your credentials more than speak for themselves.'

Daisy laughed.

'I was serious about the job offer; if it's OK with your dad, I'd be happy to pay you for your help.'

Daisy fixed him with pleading eyes and he nodded. 'Only if you promise me you'll be really careful with those tools and I don't want her using the chainsaw.'

Penny and Daisy both nodded.

'I have an errand to run tomorrow morning so come round about lunchtime,' Penny said.

'Does the errand have anything to do with Fabio?' Daisy asked, clearly still digging for dirt.

Penny flashed Henry a mischievous grin. 'Maybe.'

Obviously he had been forgiven.

Daisy looked over at Henry, sensing that something was going on between them. 'How did your important meeting with Clara go?'

'It was fine.' He watched the smile slide off Penny's face.

'Your meeting was with Clara? That's who you rushed off to see?'

'It was to talk through my designs, it was nothing,' Henry said, staring at his plate again.

'Dad, what happened to your shirt? It's all torn at the top. Did you lose a button?'

'I just got it caught in something.'

Daisy giggled. 'Is that lipstick on your neck? Wow, when you said it was fine, I didn't realise just how fine you actually meant.'

He glanced up at Penny in time to see the look of horror and disappointment register on her face before she stood up to clear the plates away.

He wanted to tell her that nothing had happened, that she didn't need to worry, but in front of Daisy it was out of the question.

A clap of thunder rumbled overhead and the tension that had dissipated had suddenly returned.

Penny got into her pyjamas later that night. Henry and Daisy had disappeared back to their own home shortly after dinner, leaving her alone, where if she had been in a proper relationship she could have spent the night cuddled up on the sofa with her boyfriend. Although she certainly wasn't in the mood to cuddle up to Henry right now. She couldn't get the thought of him and Clara together out of her mind and how guilty Henry had looked when Daisy had spotted the lipstick. He didn't even try to deny that anything had happened. She knew, however, that if he cared about her at all, he would come over once Daisy had gone to bed and try to explain. She was going to try to keep an open mind until then. She had been cheated on before and she wasn't going to let it happen again, but she wouldn't judge Henry until she heard him out.

She got into bed and had just started to read her book when she heard the soft thud of feet on the stairs.

She put her book down and watched him as he walked into the room. He looked scared as he approached the side of her bed.

'I'm sorry I wasn't there for dinner and you had to cook when I promised that I would.'

She arched an eyebrow at him; he had to do better than that. Annoyingly, very faint traces of lipstick were still present on his throat.

'Nothing happened with me and Clara, I swear. She kissed me, I told her I had a girlfriend and I walked out. I was an idiot for thinking that she actually wanted to talk about my designs and I was so eager to have an opportunity to share them with her and Edward that I couldn't see her true motive for bringing me there. I'm sorry, but you have to believe me, nothing happened. I'm not interested in her at all, or anyone else in fact. I only want to be with you.'

He shivered against the chill of the night and she instinctively pulled back the duvet, shuffling over for him to get in. He hesitated for a moment and then slid in beside her.

'You believe me?'

She nodded. 'Actually, I do. I have no reason to doubt you.'

'You have no reason to believe me either.'

She moved closer to him, so close their faces were nearly touching. His hands moved to her waist, pulling her against him, though she stopped him getting too close with her hand on his chest. 'You can tell a lot about someone from their eyes. Fear, anger, shock, deceit and love are some of the many emotions that come from the eyes.' She stared at his silvery grey eyes filled with warmth for her. 'Your eyes are telling me that you're speaking the truth.'

He smiled with relief as he pulled her closer and this time she let him. 'What are my eyes telling you now?'

She laughed. 'That you want to do all kinds of wicked and dirty things to me.'

He kissed her, sweetly, his hands caressing over her body. Her body filled with need for him but before she could get too carried away, he pulled away slightly, his eyes filled with regret.

'I can't stay.'

She smiled, stroking his face. 'I know, it's OK.'

'She's only just gone to bed. She could get up and find I'm not there. I shouldn't have come but I needed to see you.'

'It's OK. Go, I'll see you tomorrow.'

He leant his forehead against hers for a second, kissed her briefly and then slipped from the bed, giving her a smile before disappearing from the room.

They had to come clean with Daisy soon. This sneaking around was killing her.

Chapter 15

Penny grabbed her coat and took her time doing up her shoe-laces. She had put off doing this for the last few days but she knew she needed to do it now.

The sun was shining through drifts of fog, drying up all the rain from the night before and making the sea below Lilac Cottage glitter like gold.

She hadn't been into town since Tuesday, when everyone had decided to help her get ready for her big date. Who knew that the tiny piece of satin that she had been forced to buy would end up having such a devastating effect on both her and Henry? Despite telling everyone that listened that it wasn't a proper date, that they were just friends, she knew that they would all be giving her that knowing look today or grilling her about Henry's skill between the sheets. And with Henry desperately trying to keep their relationship hidden from Daisy, there wasn't a lot that she could say to the people of the town, not that she would share anything anyway, but now she needed to be even more careful. With only five days before the Christmas Eve ball, the town would be filled with people doing last-minute shopping. She sighed.

Suddenly the connecting door flew open and Henry stormed towards her.

'Daisy is in the shower and I have to go to work but I just wanted to give you something before I left,' Henry said.

'What?'

Henry gathered her in his arms and kissed her deeply. Good lord, she'd suddenly forgotten all plans for that day and only wanted to whisk Henry back to bed. When would be the next time she could make love to him? She knew any length of time would be too long. She wrapped herself around him, holding him tight and kissing him hard, but he just as suddenly pulled away.

'I really have to go to work, I can't be late on my first proper day, as much as I'd like to right now. But there's something for you to think about on your hot date with Fabio tonight.'

Penny laughed. 'I'm not. . .'

'It's OK, I get that the lure of a man in leather trousers is too much to resist, but just remember whose name you were screaming the other night.'

She smiled. 'I don't think I could ever forget. When are we going to get a repeat performance of that?'

'When you stop dating men in leather trousers.'

He kissed her on the head and walked out the back door. He turned back and gave her a wink. 'Soon, I promise.'

She smiled as she watched him go, that incredible kiss setting her up for the whole day.

She got in the car and drove down into town, the streets a hive of activity as people prepared for Christmas. In the foggy morning the Christmas lights that were strewn from the trees and hung from the lampposts and the fronts of buildings looked magical, even in the daylight, their winking orbs welcoming people into the town. The rain from the night before had frozen in the early hours of the morning and it sparkled from the roof-tops of houses and cars that lined the streets.

Penny pulled her car up outside The Pilchard, turned the engine off and took a deep breath before she stepped out of the car. She looked up at the pub sign as it swung gently in the cool sea breeze: a cheery fish smiling inanely as it leapt out of the water. Lights twinkled from the windows and even though the pub was closed it looked warm and inviting. This had been one of her favourite places to hang out in her later teen years, long before her and Chris had become friends and started dating. It was warm, cosy and traditional, with little booths to sit in. She had imagined then that she would be coming there for the rest of her life, and still propping up the bar when she was old, grey and wrinkled. She would never have thought that, due to circumstances beyond her control, she wouldn't step foot in there for eight years. Maybe it was time to rectify that.

She pushed open the door. The pub was empty as it didn't open until just before lunch, but the log fire crackled in the fireplace, ensuring the pub was welcoming for the lunchtime crowd. Kathleen was at the bar, busily going through a list, probably doing a stocktake as Penny had seen her do several times when she had come in the past.

'We're closed until eleven,' Kathleen called out as she turned around, her face going pale as she saw her.

They both stood staring at each other for the longest moment before Penny held up the bag of clothes lamely. 'I just wanted to return these.'

Kathleen stood still for a second or two longer before she walked towards her. For a moment Penny thought Kathleen might hug her, as her hands moved out, but then it seemed Kathleen changed her mind.

'Thank you.'

Penny handed over the bag and hovered awkwardly, but as there was clearly nothing more to be said she turned to go.

'Will you stay for a drink?' Kathleen blurted out. 'I'd really like it if you stayed for a drink.'

Penny turned back and nodded. 'I'd like that too.'

Kathleen went behind the bar. 'What would you like?'

'Just a tea, please. I'm driving so. . .'

'How about a hot chocolate?'

Penny smiled as she leant on the bar. 'You always were so good at making those. We used to come in here before we were legal just so we could have your hot chocolates, and you used to let us sit in the booths, making one glass last a whole hour, and you never kicked us out.'

'I liked having you lot in here, and you weren't doing any harm. The pub has always been a family place, always will be.'

Penny watched as Kathleen put a handful of marshmallows, a large spoonful of cocoa powder and a splash of milk in two tall glasses and stuck them both in the microwave while she heated some milk on the coffee machine. The microwave beeped and she pulled the glasses out, poured the hot milk into the gooey chocolatey mixture and gave it a good stir, topping it off with a good layer of squirty cream and a handful of chocolate shavings.

She passed a glass to Penny and gestured for her to go and sit by the fire. Kathleen sat opposite her on a soft leather brown armchair.

Penny took a sip, smiling at the fond memories she had of this drink and this place. She stared into the flames, wondering what she should say about what had happened in the past, or whether to say anything at all. Maybe it was best just to let it go, move on and look to the future.

'I'm sorry,' Kathleen said and Penny turned to face her. 'I am so sorry for what happened. I wanted to come and see you after the baby died, but. . . I don't know. . . I thought maybe I should leave you alone for a few days. You had your family around you and I just thought you'd need a bit of space. I planned to come and see you at the weekend but then Chris left you and I found out. . .' She trailed off.

'That he had been sleeping with Jade the entire time I was pregnant?'

'Yes. I didn't know. I swear I didn't know until after the baby had died, but when I found out I was so angry at him. Everybody was. But then what happened after, the lies he told about you, I have never been so ashamed of him before.'

Penny swallowed down the pain of that, returning her attention to the hot chocolate.

'People will believe what they want to believe and most of the town saw the lies for what they were, but as you know, there were some that believed them,' Kathleen said. 'I couldn't look at him for months, barely said a word to him. I was so embarrassed by him. God, he was hated by so many people for what he had done, but that hatred spread to me too. The looks I'd get, the comments. Even some of my friends turned against me as if it was my fault he had slept with Jade, abandoned you and told all those lies. He left the town shortly after, as you know, but I was left with all those looks and comments for months afterwards. I saw you quite a few times around town but I was never brave enough to come and say anything. I was too ashamed to come and see you personally, and eight years have passed and you've never been back in the pub since.'

'Do you blame me?'

'No, of course not. I just hoped that you didn't hate me for what happened but, as time went on, I guessed that you did.'

'I don't hate you. I hated Chris for a long while, but I never hated you. Because I never saw you again, I just presumed that you believed the lies he told you and that you wouldn't want a crazy, psychotic person in the pub.'

'Oh love, I wish I had come to see you. Maybe we could have put this to bed years ago.'

Penny nodded sadly and took another sip of the comforting hot chocolate. They had both been victims of Chris's actions.

'You know he's married now, and has a baby boy, Eric. He's five months old and Chris absolutely adores him. I guess that must be really hard for you, after seeing how badly he reacted to your baby.'

'Actually, it isn't. It was hard at the time when I saw the baby clothes and toys you had bought for him, but I hope Chris is a better person now. It was a long time ago and he was young, we both were. If he loves his little boy, as you say he does, I'm genuinely happy for him.'

'He's grown up to be a marvellous young man, and a fantastic dad. He's actually someone I can be proud of. I hope you can forgive him one day.'

'I don't hate him any more and I wish him well, though forgiveness might take a little longer.'

Kathleen nodded with understanding. 'And what about you? I hear you're seeing Henry Travis.'

Penny sighed. Nothing was secret in this town.

'He seems like a decent man.'

'He really is.'

'And I know it's early days but do you think you might have your own family one day?'

'Family comes in different guises. He has a daughter who I adore. Maybe it would be enough to just be part of their family.'

Kathleen nodded. 'Sometimes the family you pick for yourself is miles better than the one you were given.'

Penny smiled as she looked into the flames. She just had to hope that Henry and Daisy would pick her too.

It was a while later when Penny pulled back up outside her house. She had chatted to Kathleen for a few hours and, although she wouldn't be popping into the pub every week, she knew she would be always be very welcome in there from now on.

She let herself into her kitchen and smiled when she saw Jill and Daisy chatting over lunch.

'Hey.' Penny dropped a fond kiss on Jill's head.

'Hello, lovely,' Jill said. 'I made you some lunch and then I found this little waif next door, practically starving to death, so I had to feed her up too. I hope you don't mind.'

'Of course not. Can't have her wasting away.'

Daisy grinned at her as she polished off the last of her sandwich. Penny sat down next to her and gave her a friendly nudge. Daisy nudged her back.

'I saw you going into The Pilchard earlier. Everything OK?' Jill asked casually, trying not to let anything slip to nosy ears.

'It is now,' Penny said, lifting the cover off her plate and tucking into her own sandwich.

Jill smiled with understanding and watched her carefully over her mug of tea. 'You look different,' Jill said eventually, 'and I can't place what it is.'

'I had a haircut the other day,' Penny suggested, though with her hair tied back in its usual ponytail, it was unlikely to be that.

'No, it's not that. You look. . . contented and really happy.'

'I am happy.' She tilted her head to the side subtly, hopefully indicating to Jill that the reason she was happy really shouldn't be talked about in front of Daisy.

Jill picked up on it straight away and stood up to go to the kettle. 'Did you want a cup of tea?'

'Yes please.'

'She is happy, she has a hot date tonight,' Daisy said. 'With a sexy Italian of all people.'

Jill turned around. 'Oh and who might that be?'

'Fabio,' Daisy said, delighted that she had gossip to share. 'He's an ice carver, just like Penny, and very talented.'

She flicked a few buttons on her phone and turned it around to show Jill. Penny laughed as Jill watched the very bizarre proposal video. Daisy was getting enormous pleasure out of this piece of gossip and Penny was loath to burst her bubble and tell her the truth. She had politely and very firmly told Fabio that she wouldn't be going out with him when he popped round the day before, nor would she be marrying him and having his babies any time in the future. But while Daisy was fixated on this new, exciting bit of news, it might make things easier for her and Henry to secretly be together.

'Look, you, before you show Jill any more embarrassing videos or photos of me, why don't you go and get changed into something warmer than your pyjamas and then we can do a bit of carving this afternoon.'

This was the only incentive that Daisy needed. She leapt off the bench with a quick thank you for Jill and then she darted upstairs to get changed.

Penny got up and shut the connecting door and returned to her sandwich.

'Am I to presume that the reason you are practically glowing has something to do with her father and not some Italian stallion?' Jill said, passing her a mug of tea.

'You would presume correctly. We're seeing each other, it's very early days and we don't want to tell Daisy yet in case she gets upset by it, so we're just going to see how it goes over the next week or so.'

Jill's smile filled her whole face. 'And how is it going?'

Penny blushed and picked up her mug to hide behind it. Jill's face softened.

'You've fallen in love with him.'

'I think I might have.'

Jill squealed just as Daisy burst back into the room.

'What did I miss?'

'Penny was just telling me about young Fabio.'

Penny cringed a bit. This lie was going to trip her up, she just knew it.

'Come on, you, we've got some carving to be done.' Penny stood up. 'Will you be here later?'

'No, lovely, I'm getting off now, but I'll probably see you Monday.'

Penny kissed her goodbye and ushered Daisy into the cool room, hoping that the subject of Fabio would be dropped.

Henry wiped his hands on a cloth and looked at the table that was now gleaming in a coat of toffee brown varnish. It had been a brilliant day, working alongside his new colleagues, creating a table almost from scratch, and most importantly he hadn't seen Clara all day. He hoped that she had got the message the night before and would leave him alone. The factory was closing on Friday for two weeks and this was his last day at work. If he could get through the next ten minutes of work without seeing her then he would be able to have a fresh start after Christmas and hopefully he wouldn't have to deal with her again. He still had hopes of sharing his designs, but this time he would go straight to Edward or one of the designers.

He heard the click-clack of heels before he saw Clara and his heart sank. He just hoped that she would walk past him. The hope died quickly as the noise of her heels grew louder and closer and then stopped right behind him.

Clara cleared her throat annoyingly and he sighed and turned around.

'I need a word with you in my office. There's just some forms I need to go through with you.' She turned to walk away, clearly expecting him to follow.

'I thought I'd filled in all the forms,' Henry said, not moving from his spot.

'I need to go through some of the details with you,' Clara snapped, obviously not in the mood to be messed around or fobbed off today.

She stormed off and Henry watched her go. He balled up the cloth, tossed it to one side and followed her. He caught Daniel's eye as he walked past, who looked at him with confusion.

He climbed the stairs and walked through the office belonging to Audrey. She looked at him as if she had no idea why he would be going to see Clara but she didn't stop him.

He walked into Clara's office and deliberately left the door open.

He hadn't really noticed the night before, presumably because the lights from the factory had been turned off, but one wall was filled with windows overlooking the factory floor, giving her prime view of where he had been working moments before. He didn't like that she had been up here watching him.

'Close the door,' she said.

'I'd rather leave it open if it's all the same to you.'

She gave a small smug smile and got up from the desk, closing the door herself.

'Do I scare you, Henry?' Clara said as she sat back down.

'Not particularly. But I'm just about to go home, so if you can show me the issue with the forms then I can leave.' He looked pointedly at her empty desk.

'We need to fix a date for you to take me out for dinner.'

Wow. She wasn't going to beat around the bush. Well, neither was he.

'I'm not going to take you out for dinner, Clara. As I told you last night, I have a girlfriend and I don't think she would take kindly to me dating other women.'

She drummed her long gold nails on the desk, watching him carefully, the smug smile turning into something cruel.

'I don't care if you are happily married with twelve children. I'm the CEO of White Cliff Bay Furniture Company and trust me when I say I can make things very difficult for you if I so desire.'

His stomach twisted with anger. 'What are you saying?'

'Competition for your job was very fierce. You would be very easy to replace.'

Christ. He needed this job. He had moved Daisy across the country to take this job, dragged her away from his parents, her friends. There was no way he was betraying Penny, but even if he wasn't with her, he would never be blackmailed into sleeping with his boss. The thought disgusted him. Clara was beautiful but he refused to be manipulated like that.

He could feel a rage burning in his gut. He had to walk away now before he said something he would regret.

He turned and stormed out of the office. Audrey stared at him with wide eyes.

'Mr Travis, I've not finished with you yet,' Clara yelled after him. This was clearly a woman who was very used to getting what she wanted. Not with him.

He turned around and stormed back in. When he spoke, he made sure it was loud enough for Audrey to hear. 'Let me make this very clear: I am not going to take you out to dinner, I am never going to sleep with you, and if you try to blackmail me into doing so by threatening me with my job I will slap a sexual harassment suit on you so fast you won't know what's hit you. I will sue you and this company for every single penny that you have. Now I suggest you get on with your very important work and leave me to get on with the job I was hired to do.'

She went very pale and then stood up. 'How dare you. . .'

He walked out and charged down the stairs, not wanting to hear another word from her poisonous mouth. It was already past five o'clock and people were getting ready to leave, calling out goodbyes to each other as machines were turned off and work areas were tidied up. He grabbed his coat and stormed out.

He had humiliated her in front of her assistant and there was no way he was going to get away with that.

Crap.

He got into his car and slammed his fists against the steering wheel. Manipulative, evil fucking bitch.

He started his car and tore out of the car park.

He'd have to move back to his old town. He couldn't afford the rent at Penny's place on the money he got when he was self-employed.

No, he couldn't move back to where he lived before. Everything was better here, the people, the area, the school. Daisy was happy and he couldn't uproot her again. And there was his

219

relationship with Penny to think about. He didn't want to leave her. His throat felt raw at the thought of it.

He pulled up outside the house and rested his head against the steering wheel for a moment. What was he going to do?

He got out and walked around the back of the house, spotting Penny sitting at the kitchen table sketching out one of her designs. Without thinking he walked straight through her back door.

She looked up at him, smiling hugely, but her smile quickly fell from her face as she clocked his bad mood. She stood up and he gathered her in his arms and held her tight. She immediately wrapped her arms around him, one hand cupping his head, cradling him against her.

She didn't ask him why and he was grateful for that. He didn't want to talk about it. Eventually he pulled away and gave her a brief, quick kiss, leaning his forehead against hers. He was going to fight this with everything he had, because leaving Penny was not something he could even begin to comprehend.

Chapter 16

Henry walked around the outside of the house later, just as Penny came rushing out of her back door. He had calmed down a lot since he had seen Penny earlier; his resolve that Clara wasn't going to win this had helped. Ice cream in town with his daughter had also helped – she never failed to cheer him up.

'Hey, you going out for your hot date with Fabio?' Henry said.

'Ha, no. I'm going for dinner at my friend Maggie's house.'

Henry frowned as he followed her around to her car. 'As in Daniel's wife?'

Penny nodded and he stopped her with his hand on her arm. 'He invited me round for dinner too.'

Penny laughed. 'They're trying to set us up on a date.'

'They know about our date the other night though; Maggie was the one that persuaded you to get your legs and everything else waxed.'

'She didn't know it was a proper date, she had just heard that we were going out when Jade told everyone in the pub. I told her we were just friends. I think she was just hopeful it would turn out well – she certainly doesn't know how well it actually turned out for us. She's obviously trying to push it even more. I can't believe she invited us and deliberately didn't tell us the other was coming.'

Henry smiled at the interference. 'How about we have some fun with them? Get our own back for trying to set us up.'

'What did you have in mind?'

'We could go and pretend we hate each other.'

Penny laughed. 'I like the sound of that. We could still share a car though, their front door is round the side, so they wouldn't know.'

'OK, let's go in mine, you can direct me in case I get lost,' Henry suggested.

Henry got in the car and Penny got in too. They drove down the hill, through the town and pulled up on the drive at a large, smart, whitewashed house that had round windows and garish lights everywhere. Snowmen, Santas and several reindeer were lit up on the lawn and a 'Merry Christmas' sign flashed in one of the downstairs windows.

He told Penny to go ahead of him and as she knocked the door, he got out the car and slowly walked up the drive. He saw Maggie answer the door – well, he saw her huge belly first and then Maggie appeared. Maggie greeted Penny warmly and then smiled in greeting at Henry.

'Hello, I'm Maggie. It's lovely to finally meet you properly.' She reached up to kiss him on the cheek. 'It's such a funny coincidence that you're both here tonight. I had no idea Daniel had invited you round until about half an hour ago, and I invited Penny and I forgot to mention it to Daniel. But what a happy happenstance.'

Henry had to stop himself from laughing at the lie and instead he deliberately forced a small smile onto his face and flashed Penny the briefest of glares. Penny quickly looked away so Maggie wouldn't see her smile. She clearly wasn't very good at acting, though Maggie had already seen the glare from him and her smile fell from her face.

Daniel appeared in the hall as Henry and Penny stepped in and closed the front door behind them.

'Henry, so good of you to come,' Daniel said as Penny and Maggie walked off to the kitchen. Henry heard Penny whispering loudly to Maggie how she didn't like him and how she thought he was an arse. He had better act his part too.

'I can't believe you invited Penny too. She's the most annoying person in the world, she's so whiny,' Henry said, making his voice loud enough for Maggie and Penny to hear.

Daniel's face fell but, before Henry could get another word out, Maggie barrelled down the hall towards him and he had never been more terrified of anything in his life as he was in that moment.

'How dare you talk about my friend like that?' Maggie slammed her finger into his chest. 'Penny is the sweetest, most lovely, kindest, warmest person you will ever meet and I won't have you speak about her like that in my house.' She flung the front door open. 'Now get out.'

Henry made a mental note to never cross a pregnant woman, and especially not a pregnant Maggie, ever again.

In fact he was too scared now to tell the truth in case she killed him for lying to her.

Penny came rushing down the hall. 'Maggie, it's OK, we were just joking. We were just going to pretend that we hate each other to get you guys back for trying to set us up.'

Maggie looked between the two of them, her nostrils flaring. 'This was a joke?'

Henry nodded.

Penny wrapped an arm around his waist. 'We're actually seeing each other, though we are keeping it a secret for a few weeks because we want Daisy to get settled in her new home before I'm introduced as the new girlfriend.'

Henry would have preferred not to completely out their relationship, but he hoped if Penny trusted Maggie enough to keep quiet then he could too. Besides, any kind of lying to Maggie now was not going to go down well.

Maggie looked between them, wondering if they were speaking the truth, and as Henry nodded, Maggie's face split into a huge smile.

'You're together?'

Penny nodded.

Maggie squealed and threw her arms around first Penny and then Henry. 'I'm so happy for you both.'

Daniel laughed. 'Easy there, Mags, they've been on one date, they're not getting married or anything.'

'Penny, come to the kitchen with me, I want to hear all about it,' Maggie said. 'You boys can go and bond in the front room for a bit before dinner is ready.'

Daniel ushered him into the front room while giggling and whispering started in the kitchen. He wondered how much Penny was actually divulging. When he heard a squeal of excitement from Maggie, he guessed it might have been about sex rather than the nice restaurant he had taken her to.

'I'm so glad you were only joking. I was afraid I'd have to punch you for saying those things about Penny and that wouldn't have ended well for me,' Daniel said.

Maggie came waddling out the kitchen carrying two bottles of beer. She fixed Henry with a knowing smile before she left him and Daniel alone.

Daniel raised his beer bottle to Henry. 'To new friendships.'

Henry chinked the bottle against his friend's and took a big swig.

'What did Clara want to talk to you about today anyway? She never gets involved with the carpenters or any of the factory business. She doesn't seem to do anything, actually.'

Henry sat down and slowly peeled away the label on the side of the bottle. 'I'm really worried, to be honest. I don't know if I'm going to be working there much longer. She came on to me.'

Daniel sat down opposite him. 'Shit, you don't want to get involved with the boss's sister.'

'I'm with Penny so she doesn't hold any interest at all; in fact, even if I wasn't with Penny she wouldn't hold any interest for me. She tried it on with me last night but I made it very clear I wasn't available and I thought that would be the end of it. But she seems to think she has a sense of entitlement, that because she's the owner of the company that I'd be jumping at the chance to sleep with her. I told her I wasn't interested and she basically said that if I wanted to continue working there I'd reconsider.'

Daniel's eyes bulged. 'She did not say that?'

Henry nodded.

'You have to tell Edward, he would be furious.'

'Would he really believe me over his sister though? I'm the new guy, he doesn't know me. I'm hoping it won't come to that.'

'What did you say?'

'I told her if she tried to blackmail me into sleeping with her again, I would slap a sexual harassment suit on the company so fast and sue them for every penny they had.'

Daniel went very pale. 'You did what? You threatened her?'

Henry ran his fingers through his hair. 'It probably wasn't my best move. She just pissed me off. I honestly don't know whether I'll have a job to return to after Christmas and Daisy and I've only just arrived down here. If I lose my job, I don't think I can afford to stay.'

'What else could you have done? You can't let her blackmail you like that. And if you had slept with her, it would have ended very badly if Edward found out. Oh mate, I don't know what to suggest.'

Henry sighed. Everything had seemed so perfect for a few days and now this had ruined everything.

But as Penny walked in with Maggie and he pulled her down by his side, he knew there was no way he could leave White Cliff Bay now.

Penny smiled as Henry took her hand and they walked down the driveway towards his car. He had been very tactile all night, sitting next to her, holding her hand at the table, sitting with his arm around her as they chatted to Maggie and Daniel. His affection for her came so naturally and she loved it.

She was worried though. Something had happened at his work today to upset him. The fact that he had kept it to himself worried her too. Despite his smiles and easiness around her friends, there was something eating at him, she could tell, and somehow she knew it had to do with Clara.

He opened the car door for her and she slid into the passenger seat as he walked around to the driver's side.

As soon as he closed his door, he leant across towards her, cupping the back of her head with his large hands and planting a soft, sweet kiss on her lips.

'I've been wanting to do that all night,' he said, against her mouth. He started to pull away but she grabbed his shirt and pulled him back, kissing him again.

God, his kisses were so addictive, and very quickly the kiss turned into the prelude to something else: her hands were in his hair, his were wandering over her body. She reluctantly pulled away before she got too carried away right there on her friend's driveway. Henry groaned with disappointment. Frustratingly they probably couldn't even finish off the kiss when they got home.

Henry sat back in his seat, gripping the steering wheel tightly, clearly equally frustrated by their inability to finish the kiss.

He started the car and pulled out their drive.

'We, erm. . . don't have to go straight home,' Henry said.

She looked at him and laughed. 'What were you thinking, we find a secluded layby somewhere in the middle of the woods and have sex in the back of the car?'

'That's exactly what I'm thinking.'

She stared at him in shock; there were no words in her head. It wasn't exactly the sweet, gorgeously romantic experience they'd had the first time they made love but she couldn't deny that the possibility really excited her.

'I've never had sex in a car before,' Penny said.

'Me neither.'

'Really? Isn't that a rite of passage for most teenage boys?'

'Remember my later teenage years were spent raising a baby. There wasn't a lot of time for shagging in cars. Tina was the first girl I slept with, a drunken fumble at a party. There wasn't anybody else then for years.'

Henry drove through the town.

'That must have been so hard for you.'

He shrugged. 'Daisy was my priority. Women just didn't register on my radar for a long time. I was too exhausted to think about anything else. Night feeds almost killed me.'

'So no wild sex in weird and wonderful places?'

Henry thought about this for a moment. If there was any weird sex or sex in unusual places, none obviously came to mind. It made Penny feel a lot better about her complete lack of sexual experience.

'I guess I've been quite sensible. I've done the usual places, like in the shower, on the table, on the couch, on a pool table, in a garden, on a sun lounger...'

'Those are usual places?' Penny blushed.

'Well, yes. They're not weird places. One of my friends had sex in a graveyard – now that's a bit creepy if you ask me. I think mine have been quite normal. Maybe against a tree was probably the strangest place. What about you?'

Penny fiddled with a tiny hole in the knee of her jeans. 'Erm... the bed and, erm, sitting up in bed once.' Jesus, no wonder Chris went elsewhere for sex, he must have been bored out of his mind with the plain, boring sex that she had offered him. 'I never really knew what I was doing and he certainly never instigated it anywhere other than in bed.'

Henry drove up the hill quietly. 'So... we could rectify that if you want.'

'I think we better. I'm bloody miles behind everyone else in terms of wild sexual experiences.'

Henry smiled at her as he drove past the turning for her house and she bit her lip. They were really going to do this, they were going to have sex in the car. She suddenly wanted to experience all those passionate sex moments with Henry, in all the places that he had spoken about.

They drove over the hills and Henry took her hand, running his thumb over her palm in tiny little circles that just sent desire and need spiralling through her. They came to some woods and Henry pulled off into a short service road that led to an old beacon. In the day, cars would be double-parked either side of the service road as people would walk around the woods with their dogs, but now, in the middle of the night, the road was empty.

Once Henry was satisfied they were far enough away from the main road not to be spotted, he pulled onto the side of the road and parked under a tree.

He turned the engine and the lights off and they were plunged into darkness.

They sat in silence for a moment while their eyes became accustomed to the light, or the complete lack of it.

Penny was so excited and so nervous; this felt silly and wrong and wonderful all at once.

'How should we do this?' Penny asked, wondering if her innocence and naivety was a total turn-off. Maybe she should be more assertive.

She reached across the handbrake and kissed him, and as he ran his hands through her hair, she moved over to his side of the car and straddled him, accidentally pressing the horn with her bum as she positioned herself against the steering wheel. The noise was loud and alien in the middle of the woods, and it scared her enough to break the kiss.

Henry laughed and with his hands at her hips he pulled her tighter against him, away from the wheel, before kissing her again.

He unzipped her coat and slid it off her shoulders, and she shivered as the cold of the night soaked through her thin shirt to her skin.

229

'Sorry, I'll put the heating on,' Henry mumbled, leaning forwards to turn the ignition on, pushing her against the horn as he did. He carried on kissing her as he fumbled around, trying to find the heating controls. The horn went off again, hazard lights flashed and the windscreen wipers came on, making a horrible squeaking sound as they dragged across the dry windscreen.

Penny giggled. 'I'll leave my clothes on, let's just take the necessary bits off.'

Henry nodded as he moved his hands to her jeans. He undid the button and slowly unzipped her fly. But when he went to push them off her hips, it was quite clear her straddling position was not conducive to the removal of clothes.

She shuffled around so she was leaning her back against the car door and her legs were sideways across his lap, her feet in the passenger seat, as she wriggled to get her jeans off. Henry tried to help her, dragging them down her thighs, and taking her pants with them. There was just no room to manoeuvre at all.

'Let's go in the back,' Henry said, clearly getting very frustrated.

She quickly clambered off him, with her jeans still around her knees, fell through the gap between the seats and landed face down with her front on the back seat and her legs still in the front. This wasn't sexy at all. Or romantic. Henry was still trying to wrestle her skinny jeans off her legs. He gave one big yank and they came off as he fell against the wheel, sounding the horn yet again. She quickly tried to arrange herself in a better position on the back seat as Henry was fiddling with the heating controls and then he moved into the back with her. But though there was enough room for her to lie across the back seat there wasn't room for him. He knelt between her legs, his back, neck and head folded under the roof of the car; it didn't look comfortable at all. She shifted back so her head was resting against the window to try to give him more space, but that hurt her neck. Henry didn't exactly look like he was enjoying himself either.

He leant up and spent a good minute trying to prise a condom out of his jeans pocket.

'Why did you take a condom to dinner with Daniel and Maggie?' Penny said, leaning up to try to help him. 'Did you think it was that kind of dinner party?'

'I thought I might try and sneak into your house when I got back, if Daisy was asleep.'

'Planning ahead, I like it.'

He managed to get the condom out, ripped it open with his teeth and slid it on.

'This isn't all it's cracked up to be, is it?' Penny said, trying to shuffle back even more, to give him more room. He slid his hands under her bum, lifting her and folding her into a very odd angle, and she hooked one leg around his back and one over the back seat. He thrust into her just as a pair of headlights turned into the little service road, heading straight towards them. Frozen in the moment, she looked out the window over Henry's shoulder and spotted the silhouette of the blue lights on top of the car as it came closer.

'It's the police.'

'Crap.' Henry pulled out and managed with some difficulty to do his jeans back up, over his impressive bulge. He grabbed her jeans from the front of the car and quickly managed to pull them on her, dragging them up to her knees as the car stopped right behind them and a policeman got out. Penny laughed as she tried to force the jeans up the rest of her thighs. Lord knows where her pants were; hopefully nowhere in sight. She managed

231

to do the button up on her jeans just as the policeman knocked on the window. Even fully clothed, with their position in the back of the car, it was very clear what they had been doing, or about to do. Henry backed up and shuffled into a sitting position and Penny did too, and then Henry opened the back door. The policeman leant in and Penny was mortified to see it was Bob, one of her dad's oldest friends.

Bob flushed as soon as he saw her. He quickly addressed his attention to Henry instead, pretending she wasn't there.

'Sir, I saw your hazard warning lights flashing as I drove past and I came to see if there was a problem.'

'No problem, officer,' Henry said. 'We were just going to go for a walk, see if we could spot some deer.'

'Right.'

Bob glanced over to Penny again and he nodded at her. 'Penny, are you OK?'

'Yes, Bob, I'm fine. Sorry to worry you, we just stopped to see the sights.' Her hair was a tangle around her face, her shirt was all ridden up around her stomach, her shoes were off and she knew her skin was flushed; even in the illumination of the interior car light, she knew Bob had spotted all these things. She looked like she had just had the best sex of her life, which unfortunately was not the case. She had never been so embarrassed before.

'How's your dad? I was going to call him this weekend, actually.'

Oh god, she couldn't imagine how that conversation was going to go.

'He's fine. Italian life suits them.'

Bob nodded and there was an awkward silence. 'Well, it's a bit chilly tonight for a walk. There's talk of snow too so maybe you two should get off home. You don't want to be driving these roads when they are icy.'

Henry nodded and, after a few more awkward moments, Bob shuffled off, closing the door behind him.

Henry sighed and clambered into the front. Penny giggled as he picked her pants off the steering wheel and passed them to her in the back along with her shoes. She shoved her feet into her shoes and her pants in her pocket and climbed in the front seat with him.

He started the car, turned the lights on and drove up the little service road. Embarrassingly, Bob followed them, clearly escorting them out so they didn't stop on the way to have more bad sex.

They pulled out onto the main road and Henry reached for her hand. 'I'm sorry that was absolutely rubbish, though honestly, I don't see how it could have been anything else. Whenever you hear about people having sex in cars it always seems much sexier than it actually is.'

Penny let out a giggle, which then turned into a full-on laugh. 'It's been one of the funniest nights I've had in a long time.'

Henry frowned. 'Now that's a compliment I've never had before: the funniest shag I've ever had.'

'We can't all be Casanova, Henry.' Penny patted him consolingly.

'I'll do better next time.'

'I should hope so, because that was over way too quick for my liking.'

Henry continued to scowl all the way home.

They pulled up on the drive and Henry gave her a quick kiss goodnight, around the side of the house where they couldn't be spotted by Daisy, if she was still awake. Then he disappeared into his house.

Penny let herself in through her back door and Bernard gave her a cursory wag of the tail, before trotting out into the garden to relieve himself.

She saw the light go off in Henry's lounge and watched as his dark shadow disappeared upstairs.

It had been a wonderful night. With Henry's tactility over dinner, she had caught a fleeting glimpse at what life would be like when they were properly together, and she liked the look of it a lot. But beyond that the humorous side of their relationship was something she had never expected when she first met him.

Bernard came back in and threw himself down on the sofa. Penny locked the door and stalled when she saw two plates of cake crumbs and two glasses on the kitchen table. She had said to Daisy that she was welcome to sit with Bernard and watch TV in front of the fire, and to help herself to cake as there was still loads of it, but that didn't explain why there were two plates instead of one. Had Daisy had a friend round? Feeling slightly confused, she went to bed.

She lay in her room staring at the ceiling, letting her eyes become accustomed to the dark, when suddenly there was a shadow in the room with her.

Her heart leapt into her throat for a brief second before she recognised the sheer bulk of Henry, getting undressed.

'What are you doing here?'

'Finishing what we started. Daisy's fast asleep; nothing will wake her when she's that deeply asleep,' Henry said, as he lifted the duvet and climbed in next to her. He was already deliciously naked and she delighted in running her hands over his velvety skin as he quickly undressed her. 'Besides, I still have that condom we tried to use earlier, I reckon it's still good.'

Penny burst out laughing, so loud and so hard that she was sure she might wake Daisy up next door. Henry moved on top of her and she could feel his body shaking as he laughed too, though the laugh quickly turned into a groan of pleasure with what he did next.

Chapter 17

Henry was just sitting down to breakfast when Daisy emerged. She was up much earlier than normal but he knew she was a bit nervous about popping into her new school later that afternoon. Her theory was that everyone was breaking up for Christmas and would be in a good mood and probably much more open to having a new girl appear amongst them.

'Good night last night?' Daisy asked.

He smiled as he remembered the disaster that was the car sex. 'Yes, it was fun.'

Daisy sat down and frowned, and he wondered what was bothering her. 'Do you like Penny?'

Oh crap. He didn't want to lie to her but he didn't want to allude to anything either.

'Yes, I do.'

'I don't know whether I should tell you this or not but I think you should know. I think her date with Fabio last night went very well.'

Henry frowned in confusion and then remembered that Daisy genuinely believed that that was where Penny had gone the night before. He would just tell her they were joking around and that he'd had dinner with her and Maggie and Daniel.

'I heard her when she came in.'

'What do you mean?'

'Well, I heard you come back and go to your room and shortly after she must have come back, with Fabio.'

Henry felt himself go very still.

'What did you hear?'

'Dad, I heard her having sex. It was so embarrassing, but it was very obvious she was enjoying herself. And Fabio was grunting away and moaning too.'

Henry stared at her in shock. There had never been a time in his life that he had been more embarrassed than he was now. He had no words with which to fill the silence; there was nothing he could say at all.

'They were at it for ages and then when they stopped, they started again half an hour later. The man has amazing stamina. He clearly is an Italian stallion.'

It couldn't get any worse. His daughter had heard him having sex. She had heard him groaning, moaning, panting and shouting out when he had orgasmed. Twice.

He stood up and moved to the toaster, putting in her favourite crumpets and then flicking on the kettle so she wouldn't have to see his face, which he was sure was burning red.

'I'm sorry, Dad.'

Henry shrugged, still with no words to say.

'Do you want jam on your crumpets?' he finally said, hoping with everything he had that would be the end of it.

Penny knocked softly on the connecting door, which felt a bit weird considering what she had got up to the night before with her friendly neighbour. There was no answer so she popped her head around the door. There was a noise in the kitchen so she followed it. She smiled when she saw Daisy dancing around as she tidied up, listening to her iPod and singing along, by the sounds of it, to Ed Sheeran.

She walked in and tapped her on the shoulder. Daisy smiled at her and removed her headphones.

'Hey, I just wanted to wish you good luck today at school. They are going to love you, I promise you that.'

'Aw thanks,' Daisy said, throwing her arms around her and hugging her tight. Penny smiled with love for her and hugged her back. 'I am a bit nervous, but I'm only there for a few hours. I think the worst day will be the first one after Christmas, when they'll all be staring at me like I'm an animal in a zoo.'

'You should totally learn to balance a ball on your nose then, that will give them something to talk about.'

Daisy laughed. 'I'm so excited that Mr Cartwright is going to be my form teacher too, he is so cool.'

'You will love him, but I bet all the children are going to be cool too.'

Daisy moved back to the table as she wiped it down with a cloth, capturing the crumbs with her hand.

'So. . . good date last night?'

Penny stared at her in confusion for a second before she realised what Daisy meant. She felt bad for leading her to believe she was going out with Fabio when she had only been joking with Henry about going out with him.

'Oh honey, I was only messing around. I didn't really go out with Fabio. I went for dinner round my friend Maggie's place. Weirdly, her husband Daniel had invited your dad too and we didn't know the other was going. . .' She trailed off as Henry appeared in the doorway behind Daisy and started gesturing frantically.

'You went to dinner with Dad?' Daisy asked in confusion.

Henry was still waving his arms around but Penny had no idea what he was trying to say. 'Erm, yes.'

'He didn't say when I saw him this morning.'

'Maybe your dad thought that you might think it was a double date, when it definitely wasn't. It was just weird that Maggie invited me and Daniel invited your dad and they didn't know.'

'But. . . I heard you last night.'

'You heard me?'

Daisy blushed. 'Having sex.'

Oh god. Oh no. No, no, no, no, no.

'I told Dad I heard you and Fabio. . . at it last night and he seemed really upset.'

Henry had given up gesturing now.

What could she say to rescue this scenario? That Fabio had come round for a late-night booty call? That she'd had incredible sex with Daisy's dad and all the grunts and moans were in fact him? There was nothing that she could say that would make this horrible situation any better. Suddenly she had a brainwave. It wasn't the best idea – hell, it was probably the worst idea in the history of all ideas – but it was the only thing she had.

'I wasn't having sex, Daisy.'

'But I heard you.'

Penny worked her tongue around her mouth trying to create some moisture. 'I was watching porn.'

Daisy stared at her in horror. Henry stumbled out of the room backwards, gripping his mouth really hard so Daisy wouldn't hear him laugh. The clock ticked on the kitchen wall and no one said anything. Penny hadn't wanted Daisy to think that she was sleeping around, especially if she and Henry were going to come out the couple closet in a week or so. She wanted Daisy to know that she was serious about her dad and that he wasn't just a fling to her. But surely this was worse than Fabio coming round for a late-night booty call, and now any respect that Daisy had for her had gone.

'You were watching porn?'

'Well, no, not really. I put the telly on in the bedroom and fell asleep. I woke up an hour later and this couple were at it like rabbits on the screen, shouting and moaning and he was grabbing her breasts. They were sweaty and oily and. . .' Oh god, she was talking about porn with a sixteen-year-old. 'It was quite disgusting.' No, not disgusting, she didn't want Daisy to think that there was anything wrong or dirty about sex. 'I mean, not disgusting, sex isn't disgusting with two people that love each other, it's beautiful.' Penny heard a whimper of laughter from the other room. 'But the oily couples were a bit disgusting. Couple, just one couple, it wasn't an orgy. Porn films always seem to grease their couples up to make them look all shiny. I don't know how sex is possible when they are so slippery; surely the man would just slip straight off the woman and the sheets must be covered in it afterwards. The oil, I mean, not. . . *it.*' She had to stop talking but the nerves had completely disengaged her mouth from her brain now. 'I just don't get why porn films think that's attractive but they all seem to have these glossed, shiny bodies. Not that I've watched a lot of porn, you understand. I mean, I haven't watched any. I never watch it. But I've seen it. Accidentally. Late at night it's been on. The soft stuff, not hardcore porn, obviously. Just, you know, a lot of moaning and repair men turning up to fix a leaky washing machine and the couple end up doing it on the kitchen floor. That kind of stuff. That I never watch. Ever. But yes, it was on when I woke up and I turned it off immediately because it was disgusting, erm, the oiliness, that is.'

Silence again, punctuated by tiny whimpers coming from the other room.

'So, I need to go and walk Bernard.'

Daisy nodded, numbly.

'Good luck for, erm. . . later.'

Still no words from Daisy and Henry clearly wasn't going to help her out.

'I thought perhaps we could go Christmas tree shopping later? You guys need a tree and we could go and pick one and then you and your dad can decorate it.'

Daisy nodded again and Penny walked out, flashing an evil glare at Henry as she left, who was biting into a cushion to try to stop the laughter from spilling out.

Penny saw Henry pull back up onto the drive later, after he had dropped Daisy off at school. She hadn't seen him all morning, which she was thankful for. She had never been more embarrassed in her life.

He walked around the back of the house and grinned when he saw her, letting himself into her kitchen.

'Hi,' he said.

'I hate you.'

He burst out laughing. 'What did you want me to do?'

'You could have helped me.'

'You were doing fine on your own.'

241

She laughed with embarrassment. 'I talked to your daughter about porn.'

'Well, yes, probably not your finest moment, but I haven't laughed like that in forever.'

'I've probably scarred her for life.'

'I doubt it, she's a hardy sort. Besides, she does know about sex, it's not like she leads a sheltered existence. I've made sure I've talked to her about all that. I don't want her to end up pregnant at sixteen like her mum did.'

'She thinks I watch porn.'

'Oh no, I think she's very clear that you find porn disgusting.' She couldn't stop laughing. 'Did she say anything to you after?'

'No, she was probably too traumatised to say anything.'

Penny took a swipe at him and he ducked out the way, laughing loudly.

'It's not funny.'

'It really is.' He caught her by the waist and tried to kiss her on the forehead but he was laughing too much.

'Stop laughing.' Though Penny was laughing so hard, tears were running down her cheeks. 'You do realise we'll never be able to have sex again whilst she's in the house.'

'Oh, I don't know about that, you're just going to have to work really hard at being extra quiet.'

'Me?' Penny laughed incredulously. 'You're very vocal. You shout a lot.'

'You scream. That's probably scarred her more than anything.'

'Oh god. We can do it quietly, can't we?'

'Yes, I'm sure we can, and there'll be times when she isn't here and we can be as noisy as we like. So let's make the most of it now.'

She laughed.

He shuffled her back against the table and kissed her hard. She quickly realised he wasn't joking as he lifted her onto the table and attacked her clothes with great relish.

Suddenly a movement caught her eye over his shoulder and Penny stared in horror into the eyes of another woman.

'Henry, stop.'

'Not likely.'

'There's someone outside.'

Henry whirled around, protecting her half-naked body from view. Thankfully it was only the top half that was undressed and she still had her bra on, but it was quite obvious this woman had seen what they were doing.

Henry laughed nervously. 'That's my sister, Anna.'

'Shit.'

Anna was frozen to the spot, staring at them both.

Henry looked back at Penny and smiled shyly. 'Why don't you put your clothes back on and meet us next door for a coffee? I'm sure she will be delighted to meet you at last. Daisy has told her all about you.'

Henry turned back to Anna, still protecting Penny from being seen, and pointed to his house. Anna walked off, clearly not happy.

'She doesn't look delighted to meet me,' Penny said.

'Anna's lovely. I love her to bits and she's helped out so much with Daisy over the years. But occasionally she can be a right judgemental pain in the arse.'

'Well, as first impressions go, this isn't a good one,' Penny muttered, yanking her top back over her head. 'Coupled with what Daisy will undoubtedly tell her about me watching porn, I'm going to go down a storm at family events.'

Henry kissed her briefly on the lips. 'She will love you, just like I do.'

He ran off through the connecting door before Penny could say anything. She stared at the door as it closed.

Did he just say he loved her?

Chapter 18

'I just thought I'd come round and see your new place. I didn't realise I'd be interrupting anything,' Anna said, slamming her bag down on the counter and standing with her hands on her hips.

Henry sighed. It was clear that today was judgemental arse day.

He heard the connecting door open and he hated that Penny was going to get a mouthful of abuse too.

Penny came into the kitchen slowly and he reached out a hand for her. Pulling her into his side, he wrapped his arm around her waist and placed a kiss on her forehead.

'Penny, this is my sister Anna. Anna, this is my girlfriend Penny.'

Penny smiled. 'Hi.'

'Girlfriend?' Anna deliberately ignored Penny. 'You've known her less than a week. What kind of example is that to set to Daisy?'

'Daisy doesn't know,' Henry said quietly, and he watched Anna's face turn from indignation to anger.

'She doesn't know? You're sneaking around behind her back, lying to her?'

Henry bit his lip. He hated lying to Daisy and he questioned himself every day over that decision. But he could hardly tell Daisy that he had jumped into bed with his neighbour just two days after she had specifically asked him not to date her. She was happy now and he wanted to keep her that way, at least until

Christmas. Was that so bad? He hadn't come to White Cliff Bay looking for a serious relationship; in fact, any kind of relationship was supposed to be off the table. But then he had met Penny and everything had changed. Nothing seemed to make sense about Penny; he had fallen hard very quickly and nothing had ever felt like this before.

'It's just for a few days, until she's more settled and gets used to seeing us together, at least platonically. We'll tell her then.'

Penny leant into him and he held her tighter, but surprisingly she was stroking his back, trying to offer him support, when really he thought it should be the other way around.

'It didn't take you long to get *settled*. You've been here just a few days and you're sleeping together already.' Anna turned her attention to Penny. 'Did you just open your legs to him on the first night?'

'Anna!' Henry said, forcefully. There was no way he was standing for that. 'I won't let you speak to Penny like that.'

'It's OK,' Penny said. 'I know how it looks. Neither of us expected it to happen. But we have something really special.'

'Please! This isn't serious for Henry; this is all about his inability to keep it in his pants. He has never been in love, never had a girlfriend that lasted longer than a few months. You'll be no different. Why do you think he hasn't told Daisy yet? Because he knows that it's not going to last.'

'This *is* serious.' He could feel himself getting really angry and Penny's hand squeezed his, probably to try to get him to calm down. God, the last thing he wanted was for Anna to give Penny reason to doubt their relationship. 'I am very serious about Penny. I adore her and Daisy does too. I'm not keeping it a secret from Daisy because I don't think it will last. I just didn't want to upset her.'

'Then why do it at all? You promised me and her that you wouldn't be getting involved with anyone ever again.'

'That was a rash statement and you know that. You can't expect me to not have a relationship ever again because I made one terrible mistake with Emily.'

'I can expect you not to get involved with the type of person who lets you shag them across the breakfast table in the middle of the day.'

Penny let out a bark of a laugh and Henry looked down at her in confusion.

'I'm sorry, but I'm not worthy enough for him because we were about to have sex on the kitchen table? In my own home? That's the most ridiculous thing I've ever heard. You have no idea what kind of relationship me and Henry have—'

'I don't care about what kind of relationship you and my brother have. I care about Daisy and how this will affect her.'

'I care about her too,' Penny said indignantly.

If Henry had thought that Penny was going to be shy when she met Anna for the first time, he had been mistaken. He tried to suppress a smile; he liked this fiery side to her. He hadn't seen it very often but she certainly knew how to stand up for herself.

'Bullshit. You're clearly using her to get to Henry. She adores you, you're all she's spoken about for the last week, and when all this comes to an end, which it undoubtedly will, you will drop her like a hot potato. Do you have any idea how much that will hurt her?'

'I have no intention of ever doing anything to hurt Daisy. I really like her and if this thing between me and Henry comes to an end, that absolutely won't affect my relationship with her. If Henry moves out and never wants to speak to me again, she can still come up here every day and practise her ice carving. I like working with her. She's brilliant and funny and I thought that long before I was involved with Henry. I've already offered her a job: I have way too many carving jobs for me to do alone and she shows a real talent for this kind of thing.'

'What sort of person befriends a sixteen-year-old girl?'

Penny went very still next to him. 'What are you suggesting, that I'm some kind of pervert?'

Anna quickly back-pedalled. 'No, I didn't mean that, I just meant that it's a bit weird.'

'Why is it weird?' Henry said, angrily.

'Well. . .'

'You've made a snap judgement based on the fact that you saw me and Henry about to have sex, and you've come into my house and accused me of the most disgusting things. How dare you? You don't even know me. Now I suggest you get out of my house now because you're certainly not welcome any more.'

'Legally, darling, you don't have a leg to stand on there. You can't dictate which visitors Henry has in his home.'

'Penny's right,' Henry said. 'I would never presume to tell you how to live your life and I don't expect you to come in here and try to tell me how to live mine. Get out and don't come back here unless you're ready to apologise to Penny.'

Anna stared at him in shock for a moment, before she turned and grabbed her bag and stormed out.

'I'm so sorry,' Penny said, after she had gone.

'What? No, you have nothing to be sorry for. She is very over-protective of Daisy, we both are, and she's seen it go wrong for Daisy quite a few times before. But don't apologise for her issues and her bloody judgemental attitude.'

Penny sighed. 'I suck at first impressions.'

'I don't know about that. You pretty much captured me from the moment you opened the door with that huge, endearing smile on your face.'

She smiled.

'Come on, why don't you bake a cake, that'll make you feel better, and I can help.'

'I thought you wanted sex on my table.'

'We can do that too.'

She laughed and she walked off back towards her kitchen. He sighed with relief as he watched her go.

She hadn't seemed bothered by Anna saying it wouldn't last between them. He just hoped with all his heart that she knew how much she meant to him.

'She's late,' Henry said, looking at his watch for the seventeenth time in the last ten minutes.

Penny smiled with love for him and how protective he was of Daisy as he wore a hole in her kitchen floor with all his pacing.

'She's not late.'

'School finished at half past three. It can't be more than a half hour walk from there.'

'Firstly, she's probably talking to all the new friends she's made and making plans to meet up with them all over the holiday. Secondly, it might take you half an hour to walk from the town to our house, but it takes us lesser mortals a good forty-five minutes or more – we haven't all got freakishly long legs like you. It's twenty past four, I hardly think we need to call out the search and rescue just yet.'

'It's getting dark.'

She frowned with confusion.

249

'Why are you worried? It's not about her being out on her own, she's done that tons of times before.'

He sighed and sat down at the table. 'I just want to know that she got on OK today. What if she hated it? What if the kids were mean to her? I want this move to work for her. I don't want her to regret her decision to move here.'

'She is one of the most bubbly, friendliest girls I know; the other kids will love her, how can they not? Plus her hero, Mr Cartwright, is her form teacher – she is going to be over the moon about that for at least the next six months.'

'You're right, I know, there's just a lot riding on her loving her new school. I want her to be happy here.'

'She is and she will be. Stop fretting.'

Henry nodded and then looked at his watch again.

The timer went off on the oven and Henry jumped.

Penny shook her head fondly as she went to the oven and pulled out the chicken and pepper mix needed to make fajitas. She gave it a good stir, covered it with foil and put it back in the oven, turning the temperature down low just to keep it warm. It hadn't been discussed that they would have dinner together but that seemed to be the norm now. They had become domesticated very quickly and Penny loved it. But the doubt that was in her head, that doubt that had been gnawing away at her since she had seen Anna earlier that day, kept telling her not to get too involved too quickly because it would hurt all the more if it came to an end.

What if Daisy was miserable at school? Penny had known that something wasn't right at Henry's work after he had come home in a terrible state and she'd overheard him telling Daniel that he didn't know if he would have a job after Christmas and he might not be able to stay in White Cliff Bay. What if they left?

He certainly wouldn't stay just for her; he hadn't known her long enough for that. Where would that leave them?

She turned around and watched him as he tried to read the paper and surreptitiously look at his watch and the door every few moments. He wanted it to work too.

She passed Henry a block of cheese and a grater. 'Grate this, it will keep you busy for a few minutes. And when she comes in don't pounce on her, just ask her, but not as if it's a matter of life and death.'

Henry nodded solemnly.

Almost right on cue, Daisy strolled through the back door as if it was the most natural thing in the world to pitch up in Penny's kitchen after a day at school. Penny loved the ease Daisy had around her. She was smiling broadly, something that Penny saw Henry notice straightaway. He returned his attention to the cheese, sighing quietly with relief.

'Hey honey, did you have a good day?' Henry said, taking extra care not to let any worry or panic into his voice.

'I had the best day ever. Everyone was so nice. I made friends with two girls, Rebecca and Maisie, and we're going to meet up between Christmas and New Year, and Mr Cartwright is the coolest man ever and. . . I didn't realise White Cliff Senior School and White Cliff College were on the same campus.'

Penny put the fajita chicken mix on the table with the tortillas and watched Daisy get very excited about the college, which seemed an odd thing to warrant so much excitement.

Penny sat down next to Daisy. 'I'm so pleased you had a good day.'

'I did,' Daisy said, looking like she was about to burst from the excitement of it all. Henry was watching her with confusion too.

Daisy helped herself to a large portion of the chicken and suddenly leant over and whispered in Penny's ear. 'I saw Josh again.'

Penny tried and failed to suppress a smile.

'What?' Henry asked.

'Nothing,' Daisy said at the same time as Penny.

Henry scowled as he looked between them.

Daisy leant over again to whisper some more. 'He asked me to the ball.'

Ah, the reason for the giddy excitement had been explained.

Penny whispered in her ear. 'That's so cool, how exciting.'

'I know,' Daisy whispered back. 'I think I love him.'

Oh lord. How was she supposed to explain this one to Henry?

'What?' Henry said again, trying not to smile as he scowled at their secrets.

'Nothing,' Daisy giggled.

'We'll go shopping for a dress then,' Penny whispered. 'Sunday?'

Daisy nodded gleefully.

Penny tucked into her own fajita and glanced across at Henry, who was pretending to glare across the table. That glare might turn out to be a real one once he found out his daughter was going out with the tattooed, shaven-headed boy he had mistaken for a burglar a few days before.

Josh was a sensitive, sweet boy, but Penny doubted Henry would see it like that.

She would have to break it to him gently when he was in a good mood.

'I'm going out for a bit, I won't be long, I'm just popping up to Rebecca's house,' Daisy said, getting up from the kitchen table. Penny saw the grin that she had been suppressing for most of the dinner.

Henry frowned as he looked at the darkening skies outside. 'Its nearly dark out and we were going to go tree shopping.'

'We will, I'll only be half an hour. Rebecca only lives up the hill.' Daisy gestured vaguely and Penny frowned. There was no house up the hill. Lilac Cottage was the last house on the very outskirts of White Cliff Bay. The next house was a good half hour drive away on the edge of Apple Hill. Daisy was lying, she could see it in her eyes. It seemed like Daisy had secrets of her own. Henry looked at her suspiciously too.

Before Henry could protest any further, Daisy threw her coat on and with a cheery wave she raced out the door.

'She's up to something,' Henry said, as the door almost slammed back into its frame.

'Maybe she's just gone off to buy your Christmas present,' Penny suggested, knowing that wasn't it at all.

Henry scowled as he moved around the table towards her. 'Talking of that, I need to go and finish her tree decoration. Will you be OK for half an hour?'

Penny nodded and he kissed her briefly before disappearing out the back door.

Doubt niggling in her mind, she opened the front door and stepped out onto the drive. At the bottom of the driveway stood the observation hut, which was used by birdwatchers to keep an eye on the nesting cliff-dwelling birds, especially in the spring and summer months. It was also the place where some of the teenagers of the town used to hang out, especially teenage couples. She had used it herself in her youth to meet up with one or two boys. They'd sit, talk and listen to music. For her nothing further than a few kisses had happened in that hut but, with a small gas fire, gas lamps, a soft bench to lie on, it had been the place where several of her peers had lost their virginity. It was silhouetted against the pale twilight sky and, as she watched, flickering lights suddenly came on inside.

That's where Daisy had gone. It was entirely possible that Daisy had gone there to meet up with her new friends Maisie and Rebecca. But that didn't explain the two plates of cake crumbs and two glasses the night before. Her guess would be that Daisy was meeting up with Josh. Now, should she go down there and catch them in the act of doing lord knows what? Should she go and tell Henry that his daughter was currently lying in the aptly named 'Love Shack' with a seventeen-year-old tattooed thug, at least in his mind, or should she just pretend she knew nothing? Daisy was a sensible girl and any bridges that Penny had built with her would be destroyed if she marched straight into that hut now acting like an over-protective mum. Henry's relationship with Daisy would be strained too if he found out and reacted in the way that Penny thought he would. And knowing Josh and his shy, sweet nature, they probably weren't doing anything beyond holding hands. It was probably best to do nothing for now and get Daisy on her own later and maybe have a little word.

'Come on, hurry up, all the best trees will be gone,' Daisy said as Penny tried to find a parking space at the tree farm that was big enough to hold her freezer van. Henry had had to help her deliver two ice carvings after dinner and it didn't make sense to go back to the house to drop the van off. Plus, as the van was so big, it meant they could use it to stick the tree in the back.

'I can't just stick the van anywhere, plus they have hundreds of trees, I think there'll be plenty of choice.'

'There'll only be little ones left.'

'You can only really get a little one – the annexe is quite small.'

'We always get the biggest, fattest tree we can find.' Daisy bounced up and down in her seat like a small child. Penny loved her enthusiasm for life. 'Will you get a tree?'

'I'll probably get a small one too.'

'Noooo, you have all that space in front of the window, or behind the sofa. You could get a massive one. I know, why don't we get a shared one and we can all decorate it together?'

Penny parked the car and tried to dispel the huge lump of emotion that had lodged in her throat with that simple statement of togetherness from Daisy. She had accepted Penny into their little family so easily and readily.

Penny nodded. 'OK.'

'Yayyyy!' Daisy bounced out the van and set off at a sprint towards the plethora of trees.

As soon as she was out of sight, Henry leant across and kissed her sweetly.

'She adores you,' he whispered. 'And I do too.'

He got out and lumbered across the grass after his daughter. Penny smiled as she watched him go. This was turning out to be the best Christmas ever.

She got out and walked across the grass. It was snowing lightly again and she looked up at the occasional star that shone through the cloud-filled sky as the soft flakes dusted her cheeks.

She caught up with Henry and had to shove her hands in her pockets so she wasn't tempted to hold his hand.

The trees were stacked in size order and she watched as Daisy walked past the smaller ones and headed straight for the big ones at the end of the farm. They reached the part that sold the biggest trees and, although all of these were way too big for the house, she didn't have the heart to say anything, not when she had been inducted into their little decorating team. Daisy was going from tree to tree, feeling the needles, smelling them, looking at the labels. Penny had never bothered to look at the trees before, she had just bought the first smallest one she had seen and that was it.

'Surely all the trees are the same,' Penny said.

'No, definitely not,' Daisy said. 'There's three main types: a pine, a fir or a spruce. The spruce is generally rubbish. There are several different types of fir and pine trees, and we want one that has a good needle retention, even without water. You want soft needles too and something that smells good. Generally we are looking for a Nordman or a Noble fir, but I'd settle for a White Pine.'

Penny glanced at Henry as Daisy disappeared around the back of the tree. 'She knows her trees?'

He nodded. 'She takes this part very seriously, and the fact that you've been invited to join us shows how much she likes you.'

Penny smiled.

'OK, this is the one,' Daisy said, triumphantly, lovingly stroking the winning tree.

Penny looked up and up. It had to be at least twelve feet high.

'Daisy, that's never going to fit in my house, let alone yours.'

'It will if we stick it under the stairs – you have that space going up to the first floor – and so what if the top sticks through the bannister a bit, or rests on the ceiling? This is going to look fab.'

Henry was already moving off to tell one of the staff which tree he wanted, knowing that Daisy wasn't to be talked out of it.

Before Penny could protest any further, the tree was bagged up into a big net and between the three of them, Henry carrying most of the weight, they just about managed to get the tree into the van, with the top three feet sticking out the back.

Henry secured the doors to make sure they weren't going to swing open and Penny drove them home.

They struggled to get the tree in as Bernard, showing the most life she'd ever seen from him, ran around barking at them as they brought the invader into his home.

They stuck it in the corner so the top of the tree protruded up somewhere on the first floor at the top of the stairs.

There were never going to be enough decorations in the world to fill this thing. Penny guessed they'd have to go for a minimalist look.

'I'll get the decorations,' Daisy said, running off to the shed where lots of their boxes were stored.

'We should probably just stick to one colour. I have lots of silver baubles upstairs, we could have a silver theme. . .' She trailed off as Henry was looking at her incredulously.

'A silver theme? Erm, our decorations are an eclectic mix; there certainly isn't a theme to them.'

'But it will look really busy.'

He grinned. 'We like busy. Why don't you put some Christmas music on and heat up some of your wonderful mince pies, and I'll go and help Daisy with the decorations.'

She frowned slightly as she watched him go. She couldn't pick holes in their tradition, not after she had been accepted so easily into the inner sanctum of the tree – decorating team.

A multi-coloured tree certainly wouldn't go with her rather tasteful green and white light garlands and decorations, but she would just have to let it go.

She built a fire in the fireplace, put on some Christmas songs and went to sort out the mince pies just as Daisy came back, weighed down by three large boxes.

She glanced down to the shed, where Henry was still rooting around trying to find the right boxes.

'Daisy.'

Daisy dumped the boxes on the table, grinning from ear to ear. 'Yep?'

'Are you seeing Josh?'

'Yes. Don't tell Dad.'

Penny's eyes bulged, wishing she'd never asked. 'Are you hanging out at the Love Shack?'

Daisy laughed. 'The what?'

'The birdwatchers' hut at the end of the drive. That's what we called it when we were teenagers. All the kids used to hang out there and kiss and. . .' She was not going to talk to her about sex again.

'Yes, but we just talk and stuff, it's no big deal. Just don't tell Dad because he'll freak out. How are things between you two anyway?'

Penny noted how quickly the tables had turned. She wasn't going to lie to Daisy, even if she couldn't be completely honest. 'Good. I really like him.'

Daisy studied her for a moment and then smiled. 'He likes you too.'

Penny bit her lip. Did she know something was going on between them? She was a smart girl, she had probably worked it out by now, but was she OK with it?

There was no time to discuss either topic because Henry burst through the back door, juggling five large boxes. Daisy picked up her own boxes and scurried through to the lounge.

By the time Penny came back in with the plates of mince pies, several of the decorations had made it from the box to the tree and Henry and Daisy were jive dancing with each other to 'Rocking Around the Christmas Tree'.

She watched them with a smile. They were so close and she just hoped that she could fit into that somehow.

She put the plates down and Henry grabbed her for a rock and roll style dance, twirling her around as Daisy laughed at them and resumed her decorating. Penny laughed as she was spun out and twirled back, and she clung to Henry feeling dizzy and giddy with it all. Finally the song ended and something much slower came on, which didn't seem appropriate to dance to with Daisy in the room, so Henry released her awkwardly.

Penny looked through the boxes of decorations and the ones that were slowly filling the tree. There was a colourful mix of decorations, some that Daisy had clearly made as a child, with tiny handprint Christmas trees covered in glitter, snowmen made from lots of cotton wool, and toilet roll tube Santas. There were some rather eccentric shop-bought decorations ranging from neon-coloured candy canes, ceramic Santa-clad teddy bears, and angels dressed in leather biker gear. There were also some beautiful wooden ones that had evidently been handcarved by Henry and Daisy. This tree was a huge cacophony of colour celebrating their rich, vibrant history together. Penny loved every single piece of it, even the mooning Santa that Daisy hung pride of place right in the middle of the tree. But it did make her a bit sad that there wasn't a part of her on this tree.

'Why don't you get some of your decorations down?' Henry said softly, clearly reading her mind as he had a knack for doing.

She shook her head. Her tree decorations were boring round baubles that held no special meaning or significance to her and it would seem odd to dilute their decorations with her dull ones. She would be a part of the tree by helping to decorate it.

She picked up a gold-painted fir cone covered in glitter with a scarlet ribbon tied at the top and hung it from one of the branches, feeling the smile grow on her face as slowly every branch began to sparkle with colour and glitter. Daisy moved upstairs to lean over the bannister and decorate the top branches as Henry started wrapping lights around every part of the tree.

All too soon the tree was finished and Daisy raced down-stairs for the big lights switch on.

'Five, four, three, two, one,' Daisy yelled and flicked the switch.

The tree was suddenly lit up with over a thousand lights, all in different colours. Some twinkled discreetly, where some flashed on and off to the beat of an unheard tune.

Penny stepped back to admire their handiwork. It was garish and messy and fanciful and silly and the best Christmas tree she had ever seen.

Daisy had long since gone to bed, though Penny suspected it was to give them some time alone. For someone who had been so against them getting together at the beginning, she seemed to be pushing them together now. The music had changed from that of Slade and The Pogues to sweeter, softer Christmas songs, and she was dancing slowly in the arms of the most wonderful man she had ever met.

She rested her head on his chest, listening to the steady beat of his heart. She had tried to hold back, to not fall so deeply in order to guard her heart, but she had failed at every single turn.

She looked up at him, his beautiful face illuminated in the glow of a thousand fairy lights, and he bent his head and kissed her softly.

She was in love with him, she couldn't deny it any more. Completely and utterly in love with him.

He pulled back ever so slightly so that, when he spoke, his mouth was still touching her lips.

'I really want to make love to you right now. Can you be quiet?'

She smiled. 'Can you?'

'Let's see.' He took her hand and led her upstairs.

She wasn't scared any more. This was where she was supposed to be. Everything was perfect. And Anna or Daisy or Clara wouldn't change that. She loved him and she was pretty sure he felt the same way.

Chapter 19

'Tell me again why I agreed to this,' Henry said as he pulled the car into a space behind the marquee the next day.

The car park was already filling up nicely, the annual festivities attracting a lot of attention. It was a good thing because, like a lot of the events leading up to the ball, it was raising a lot of money for charity. Though Penny could understand Henry's reticence. While she had been to watch the Giant Gingerbread House Race many times over the years, she had never been on one of the teams before.

'Because Edward asked you to do it and you didn't want your boss to know that you are secretly an anti-social grumpy sod,' Penny said and Daisy let out a bark of a laugh from the back seat.

'She's got your number, hasn't she, Dad.'

'More to the point, why am I doing it?' said Penny. 'It's supposed to be families of staff members from White Cliff Bay Furniture Company and I don't qualify for that.'

Daisy scrabbled out the back of the car and closed the door.

'You will qualify soon, so stop your whingeing. Consider it practice,' Henry said, smiling at her.

Her heart soared at the simplicity of that comment, while he clearly had no idea that he had made her entire day.

He hesitated for a moment, staring at Edward at the entrance of the marquee. He was nervous about today and she didn't know why, but she knew it wasn't just about doing something silly in front of an audience. Why was he so scared he would lose his job so soon after he had got it? What had happened a few days before that would make him so wary and why hadn't he talked to her about it? He was trying to put on a brave face for her and for Daisy, but Penny would rather he talk to her about his worries. She couldn't escape the feeling that this had something to do with Clara.

After a moment, he got out and Penny followed him.

Up ahead of them Penny saw Maggie, waddling along with a boy in each hand and Daniel with his arm around her waist. Penny smiled wistfully at the proper little happy family.

She looked over at Henry and Daisy, and he smiled at her over Daisy's head. They weren't the orthodox family of high school sweethearts like Maggie and Daniel were, and they weren't married and didn't have children together, but Penny couldn't be happier to be part of Henry's family and to have Daisy as her sort of step-daughter. Maybe it was getting too far ahead of herself to imagine that after only knowing Henry for a week, but she couldn't help it.

As one of Maggie's boys lagged behind for a second, Maggie turned to see what had caught his attention and, spotting Penny, she waved madly. She left the boys with Daniel and came over.

'You're going down, Meadows,' Maggie said, giving Penny a fond kiss on the cheek. 'Our team has won for the last three years, there's a lot riding on our title. We won't be giving it up so easily.'

'But you are slightly hindered this year; your little bump may get in the way of decorating and building.'

'I'm going to be directing the boys, so we actually have the advantage as I'll be an outsider looking in. Who's your project director?'

'Probably Henry – you know what I'm like with even the simplest of flat-pack furniture. Quite why he picked me to be on his team I don't know.'

Maggie linked arms with Penny and leant in to whisper in her ear. 'You know why.'

'Hey, no colluding with the enemy.' Henry came over and kissed Maggie on the cheek.

'Oi! Hands off my wife, Travis,' Daniel called and Henry laughed, holding his hands up innocently.

'Maggie, this is my daughter Daisy. Daisy, this is our mortal enemy – well, for this afternoon at least.'

Daisy smiled at Maggie, shyly.

'We'll have to all go out for a girly pampering day after Christmas, before this little one arrives. We can have our nails done and our hair and make-up. What do you think, Daisy?' Maggie said and Penny smiled with love for her friend for including Daisy like that.

'Yeah, that'll be great.' Daisy grinned.

Edward was standing at the entrance to the marquee, welcoming all the White Cliff Bay employees as they came in. Penny noted he knew everyone's names and many of the wives and children's names too. As they approached, she could see all the spectators filing in through a different entrance.

Maggie re-joined Daniel at the entrance and Edward chatted to them briefly before they went inside.

Edward turned to them and smiled warmly.

'Henry, I'm so pleased you agreed to be a part of this today. We have been holding this event for years and it always makes some decent money for charity. It's good fun too, so don't feel anyone is going to judge you on your skills today. Working with icing is very different to working with our normal furniture glue.'

'Are you taking part, sir?'

'Edward, please. And yes, my family and I always take part every year. We never win though.'

'Ah, maybe this year.'

'Maybe. And this must be your lovely family.' Edward smiled at Penny and Daisy.

Penny froze, not sure what to say, whether to confirm or deny it. Were there really strict rules that meant only families were allowed to take part? Would Henry get into trouble for having someone who wasn't his family on his team? Should she be holding hands with Henry and pretending to be the adoring wife?

'Yes, this is Penny and Daisy,' Henry said, without missing a beat.

Edward shook both their hands. 'Well, I hope you both have fun today, may the best team win.' He quickly consulted his clipboard. 'You're in bay six.'

Henry ushered them inside. As soon as they were out of hearing distance, Daisy wrapped an arm around Penny's shoulders.

'Hear that? You're our family now, you're stuck with us.'

Penny's heart leapt with happiness. 'I can't think of a nicer family to be stuck with.'

Henry smiled at them as they stepped into their designated bay before turning his attention to the materials and tools.

He prodded the plastic gingerbread panels, feeling the weight of them, and looked at the oversized plastic sweets, which were arranged in neat piles around the edge of their bay, some of them spilling out of a large cardboard box. He gave the icing a stir, letting the mixture fall back into the bowl as he judged its consistency.

'How does this work then, how do we win?' Daisy asked, obviously taking the competition as seriously as her dad.

'Well, we get points for being the fastest to finish. First team to finish gets ten points, then the second team to finish will get nine points, and it goes down incrementally, so even if we are last to finish we still get points. The structure has to be sturdy too: if you finish first but your house collapses before the end of the competition then you can be disqualified if there is no time for you to fix it. We then get points for style, creativity and originality, which are judged by Linda from the bakery and Summer from the sweet shop. They will award points out of ten for each team too. There are mini prizes awarded for the fastest team and the best team in the design stakes, and then an overall winner.'

'Surely the overall winner would be one of the mini prize winners,' Daisy said, picking up a giant plastic Jelly Tot and playing with it in her hands.

'Not necessarily. Getting high points for finishing first but low points in design would give you an average overall score, where getting an average score for both, say seven or eight, would give you a much higher score overall. Basically we want to work quickly but not forsake the design aspect too; we can't afford to have it look shoddy.'

The spectators had already filled up the seats but still more were coming in, happy to pay to stand and watch.

The inside of the marquee was already decorated with tiny fairy lights, hung in looped boughs across the windows. It was all going to look magical once it was set up for the ball, which was only three days away.

'Are there any rules?' Henry said.

'No, you can't help or hinder another group and other than the fact our gingerbread house has to still be standing at the end of the race, we can do whatever we want.'

'We need a strategy,' Daisy said. 'We need to do something different to everyone else.'

Henry stood up and joined their little huddle. 'What are you suggesting?'

Daisy looked around, thoughtfully. 'We can use everything in the bay, right?'

Penny nodded.

'How about that cardboard box?' Daisy asked.

Penny looked over at the huge box that was filled with some of the smaller foam and plastic sweets.

'We could use it. What were you thinking?'

'A porch or a dormer.'

'A dormer would be tricky to do, but I love the idea of a porch. We can decorate it too so it doesn't just look like a box,' Henry said.

'We can use the rope as some kind of snowy garland that we can drape from the roof,' Penny said, getting into the spirit of a little bit of cheating.

'Let's do it,' Henry said, that wonderful look of mischief in his eyes.

'Ladies and gentlemen,' Edward called over the microphone. 'Please will you take your seats, the Giant Gingerbread House Race is about to start.'

There were cheers and claps from the crowds and then Edward called for silence.

'Thank you all for coming today. As most of you are aware, we do this event every year to raise money for whichever charity is being supported by the Christmas ball. This year we are raising money for Kaleidoscope, who research the causes of miscarriages, stillbirths and premature babies, and offer support and counselling to those families that have been affected.'

There was a huge round of applause from the crowd and Penny felt a lump in her throat that they were helping a charity that was so important to her. She caught Maggie's eye across the room and smiled at her for choosing that charity.

Edward introduced the teams briefly, again introducing Penny as part of Henry's family, which caused a few murmurs of interest amongst the crowd. He explained the rules, pretty much echoing everything that Penny had said, and then he started a countdown.

'We'll leave the rope till last so people don't copy our idea, the cardboard box too,' Henry whispered over the countdown. 'We'll just build the house first.'

Penny nodded, suddenly excited about their design and a little bit of rule breaking.

'. . .Three, two, one, go!' Edward shouted.

Henry and Daisy immediately grabbed two panels, one back panel and one of the sides, positioning them so they were at a right angle to each other. They were a perfect team, each knowing what the other was going to do before they did it. Penny realised if everything went according to plan with her and Henry's relationship, she would be joining their little team soon too.

She quickly started spooning the icing mixture into the piping bag as Henry got the two panels perfectly lined up.

Penny started squeezing the icing down the join, hopefully cementing the two panels together. As Henry held it firm while it dried a bit, Penny ran around and piped the icing down the other side of his panel.

'It's setting really quickly, what is this stuff?' Henry said, tentatively letting go of the panel.

'I don't know, it's not like any icing I've ever seen before. If I were you, I wouldn't eat it,' Penny said as she hauled over the front panel with a space for the door. Daisy quickly ran around to grab the end of Penny's panel.

Suddenly Penny saw Henry glance across the marquee as if he had spotted something, and whatever he saw wasn't good. She looked over to see what the other teams were doing, convinced they had also decided to use the cardboard box too, and saw Clara, striding between the teams. A look of panic crossed his face, which deepened when he saw that Penny had seen it too, before he quickly returned his attention to the house.

Henry had told Clara that he had a girlfriend. That surely should be the end of it. So what would cause Henry to be so worried?

Henry focussed on securing the front panel to the side they had already used, ignoring the questioning gaze from Penny as she piped the icing into the join.

This was not going to end well for him. Clara was an incredibly proud and arrogant person. The rejection and then the embarrassment in front of her assistant was going to be the final nail in his coffin.

But surely Clara wouldn't make a scene here today, not in front of Daisy and Penny, and certainly not in front of all these people.

He glanced over again. Clara was deliberately stopping to talk to each of the teams. On the surface, the audience watching would think that one of the managing directors of the

269

company was just being sociable, cheering the teams on, but the look of surprise from the employees she was interacting with and even from Edward showed she had never done anything like that before. Henry knew why: it was completely tactical. If she was seen talking to every team then when she came over to talk to him, which she undoubtedly would, no one would be suspicious.

He looked over at Penny, who was watching him carefully. Shit, he should have told her. Now it looked even more suspicious when nothing had actually happened.

'Grab the other bit, Daisy,' Henry said and Daisy ran off to grab the panel.

Henry moved to the back on the pretence of checking the join and Penny followed.

'She's blackmailing me to sleep with her,' he whispered, then continued, 'if I don't, I lose my job. If I do I'll probably lose my job, so it's a win-win situation all round.'

She stared at him in shock.

'Daisy, can you hold that side panel against the front?' Henry called over, directing her to the furthest corner away from them.

'Have you told Edward?' Penny said.

He shook his head.

'If you don't tell him then I will. I'm not letting her get away with that.'

'Shit, Penny, that's not how I want to resolve this situation. He isn't going to believe me over his sister. If I go to him to complain about Clara I'll likely get the sack from him.'

'Then how did you plan to resolve it?'

'I told her I'd slap a sexual harassment suit on her if she tries to blackmail me again.'

'And will you?'

'Well, I'm not going to sleep with her, if that's what you're thinking,' he hissed. 'She can't possibly sack me, Edward would want to know why. I'm sure if I keep rejecting her she'll just go away.'

'That's why you're as skittish as a kitten about her coming over here then. Because you're confident that she's just going to go away?'

He moved away, angry that everything was crashing down around him and there didn't seem to be any way to stop it. Penny caught his arm and pulled him back.

'You need to fight for this. If you want this job, if you want anything badly enough, then you fight for it. Don't just roll over and play dead.'

Henry nodded, though he wasn't sure what he could do to fight Clara. He glanced over at her again and he caught her eye. She smirked to herself as she moved to the team in the next bay. Henry saying no had provided her with a challenge that she wasn't going to back down from.

Clara stepped up to their bay; the only thing separating them was the low rope barrier.

'This is looking good,' Clara remarked cheerfully, though her eyes were firmly on him and not the house.

He returned his attention to the house as Penny helped to join the final side together, piping the icing down the join while he and Daisy held the panels in place.

'Henry, might I have a word?' Clara called over.

'I'm busy,' Henry snapped and watched Daisy's mouth fall open at his rudeness to his boss.

He glanced over at Penny, whose face was switching between concern, worry and anger.

He had to resolve this once and for all.

Leaving the girls to work on their own for a moment, he stepped over the little rope fence towards Clara and moved a few steps away so no one in the audience could hear them either.

'I told you to leave me alone.'

'I'm not used to people saying no to me.' Clara smiled, flicking her hair over her shoulder.

'And are you used to getting sued for sexual harassment? Because I told you if you bothered me again about this, that's the direction I would take it.'

'Oh please, Henry. If you were going to do that you would have done it already; you'd have marched straight from my office to Edward's or human resources and complained to somebody, but you haven't. And that's because you secretly want this.'

'I'd rather gouge out my own eyeballs with a fork than sleep with you or have anything to do with you.'

'Yet one word from me and you're over here talking to me instead of working alongside your *pretty* girlfriend.'

Henry glanced over at Penny, who was studiously not looking at him. 'Look, why are you doing this? You're very attractive, you can have any man you choose. Why go for someone who is already taken?'

'You're right, Henry, I can have any man I choose and I choose you. Let's cut the crap, you and I both know you're going to sleep with me so stop trying to put me off. I'll be in my office at six o'clock tonight. The factory will be empty but I'll leave the side door open.'

'I'm not—'

'You will be there or I will make your life a living hell. I'm sure your little girlfriend will be delighted to hear of how you fucked me over the desk the other day. I could give her a very detailed account of that, if you don't show later. Or perhaps I could tell her that that was how you got the job in the first place.'

Henry wanted to tell her to go ahead, but was his and Penny's relationship strong enough to withstand that when they barely knew each other? Did Penny trust him enough to believe him over Clara?

He knew what he had to do and he felt sick at the thought of it. He nodded. 'OK, six o'clock. Wear something sexy and not a lot else.'

Her eyes lit up that he had been bought so easily. She licked her lips and nodded before she walked out.

Chapter 20

Henry returned to the gingerbread house and Penny looked at him hopefully as Daisy ran off to get a few more oversized sweets.

'Don't worry, I've sorted it. She won't bother us again.'

'Really? Because she certainly walked off with a skip in her step.'

'I've sorted it,' Henry repeated.

He threw himself into building the house, hoisting Daisy up so she could help to attach the roof and do the icing at the top, helping with the decorations and the best placement of the big foam sweets for an aesthetic appeal. Lastly, as several teams had already finished, they added the cardboard box to the front, making a short porch, and quickly added decorations and icing to that too. He barely heard the cheers from the audience as they saw what they were doing or the good-natured calls of cheating from the other teams; his mind was only on what he had to do after this was finished. It was scummy, he knew that, and he'd probably end up with no job afterwards anyway, but it was the only way to stop this before it got any further.

The other teams finished and the judges walked around to make their decisions, but he was barely aware of any of it. His heart was hammering against his chest. For their ingenuity in using the cardboard box as the porch they won first place in the design stakes, something that Daisy and Penny were over the moon about, but Henry couldn't concentrate, could barely even muster a smile as the hamper of chocolate and other goodies was handed over. They didn't win overall because they had been one of the last teams to complete their house. Daniel and Maggie's team won again but Henry was so distracted he even forgot to clap. He was finding it difficult to breathe now as panic slowly set in.

Edward awarded the final prizes, said a few more words to the crowd and then suddenly people were leaving.

He looked at his watch: it was already gone half past five. He needed to act now.

As the last of the crowds dispersed and people shouted out their goodbyes to each other, Henry left Penny and Daisy and marched straight over to Edward. But as he got close, he noticed that Audrey, Clara's assistant, was talking to him. Crap. He hadn't accounted for this. What was she telling him? If she was a friend of Clara's then she certainly wouldn't be painting him in a very good light for what he had said to Clara in the office the other day. But whatever she was saying, he wasn't going to turn back or change his mind.

He approached and Edward was clearly furious. Edward saw him come closer and his expression of anger only deepened.

'Henry, is this true?'

Henry swallowed. 'It depends what Audrey has told you. I can certainly tell you my version if you'd like to hear it.'

Edward nodded, his eyebrows slashing down into a deep frown as Henry explained everything. He had never seen Edward so angry before, and Henry tried to imagine what he would feel if someone came up to him and said these things about Anna. Henry would most likely take a swing for them and

Edward looked about ready to do the same. Finally he finished. Well, most of it.

'That's pretty much what Audrey just told me. She told Clara that if she doesn't leave you alone she would tell me, and after seeing Clara with you today, Audrey knew it had gone too far.'

'She threatened me with my job if I told you, but I'd rather lose it than let her get away with that,' Audrey said, clearly as terrified about telling Edward as Henry had been.

'I know you have no reason to believe me,' Henry said. 'I've worked for you for one day, but I have no reason to lie to you. I want this job, I moved across the country to take this job and I would never do anything to risk losing it, but I will not be black-mailed into sleeping with her so I can keep it. Sadly, I can prove I'm not lying too. Right now, she is waiting in her office for me to come and sleep with her. She told me to meet her there at six or she would tell my girlfriend that we've been sleeping together. I agreed knowing that I was never going to go, and thought you might like to go in my place. You'll be able to see that I'm not lying about this. Her being there should be all the proof you need.'

'Henry, I don't need any proof. I believe you. Sadly, it's not the first time this has happened. Although I've only heard rumours before and none of the men were actually brave enough to come and tell me about it. I don't know if any of them slept with her to keep their jobs; I'd like to think they slept with her because they wanted to, not because they were forced to. Without any com-plaints or proof there was very little I could do to stop it other than talk to her, but she always insisted she had never done any-thing wrong. I will go and see her now, and I will put a stop to this. You have my sincere apologies that this has happened but I assure you it will never happen again, to you or to anyone else. Please rest assured, both of you, that your jobs are safe, but I would ask that you please keep this to yourselves. The reputation of White Cliff Bay Furniture Company is a very good one and I would hate something like this to tarnish the company or get out into the local or national presses.'

Henry and Audrey nodded.

Edward said goodbye and Henry thanked Audrey for her honesty. He would have told Edward anyway, but it was easier having two of them corroborate the same story.

He walked back over to Penny, feeling like a huge weight had been lifted off his shoulders. He should have told Edward the other day rather than dragging it out like this. It could have been over so much sooner.

Daisy was nowhere to be seen as he approached. Penny was watching him carefully.

'Daisy has gone off to see an art exhibition in town with one of her new friends – apparently Jackson Cartwright has some paintings in the town hall so she wants to see it and then they are going for pizza afterwards. I hope you don't mind, I said it was OK. I gave her some money and Rebecca's mum said she would drop Daisy off later and...'

She trailed off as he suddenly wrapped himself around her, holding her close to him and not caring who saw.

It was over and now everything could get back to being perfect again with this incredible, patient, beautiful woman.

Penny tried to watch Henry talking to Edward outside the lounge window without letting Daisy notice how worried she was. They had come back from dropping off a couple of ice sculptures earlier and Edward had been waiting for them, awkwardly talking with Daisy, who had also returned in their absence.

Daisy was sitting next to her now, giving Bernard all the attention in the world, and she clearly had no idea what was going on other than Henry was talking to his boss. Edward had obviously been very diplomatic with whatever he had talked to her about.

Whatever was going on, they both looked very serious.

She watched Edward walk off and Henry wave him goodbye before he let himself back in through the front door. He didn't say anything but the look he gave her was one of pure relief. It really was over, and by the looks of things his job was safe too. Henry hadn't said a lot about what had happened after the Gingerbread House Race, or what Clara had said to him, just that he had told Edward everything and he would just have to wait and see what would happen next.

'Let's all go out for dinner tonight,' Henry said, smiling hugely.

'I've already had enough pizza to last me a lifetime,' Daisy said. 'You guys go out though.' She waggled her eyebrows mischievously.

Penny blushed. Daisy seemed dead keen on them getting together, which was quite a leap from the conversation Penny had had with her the week before.

'You should come out with us anyway,' Penny said. 'You can have dessert. Don't stay here on your own on a Saturday night.'

'I'm fine. *X Factor* is on in a bit and I said I'd Skype Melissa anyway and watch it with her. You go and enjoy yourselves.'

'Just me and you then,' Henry said, trying to keep the amusement off his face at his daughter's meddling.

'Well, give me a hand loading the van with the ice blocks I need for the ice carving workshop tomorrow and then I'll get changed.'

Henry nodded and they walked into the freezer. He helped her load several small blocks that she had cut in preparation for the workshop onto a trolley and they wheeled it around to the van together.

'Are you going to tell me what happened?' Penny whispered, just in case Daisy could hear them.

'No, I'll tell you in the car. I don't want Daisy to hear this.'

They loaded the blocks onto the van, wrapping each piece in bubble wrap so they didn't stick to the van or each other. Then Penny went to get changed.

She wanted something smart but not overly dressy for what was probably going to end up as a meal in a pub, so she just grabbed a nice jumper, threw on a little bit of make-up and brushed her hair into a plait. Henry had seen her first thing in the morning when her hair was everywhere, he'd seen her in her definitely not sexy pyjamas and in her usual jeans and hoodies, and he still seemed to really like her.

She ran downstairs, they said their goodbyes to Daisy and got in the car.

'So come on, out with it,' Penny said as Henry drove down the bumpy driveway.

'OK, but I don't want you to think less of me. Part of me thinks it was a pretty shitty thing to do. Clara wasn't taking no for an answer – the more I rejected her, the more of a challenge she saw me as. She told me to meet her in her office tonight or she'd make my life hell. So I agreed.'

Penny swallowed down the sudden fear that clutched at her throat. Had he agreed to sleep with her in order to get her off his back once and for all? No, he would never do that.

Henry glanced over. 'I had no intention of ever meeting her. I wanted proof for when I told Edward just in case he didn't believe me. I told him everything and Audrey, Clara's assistant, backed up my story too. I told him where he could find her, that she was waiting for me, but he believed me without that. I feel bad that I set her up like that when I didn't need to. Anyway, Edward went to talk to her about it and found her in a very compromising position, half naked, sprawled across her desk from what I can gather. She must have been mortified.'

'Don't you feel sorry for her, don't you dare,' Penny said angrily. 'She did this, no one else, only her. She blackmailed you to sleep with her and threatened you with your job too. What kind of scuzzy lowlife does that? If that had been the other way round and you had blackmailed her, people would look at you like a sick monster because you're this big man bullying some little woman into sleeping with you. Why is it any different that she was the one that was bullying you? She deserves everything that she gets.'

'Well, I still feel a bit bad, especially as Edward fired her on the spot.'

'He fired her? His sister? How did he do that? They both have control of the company. I didn't think Edward had more power than she did.'

'Well, apparently he does. The company was originally offered to him by his dad as Clara had no interest in it, but she kicked up such a fuss that their dad was forced to make her managing director too, but he ensured that there was a sixty–forty split in the shares of the company, with Edward having the bigger share so that he would always have the deciding vote in the big decisions for the company. Clara's never done anything for the company, he openly admitted to me that he has no idea what she does all day in her office and that she's been a dead weight for the company for years, but she is his sister so he just let it go. Anyway, he's sacked her now. He stayed with her whilst she cleared out her things and took her key off her. She won't be back. It caused a massive row between them and I feel bad for that too. I'm not sure if sacking her was an overreaction on his part or not. I feel like she should have had a warning first but apparently Edward has heard rumours that she's done this kind of thing before, but he could never prove anything. Maybe he just wanted to get rid of her and this was the excuse he needed. But Audrey will be relocated to another department in the factory and I still have my job, so I guess you were right. Fighting for it actually made a difference.'

Penny smiled. 'I'm glad it all worked out for you and I'm sorry that you had to go through that at all. But don't feel bad about how it ended for her. She brought this on herself and if it wasn't you it would have been some other poor man. It would have ended this way eventually. Plus, Jill's family are completely loaded. Clara is not exactly going to end up out on the streets after losing her job. I think she'll be fine.'

'Oh god, Jill. . . I forgot that she is Clara's step-mum. Do you think she'll hate me for this?'

'I doubt it, there has never been any love lost between her and Clara. Besides, this isn't your fault, stop thinking that it is.'

Henry nodded as he drove down through the town and out the other side to The Bubble and Froth, a lovely little pub on the furthest reaches of the town that sat nestled in Silver Cove, right on the beach, amongst a cluster of houses. The pub was owned by her brother's friend Seb and served the most amazing food.

They walked in and Penny admired the gorgeous huge Christmas tree that took pride of place in one corner of the room. It was tastefully decorated and looked almost boring in comparison to the wonderful monstrosity currently sitting in her lounge.

Henry held out Penny's chair for her and she smiled at his impeccable manners before he sat down opposite her.

'You look lovely tonight.' He reached across the table and took her hand.

'Thank you.' Penny glanced around the pub, wondering if people were watching them. This was the first time they had properly been out as a couple in White Cliff Bay, but they had already been seen at the tree farm and paraded as a family that day at the gingerbread competition. It seemed that their togetherness was old news as no one was looking in their direction at all. She looked at the empty chair at their table and felt a pang of guilt. 'I feel bad that Daisy is at home alone.'

'You did ask her to come with us and it was her idea that we came out without her. I think she likes the idea of us being together, which is a huge U-turn from asking me not to date you last week. She certainly didn't stay at home because she wanted to watch *X Factor* – she hates it, she's never watched a single episode in her life.'

'Well, I hope it's that she wants us to get together and she doesn't feel awkward being a third wheel around us.'

Henry frowned. 'I hope she doesn't feel like that either. I certainly didn't get that sense when she was pushing me out the door and telling me to have a good time, but I'll talk to her just in case.'

Amy, one of the girls who worked in the pub, came and took their drinks orders.

'I was thinking about Christmas Day. Do you have any plans?' Henry said after Amy had gone.

'I'm not sure yet, I might go to my brother's, but he doesn't like Bernard in his house so if I did go I'd probably just go in the evening – I couldn't leave Bernard alone all day. Jill always invites me round but I feel in the way of the big family dinners I know she has. I'm happy to stay in on my own, there's always some gorgeously trashy Christmas movies to watch and lots of food to eat. Will you go to Anna's?'

'We've been invited but. . . I was thinking it'd be nice to spend Christmas on our own this year. We're always at my mum and dad's or at Anna's. It would be lovely to spend it with just me and Daisy. It's always a tradition that I make mince pies on Christmas Day and we eat them fresh from the oven. They taste awful as I can never get them right but we always do it. One year I suggested that I didn't do it as my pie-making skills were so bad, but Daisy insisted.'

Penny smiled at that lovely idea of it just being the two of them and their traditions.

'When I suggested to Daisy that we stayed at home this year, she loved the idea and she also said it would be great to have one or two friends over for lunch, and then maybe go to see Anna in the evening. I'm guessing she wants someone else to share the burden of the bad mince pies, but want to guess who she wanted to invite over for lunch?'

Penny felt her smile widen.

'Well, Bernard was her first choice, but you were a close second.'

Penny laughed. 'I would love to come for Christmas lunch and I know Bernard would too.'

'Well, that's settled then.'

They took a few moments to choose their food and Penny couldn't help the huge smile spreading over her face as she stared at the choices. This night couldn't have turned out any more perfect.

Suddenly Henry's phone vibrated on the table between them. He glanced at the caller ID, frowned and quickly answered.

'Daisy, are you OK?' Henry asked.

Penny couldn't hear the words but after a few moments of her talking Henry was already out of his seat, yanking on his coat, so Penny quickly followed suit.

'OK, honey, don't worry. We're on our way home now, we'll be with you in about ten or fifteen minutes.'

Penny threw some cash down on the table to cover the drinks and waved at Seb and Amy behind the bar to say they were leaving. Henry grabbed her hand and marched out, still talking to Daisy on the phone.

'Hang on, Daisy.' He held the phone away from his head and covered the mouthpiece so Daisy couldn't hear him. 'Do you have any candles?'

'Yes, in the drawer to the left of the cooker. Why, what's going on?'

'There's been a power cut and she's freaking the fuck out. I'm sorry about our evening.'

'Don't apologise, it's fine. If I was home alone when the power went out, I'd be freaking out too. Let me talk to her, you can drive,' Penny said, sliding into his car.

Henry passed her the phone as he slammed the car into gear and sped out the car park.

'Daisy, it's me, are you OK?'

'No.'

Penny cleared her throat. 'Are you alone?' Henry gave her an odd look but it was entirely possible Josh had come round while they were out, another reason why Daisy had pushed them out the door so hurriedly.

'Yes. Josh couldn't come. I'm in pitch darkness, all the lights went out and I'm really fucking scared. . . Don't tell my dad I swore.'

'I won't. OK, what are you scared about: aliens, ghosts, mad axe murderers?'

'Don't give her ideas,' Henry hissed.

'Yes, all those things,' Daisy cried.

'OK, the house isn't haunted, I promise you that. I've lived there my whole life and never seen a dodgy shadow or had anything moved or go missing. If there's such a thing as ghosts they don't live in my house. If aliens were going to come down and destroy the human race, I think they'd likely start with the White House or the Houses of Parliament or the cast of *The Only Way Is Essex*, rather than a little house in the middle of nowhere with one girl and one lazy fat dog.'

Daisy giggled. 'You have a fair point.'

'And statistically you are more likely to be murdered by someone you know than by a stranger, and as the only people you know in White Cliff Bay are racing along the roads to get to you as we speak, and Anna, who is tucked up at home looking after her babies, I think you are safe from that too.'

'What if it is a stranger and they're in the house with me right now?'

'Do you know what the crime rate in White Cliff Bay is? I do, because I had to sit and listen to the yearly crime figures at the White Cliff Bay town council annual meeting two weeks ago.'

Henry took a corner hard and Penny banged her head against the window. She placed a calming hand on his leg; the last thing Daisy needed right now was for them to end up in a ditch because of Henry's erratic driving. She felt the car slow minutely.

'So the crime figures. There were five crimes committed in White Cliff Bay this year. Two of them were kids playing music too loudly on Silver Cove beach in the summer; one was a cow getting out of a field and trampling over someone's garden; Mrs Jacobs complained to the police when her neighbour came home drunk one night and accidentally trod on one of her gnomes; and an umbrella was reported stolen from a pub. Apparently it had been left to dry in a rack by the door and when Mr Sampson came to collect it on his way home it had been taken. It was, however, returned to the pub a few days later, so Mr Sampson was reunited with it and no further action was taken. That's it as far as crime goes in White Cliff Bay. We don't have axe murderers.'

'What if the axe murderer is from out of town?' Daisy said, slightly mollified.

'Well, that's entirely possible. You are completely out the way though there. You know it takes a good two minutes to drive from the main road to our house, longer to walk with a heavy axe.'

Henry put his foot down and she was thrown back in her seat.

They reached part of the town that was in complete darkness and people were out on the streets with candles and lamps, obviously making a big party out of it all.

'You can't even see our house from the main road,' Penny went on, trying to calm Henry down too. 'I can't see someone making that journey just to kill a stranger.'

'I suppose not.'

In the background, Penny suddenly heard Bernard barking furiously, immediately undoing all Penny's hard work to calm Daisy down. Daisy gave a little whimper of panic.

'It's rabbits, I promise you, Bernard hates them. There is no one in the house with you. Look, where are you?'

'In my bedroom.'

'OK, so you have that white chest of drawers right next to the door – can you push it in front of the door?'

'Hang on.'

Penny listened as she heard a few grunts and the sound of furniture being dragged across the floor, and then Daisy came back on the line.

'Done it.'

'OK, you're safe now. No one is going to get through that door and we will be home in five minutes. Well, probably two with the rate your dad is driving.'

'Is he scared?'

'He knows you're upset, he just wants to be there for you.'

'Is he clenching his jaw?'

Penny glanced over him. He was scared, there was no doubt about that. His hands were gripping the steering wheel so tightly his knuckles were white. His jaw was clenched and his eyes were determinedly on the road. Perhaps all the talk of axe murderers had done more damage than good because he was clearly more upset than Daisy was.

'No, he's fine.'

Daisy laughed. 'You're such a liar.' The laughter faded from her voice. 'Dad doesn't do scared very often.'

'He does when it comes to you, honey.'

She somehow knew Daisy was smiling at that.

'Bernard has stopped barking,' Daisy said. There was an edge to her voice.

'Because the daft sod has got tired of barking at the rabbits and probably fallen asleep again. Next time we go out you can have Bernard in your room with you; he'd protect you from any axe murderers.'

'Is he a good guard dog?'

'Is he heck, but his farts are lethal, enough to scare away the bravest of men. Plus he's really good at shagging anything that moves. Bernard could shag the axe murderer whilst you made your getaway, but the farts would probably kill the axe murderer before he came anywhere near your bedroom.'

Daisy laughed.

'We're pulling into the driveway now, we'll be there in two minutes, just stay in your room until we get there.'

They bounced down the dirt track, slamming through pot holes in a way that couldn't possibly be good for the car. She sort of expected this overreaction from Daisy, but not from Henry; it was clear to see that Daisy was his entire world.

The house loomed up over the edge of the hill and, shrouded in darkness, it did look slightly foreboding and sinister.

He skidded to a halt at the side of the house, narrowly missing the back of her freezer van.

They got out and he ran around the back before she could stop him. It'd be too dark around there to see the key hole, whereas at least she had the moon to help her get in the front door. She quickly let herself in and ran past Bernard, who was snoring loudly on the sofa. She pushed through the connecting door and raced up the stairs. She wasn't scared for Daisy's safety, she just wanted to get to her as soon as possible.

'Daisy, it's me, open the door.'

There was a second's hesitation and then she heard the drawers being dragged away from the door. The door was flung open and in the limited light from the moon she saw a glint of blonde hair before Daisy's body slammed hard into hers. Daisy wrapped her arms around her and Penny held her tight.

'You're OK, we're here now.'

'I'm so sorry, I'm such a tit. I should have grown out of being scared of the dark a long time ago.'

Penny heard a thunder of feet as Henry came rushing up the stairs.

'Hey, it's not silly to be scared of the dark. Trust me, if I was here in the house alone and the lights went out, I'd be shitting myself too. Don't tell your dad I swore.'

Daisy giggled against her.

'Too late, I already heard,' Henry said, wrapping them both in a huge bear hug and squashing Daisy between them.

Oh god. It was beyond silly to attach anything to that hug but Penny couldn't help smiling to herself. This was what it would feel like to be part of their family and it felt wonderful. It wasn't so much having children that she had always missed, it was this feeling of togetherness and belonging that she had never had before. She released one of her arms and wrapped it around Henry, and he shifted her and Daisy tighter against him.

'I can't breathe,' Daisy protested from somewhere between them, and after a few moments Henry reluctantly let them go.

Henry held Daisy at arm's length, as if checking her for injuries, and Penny found herself smiling at how completely over-protective he was.

'Why don't we all go into my lounge and we can light a fire and some candles? I have some marshmallows we could toast too.'

Henry nodded and led the way down the stairs, holding Daisy's hand. Daisy reached back and held Penny's hand, and they walked down the stairs in a chain and back into her lounge.

'Henry, why don't you build a fire and I'll grab some candles?' Penny suggested once she had turfed Bernard off the sofa and situated Daisy there.

Henry set about throwing in logs and twigs and Penny returned to the kitchen to grab some matches and candles. She lit all of the ones she had, attaching some of the taper candles to little dishes, and then positioned a few around the kitchen and brought the rest into the front room.

The fire was burning quite well by this point and coupled with the candles it sent a warm, golden glow around the room.

Henry sat down on the sofa and pulled Daisy into his arms, just as he had done with Penny the first night they had kissed. Penny sat down behind Daisy, leaning into her and stroking her back.

'All that bloody talk of axe murderers scared the crap out of me,' Henry muttered, kissing Daisy's head and linking hands with Penny. He stared at her, his eyes filled with emotions Penny couldn't comprehend.

'It made me laugh,' Daisy said, pressed against his chest, completely unaware of the staring competition going on over her head.

'That was the general idea,' Penny said, defensively, unsure if Henry was angry with her, although the way he was caressing her hand said otherwise.

290

Henry smiled slightly at her then returned his attention to his daughter, though he kept his hand entwined with Penny's.

Henry woke up later with a crick in his neck and his two favourite girls in his arms. Penny had got up earlier to cook them all some food, which they'd eaten in front of the fire and then they'd resumed their positions on the sofa in one big group hug. He knew that Daisy and Penny were mostly trying to reassure him rather than Daisy needing that reassurance. She had been laughing and joking with Penny over dinner, whereas his heart refused to calm down.

It was ridiculous to react that way over a power cut, but knowing how scared Daisy had been had scared the crap out of him too. He'd always reacted badly whenever Daisy got hurt. He remembered when she had fallen off her bike as a kid and badly scraped her knee and he'd rushed her off to hospital. He'd nearly punched the dentist once when Henry had mistakenly taken Daisy's scream of terror for one of pain and the dentist had barely even touched her. When it came to Daisy he knew he was completely over-protective and irrational but there was nothing he could do about it.

He looked down at Penny, her face tucked under Daisy's armpit, her arm wrapped tightly around Daisy's back. Their evening hadn't gone anywhere near as planned but somehow this was miles better. Penny had accepted Daisy into their relationship as if it was the easiest thing in the world to suddenly have a teenage girl to factor into the equation. It would normally take weeks or sometimes months before he introduced his previous girlfriends to Daisy, and there had always been an awkwardness between them. Even the ones who had faked liking Daisy to get on his good side had never had the ease that Penny and Daisy had with each other. Daisy adored Penny and the feeling was quite obviously completely mutual.

He ran his fingers through Penny's hair, feeling the softness of it. She opened her eyes blearily to look at him and he just wanted to lean forwards and kiss her, which he would have done if he hadn't had the dead weight of his daughter lying on his chest.

'I'm going to take Daisy to bed,' Henry whispered.

Penny nodded and scooted back off of Daisy.

With some difficulty, he managed to extricate himself from Daisy, stood up and then he scooped her up. Penny smiled up at him sleepily and he smiled back before he walked out and carried Daisy up the stairs. A minute later he came back for Penny, who was fast asleep again, still on the sofa. He scooped her up too.

'What are you doing?' she mumbled.

'Taking you to bed.'

'Oh.' She snuggled into his neck as he walked up the stairs. 'I'm not really awake enough for that.'

He felt her breathing immediately becoming heavy again.

'I can't stay, not tonight. I don't want Daisy waking up and finding me gone.'

'K,' Penny whispered.

He laid her down on her bed and she nestled into her pillow, her eyes closed as she drifted off.

'I fell in love with you a little bit tonight. Although maybe I should say I fell in love with you a little more. The way you handled Daisy was brilliant; even I wouldn't have handled it like that. Well, I didn't, you saw what a mess I was over something as ridiculous as a power cut. But you. . . you just kept talking to her, making her laugh, made her see sense. You were wonderful.

I love how you are with her, but not just with her, I just love how you are. I'm not really making a lot of sense, am I?'

There was no answer from Penny at all and, judging by her heavy breathing, she was somewhere else entirely, certainly not in the room with him.

He bent over and kissed her on the head and left her to sleep.

Chapter 21

Penny stared at the silvery dress in wonder. In the lights of the shop changing room it sparkled as if the whole thing was made from tiny twinkly fairy lights. It gathered under the breast in a cluster of large black gemstones and then flared out to the floor, covering all her lumps and bumps. It was simple, elegant, utterly stunning and cost more than she would pay for groceries in a month.

'You should buy it,' Daisy said, next to her, twirling back and forth in a gorgeous red velvet floor-length dress.

'It's over five hundred pounds. I cannot justify paying that for a dress I'm only going to wear once.'

'Why, brides do that all the time. Besides, can you imagine Dad's face when he sees you in it? I think he might just drop to one knee and ask you to marry him there and then, you look so beautiful in it.'

Penny laughed.

'I'm totally serious.'

'And how would you feel about that?' Penny asked carefully, trying hard not to sound like she was too bothered about the answer.

'I think you'd both be really good for each other, if he can get past his fear of letting anyone in. I don't want him to hurt you and I told him that, but he really likes you and I've never seen him that way about any woman before. Maybe you can be the one that changes him. But if you do end up married you have to promise me that you'll let me be bridesmaid.'

Penny wanted to tell Daisy that they were already dating but that was something that Henry would have to do himself. But clearly, with Daisy's blessing, they might be able to tell her sooner rather than later.

Penny went back into the cubicle, unzipped the dress and carefully hung it back on the hanger. She came back out and Daisy was already dressed and waiting for her.

'Are you getting the red one?'

Daisy pulled a face. 'I've already spent all my pocket money on the green one.'

'Well, let me treat you to that one. It's loads cheaper than the silver dress and then you have a choice come Christmas Eve.'

'No, I can't let you buy it for me.'

'Consider it your Christmas present. Come on, we need to get back home so we can pick up the freezer van before the ice carving workshop.'

'Are you getting the silver dress?'

'No, I have a lovely little black dress that I wear every year to the ball. I have some new shoes to go with it, that'll have to do.'

Penny paid and they left the shop. She smiled when Daisy linked arms with her. They had spent a wonderful morning together, wandering between the shops, chatting, stopping for Christmas cake in Linda's bakery. They just sort of clicked and Penny genuinely loved spending time with her.

'Oh look, there's Anna,' Daisy pointed out and ran over to give her aunt a hug. Penny hesitated and reluctantly walked over. Bea was with her and presumably baby Oliver was asleep in the pram.

Bea waved at her when she saw her and Penny bent down to talk to her so she wouldn't have to talk to Anna.

'Hello Bea.'

'Hi Penny,' Bea said and Penny was aware of Anna and Daisy stopping talking above her head.

'Are you looking forward to Christmas?'

Bea nodded. 'Can you teach me how to say "Happy Christmas" with my hands?'

'With sign language? Yes I can.' She carefully signed the two words and Bea copied her. 'That's it. Now you can tell Tilly in the bakery what your name is and wish her a happy Christmas.'

'Thank you. Will you teach me more words?'

'I tell you what, every time I see you, I'll teach you something new. Do you want another one before you go?'

Bea nodded keenly.

Penny signed a word slowly and Bea copied her again, getting the hang of it very quickly.

'What does that mean?'

'Chocolate.'

Bea giggled.

'Tell you what, Bea,' Anna said, 'Daisy can take you to the bakery and if Tilly is in there you can ask for some chocolate *cake*,' Anna said, signing the word for cake.

Bea nodded enthusiastically and Anna gave Daisy some money. Daisy scooped Bea up and ran across the road to the shop, leaving Penny and Anna alone.

Penny stood up so Anna wasn't towering over her. She was tall like her brother, obviously inheriting those genes too.

'I've been watching you and Daisy for the last hour,' Anna said.

'You've been following us?' Penny was incredulous.

'Spying would be a more accurate description.' Anna half smiled. 'She loves you and I can see you genuinely like having her around. I have to remember she is a brilliant judge of character.

She didn't like any of Henry's girlfriends, even when we all thought they were lovely, and they turned out to be terrible, so if she likes you then maybe I should trust her too.'

'Is that your version of an apology?'

Anna sighed, obviously finding it hard to say. 'I love her. I love them both and I don't want to see them getting hurt, especially Daisy and especially after what happened last time with Emily. So I'm sorry if I overreacted. It came from the right place, even though I know that doesn't excuse it.'

Penny smiled. 'Apology accepted. And I'm sorry for kicking you out of the house.'

Anna shrugged as she turned to walk up the road alongside Penny. 'I totally deserved it. When will you tell Daisy?'

'Soon, I hope. She wants us to get together too, so I hope Henry tells her soon, maybe after Christmas. It's been a pain in the arse hiding it.'

Anna laughed. 'I can imagine. Henry is rubbish at keeping secrets too, he always was as a child, so I imagine it's causing him all sorts of headaches.'

'Did you two get on as children?'

'Yes. Well, not always. We used to have the best time playing together, but we'd fight like cat and dog too. Still do, actually, although we get on really well most of the time.'

'Is it true that you still have food fights?'

'Ha, yes we do, but only when he annoys me. It's hardly a good example for the children though, is it?'

'I don't know, it's certainly one way to sort out any disagreements without resorting to violence and swearing and shouting.'

They turned to wait for Daisy and Bea, watching as they came running out the shop towards them.

'I think Bea might be a good judge of character too,' Anna said.

'Because she likes me?'

'Because she talked to you. She never talks to anyone outside the house. Not even me.'

Penny took a few moments to let that sink in and how worrying that must be for Anna.

'Maybe you could teach her some more sign language. If she isn't brave enough to talk to people at least she can communicate in a way that a lot of other people in the town can understand, even if she's only signing with you.'

Anna smiled and scooped Bea up, who was covered in chocolate already. 'I think that is a brilliant idea. We better go.' She hesitated for a moment before she turned back. 'You'd be very welcome to join Henry and Daisy when they come to us on Christmas Day night.'

'Oh you should,' Daisy said, biting into her cake. 'We always play games in the evening.'

'Thank you, that's very kind. I may be at my brother's but I might visit him late afternoon and then maybe come to you in the evening.'

'You'd be welcome any time.'

Penny watched her go with a smile and then suddenly realised the time.

'Come on, Daisy, we'll be late for the ice carving workshop and, trust me, Maggie is not the sort of person you ever get on the wrong side of.'

'I'm really excited,' Daisy said as she jogged up and down on the spot to keep warm.

Penny blew on her fingers, trying to find the excitement that Daisy had for working at such low temperatures. Working in the cool room in her house was always a bit chilly, but working in a flimsy outdoor marquee with no heaters was a new level of cold. The weather seemed to have got colder and bitterer over the last few days. Maggie, in her wisdom as chief organiser extraordinaire, had decided that Penny didn't need heaters for her ice carving workshop in case the ice melted while people were working on them. Something Penny had only just found out now. With all the stress of the ball and the other events Maggie was organising, as well as being completely exhausted from being heavily pregnant, Penny didn't want to bring up the fact that her blocks of ice would take five hours before they would even start to melt, even in a warm room filled with people. For an hour-long workshop a little heat was not going to be an issue; in fact, the lack of heat might cause problems for the participants.

'How many people do you think will come?' Daisy asked.

'I don't know. I've never done anything like this before. I've done a few private parties before for hen parties and stag nights, and I've done a few corporate team-building-type events, but I've never just put out an open invitation for anyone to come along and have a go. It was Maggie's idea, she said it would be another thing that would raise money for charity. And she's not someone you ever say no to.'

Daisy smiled as she glanced over at Maggie on the phone. 'No, I get that impression too. So how does this work, you just show people how to do it and let them get on with it?'

'Pretty much. I'll show them the basic skills. I have some templates here if anyone wants to use them and then I'll just go round and give them pointers as they work. I'm not honestly expecting great things from anyone. People will just want to have some fun having a go. Whenever I've done the hen or stag parties, everyone always does willies.'

Daisy burst out laughing. 'Seriously?'

'Yeah.'

'What, *everyone*?'

'Yes, pretty much. Grannies, mother of the bride, the men, they all like to carve willies. I don't know why. The first time I did a hen party I just presumed I had a group of ladies that had a bit of a dirty sense of humour, but I've done maybe ten or twenty parties over the years, and every single time I get willies.'

'That's hilarious.'

Penny smiled. 'I'm hoping the people of White Cliff Bay might be more discerning and I might get a few Christmas crackers or bells or trees, but I imagine I'll probably just get a load of willies. Maggie has a local press photographer coming to record the sculptures at the end so I need you to create something tasteful to make sure he won't be photographing a load of willies.'

'What's all this talk of willies?' Henry said, carrying over three small ice blocks and setting them up on the tables. 'Are you corrupting my daughter?'

Daisy giggled. 'Wellies, Dad, not willies. You need to get your ears checked, old man.'

Henry slung an arm around her neck and strangled her against his chest. 'Less of the old, you, and stop talking about willies with my innocent daughter.'

Penny laughed. 'You're the only one mentioning willies. Daisy was telling the truth, we were talking about how I needed a new pair of wellies and what colour to get.'

She tried but failed to look innocent as Henry pretended to glare at her.

'And what colour did you decide on?'

'Pink,' Daisy said.

'Purple,' Penny said at the same time, and then hid her smile behind her water bottle.

'Pinky purple,' Daisy said, unable to control her laughter as they carried on the lie.

Henry suppressed a smile as he walked back to the freezer van to collect more blocks.

'We should talk about something else sordid for when he comes back,' Daisy said. 'How about drugs or prostitution or bestiality?'

Penny spat out her drink. 'I think you're the one who will be corrupting me, not the other way round. Bloody hell.'

'Don't swear in front of my daughter,' Henry said as he came back, and Penny burst out laughing at what he had just missed.

'Yeah, Penny, my innocent ears don't need to hear words like that.'

Penny was about to defend herself when a family with a young child walked through the doors. The posters had been very clear about the age limit. With the sharp tools that were being used, no one under the age of eighteen was allowed to participate for legal reasons. Daisy was the exception to that rule and only because Penny had taken full responsibility for her and told Maggie how good she was. Penny hoped this family hadn't turned up wanting their little children to have a go. Maggie, as efficient as ever, went to greet them as a few other people walked through the doors of the marquee.

At least with more people inside the marquee it might start to warm up a bit, although they would need hundreds more people to make a difference to the temperature. It was so bitterly cold Penny worried about whether people would really enjoy themselves or even be able to hold and use the tools properly.

A few more people arrived, some of them Penny knew from around the town: Libby, Maggie's sister Hazel, surprisingly old Suzanna from the chemist, other people she didn't know. Maggie was taking payment and issuing them with instructions to find a pair of gloves and a table. The marquee was still almost empty. With Christmas only three days away the people of the town were most likely using the day for last-minute shopping or visiting relatives. As the time they were supposed to start came and went and no one else arrived, Penny guessed that was it. There were ten of them eager to learn, which was a nice number to teach, but not the hugely successful event that Maggie had hoped it would be. The participants were all huddled inside their coats looking miserable in the cold.

Henry looked around the group anxiously. 'Why don't I take orders from these guys for some hot drinks? There's a coffee shop just down the road, I could be there and back in about fifteen minutes.'

'That'll be perfect, thank you so much,' Penny said, leaning up to kiss him on the cheek and stopping just in time before anyone noticed. Henry smiled at what she had just been about to do.

'Soon, I promise,' he whispered. He touched her hand just briefly but it was enough for her to know that he wanted to kiss her too.

He went around and took orders from everybody. They were all beyond grateful at the prospect of something hot to warm themselves up.

After he had left, Penny introduced herself and gave a short demonstration of how to draw the thing they wanted to carve and which tools to use to turn that 2D drawing into a 3D sculpture. She only had basic tools available for them to use and certainly no chainsaws, so she was confident enough to be able to walk around and work with each member of the group one on one, leaving the others to fend for themselves until she got around to them.

There were three girls in their early twenties who had come together and were giggling about what they were going to carve. Penny smiled, knowing that they at least would be producing willies.

She walked past Daisy, stopping briefly to examine what she was drawing on the side of her block.

'Don't worry, it's not going to be a willy,' Daisy said.

'Nothing else dodgy either, if you don't mind. Your dad will never forgive me.'

Daisy smiled and carried on with her carving. Penny left her to it. A quick circuit of the tables proved that seven of the ten members of the group were in fact doing willies and finding themselves very original and funny for having thought of it. Libby was using the template to make a square boxed cracker and one man was trying his hand, not very successfully, on a tree.

She stopped in the middle, watching her students immersed in their work and smiled at what a lovely feeling it was to see her tuition in progress, to see them enjoying themselves because of what she had shown them. Maybe she really would take Jackson Cartwright up on his offer to come in and teach his students.

But it *was* too cold and although her students were having fun with the new challenge, she could see many of them were having to stop to blow on their hands. Working at low temperatures was never fun. She had sometimes been forced, for one reason or another, to carve inside her walk-in freezer, but she could only stand it for short periods before her hands and feet got too cold to work, despite wearing gloves and steel-toecapped fur boots. Even Daisy, who was used to working in the cool room with her, was having to stop momentarily to put her tools down and rub her hands together. She had rolled her sleeves up, as she did every time she worked, and her bare forearms were exposing her to the cold more than was necessary.

Outside snow was falling in big fat flakes. Though the ground was too wet for it to be able to settle, it certainly proved how cold it was.

Suddenly there was a cry of pain and Penny whirled around to see Daisy cradling her arm. Penny rushed over to see that she had cut her arm. It wasn't bad but it had obviously come about from her hands being too cold and numb to hold the tools properly. The gloves Daisy had been wearing were too big for her to grip the tools and they were letting cold through the gaps too.

'Are you OK?' Penny asked, wrapping a comforting arm around her shoulders.

Daisy nodded, giving her a weak smile. 'It bloody hurts. Don't tell Dad I swore.'

Penny laughed. If Daisy could joke about that then she was fine. She looked around at the group. Henry should be back soon with their drinks to warm them up but Penny wondered whether she should call a halt to the workshop. For some of these guys who weren't used to working in cold temperatures, they could end up hurting themselves just as Daisy had done.

Penny turned to grab the first aid kit just as Henry walked back into the marquee. His face fell as he saw Daisy holding her arm.

'Oh crap,' Daisy muttered. 'I'll make a distraction, while you run away.'

'What?' Penny said, but the angry look on Henry's face told her everything she needed to know. This was not going to go down well. She focussed her attention on pulling out a large plaster from the first aid box and managed to use an antiseptic wipe to clean up the excess blood before Henry could get there. But he was suddenly by her side.

His breath was accelerated, fearful as he stared at the cut, which could only have been an inch in length.

'What the hell happened?' he said through gritted teeth.

'Dad, it was just an accident, it was my own stupid fault.'

Henry's gaze turned accusingly towards Penny. 'I thought you said it was safe.'

'It's too cold in here, I'm sorry,' Penny said, returning her attention to the cut as she carefully and gently applied the plaster to the wound.

'I'm going to take Daisy home,' Henry said, clearly trying to keep his temper in check.

Daisy's shoulders slumped.

'I think you're overreacting slightly.'

'I'm overreacting?' Henry said, incredulously.

'Yes, you're being an over-bearing, over-protective arse. It's a tiny scratch and I don't appreciate you looking at me as if I'm an evil monster,' Penny said, snapping the lid closed on the first aid box. After a second or two, she was surprised to see a smile pull at his lips.

Daisy stared at them in shock.

Penny smirked, sensing the tension had gone. She took the first aid kit back to where the rest of her stuff was and he followed her.

'An arse?'

Confident that they were out of earshot from everyone else, she turned around to talk to him. 'Yes, and why don't you take that gorgeous arse of yours and deliver the hot drinks for me and then sit over here out the way? Let Daisy get on with her ice carving, she will learn from her mistakes and be more careful about how she uses the tools. Plus I'll keep an eye on her.'

Henry nodded, suddenly a whole lot calmer. 'I'm sorry.'

She smiled. 'It's OK.'

Penny went back over to Daisy. 'Are you OK to carry on? You can sit out if you want to?'

Daisy shook her head. 'No, I'm fine.' She glanced over at Henry, who was doing as he had been told and dishing out the drinks. 'No one has ever stood up to him like that before. I expected him to go ballistic. As I said, you're good for him.'

Penny looked over at him. She had never stood up for herself before either, preferring to keep her head down in an argument. He had taught her that she should never accept being treated badly by anyone. She smiled. He was good for her too.

Chapter 22

Penny was up in her bedroom later that afternoon, fighting with changing the duvet cover on her bed, when there was a tentative knock on the bedroom door. Henry had stayed down in the town when she and Daisy had returned home, needing to do some Christmas shopping, and he probably wouldn't knock anyway, he had already seen her in all her glory.

She opened the door and was surprised to see Daisy, her hair and make-up done flawlessly. Daisy grinned at her, though it didn't quite meet her eyes.

'I'm meeting up with Josh. Can you tell Dad that I've gone to see Rebecca or something?'

'Daisy, that's not fair, asking me to lie and cover for you. I feel bad enough as it is not telling him what I know without adding lies to my list of crimes too. You need to. . .' Penny trailed off, seeing the worry on her face. 'What's wrong?'

Daisy came in and sat on Penny's bed. 'I told Rebecca that you called the old hut the Love Shack and Rebecca said that everyone knows it as that. She said a lot of the teenage boys take their girlfriends there to have sex. Josh suggested we hang out there. What if he wants to sleep with me?'

Penny sat down heavily on the bed next to her. There was no manual for dealing with this kind of thing. She wished Henry was here but she knew he wouldn't deal with it in the best way, which was probably why Daisy had come to her.

'How many times have you seen Josh now, since the ice carving competition?'

'How many dates? Three. I think I love him.'

Penny suppressed a smile at the simplicity of teenage love, although it was never simple at the time.

'I'm not ready to sleep with him yet.'

'Then you tell him that.'

'What if he dumps me because of it? I've never had a boyfriend. No boy has ever paid attention to me before, as if I'm not worth even talking to. And maybe I'm not if my mum left me when I was only two months old. Josh doesn't think I'm worthless or ugly. He loves me exactly as I am and I couldn't bear it if he rejected me too.'

Penny's heart ached for Daisy. The damage her mum had done was far-reaching and was something it would take Daisy a large part of her life to get over.

'You are beautiful and intelligent and kind and funny and Henry loves you so much. He doesn't think you are worthless; you are the single most important person in his life. If Henry and I ever get together and get married, I will be proud to have you as my step-daughter. Your mum missed out big time when she walked out on you, but that is a reflection on her, not you. If Josh can't see how incredible you are then that is his loss, not yours.'

Daisy stared at her for a moment and then threw her arms around her neck and hugged her tight. Penny wrapped her arms around her too, stroking her back. Finally Daisy pulled away.

'Tell me, has Josh mentioned that he wants to sleep with you at all?'

Daisy shook her head. Penny knew how painfully shy Josh was; it probably hadn't even crossed his mind to take it any further.

'Have you guys done anything other than kiss?'

Daisy blushed. 'No, we generally just talk and listen to music. We've kissed a bit but he is so sweet and respectful. Rebecca says that Lucas, her boyfriend, always gropes her boobs, but Josh hasn't touched my boobs at all.'

Penny noticed the look of disappointment on Daisy's face. 'Do you want him to?'

'Yes. Maybe. I don't know. They're a bit small.' Daisy looked down at her chest. 'Rebecca says it feels nice.'

Oh lord. What would Henry's reaction be to this conversation? He would probably ground Daisy for life and stop her from seeing Josh and Rebecca ever again.

'Does it feel nice?'

Shit. Penny had a brief flashback to Friday night, Henry kissing her breasts, taking her nipple into his mouth. 'Yes, it does, but that's not something you should do unless you feel completely comfortable with it.'

'Sometimes I want to do more than kissing with him but I'm scared. I don't know what I'm doing and I certainly don't want to get it wrong. And I just don't know whether I'm ready for all that yet. But he is so lovely and he hasn't had a girlfriend before. I want to share my first time with him.'

'My first time I was a lot older than you are now. I was twenty years old and it was a very quick and mostly uncomfortable fumble in my boyfriend's bedroom before he ran downstairs to have dinner with his mum and dad. But the first time with. . . my second boyfriend was beautiful and sweet and far more pleasurable. I was nervous but he was so kind and gentle. He made the whole experience about me and what I wanted and needed. In many ways I wish I had waited to share my first time with him instead. Your first time should be wonderful and it should be somewhere romantic, not some wooden shack where countless other couples have lost their virginity. But most importantly it needs to be with someone you love and trust completely.'

'I do love and trust him.'

'OK, but you've only been dating for a few days. Just take your time to really get to know him and when you are ready, if you trust him, maybe you can talk to him about your fears. But never ever do anything that you aren't comfortable with or not ready to do. If he truly loves you, he will wait until you are ready.'

Daisy nodded solemnly. 'I should go, he's probably waiting for me.'

Daisy stood up and Penny experienced a brief moment of panic, of wanting to take her up to the loft and lock her up there until she was at least twenty-five. Should she stop her going, get her to stay at home until Henry came back, and then he could deal with this in whatever way he saw fit? He was her dad after all. Penny was just the landlady.

Daisy moved to the door. 'Thanks for this. You won't tell my dad, will you?'

Penny swallowed and shook her head. 'Look, wait a second.' She moved to the drawer near her bed and pulled out a small handful of condoms. 'I really don't think you should sleep with Josh, not for a few weeks or months yet, not until you're ready. But if you do sleep with him in the future, just be safe, OK?'

Daisy stared at the condoms, her pale skin blushing bright red, telling Penny that Daisy was nowhere near ready to make that commitment yet. Daisy grabbed the condoms and shoved them in her bag.

'Just tell him you're not ready, I'm sure he will understand.'

Daisy nodded and, with a small smile, she walked out.

Penny stood in the doorway of her bedroom, watching Daisy disappear down the stairs. A few seconds later she heard the back door close. What the hell had she done?

Henry was walking back up the hill towards his home, whistling happily to himself. Life was pretty damned perfect right now. He had sorted out his problems with Clara at work, and while Edward had been in the office sacking his sister he had stumbled across Henry's designs and had just phoned him to say he had taken them home to look at and really liked them. He was going to set up a meeting with one of the designers after Christmas and this time Edward would sit in on the meeting too. Daisy was really happy here in White Cliff Bay and he had the most wonderful girlfriend, who he knew he was falling in love with. With only two days until the Christmas Eve ball, it couldn't get any better.

He was taking a shortcut over the grass, passing by the wooden shack at the end of the drive to his house, when he saw Penny a hundred yards away, walking Bernard. He waved at her and she stared at him as if he had three heads.

There was soft music coming from inside the shack and giggling. He smiled to himself. There was obviously a couple in there making the most of this secluded spot. He heard the giggle again as he passed the front door and stopped dead.

He recognised that giggle. He had heard that giggle every day for the last sixteen years. He doubled back a few paces and yanked open the door. His heart dropped into his stomach. Daisy was lying on the bench with Josh lying entirely on top of her as they kissed.

They broke apart and Daisy paled when she saw him. His eyes turned to Josh as he scrambled up off his daughter. He was momentarily relieved to see they both still had their clothes on.

'What the bloody hell do you think you're doing with my daughter?' he spat, unable to control the rage that was boiling through him.

'Dad, we were just kissing.' Daisy sat up. Her t-shirt had fallen off her shoulder revealing her pale skin and a black lacy bra strap had also slid down her arm too. Had his hands been on her? The thought of this boy mauling her made him sick.

Suddenly Penny arrived in the hut, out of breath. 'Henry, calm down, please.'

He barely heard her, his eyes snapping back to Josh as he wrapped his arm around Daisy's shoulders. 'Get your hands off my daughter before I break them.'

'Henry!' Penny said, incredulously. 'He's a child.'

'Dad, don't talk to him like that. Josh, just go, please. I don't want you to get hurt.'

Josh stood up. The boy was huge and Henry's stomach rolled with the thought of Josh and Daisy together.

Inexplicably Josh moved to stand between Henry and Daisy. 'I'm not leaving you with him when he's this angry. I'm not going to let you hurt her.'

Henry was staggered by this. The thought that he could hurt his own daughter was laughable. Sure, he wanted to punch or kick something, but he could never do anything to hurt Daisy. But what was even more disturbing was Josh's protective attitude towards her. Henry expected him to run away as soon as he had stepped foot in the hut but Josh clearly really cared about Daisy and that threw him even more.

Penny placed a hand on his arm. 'Henry, they were just kissing.'

He ignored her and turned his attention back to Daisy. 'Get up, we're going home and you're never going to see him again.' Somewhere at the back of his head he knew he was being unreasonable but he couldn't engage with the rational part of his brain right now.

'Dad! We're in love.'

'In love? It's been a week!'

'So?'

His sixteen-year-old daughter was in love. How had this happened? It seemed like only yesterday he'd been putting her hair in pigtails and taking her off for her first day in school. He had to calm down, he was reacting really badly to this. It had just shocked him to find his daughter in that position. Penny was right, they were just kissing. He took a deep breath and let it out slowly.

Daisy looked at Penny. 'I can't believe you told him, you promised to keep it a secret.'

'I didn't tell him, I swear.'

Rage exploded in his gut again as he rounded on Penny. 'You knew? You knew she was seeing Josh and you never told me?'

Penny paled guiltily. 'I... I wanted to but...'

Henry turned away and snatched up Daisy's bag. 'We're going home.'

The bag caught on the leg of a chair and the contents spilt out on the floor, including three condoms.

Everyone stared at the condoms in shock.

Finally Henry found his voice. 'Just kissing, eh?'

'I gave them to her,' Penny said, quickly.

'You gave my daughter fucking condoms? You knew she was dating Josh and not only did you let her come down here to see him, but you pushed her out the door with a handful of condoms and told her to have a good time. Who the hell do you think you are?'

Penny took a step back away from him, wounded by his words.

'I wasn't going to sleep with him,' Daisy said. 'I talked to Penny about it and she told me how wonderful her first time was with her second boyfriend, how special it was and how important it was that I waited until I was ready. I wanted my first time to be beautiful like that, I didn't want to be like you that had a drunken fumble at a party, which you regretted for the rest of your life.'

Daisy ran out and Henry went to follow her but Penny snagged his arm. 'Wait a second.'

He removed his arm from his grasp, her betrayal burning in his gut. She should never have kept it secret. If he had known about this he could have had a civilised conversation with his daughter about sex. He should never have found out like this. His eyes strayed to the condoms again and the anger bubbled back to the surface.

'Stay away from my daughter and stay away from me. I never want to see you again.'

He stormed out the hut, ignoring the devastation on Penny's face.

It was hours later by the time Penny went home. Not wanting to face Henry, she had walked the cliffs with Bernard until hours after it had gone dark. She had also cried every tear she

314

had. Finally, when the tears had subsided and only a numb pain remained, Penny made her way back home.

It was ridiculous to fall so hard, so quickly for Henry. It shouldn't hurt this badly after only knowing him for a week, but even knowing how silly it was to have these feelings, there was nothing she could do to stop it.

She let herself in through the back door and her eyes immediately glanced over to the connecting door. Their lights were off and the house was silent. Henry's car was still parked outside so they hadn't gone out or, even worse, packed up and left.

She grabbed her keys for her freezer van so she could unload the remaining smaller blocks that hadn't been used at the workshop earlier back into her walk-in freezer. Luckily she had cut the normal-sized big blocks up into smaller pieces for the workshop so she could carry them on her own, even if they were still heavy.

She carried them into the cool room one at a time and then opened the freezer door. Weirdly, the door stuck but she gave it several big yanks and eventually it came away from the frame.

Inside, a large pool of water had frozen on the floor, creating a mini ice skating rink inside her freezer.

She stared in horror as the reality of the situation settled in. Not only had several large blocks of ice for future carvings melted away to nothing but so had a carving for a corporate party the following night, her competition piece for the Christmas Eve ball and a carving ordered by a man who was going to propose to his girlfriend on Tuesday night. She felt sick. Out of the three carvings that had gone, the proposal one was the worst because she knew her oversized diamond ring was the finale in a whole trail of romantic gestures the man had organised. She couldn't let him down. If these had melted due to the power cut the night before, then the ice in the block maker machines would have melted too. And they would take three days to refreeze. They might be ready by Tuesday night but not in time for her to carve before the proposal.

She looked at the five smaller blocks sitting in the cool room. She could fuse three of them together to make one big block. The join lines would be quite prominent but she could still create a large ring out of it and surely the man wouldn't mind as long the gesture was the same. She would refund him if he was upset with the quality but at least he would have the oversized diamond ring. She would have to call the organisers of the corporate party to cancel the other order.

She quickly brought the smaller blocks into the freezer, wet the ends and clamped three of them together to make one big block. It would be ready for her to carve by the next day.

She walked out into the kitchen and saw Daisy waiting for her.

As soon as Daisy saw her, she burst into tears.

Penny rushed over and quickly took her in her arms as Daisy sobbed against her.

'Hey, what's with all these tears?' Penny said, stroking the back of her head.

'I'm so sorry. All of this is my fault. I should never have hid it from Dad and I should never have asked you to cover for me. . .'

'You have nothing to be sorry for.'

'But now my dad hates you.'

It was like a punch to the gut all over again. Henry did hate her, she had seen it in his eyes. That was the worst part of it, seeing that look in his eyes had confirmed that he had never felt for her what she felt for him. Penny hadn't manipulated Daisy into thinking that she liked her or used Daisy to get to her dad or even told Daisy a nasty pack of lies like Henry's previous girlfriend had. Although Henry had every right to be angry at her, she didn't deserve that kind of anger. She had done the best thing she could for Daisy, but Henry was treating her like she was the lowest form of scum.

She swallowed down the pain as she prepared to lie to Daisy. 'He doesn't hate me. He was angry and he had every right to be.'

'I thought you two would get together and I've ruined that now.'

'You've not ruined anything.'

'I'm not talking to him if that helps,' Daisy said.

Penny somehow found the energy to smile slightly at that. 'Honey, I don't want you hating your dad over this. This is between me and him, and I never want to be the person that comes between you two.'

Daisy held her tighter as she cried. 'Will you forgive him? When he apologises, which he will because I'll make him. You will forgive him, won't you?'

Penny pulled back slightly and kissed Daisy's forehead. 'Whatever happens between me and Henry, me and you will still be friends, you don't ever need to worry about that.'

Daisy stared at her for a moment before fresh tears filled her eyes. 'You won't forgive him, will you?'

Penny decided for once she was going to be honest with her and she shook her head. 'I don't think I can.'

'Why?' Daisy cried.

Anger suddenly replaced all the pain she was feeling. 'Because my last boyfriend treated me so badly and I'm not going to put up with it again. Your dad always told me I deserved better and I do. No one gets to treat me like a piece of shit and then come crawling back and apologise for it later. If you care for someone, you'd never treat them like that in the first place.'

A noise at the connecting door made them both look up. Henry was standing there but, silhouetted in the darkness, Penny had no idea what expression was on his face.

'You better go,' Penny said to Daisy. 'But remember what I said, it's not going to change things between us.'

Daisy sniffed and nodded, and then she walked towards the door.

Penny didn't wait to see if Henry would say anything to her once Daisy had gone upstairs. She turned away and went to bed.

Penny woke to movement in her kitchen the next morning and wondering if it might be Henry – maybe even half hoping – she pulled on her robe and walked downstairs. She was only slightly disappointed to see Jill banging around and making breakfast.

Jill smiled hugely when she saw her and gave her a big hug. She pulled back slightly and her face fell.

'You've been crying, what's happened?'

Penny shook her head. 'It doesn't matter.'

'It obviously does.'

There was a noise from upstairs in the annexe as someone got out of bed and suddenly Penny didn't want to be there. Either Henry was going to come downstairs and shout at her some more, apologise profusely or ignore her completely, and she didn't want to be there for any of that.

She still had that proposal carving she needed to do, but that could wait until later.

'What did you have planned for today?'

Jill picked up on her urgency straight away. 'I. . . was going to take you out for the day.'

Penny smiled with love for her. 'I'd really like that.'

'Well, go and get dressed then, while I put these breakfast things away.'

Penny nodded with gratitude and ran upstairs.

The amazing scents of the Christmas market in the next town of Apple Hill could be smelt from the very back of the car park, and it was all the more magical with the snow that was falling quite heavily around them, settling on the car roofs and in the grass.

They walked through the marquee entrance and were met with a wall of warmth and the rich smells of sweet honey, spiced wines, fruits, chocolates, fudge, breads and so many other things that Penny couldn't discern them.

The place was packed. Christmas Eve was tomorrow and everyone was running around trying to take care of last-minute shopping and preparations.

Over a breakfast of bacon sandwiches made with a special whisky bread, which tasted amazing, Penny told Jill what had happened the day before.

Jill finished off the remains of her sandwich and licked her fingers. 'My lovely Penny, although that was a massive over-reaction from him, being a parent does funny things to you. I guarantee you that he is regretting what happened yesterday afternoon right now and working out a way to apologise to you.'

'He can stick his apology up his arse, I'm not interested.'

Jill shook her head. 'I don't know a single parent who has never overreacted when it came to the safety and protection of their children. The first child is the worst – by the time you've had two or three you become much more mellow. But Henry never had that, he only ever had one, and she is his entire world, you can see that. I never had children but I love you and your brother as if you were my own, and I would quite simply die for you if it meant you were happy, healthy and safe. One day you might have children of your own and you shouldn't judge a parent until you've walked a mile in their shoes, until you've felt that unwavering, all-consuming love for a child that makes you act rashly and insensitively at times. It was a shock for him to find his daughter like that and it must have hurt him that you didn't tell him.' Jill raised her hand to stop Penny interrupting. 'Though I understand why you did it. Any relationship has arguments and rows, but you forgive each other and you move on, you don't throw away the man you love at the first hurdle. When he apologises, tell him he is an arse, tell him how much he hurt you, but then forgive him and never look back.'

Penny shook her head. She couldn't forgive Henry, not yet anyway. She was still too angry for that.

Jill patted her on the hand and stood up. 'Come on, I want to see the delights this market has to offer.'

There was no more mention of it after that; Jill knew when to sow the seed of what Penny should do and when to leave her alone to think about it. Instead they moved from stall to stall admiring the scented candles, tasting all the fudge, chocolate, honeycomb, sweets, breads, sweetened nuts, jams and cheeses. Penny drank lots of hot spiced apple cider and mulled wine, enough to make her feel warm and contented. There were several stalls selling mince pies, all of them with different flavours and spices and unique ingredients, and Penny bought and ate several tiny chocolate mince pies. They admired the tree decorations made from glass, wood and even the tacky plastic ones, and they all reminded Penny of the wonderful tree sitting in her lounge. There was even a stall that sold gingerbread house kits and some beautiful ready-made ones. It was almost as if Jill had deliberately brought her here to remind her of all the amazing memories she had shared with Henry in the last week.

By the time they left, Penny had eaten her weight in free samples, had gone back for several more glasses of the delicious spiced hot apple cider and was weighed down with bags of purchases she had no recollection of buying.

By the time Jill dropped her off at home, she was feeling a little bit drunk and certainly not in any mood to face Henry in whatever mood he was in, so she dumped her bags in the lounge and went off to bed for an afternoon nap.

She woke later and it was already dark outside, the snow still falling heavily outside the window.

Her head was still feeling a bit fuzzy and she quite fancied staying in bed until Christmas was over. Tomorrow was Christmas Eve, the night of the ball. She could easily stay in bed for two more days. No one would care anyway.

Suddenly she remembered the proposal carving that she needed to do before tomorrow night. As she had agreed to help Maggie with a lot of the setting up for the ball the next day, she couldn't lie in bed feeling sorry for herself any longer.

She got changed into slightly warmer clothes and went down to the freezer.

She opened the freezer door, the bloody thing sticking again, and looked inside. Once the proposal carving had been delivered she would have to defrost the whole freezer and clean the door and the floor before she put any more carvings in there. The pool of frozen water in the freezer was dangerous.

She looked at the three blocks of ice she had clamped together the night before and sighed. In her haste to rectify the situation, and with her mind still on Henry and Daisy, she hadn't put the block on top of her trolley. As it was too heavy to lift on her own and there was no way she was asking Henry to help her move it, she resigned herself to carving it in the freezer. The diamond ring carving at least would be fairly easy and quick to carve, so she wouldn't be in there too long, and once the ice had been carved away so it was hollow in the middle, she was confident she would be able to move it on her own the next day.

She grabbed the tools from the cool room and shut herself in, not totally confident that the three blocks of ice, forged into one piece, would hold together once she started working on it. At least in the cold of the freezer they would be less likely to break.

She scrolled through the tunes on her iPhone until she found something that was not remotely Christmassy and then started to carve. She marked out the basic ring shape and then used the chainsaw to chop off the bits that she wouldn't need, including the middle. She made the ring a lot thicker than she had originally intended because she needed the strength of a thick ring. She spent a while getting the ring part as flawless and smooth as she could but it really was cold in here and her fingers were becoming numb, even through the gloves.

She pushed on, knowing she needed to finish it tonight, and at least while she was in here, focussing on the design and the carving, she wouldn't have to go out there and think about Henry and how this might actually turn out to be the worst Christmas ever. She was undoubtedly going to spend it alone and, although in previous years, when she had been alone, that had been fine, being in love with a man who hated her and being dumped by him just a few days before the big day made things infinitely worse.

She was feeling sleepy now, the alcohol no doubt still leaving its mark. She rarely ever drank so when she did she always felt hungover a few hours later rather than the next day. She would finish here and go back to bed.

She ignored the cold that was settling into her body and took her time with the detail of the claw that would hold the giant diamond, making sure the facets of the diamond were smooth and polished.

Finally she stepped back to admire the finished piece.

It really was cold in here and maybe it was the time she had spent in there but it felt a lot colder than it should. Her arms and legs were almost painfully cold, her fingers were practically numb, her eyes felt heavy. She had never had such an adverse reaction to working inside the freezer before.

She checked the temperature gauge by the door and swore. After the power cut on Saturday the freezer had reset itself at its coldest temperature, which was about twenty degrees colder than it should be. No wonder she was in so much pain. It also explained why she felt so tired; it wasn't the alcohol, her body was shutting down.

She needed a nice warm bath – she knew that going from extreme cold to extreme heat would not be good for the body so she'd have to warm herself up gently.

She picked up all her tools and pushed the door, but it didn't budge. Confused, she tried the door again and it still didn't move. She put the tools down and tried again. It didn't shift an inch. Shit. She threw her weight against the door in a panic, but it still didn't move. The handle wasn't turning properly from the inside, partly frozen from the intense cold, and her hands were too numb to apply any real pressure to it.

Leaning onto one of the shelves, she tried to kick the door handle with her feet, but that didn't work either.

She banged on the door and shouted as loud as she could, but there was no noise from the room outside and no one came to rescue her.

She banged again, shouting, yelling, throwing her weight against it time and time again, but she was trapped.

She quickly dug her phone out of her pocket and scrolled through her contacts. Who could she call? Henry or Daisy were the obvious choices; if they were next door they could come and let her out, but Henry wasn't speaking to her and she didn't have Daisy's number.

Maggie was twenty minutes away, Jill would be about half an hour and her brother was a good fifty minutes from her house.

The phone beeped feebly to say she was running out of battery. Shit, could anything else go wrong?

She quickly dialled Henry's number. He would be angry but he wouldn't leave her in here to freeze to death.

It rang a few times and to her surprise he answered straight away.

'Hello?'

She tried to judge his tone – was he still angry, upset, regretful? Now was not the time to get into any of that.

'Henry, are you in your house? I need your help.'

'No.'

One-word answers weren't good; he clearly hadn't forgiven her yet. She was so mad at him, she didn't even want to speak to him right now. And if he was out then he couldn't even help her.

The phone beeped, indicating that it was about to die any second.

'How far away are you?'

His voice softened slightly with concern as he sensed the panic.

'What's wrong?'

'Is Daisy at home?'

'No, she's at Anna's. What's wrong?'

'I'm trapped in the freezer.'

'How are you trapped?'

'The door is stuck. After the power cut the freezer reset itself and it's colder in here than it should be. I had to carve in here and I've been in here for nearly two hours and now I can't get out.'

Henry was silent for a moment and then the phone rang off.

She stared at the phone in horror. Was he coming, was he not coming?

She tried to phone him again but before it even rang her mobile died.

Crap.

She had to get out of here. She threw herself at the door a few more times but it didn't move at all.

OK, so she had to remember how to survive extreme temperatures. She had looked into it once when she had been trying to find out how long it was safe for her to work in the freezer. She didn't think moving around was a good idea because that kept blood pumping around the extremities but away from the vital organs, so she just had to stay still. She sat down in the corner of

325

the room and curled herself up into a tight ball, knees up to her chest, her arms wrapped around them.

Henry had to be coming. No matter how angry he was, he wouldn't leave her to freeze to death. He would come and save her. It just depended on whether he could get to her in time.

Chapter 23

Henry skidded to a halt outside the house. It had taken him nearly half an hour to get home. He should have called the fire brigade or the police or someone, anyone would have got there quicker than he could have done, but he knew the satnav didn't actually take anyone directly to the house and, remembering what a pain in the arse it had been for him to find the place on his first day, he didn't want to waste time explaining where the property was. He had phoned Daisy to get her to cycle home, but neither she nor Anna had answered the phone, and Anna didn't have a car as Steve had taken theirs to come and meet him.

He raced around the back of the house and barged through the back door and into the cool room. He yanked at the freezer door. It was stuck but he pulled at it hard and it eventually opened. Penny was sitting in the corner of the room, huddled up into a ball. She wasn't moving. The bottom dropped out of his world.

He ran to her side and shook her but there was no response. He quickly scooped her up and carried her out as she flopped uselessly against his arms. Should he call an ambulance? Should he just drive her to a hospital himself? It was over a forty-five-minute drive from here to the nearest hospital, probably closer to an hour. He knew phone reception was sporadic and he didn't want to leave her while he ran down to the shed to make the call.

The most important thing was to get her warm. He laid her in front of the fireplace and quickly built a fire in the grate. As it flickered and roared into life he covered her with a blanket, ran upstairs and grabbed the thick duvet off her bed.

Her clothes were icy cold and he knew he had to get her out of them if she was going to warm up. She was so still and it scared the crap out of him to see her like a frozen Sleeping Beauty. He yanked the zip down on her jacket and dragged it off her body. The long-sleeved t-shirt she was wearing underneath was also cold so that came off too. He yanked her boots off and pulled her waterproof trousers and her leggings off so she was just left in her underwear. Ripping his shirt off, he lay on top of her, covering them both with the duvet.

'Penny, can you hear me?'

She didn't move; he wasn't even sure if she was breathing. He put his face next to hers and could feel tiny shallow breaths on his cheek. He rubbed her arms desperately. She was so cold and she didn't seem to be getting any warmer.

'Penny, come on, open your eyes and look at me,' he begged.

The fire was roaring now and he could feel the heat through the duvet and on his face. She had to feel it too.

'Penny, if you don't open your eyes now, I'll never speak to you again. Do you hear me? Open your fucking eyes.'

To his surprise she did and he nearly wept with relief. She stared past him, her gaze not focussing on him at all, and he grabbed her face hard. 'Look at me.'

She blinked blearily a few times and then her eyes locked with his.

'You came,' she whispered, her eyes filling with tears. 'I thought you didn't care.'

'Of course I fucking care. You know how much you mean to me.'

She shook her head as he carried on gently rubbing her arms. 'Not really. You said you never wanted to see me again.'

'I was angry. I didn't mean it. Jesus, Penny, how could you believe that I didn't care?'

'You were quite adamant. And I hated you a little bit for it too. You said we were finished.'

'No, we're not,' he snapped, before realising his concern for her and relief that she was OK were now quickly turning into anger too. 'Christ, you scared the crap out of me.'

He found himself burying his face in her neck, wrapping his arms around her and pulling her tightly against him. He had nearly lost her. He closed his eyes and breathed her in, relishing the feel of her pulse hammering against his lips, proving she was very much alive.

'Am I naked?'

He looked up. 'I was trying to keep you warm.'

'By undressing me?'

'Body heat is supposed to be the best way to combat hypothermia.'

'Are you naked too?'

'I have my jeans on.'

'Did you just strip me naked so you could perv over me?'

'It didn't cross my mind.'

'Really? So if I was a man, the first thing you would have done would be to strip me naked and lie on top of me?'

Henry hesitated. 'Possibly. Probably not. It's not like I haven't seen your body before. If we weren't in a relationship, I wouldn't have stripped you.'

'We're not in a relationship, you dumped me, remember?'

'I didn't dump you. I was angry at you, there's a big difference.'

She shook her head. 'I'm grateful that you came to rescue me, but I didn't call you because I wanted to get back together with you, I called you because I thought you might be next door and you were the nearest person. I'd quite honestly be happy if I never saw you again.'

Pain squeezed at his chest with that comment. But then how could he expect anything different? He had yelled at her, told her never wanted to see her again. But would she really throw it all away over one stupid, thoughtless moment?

She suddenly looked angry. 'You have no right to be hurt over this, everything was perfect and you ruined it. You promised that you would never hurt me and you did.'

He gritted his teeth. 'Shit, I'm sorry, I never meant to hurt you.' He kissed her softly but she didn't kiss him back. He looked at her but her eyes were hard. He kissed her again but she still didn't respond. Panic surged through him again. He'd lost her. She was alive and breathing and wrapped in his arms but he had lost her due to his stupid temper.

'I'm sorry.' He kissed her throat, trailing tiny kisses across her collarbone. 'I talked to Daisy, she told me everything you said to her. You were wonderful, you handled it so much better than I ever would. I was just blindsided. I never expected for one second to walk in there and find her in that compromising position with the condoms that you gave her. It was a shock and I know I overreacted but I'm so sorry.'

Tears filled her eyes again. 'I don't think I can do this, Henry. If you really cared about me as much as I care about you, you wouldn't shout at me like that. You wouldn't get so angry that you finished with me.'

Henry stared at her. It was over. She wasn't prepared to fight for him. Well, he was damned well going to fight for her.

'Wait a minute. I love you. I fucking love you so much. I thought you loved me too. Daisy told me what you said about making love to your second boyfriend and how perfect and beautiful it was. I know you meant me, and it was perfect and beautiful because we were made for each other. When you love someone you love everything about them, you love them when they're sad or angry or stubborn or overreact. You love them through the good times and the bad. When you love someone, you love them when they snort with laughter, when they turn up in your house for dinner with their hair like a tangled bush, you love them when you kiss them with morning breath, you love them when they make cakes just because they're angry, you love them because they make you laugh and cry. I love you and if you love me you'll forgive me.'

He watched her face soften slightly.

'I'm sorry, I really am.' He kissed her and was relieved that after a few seconds she kissed him back. 'We're OK, aren't we?'

She raised a weak hand to run through his hair and eventually nodded, and he kissed her again. He pulled her tighter against him. After just a few moments the kisses turned to something more; it was needful and the need had come from her.

Her hands wandered down his back to the top of his jeans and slid around his hips to the front.

He pulled back slightly. 'Penny, I think we should get you to a hospital, just in case. I . . .'

She kissed him again and he hated that she was crying, that he had caused her to cry.

She fumbled at the front of his jeans again and he helped her, wriggling out of them as quick as he could.

331

He knelt up and pulled her up too, his mouth not leaving hers as he dragged her bra off her and her knickers. He lifted her onto his lap and as she straddled him, he pushed inside her. She wrapped her arms around his neck, kissing him hard, and without any space between them, they started to move. It was fast and urgent and desperate and, as they both tumbled over the edge, he knew he could never let her go.

Penny lay on top of Henry's chest watching the flames dwindle and die as he played with her hair. Her breathing was just about returning to normal.

'I think we're OK,' Penny said.

'I am sorry. I promise I'll never shout at you again,' Henry said, running his hands down her back.

She looked up at him. 'Don't make promises you can't keep. We will have rows and we will shout at each other, but you can't break up with me every time you get angry. It's not fair.'

'I know, I'm sorry. I'm not handling any of this well. I've not had a relationship like this before. Even with the semi-serious relationships, they never felt like this.'

The back door slammed open. 'Penny, Dad!' Daisy shouted, her voice filled with panic.

Penny scrabbled up, grabbing the blanket, leaving Henry to cover himself with the duvet as he stood up quickly too. Daisy ran to the cool room door but before she opened it she spotted them. Daisy's face showed a myriad of emotions, from relief that Penny was alive, to disappointment, hurt, humiliation and finally anger.

Chapter 24

'You've been sleeping together?'

'It's not what it looks like,' Henry said, wrapping the duvet around his hips. 'I was trying to keep her warm.'

Penny stared at him in horror. Now was the time to apologise for keeping it from Daisy, explain why they had done it and come clean, not lie about it even more.

'Jesus, Dad, don't lie to me. How long has it been going on?'

'About a week,' Penny said.

Henry glared at her then moved towards Daisy. 'Look, we didn't want to upset you.'

'So you lied about it, sneaked around behind my back, treated me like a child? Why the hell wouldn't you tell me?'

'Because you asked me not to date her and—'

'And look at how well you respected my wishes.'

'Listen, love, you were happy here and you were scared that I would cock it up with Penny and we'd have to move out. I just wanted to get to Christmas, give you a bit more time to settle in, before I told you how important Penny was to me.'

Daisy, clearly not sure who she should be more angry at, turned her attention to Penny. 'And that's why you were being so nice to me, teaching me about ice carving and taking me out, buying me clothes – you were just using me to get to my dad.'

Penny was horrified. She stepped towards her, wishing more than anything that she didn't have to have this conversation naked, with only a blanket to protect her modesty. 'No, Daisy, honey. I would never do that. I genuinely love spending time with you,

you make me laugh, you're so creative and I love how insightful and kind you are. I was happy to spend time with you long before me and your dad got together. If we broke up now, I'd still be happy to teach you about ice carving and take Bernard for walks with you, I said that the other night after Henry had shouted at me. I would never be that manipulative to get what I want. And I know you've only known me a short time, but you should know that what you see is who I am, there has never been a hidden agenda with me.'

Daisy was clearly not to be talked round. She turned her attention back to her dad. 'What is it with you and women? Is sex so important to you that you can't stay single for longer than a few months?'

Henry looked furious. 'Damn it, Daisy, this isn't just sex, I'm not just messing around here. I love her. I'm in love with Penny. I have been for a while.'

There was a silence in the room then, punctuated only by Bernard snuffling on the sofa.

'You love her?' Daisy said, quietly.

'Yes.'

'After one week. You hypocrite. You belittled what I had with Josh, saying I hadn't known him for long enough, but somehow you fell in love in a week too. And that isn't something that you thought you should tell me?'

'We were going to tell you, after Christmas. I just wanted you to feel a bit more settled here before I told you this was the woman that I wanted to marry.'

Penny felt tears spring to her eyes. He loved her and wanted to marry her? She wanted to kiss him and hold him but she couldn't.

Daisy stared at them and then stormed off, slamming the connecting door between them.

'Shit,' Henry said, quickly dropping the duvet and getting dressed. 'Shit, shit, shit.'

Tugging his shirt on and doing up a few cursory buttons, he made to run after Daisy, but he came back and kissed her briefly.

'I love you and I'm going to fix this so we can be together properly without any secrets. Trust me on that.'

Penny nodded and he kissed her on the forehead and left, closing the connecting door between them.

She heard his footsteps thunder up the stairs and more shouting between the two of them, though she couldn't make out the words. He had to make this right because she loved him too and she couldn't lose him before they had even started.

Penny stared out the bedroom window at the muted early morning sky as the snow fell thick and fast, swirling and dancing in the wind.

She hadn't been able to sleep much, hoping that Henry would appear in her bedroom and tell her it was all sorted out. But he never came.

Surely he wouldn't let this come between them. But Daisy had also been the only reason he had broken up with his previous girlfriends. She would always come first for him.

Her head hurt. After the stress of thinking that her and Henry were finished, to getting back together with him, and now this, it felt like they were over again.

Tonight was the Christmas Eve ball and it looked like she'd be going alone if Henry couldn't right things with Daisy.

She got out of bed and went into the shower, feeling thoroughly deflated, especially as the night before Henry had told her he loved her.

She walked back into the bedroom and saw her phone was flashing silently on the bedside table.

She grabbed it and noticed she'd had three missed calls from Maggie. She also noticed it was a lot later in the day than she had originally thought; the snow had made it much darker and she must have slept a little late that morning without realising it. She quickly phoned Maggie back.

When her friend answered it was clear that she had gone into full-blown panic mode. 'Penny, the bloody, pissing, sodding snow. Everything is ruined, every fucking thing.'

'Maggie, what's wrong, what do you mean?'

She moved to the window and froze in shock. Everywhere, as far as the eye could see in every direction, was covered in a thick blanket of snow. On top of her van's roof was almost two foot of the stuff and the wheels were almost buried too.

'The ball will have to be cancelled. Everything was due to arrive today: the tables, chairs, the food, the DJ, the heaters, even most of the waiters and waitresses were coming from different towns,' Maggie said, and Penny could tell that she was almost crying with the frustration of it all. 'Half the ice carvers lost their sculptures due to the power cut the other night and that was going to be the main decoration for the evening.'

'Hang on a minute. We are not cancelling the ball. We're not. Not after all your hard work and planning. We've had a ball in the town as far back as I can remember and we're not going to cancel just because of a little bit of snow.'

'It's more than just a little bit of snow, Penny,' Maggie snapped.

Penny ignored the anger in her best friend's voice. 'Give me five minutes to have a think about this and I'll call you back.'

Penny hung up and paced the room for a moment before scrolling through her phone. The town council had a telephone tree for when they needed to arrange a meeting or if there was a problem in the town like a faulty traffic light that people were being asked to avoid or an escaped cow when people were asked to help round it up. This counted as a really big problem.

She quickly composed a text explaining the problem and asked for help. She included her mobile number on the bottom so people would reply to her and not the person who had forwarded on the text. She sent it to the five people on her part of the tree, knowing that within half an hour almost every member of the town would be informed and many of their friends and family too, which would cover almost the entire town.

She got dressed quickly while she waited. As she pulled her jeans on, the phone beeped. As she did up her belt the phone beeped again, seven times in quick succession. She pulled her snow boots on and quickly did up the laces as the phone beeped again and again and again.

She picked it up, seeing that she already had over thirty messages. Wow these guys were quick.

There were offers of food from most people, mainly sandwiches, crisps and cakes, but probably enough to keep everybody satisfied tonight. Everyone who replied said they would bring their own soft and alcoholic drinks. Kathleen from The Pilchard was offering all her tables, chairs and outdoor patio heaters if someone could come and pick them up. The landlords from The Bubble and Froth, The Mermaid and The Smuggler's Inn were all offering the same thing as they were all going to be closed for the night anyway due to the ball. They were all donating bottles of wine and soft drinks too. Someone had an iPod and excellent speakers they often used for parties with a huge range of music, mostly light pop stuff that everyone could sing along to. There was a small digging team already down in the town that were digging out the main roads and the side roads leading up to the marquee. Thankfully most of the main roads in the town had been gritted the night before, even if the roads leading into the town hadn't been, so they didn't have mountains of the stuff to get rid of.

She quickly typed a reply, including everyone who had texted her and the five people on her part of the telephone tree. She explained that food was covered, asked if anyone willing to help with the digging could go down to the town with a spade and if anyone had access to a big van that could go round and collect all the tables and chairs. She also asked if anyone could donate some tablecloths and candles too. She waited a moment to see if she got any replies and, within a few minutes, several texts had come in with whole families agreeing to be part of the digging team, two people with large vans had offered their help with collecting the tables and several people had said they would bring tablecloths and candles to the marquee.

Although it wasn't anything like what Maggie had planned, the ball could at least go ahead in one way or another.

She called her friend back.

'Maggie, I have food planned, sandwiches and cake, and people are bringing their own drinks and. . .'

'People have paid forty pounds for these tickets and we're going to give them sandwiches? They'll be asking for their money back.'

'No, they won't, it's for charity and the people in this town care about the ball. No one will give a shit whether they are eating sandwiches or some chicken stuffed with spinach and cheese. And sandwiches is better than no food at all. Now stop being so moany and listen to what I've sorted out.'

Maggie was silent for a moment. 'OK,' she said, quietly, suitably chastised.

Penny explained the plan and that she was going to get down to the marquee to help set up as things started to arrive. Maggie agreed to meet her there as soon as she could get through the town.

Penny hung up.

That would be a problem for her too. Her little car was no match for the amount of snow that was sitting on her driveway and the freezer van was too old and weak to make it through either. Once she got to the main road she would probably be OK, but her drive was so long it would take the next three or four hours to dig her car out. Henry's Range Rover might be able to get out and the Christmas ball needed all the help it could get at the moment.

She pulled her coat, hat and gloves on and ran downstairs. She hovered for a moment outside the connecting door. It was silent on the other side. Had they perhaps killed each other the night before?

She knocked tentatively on the door and a huge shadow loomed near the window for a second before it was opened. Henry smiled briefly at her before the smile faded and vanished. He looked tired and unbelievably sad. Behind him, Penny could see Daisy reading on the sofa, studiously ignoring both of them.

'Henry, I need your help. The snow has caused massive problems for the ball, no one can get to the town to deliver the tables and chairs and food. I have a plan forming but I need to get down to the town to help.'

'You want me to take you down?'

'Yes, sorry.' She glanced at Daisy. 'I know this isn't the best time but my car just won't make it.'

Henry grabbed his coat and shoes straight away, not even questioning it, but to Penny's great surprise Daisy was getting into her coat and shoes too.

Henry glanced at Penny and shrugged subtly. He wasn't about to argue.

Between them they managed to dig the wheels out and they bundled into the car. It had stopped snowing and the sun was now trying to make an appearance.

Henry manoeuvred the car slowly down the drive. The car was struggling but at least they were making steady progress. Finally they hit the road that would take them to the town. It was covered in snow but because the gritter lorry had obviously been out the night before it wasn't as bad as her drive.

They drove in complete silence down to the town and Penny had no idea what to say to make this situation any better. The fact that Daisy was coming with them to help with the ball stood for something, but Penny still didn't know where she stood in her relationship with Henry.

As they rounded a corner, Penny got her first glimpse of the town. Every rooftop glistened under a layer of sparkly cotton wool; it looked like something from a movie set as it twinkled in the midday sun. She had never seen the town look so beautiful before and it was a dramatic sight framed against the inky blue backdrop of the sea.

'Look,' Penny pointed out to Daisy, forgetting for a moment that they weren't on speaking terms.

Daisy leant forwards and for a second, just a brief moment, her face reflected the awe of the scene, before the sullen grumpiness returned and Daisy sat back in her seat.

Penny sat and stared at the town for a moment before she swivelled around to talk to Daisy.

'I am really sorry that we lied to you, it was never our intention to hurt you. Everything happened between me and your dad so quickly and neither of us expected it to. We just wanted you to get a bit more settled in, make some friends, be comfortable here before we suddenly announced that we were dating. I'm so sorry, I really am.'

Daisy looked out the window and refused to even acknowledge that Penny had spoken. Penny glanced back at Henry, who shook his head in warning, telling her not to push it any further.

Penny sat back in her seat and sighed. 'We need to stop at The Pilchard first, pick up a few outdoor heaters and take them to the marquee so we can start warming up the place.'

Henry nodded.

As they got closer to the main town centre, the roads became a lot clearer. There were loads of people on the street digging the snow off the roads and it made Penny smile to see how everyone was laughing and joking with each other. This was not a problem for the people of White Cliff Bay, this was a day out or an adventure.

They stopped at The Pilchard and with Daisy's help and a few passers-by they managed to load four heaters into the back of the Range Rover.

They drove up to the marquee, which was in a field on the headland overlooking Silver Cove beach. The road hadn't quite been cleared in that part of the town but, with a little help from the sun that seemed to be melting some of the snow and Henry's car, they soon made short work of it.

They unloaded the heaters and Henry helped to set them up. Luckily the power generator and cables had all been delivered along with the marquee a few days before and the Portaloos, Penny knew, had been delivered the day before, so that was something.

'I'm going to help with the digging,' Daisy announced, walking out the marquee before Henry could say anything.

'I'll get some more heaters from the other pubs. The sooner this place is warm the better.'

Penny nodded and watched him go. He hadn't kissed her. He'd given her no sign at all that everything was going to be OK between them.

A van arrived and several tables were unloaded, and Penny had to force her attention away from her crumbling relationship to make sure they were set up in the right place.

With no crumb of hope from Henry, Daisy still walking around under a black cloud and the marquee nowhere near ready, it was going to be a long day.

Chapter 25

Penny stepped out the bath and towelled herself off. She had no idea what she was going to wear to the ball that night. She supposed she would go for the black dress she wore to the ball every year. It didn't seem right somehow to wear the green dress she had worn on her first date with Henry when she wasn't going to the ball with him.

At least the ball was going ahead, thanks to every single person in the town who had turned up to help, either by bringing food, helping to clear the snow or helping her and Maggie to set up the tables, chairs and decorations. She felt good about it, the community spirit, the fact that the charity would still get their money. But she still couldn't raise a smile about her relationship with Henry.

She had barely seen him for the rest of the day. He'd returned once with more heaters but disappeared again without saying a word. He'd texted her later to say he had got caught transporting people around the town and, although lots of people had come and gone with food and cake, she hadn't seen him again. She had no idea whether he'd even come home yet or was still helping out somewhere. She'd got a lift home from one of the local farmers in the end. She didn't know whether they were ever going to get past this. They loved each other, but his fear of upsetting Daisy seemed to far outweigh any feelings he had for Penny. She wanted Daisy to be happy with them being together too but she was getting a little bit frustrated that Henry would allow his sixteen-year-old daughter – or rather the fear of hurting her – to dictate to him how he lived his life. And although she understood the history behind him being scared, there was a part of her that wanted him to fight for her, to put her on an equal footing with his daughter, not ten spaces behind.

She walked out into the bedroom and stopped. Lying on the bed was the beautiful silver dress she had tried on the other day with Daisy.

Resting on top of the dress was a little paper heart, with the words, *Put this on and meet me downstairs, Henry x.*

She found herself smiling. Was she really going to go to the ball with her prince? Had he spoken to Daisy and straightened it all out?

She was tempted to run downstairs now and ask him, but she supposed she should get ready first. She dressed quickly, threw on some make-up and swept her hair up on top of her head.

She opened the bedroom door and was thrown by the trail of rose petals that led from her door and down the stairs, as if she was unable to find her way down on her own.

She stepped down the stairs and saw hundreds of candles flickering in the darkness of her lounge, but standing in the middle of them all was Henry dressed in a tux. She stopped half-way down the stairs and stared at him. If there was a finer sight in the world than Henry Travis in a tuxedo, she was yet to see it.

'You look so beautiful,' Henry said, softly, coming to the bottom of the stairs and holding out his hand for her.

She took it, her heart beating wildly as he pulled her into the middle of the lounge.

He kissed her gently on the cheek and then went down on one knee.

Her heart stopped, blood rushed to her head, making her immediately dizzy. 'Henry, shit, no, you can't.'

'Don't worry, it's not that.'

She laughed in relief.

'I've thought about this a lot over the last few days, before I shouted at you and made you cry, and before I made my daughter hate me because I lied to her, before any of that happened, I wanted to tell you how I felt. And I didn't want to just say the words in passing, as if I was asking you what your favourite colour is, and I certainly didn't want to throw the words out while I was trying to get you warm again after you nearly died of hypothermia. I wanted something bigger than that because what I felt for you was so much bigger than anything I've ever felt before.'

He pulled a little black box out of his pocket and, despite knowing this wasn't a proposal, her breath hitched at the sight of it.

He opened it and offered it up to her. Two hearts entwined with each other lay on the black velvet: one wooden heart, one made from crystal. There was a scarlet ribbon tied around the top, but it was the curly words engraved into the wooden heart that caught her attention the most. *I love you*. She ran her fingers lightly over it, the lines of the wood and the shine of the varnish reflecting the lights of the candles beautifully.

'And this heart –' he pointed to the crystal – 'you have to pretend it's made from ice, a special kind that will never melt.'

She smiled at the significance of the ice and the wood entwined – her world and his.

'And I thought you should have something that was yours on our tree.'

'I can't believe you did all this just to tell me you love me.'

'I do love you, Penny. I fell completely and utterly in love with you almost from the very first time we met. I have never met anyone so kind, so pure and sweet as you before. You make me laugh, a lot, I could talk to you for hours and never get bored, and I have never felt for anyone the way I feel with you. You are right, you deserve the very best, and I'm going to do everything I can to give it to you.'

She knelt down so she was face to face with him.

'I love you too. You've changed my life in such a short time. I told myself repeatedly that I didn't need a man or a family to make me happy. And in reality I don't *need* one, but I do want one. My idea of a family was marriage and babies, and that's changed now. I want to be part of your family and I want to be with you more than anything else in the world. You make me happy, happier than I've ever been, and I want to make you happy too.'

He kissed her and then pulled back slightly. 'I'm not ruling out babies either. I know I've done the sleepless nights and the nappy changes but I'd love to do it all again with you.'

'Really?'

He smiled and nodded. 'Just. . . not yet, eh? Let's give it a few months before we think about that.'

'OK.'

'Now, shall we hang your decoration on the tree and go to the ball?'

'What about Daisy?'

His face fell. 'She's still not speaking to me, I've tried everything but she flat-out refuses to talk. I'm gutted. She's at Anna's and I think she'll be going to the ball with them. But we've not had much chance to see each other today. I'm going to sort it out with her tonight. There's no way I'm spending Christmas not talking to her. And I'm going with you to the ball and she will see that I'm serious about you and that I love you.'

She smiled. 'OK.'

She stood up and offered out her hand for his. He took it and pulled himself up.

'The next time I get down on one knee for you, it will be the real thing.'

346

Her smile grew and she didn't think she would ever stop smiling tonight.

Holding her hand, he led her over to the tree. 'Where would you like to hang it?'

Penny considered it for a moment. 'How about here, between the Santa that's showing his bum and the angel that Daisy made from an old washing-up bottle?'

'I think that's a bat from Halloween, actually, but yes, good choice.'

Henry took it from the box and passed it to her. She hung it on the branch and it glistened and sparkled under the fairy lights.

'Perfect.'

Henry helped her to put her coat on and then led her out.

'Wait. We need to deliver a carving.'

'Tonight? Now? Won't everyone be at the ball?'

'This is a proposal carving, and I think they'll probably be at the ball after or before as I have to place it quite near, but I can't ruin this guy's big moment. We can wrap it up and take it in your car, just don't put your heating on full blast.'

Henry helped her to wrap it up and carry it out and they drove down to the town. Under the glow of the silvery moon, White Cliff Bay twinkled and shone, still buried under a blanket of snow. It was magical, ethereal in its beauty.

The streets were completely deserted as everyone else was clearly already at the ball. They positioned the proposal carving around the back of the marquee at the end of the thin cliff path that led up from Silver Cove beach and then drove around to the car park, which was already overflowing with cars. After finally finding a space, Henry escorted her inside.

Near the entrance stood two ice carvings, the only ones to survive the power cut or to make it through the snow. Octavia

347

had carved a stunning full-sized Santa, sitting on a chair checking his naughty and nice list. It was incredible. Next to it Melody had carved a beautiful reindeer. It wasn't the big competition of previous years but at least Octavia would rightfully win this one and Melody would come second, which would mean an honourable mention for the newcomer in the Ice Carving Federation magazine, even if it was by default.

They moved further into the marquee. The place was packed, people were chatting at the makeshift bar, sitting down at a hodgepodge of tables covered in a colourful array of tablecloths and donated table decorations, none of which matched, and several people were up on the dance floor, swaying gently to the sounds of 'Have Yourself a Merry Little Christmas' by Frank Sinatra. But Penny could see that every single person seemed to be enjoying themselves. They didn't care that the food was mostly sandwiches, or that the music came from an iPod instead of a DJ, or that none of the tables and chairs matched. The ball had happened because every single one of these people had helped to put it on. She could see Jill looking stunning in a long blue sequinned dress as her husband Thomas twirled her around the floor. Maggie was dancing with one of her boys and Edward waved at them as he danced with his wife. She loved this town with its crazy, nosy, caring people, and now she had one more reason to love it too.

She squeezed Henry's hand and he smiled at her. She wanted to find Daisy and hug her too, though she doubted that would happen any time soon.

'Can you see Daisy?' Henry asked.

'Yes, she's over by the buffet with Josh. She's already seen us and is pretending she hasn't.' Penny saw the scowl on his face as he saw Josh with his arm around Daisy's shoulders. 'Don't make a big deal over this, he is lovely and you certainly don't want to make the situation worse between the two of you by going all "over-protective dad" again.'

'I need to talk to her but shall we dance first?' Henry asked and she nodded.

He swept her onto the dance floor, and with his arms around her waist and her head on his chest, in front of the whole town, they started to move slowly around the floor.

She looked up and he smiled at her. He bent his head down to kiss her when suddenly a large, mayonnaise-covered prawn splattered against Henry's forehead. He looked up in confusion as the prawn slithered down his cheek and Penny managed to catch it before it hit his tux or her dress.

They looked around to see Daisy standing on the dance floor with her hands on her hips.

'Don't ever lie to me again,' Daisy said, a smirk fighting on her lips, and Henry let out a booming laugh. With one arm still wrapped around Penny, he used the other arm to hook Daisy by the waist and brought her in for a group hug. Penny wrapped an arm around her too.

Henry kissed Daisy on the forehead. 'You are the best thing that has ever happened to me and I have never regretted having you, not for one second. I would never do anything to deliberately hurt you. I love you so much and me being in love with Penny doesn't mean I love you any less.'

'I know that, Dad.'

'And I love you too,' Penny said. 'If that's OK?'

Daisy nodded and hugged them both tight.

Penny leant her head against Henry's chest again and watched the twinkling fairy lights over Daisy's head.

It had turned out to be a perfect Christmas after all.

Epilogue

Christmas Day

Penny lay on the sofa watching the flames dance in the fireplace. She had eaten way too much turkey, chocolate and Christmas pudding, not all at the same time but close enough. She felt uncomfortably full and bloated. Daisy was lying next to her, her head on Penny's belly, which wasn't helping the full feeling but Penny didn't care. She had never felt so blissfully happy as she did at that moment. She ran her fingers through Daisy's hair, stroking her head affectionately. Anna, Steve, Bea and Oliver were coming round later that night but right now it was just the three of them, which suited Penny just fine, spending Christmas Day with her gorgeous new family.

'That snow is coming down hard,' Henry said, staring out the window with Bernard lying sprawled out upside down on his lap.

Penny transferred her attention to the fat flakes of snow that were swirling in the darkening sky outside. 'Stop worrying.'

'I'm not worrying,' Henry said, failing to keep the note of tension from his voice.

Daisy giggled, the vibrations of her laughter travelling straight through Penny's belly. 'You're the world's worst worrier, and I love you for it, but I am relieved that some of your over-protectiveness has transferred to Penny recently. Lets me off the hook a bit.'

'I still worry about you. Worrying about Penny doesn't mean I worry about you any less and don't think that this –' he gestured at Penny – 'means I'm going to be more relaxed about you going out with Josh. No. . . *shenanigans* until you're at least thirty.'

Penny laughed. 'Daisy is far more sensible than you.'

'Daisy I trust, it's Josh that I doubt. I remember what it's like to be a teenage boy: pretty much the only thing they think of is sex.'

Penny bit her tongue, stopping herself from saying that hadn't changed for Henry; it had been a long time since he had been a teenager and he still had a huge sexual appetite. Henry blushed, clearly knowing what Penny had been thinking.

'Dad, Josh is still terrified of you ever since you threw him to the ground. I imagine he'll still be too scared to go near me on my wedding night. I really don't think you have anything to worry about just yet.'

Henry seemed placated slightly as he turned his attention back to the snow, the frown returning to his face.

Bernard woke, stretched sleepily, kicking Henry in the face – which did nothing to detract his attention from the snow – fell off his lap and curled up in front of the fire.

Penny sat up with some difficulty, planted a kiss on Daisy's head and walked over to Henry, his eyes immediately on hers, aware of her every move. He pulled her onto his lap and she gently kissed his scowl.

'What are you worried about?'

He ran his hands over her stomach. 'Everything: the snow coming down too heavily and us not being able to get out if we need to, what the roads will be like if we need to travel on them, whether we have everything we need here if we do get snowed in. . .'

Penny kissed him softly on the mouth. 'We're going to be fine. There's something else bothering you, you've been on edge all day.'

The timer went off on the oven, indicating that the mince pies that Henry had made fresh earlier that day were cooked.

351

Henry looked over to the oven anxiously and then back at Penny. 'I'm worried you won't like my mince pies.'

Penny laughed as he scooted her off his lap, planting a quick kiss on her lips, and ran into the kitchen.

Daisy groaned. 'Dad's mince pies are the worst. I never know how someone can go so drastically wrong with mince from a jar and roll-out puff pastry, but he does, every single time.'

'These ones are different,' Henry called from the kitchen as he plated some pies up straight from the oven.

'I think I'll leave mine till later,' Penny called, although the delicious scents did smell tantalisingly good.

'No, you have to at least try it, let me know if I'm on the right lines.'

He came in with two plates, passed one to Daisy and then sank down on one knee to present his mince pie dramatically to Penny. Despite the huge quantities of food that she had eaten less than an hour before, she still reached for it keenly; it smelt wonderful.

Just as she was about to pick it up, she noticed something sparkle from the top of it. Realising almost immediately that it was a diamond ring, her eyes snapped up to meet his.

'Penny Meadows, I fell in love with you a little over a year ago over your delicious mince pies, and I was wondering if today, over my probably not so delicious mince pie, you would do me the honour of agreeing to be my wife.'

Penny stared at the ring, her heart thundering against her chest. It wasn't that unexpected, she'd known they were heading this way almost from the first time they had kissed, but she hadn't expected it to come today and certainly not over a mince pie.

'Good god, Dad, it took you bloody long enough. I thought you were going to end up waiting until she popped out a whole football team of kids before you proposed.'

352

'Well, I didn't want to rush into anything,' Henry said, not taking his eyes off Penny for a second. His mouth quirked up into a mischievous smile. 'I had to make sure she was the right one.'

Penny smiled.

'I love you, Penny Meadows, I always have. Will you marry me?'

Penny plucked the ring from the pie and sucked the mince off the bottom. It tasted disgusting, like burnt treacle. She slid the ring onto her finger.

'I love you with everything I have – of course the answer is yes.'

She leant forwards to kiss him and he wrapped his arms around her, holding her tight. Inside her belly, a little foot kicked out and she laughed against his lips. 'I think your son approves too.'

Henry laughed and knelt forwards to kiss her oversized belly. 'She said yes,' he whispered.

'He's probably wondering what took you so long too,' Daisy said from the sofa as she took a big bite of the pie with a huge smile on her face. The smile quickly fell off though as she shuddered with disgust. 'Dad, this is gross.'

'My work here is done.'

Daisy stood up and came over to hug them both. 'Congratulations. I'm really happy for you both.'

Henry sat on the chair and pulled Penny onto his lap, stroking her large belly and admiring the ring.

Daisy sat on the arm of the chair stroking her belly fondly too. Penny watched her wonderful little family as she played with the wooden star necklace that Henry had made for her. She remembered the wish she had made on the shooting star the year before and smiled knowing that every wish she'd made had finally come true.

Dear Reader,

Thank you so much for reading *Christmas at Lilac Cottage*. I had so much fun creating this story and I hope you enjoyed reading it as much as I enjoyed writing it.

One of the best parts of writing comes from seeing the reaction from readers. Did it make you smile or laugh, did it make you cry, hopefully happy tears? Did you fall in love with Henry and Penny? Did you like the gorgeous town of White Cliff Bay? If you enjoyed the story, I would absolutely love it if you could leave a short review or get in touch with me on social media, where you can also hear about other things I'm up to.

Thank you for reading and I hope you have a wonderful, cosy Christmas.

Love Holly x

@hollymartin00

@BonnierZaffre

hollymartinauthor

hollymartinwriter.wordpress.com

Acknowledgements

To my family: my mom, my biggest fan, who reads every word I have written a hundred times over and loves it every single time, my dad, my brother Lee and my sister-in-law Julie, for your support, love, encouragement and endless excitement for my stories.

For my twinnie, the gorgeous Aven Ellis, for just being my wonderful friend, for your endless support, for cheering me on and for keeping me entertained with wonderful stories and pictures of hot men. Although we have never met, you are my best friend and I love you dearly.

Huge thank you to my wonderful, incredible friends Kirsty Maclennan, Megan Milliken and Victoria Stone for the endless support and love. You are amazing.

To my friends Gareth and Mandie, for your support, patience and enthusiasm. My lovely friends Jac, Verity and Jodie, who listen to me talk about my books endlessly and get excited about it every single time.

For Sharon Sant for just being there always and your wonderful friendship.

To my wonderful agent Madeleine Milburn for just being amazing and fighting my corner, and for your unending patience with my constant questions.

To my editor Claire for helping to make this book so much better, for putting up with all my crazy throughout the whole process, for replying to every single email and for listening to me freak out with complete and utter patience. Thank you to Kim Nash for the tireless promoting, tweeting and general cheerleading. Thank you to all the other wonderful people at Bookouture: Oliver Rhodes, the editing team and the wonderful designers who created this absolutely gorgeous cover.

To the wonderful team at Bonnier Zaffre who have helped to realise my dream of seeing my books in shops.

To Oliver Mallinson and the RNLI for helping me with the details of the lifeboat rescue.

To Clair at Global Ice Sculptures & Ice Styling for answering all my questions about ice carving – it was the most fascinating morning listening to you explain the process and watching the carvings being done.

To the CASG, the best writing group in the world, you wonderful, talented, supportive bunch of authors. I feel very blessed to know you all, you guys are the very best.

To the wonderful Bookouture authors for all your encouragement and support.

And some other gorgeous people who have encouraged, supported, promoted, got excited or just listened: Rebecca Pugh, Lisa Dickenson, Sharon Wilden, Kelly Rufus, Simona Elena, Erin McEwan, Katey Beeden, Maryline, Jo Hughes, Dawn Crooks, Laura Delve, Jill Stratton, Tay Pickering, Emma Poulloura, Aga Klar, Catriona Merryweather, Lynsey James, Lindsay Hill, Ana, Alba Forcadell, Dawn Brierley, Sophie Hedley, Cesca Major, Rachael Lucas, Kat Black, Helen Redfern, Katy Gough, Emily Kerr, Jaimie Admans, Kate Gordon, Pernille Hughes, Louise Wykes, Paris Baker, Silke Auwers, The Blossom Twins, Daniel Riding, Pat Elliott, Shaun, Mark Rumsey, James Brown, Arron Davenport.

To all those involved in the blog tour. To anyone who has read my book and taken the time to tell me you've enjoyed it or wrote a review, thank you so much.

Thank you, I love you all.

Holly's Mince Pie Cakes

I love making mince pies. As a child my mum taught me how to make my own pastry by rubbing the butter into the flour. I love the shop-bought ones, too; they're so fruity, smell so good and aren't like anything else you can buy. You know Christmas has come early when they start to appear on the shelves.

My other great love in the kitchen is making fairy cakes. Every Sunday in my house when I was growing up was spent making them, mainly so I could eat the leftover cake mixture from the bowl – I used to make sure there was a lot!

I thought I would combine my two favourite bakes and what appeared was utterly delicious, so here is my quick and easy recipe for mince pie cakes for you to enjoy too.

*Makes 12 cakes

Ingredients
100g soft butter
100g sugar
100g self-raising flour
2 eggs
A generous splash of milk
A jar of mincemeat

How to do it

- Preheat the oven to 180°C/gas mark 4.

- Grease 12 paper cupcake cases and pop them into a 12-hole fairy-cake tin.

- Beat the butter and sugar together until creamy.

- Add the flour, eggs and milk and beat again. The mixture should be quite wet and sloppy. By all means dip a spoon in (or your finger!) and have a taste.

- Take a small spoonful of the mixture and half-fill each cake case.

- Add a teaspoonful of mincemeat to each half-filled cake case.

- Finish each cake with a large spoonful of cake mixture, covering the mincemeat, so you have the mincemeat in the middle of the cake. (Ensure there is enough raw cake mixture left over to indulge in while your cakes are baking!)

- Bake in the oven for about 20 minutes. The cakes, when cooked, should be golden brown and springy to the touch.

Be warned: the mincemeat will be very hot straight from the oven so leave the cakes for twenty minutes or so to cool before you tuck into them.

Enjoy!

Q&A with Holly Martin

Congratulations on having written *Christmas at Lilac Cottage*! Thank you for agreeing to answer some questions about your writing for your many fans.

 When did you first start writing? And when did you first start thinking of yourself as a writer?

I've always written stories – from when I was a child – and I remember getting a typewriter as a Christmas present when I was nine. The first story I remember writing was a fanfiction story; my own version of *The Animals of Farthing Wood* by Colin Dann. I also remember writing a shipwreck story about a girl who ended up on a desert island. When I was eighteen and at university, I wrote a funny story about student life. I started writing chick lit about seven years ago and I've just never stopped.

 White Cliff Bay is described beautifully – it leaps from the page and we can almost smell the salt in the air. Was this based on somewhere you've been?

White Cliff Bay is an amalgamation of many cutesy seaside towns in Cornwall and Devon, which I went to many times when I was growing up and have returned to since being older. I love St Ives and that was in my mind when I started planning this story. When I was researching this book, I stayed in Polperro in Cornwall and with its whitewashed houses that seemed to tumble down the steep hillsides it ticked so many of the boxes for me and gave me lots of inspiration for my stories. Everyone knew everyone there, and people said that the shops ran on 'Cornish time', which generally meant they opened and closed whenever they saw fit. They might open around half-ten, close for a few hours over lunch and open up again for a few more in the afternoon. Everything was so much slower and laidback in Polperro and I couldn't help falling in love with the place. I stayed in Brixham too and the pretty, coloured houses and friendliness of the locals was something I completely adored – so much so I've recently moved there.

 Which was your favourite scene in the book to write, and why? Was there anything you edited out of the book?
I love writing comedy and when I'm sitting at the computer chuckling away then hopefully I'm doing something right. One of my favourite scenes was the 'porn' scene; it made me laugh to write how Penny is desperately trying to make an awkward situation better and just keeps making it worse, digging herself deeper and deeper into trouble.

In terms of editing out a scene, there wasn't a lot that came out of the original. Chick-lit stories generally follow one of two patterns: girl meets boy and because of complications they don't get together until the end or, in the case of *Christmas at Lilac Cottage*, girl meets boy, they hit it off and *do* get together but then there has to be a 'black moment' before the end, something that pulls the couple apart. It's this black moment that I find the hardest to write. By the time I get to the end, I've fallen completely in love with my characters and I just want them to be together and live happily ever after. Even though I know the story would be very dull without any conflict, I hate writing the part which breaks the couple up; it feels somehow disloyal. So the black moment between Henry and Penny was changed a few times before I was happy with it.

 Like your readers, Penny also loves to curl up with a great romance. Which escapist reads have you enjoyed recently? Do you have any favourite authors who inspire your writing?

I love stories by Katie Fforde and Jill Mansell. I think I've read every one of their books and they were both a huge inspiration for me. I wanted to write gorgeous cosy stories like they do. I also love Aven Ellis and Lisa Dickenson. I love Christmas stories and every year I fill my Kindle with almost every Christmas romance I can get my hands on and find I'm still reading them long after the day itself.

Which of your characters would you most like to spend a Christmas Day with? And if you could invite a character from another novel, too, who would it be, and why?

One of my favourite characters is George from *Snowflakes on Silver Cove*. He is funny and very down to earth, not like any of the big, strong men I normally write about. He also adores everything about Christmas – his house is filled with Christmas decorations, he wears Christmas jumpers with pride, he has a fleet of life-size reindeer in his front room and I found his love for the whole season really adorable. I think I would also invite Hermione from Harry Potter; we could have a really good chat about the magical world us Muggles are not privy to and I think she could magic up a decent Christmas lunch too.

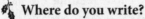

Where do you write?

I used to write in a conservatory and I'd get very easily distracted by the birds and the antics of the squirrels. Since I moved house, though, I now have my own office. At the time of writing, I'm staring at the most hideous carpet I've ever seen and some pretty disgusting wallpaper. But I love that I have my dedicated space and I can't wait to make it my own.

Do you have a favourite Christmas carol or song?

I love 'Fairytale of New York' by The Pogues, especially that part of the song that talks about building his dreams around hers, and I love 'All I Want for Christmas is You' by Mariah Carey.

Who would you like to play Penny and Henry in a film adaptation of *Christmas at Lilac Cottage*?

It's hard to find the perfect Henry; he is so big, not only in height but in stature too. And it has to be someone who is divinely handsome as well! So I would probably go with the stunningly beautiful Chris Hemsworth or Joe Manganiello or Karl Urban, who all have that rugged-sexy-muscular look. And if one of them did get the part, I would have to go down to the film set every day and make sure that they 'got' the role. It would be a hardship but I'm prepared to put the hours in. I think I would have someone like Emma Watson or Keira Knightley to play Penny; both really cute but seemingly very down to earth.